IF I KNEW YOU WERE GOING TO BE THIS BEAUTIFUL, I NEVER WOULD HAVE LET YOU GO

JUDY CHICUREL

TINDER
PRESS

Published by arrangement with G.P. Putnam's Sons,
a member of Penguin Group (USA) LLC,
A Penguin Random House Company

First published in Great Britain in 2014
by TINDER PRESS
An imprint of HEADLINE PUBLISHING GROUP

1

Cataloguing in Publication Data is available from the British Library

ISBN 978 1 4722 2165 0 (Hardback)
ISBN 978 1 4722 2166 7 (Trade Paperback)

Typeset in Century Schoolbook by
Palimpsest Book Production Ltd, Falkirk, Stirlingshire

Printed and bound in Great Britain by Clays Ltd, St Ives plc

Papers used by Headline are from well-managed forests
and other responsible sources

HEADLINE PUBLISHING GROUP
An Hachette UK Company
338 Euston Road
London NW1 3BH

www.tinderpress.co.uk
www.headline.co.uk
www.hachette.co.uk

IF I KNEW YOU
WERE GOING
TO BE THIS
BEAUTIFUL,
I NEVER WOULD
HAVE LET YOU GO

For David.
And for my father, Michael (1919–2005),
who always believed.

ONE

summer wind

'So she says to me, "Young man, you got maniacs hanging around your store," and I tell her, "You're right, lady, you're a hundred percent right. I got maniacs outside my store, I got them inside my store, I got maniacs on the roof," I tell her.'

Desi flicked a length of ash into the ashtray we were sharing. The end of his cigar was slick with saliva. He shifted it to the side of his mouth and continued. 'What am I gonna do, argue with her? Kill her? I mean, please, some of these people should maybe look in their own backyards before they come around here making comments. There's an old Italian saying, "Don't spit up in the air, because it's liable to come back down and hit you in the face."'

'I have no idea what that means,' I said.

'It means what it means, man,' Mitch called from the other end of the counter. 'Everybody's everything. Can you dig it?' He had a six-pack of Pabst Blue Ribbon under the arm with

1

the rainbow tattoo and was taking a Camel non-filter from a freshly opened pack he'd just purchased. He tapped his cane twice against the counter and then winked at me before hobbling out the door. Mitch lived at the opposite end of Comanche Street, in one of the rooms at The Starlight Hotel that looked out over the ocean and smelled of mildew and seaweed. This was the third six-pack of the day he'd bought at Eddy's; he had to make separate trips because he could only carry one at a time. It was close to the end of the month, when his disability check ran out, which was why he was buying six-packs instead of sitting on the corner barstool by the jukebox in the hotel lounge.

Desi shook his head, mopping up a puddle of liquid on the counter. 'Yeah, yeah, just ask Peg Leg Pete over there,' he muttered as the door closed behind Mitch.

'Don't call him that, man,' I said. 'I thought you liked him. I thought you were friends.' I felt a vague panic that this might not be so.

'Hey, hey, did I say I didn't like the guy? I love the guy,' Desi said, wringing out the rag, running it under the faucet behind the counter. 'But he's not the only one sacrificed for his country. A lost leg is not an excuse for a lost life. And besides, he only lost half a leg.'

'Desi, Jesus—'

'Don't "Jesus" me, what are we, in church? And what are you, his mother? Half a leg, no leg, whatever, he don't need you to defend him. He can take care of himself.' He shook his head. 'You kids, you think you know everything.'

'I don't think I know everything,' I said wearily. Most of the time, I didn't think I knew anything.

2

'Yeah, well, you,' Desi said, moving down the counter to the cash register to ring up Mr. Meaney's *Daily News*. 'You're different from the other kids around here. You want my advice? Get out of Dodge. Now. Pronto.' My stomach winced. I was glad no one else was around to hear him; Mr. Meaney didn't count. I'd been hanging around Comanche Street for three years and there were still times when it felt like I was watching a movie starring everyone I knew in the world, except me. The feeling would come up on me even when I was surrounded by a million people: in school, on the beach, sitting at the counter in Eddy's.

Desi owned Eddy's, the candy store on the corner of Comanche Street and Lighthouse Avenue in the Trunk end of Elephant Beach. The original Eddy had long since retired and moved to Florida, but Desi wouldn't change the name. 'Believe me, it's not worth the trouble,' he said. 'Guy was here, what, twenty-five years? I pay for the sign, I change the lettering on the window, and then what? People are still gonna call it Eddy's.' He was right. They did.

Sometimes in February, I'd be sitting in Earth Science class or World History, and outside the windows, frozen snow would be bordering the sidewalk and the sky would be gunmetal gray and I'd start thinking about having a chocolate egg cream at Eddy's, and suddenly summer didn't feel so far away. If I thought hard enough, I could taste the edge of the chocolate syrup at the back of my throat and it would make me homesick for sitting at the counter, drinking an egg cream and smoking a cigarette underneath the creaky ceiling fan that never did much except push the stillborn air back and forth, while everyone was hanging out by the magazine racks

3

if the cops were patrolling Comanche Street, or sitting on the garbage cans on the side of the store where, when it was hot enough, you could smell the pavement melting. Sometimes Desi's wife, Angie, would open the side door and start sweeping people away, saying, 'Look at youse, loafing, what would your mother say, she saw you sitting on a trash can in the middle of the day?' And Billy Mackey or someone would say, 'She'd say, "Where do you think you are, Eddy's?"' Then everyone would laugh and Angie would chase whoever said it with the broom, sometimes down to the end of the block, right up to the edge of the ocean.

Eddy's was open only in summer, from Memorial Day to Labor Day, sometimes until the end of September if the weather stayed warm. Desi and Angie and their kids, Gina and Vinny, moved down from Queens to Elephant Beach and lived in the rooms over the store, where they had a faint view of the ocean. On Sundays, when Vinny or Angie worked the counter, Desi would walk down to Comanche Street beach and put up a red, white and green umbrella ('the Italian flag') and stretch out on a lounge chair, wearing huge black sunglasses, a white cotton sun hat, polka-dot bathing trunks that looked like underwear, and white tennis shoes because once he'd cut his toe on a broken shell and needed stitches. He'd lie out on that lounge chair like a king, smoking a cigar, turning up his portable radio every time a Sinatra song came on. If any of us tried talking to him, even to say hello, he'd say, 'Beat it. Today I'm incognito.'

'I'll tell you what the trouble is with you kids,' Desi said now, walking back to where I was sitting. He took my empty glass and started mixing me another egg cream. He squirted seltzer and chocolate sauce into the glass and stirred it to a frenzy. He slid it back across the counter and I tasted it and it was perfect.

'The trouble with all a youse is you don't know how to shut up. I mean, who am I, Helen Keller? I can't see or hear what goes on the other side of the counter? It's sex and drugs and rock 'n' roll all day long and mostly sex, and now it's not just the guys talking.' His voice dropped a shocked octave lower. 'It's the girls. The *girls*. "So-and-so got so-and-so pregnant," "So-and-so had an abortion," I mean, please, what do I need to hear this for? Look at that little girl, what's her name, the one got knocked up didn't even finish high school, waddling in here like a pregnant duck. Nothing's sacred, *nothing*. And then you wonder why.' Desi shook his head. 'Believe me, there was just as much sex around when your mother and I were young. Thing is, we weren't talking about it. We were doing it.'

We both looked up as the door banged open and then just as quickly banged shut. Desi shrugged.

'False alarm,' he said.

He opened the ice-cream freezer and the cold heat from the freezer melted into the air. He began scooping ice cream into a glass sundae dish, vanilla, coffee, mint chocolate chip, and then covered the ice cream with a layer of chocolate sauce, then a layer of marshmallow topping, and finally a few healthy squirts of Reddi-wip. He picked up a spoon and casually began digging in. Angie hated that Desi could eat like that and never gain an ounce. She said that all she had to do was look at food and she gained ten pounds. Desi said she did a lot more than look, but only when Angie wasn't around.

5

I glanced up at the Coca-Cola clock behind the counter, wondering where everyone was. I'd left the A&P, where I worked, at three o'clock and figured I'd hang out at Comanche Street until it was time to go home for dinner. It was one of those dirty, overcast days in early summer and no one was at any of the usual places. They were probably at somebody's house, in Billy's basement, or maybe at Nanny's. I thought about calling but the taste of the egg cream, the whoosh of the overhead fan, Desi's familiar gluttony were all reassuring. Part of me was afraid I might be missing something, but I was always afraid of missing something. We all were. That's why we raced through family dinners, snuck out of bedroom windows, took dogs out for walks that lasted three hours, said we had school projects and had to hang out at the library until it closed at nine o'clock at night.

The way I felt now, though, unless Luke was involved, there wasn't that much for me to miss. Part of me was hoping he'd come into Eddy's to buy cigarettes or the latest surfing magazine. Something. I'd only seen him once since he got back from Vietnam last Sunday, right here in Eddy's. I hadn't been prepared, though; I hadn't washed my hair or gotten my tan yet, and I hid in one of the phone booths in back until he left. Since the summer before tenth grade, I'd been watching Luke McCallister, from street corners, car windows, in movie theaters, where some girl would have her arm draped around his back and I'd watch that arm instead of the movie, wanting to cut it off. I'd comfort myself that she was hanging all over him, that if he'd really been into her, it would have been the other way around. Luke was three years older, his world wider than Comanche Street and the lounge at The Starlight

Hotel, all the places we hung out. But I was eighteen now, almost finished with school and ready for real life. It was summer, and anything was possible.

'Mystery,' Desi said, and I jumped a little, thinking he could read my mind. That's exactly what I was thinking about Luke, that he was more of a mystery now than before he'd left for the jungle two years ago. I looked at Desi, who was scraping the last little bits of marshmallow sauce from the sundae dish. He pointed the stem of his spoon toward me.

'You gotta have mystery, otherwise you got nothing.'

I slurped the remains of my egg cream through the straw, making it last. Then I lit a cigarette. 'I still have no idea what you're talking about,' I said. 'Speaking of mysteries.'

Desi sighed. He carried the sundae dish over to the sink and rinsed it, then set it in the drain on the side. He came over to where I was sitting and put his palms flat down on the counter and stared at me, hard. 'Here's what I'm talking about,' he said. 'A girl comes in here, she's got on a nice blouse, maybe see-through, maybe she's not wearing a bra, I don't know. I look, I'm excited, I start imagining possibilities. But a girl comes in here topless, her jugs bouncing all over the counter? That's it for me. I'm immediately turned off. Why? Because now I got nothing. There's nothing left to my imagination. There's no mystery, you see what I'm saying here?'

I rolled my eyes. 'Yeah, right. Like some girl would come in here topless and sit down at the counter and you'd have no interest.' But I could see that Desi wasn't listening. He was just standing there, leaning against the counter with this dreamy little smile on his face.

7

'What?' I asked finally.

'Nothing,' he said after a moment. 'I was just—' He picked up his cigar from the ashtray and relit the stub. 'There was this girl, see. Back in Howard Beach. Before I started going with Angie. She used to wear this sky-blue sweater when she came around the corner.' He took a long pull from the cigar. 'Little teeny-tiny pearl buttons, all the way up to her neck.' Embers spilled from the cigar stub and showered the counter.

'All those buttons,' Desi said, gazing through the smoke, as if he was watching someone walking toward him. He put the cigar back in the ashtray and sighed again. He picked up the rag and began wiping the dead embers off the counter.

'Ah, you kids,' he said. 'You think you invented it. All of it! Everything. You think you invented *life*.'

TWO

babies

Everyone was waiting for Maggie Mayhew's baby to be born. It seemed as though she'd been pregnant forever; walking down the aisle of St. Timothy's Church last winter, her belly already starting to swell under her paisley granny gown. She'd cradled against her breasts a bouquet of tall lilies, which left rust stains that never washed out of the bodice of her wedding dress. Now she was past due, and the fat joints that Matty, her husband, had rolled and saved to hand out instead of cigars had long been smoked.

'You're so big, does that mean a boy?' Nanny asked when we stopped by on our way to the beach. Maggie was her cousin, a couple of years older than we were; she was already working as a secretary in Manhattan, at an advertising agency on Madison Avenue.

Maggie smiled. 'That's so sexist,' she said gently. 'Girls can be big, too. Girls can do big things. My girl will.' She patted her belly, rippling with life underneath her peasant blouse.

'Someone should ask her if girls do such big fucking things why she sits in the house every night while Matty's out with the boys,' Liz said later, when we were walking up the block to where the Buick Skylark her father had given her as a graduation present was parked. It was June, and up and down Comanche Street, shuttered bungalows were being opened by families coming down from the city for the summer. 'I wouldn't put up with that shit.'

'He really loves her, though,' Nanny said. 'You should have seen at the wedding, the minute the priest finished, Matty grabbed her and gave her this, like, earthshaking kiss. He wouldn't let her go.'

'You think this home birth was her idea or Matty's?' Liz said. 'I think it was his. I think she'll do anything he tells her to do.'

Maggie and Matty lived in a bungalow at the end of Comanche Street, with her brothers, Raven and Cha-Cha. At night, you'd see Matty and Raven walking to the beach to get high before heading out to the bars, huddled into their faded jean jackets against the late spring chill, while Maggie sat on the sagging steps of the bungalow, hands resting on the rising slope of her stomach.

'You should have heard Aunt Francie,' Nanny said. 'She was over our house ranting the other day, saying she screamed until her lungs hurt that they had to go to the hospital, this was the twentieth century, for chrissake, but Maggie stood her ground for once, told her, "Ma, it's my baby, I'll have it however the hell I want." I don't know if she's really brave or just plain crazy.' Liz and I had grown up in Elephant Beach, but Nanny and all her cousins were originally city

10

people, from Washington Heights, way up at the tip of Manhattan. Their parents had moved them to Long Island to escape the gangs and the drugs and other bad influences, but the kids had brought it all with them.

'Well, women did it for years,' Liz said. 'Years and years. Of course, the attending physicians weren't a bunch of stoned potheads and a speed freak. But I'll tell you the truth, when my time comes, it's gonna be, "Give me the drugs, man, give me the drugs."'

I heard a crackling sound and blinked. Liz was snapping her fingers in front of my eyes. 'Earth to Katie, earth to Katie,' she chanted. 'Spacewoman, where are you?'

'Just thinking,' I said, and was saved by Mitch coming down the street from the opposite direction, his bad leg stuttering behind his good one. He was singing 'It's All Over Now.' Mitch was a Stones freak; he played 'Satisfaction' and 'You Can't Always Get What You Want' on the jukebox at The Starlight Lounge about twenty times a night. He was carrying a paper bag from Eddy's.

'Hiya, handsome,' Liz said, and we all waved and whistled.

Mitch laughed out loud. 'Hey, little foxes,' he said, grinning broadly. He twirled his cane outward with a flourish and bowed from the waist, almost falling over but saving himself just in time. He blew us a kiss and kept walking down Comanche Street, singing.

'Man, what a waste of skin,' Liz said when he was past us.

'Guy loses his leg in Nam, gets the Purple Heart, you call him a waste of skin?' Nanny always got emotional about the war; her cousin, Sean, died in Vietnam just last year, and

11

another cousin, Quinn, was in the army but so far hadn't been out of Fort Worth, Texas.

'I'm not talking about his leg,' Liz said. 'Please, what do you take me for? His leg I can deal with. But he's, like, three sheets to the wind and it's not even noon yet.'

'Which makes him so different from everyone else around here,' I said.

'Yeah, but we're still young, we'll outgrow it,' Liz said. 'Mitch is, what, pushing thirty? That's old to still be drinking your breakfast. But he's so sexy, right? He reminds me of Clint Eastwood in that movie we saw last year, what was the name of it? Where he plays a Yankee soldier whose leg gets amputated—'

'*The Beguiled,*' I said.

'Yeah! That's the one,' Liz said. 'You don't think he looks like Clint? A Clint who's fucked up most of the time? Those eyes, and he has the sexiest wrists—'

'"Wrists?"' Nanny rolled her eyes. 'What, are *you* three sheets to the wind?'

'I noticed it one night when I was standing next to him at the bar,' Liz said. 'He was lighting a cigarette, and I swear, if I wasn't so into Cory—'

Nanny and I looked at each other. Cory McGill was Liz's big love, but how he felt about her was another story.

I was glad that Mitch had come along, though, so I didn't have to tell them I was thinking about Luke. Even my best friends didn't know how I felt; I didn't want it all over the earth before anything happened. His brother, Conor, said that Luke was not himself, that he stayed in his room all day and then went out late at night and must have walked the beach because the floor of his room was covered with sand. He slept most of the time, or gazed out the window, smoking. One night, Conor came home and found Luke sitting by the window. When he asked if something was wrong, Luke said, 'Nothing, man, just happy to be home,' and told Conor to go to sleep. The windowsill had been filled with cigarette butts. His bags were still stacked by the closet door, waiting to be opened. 'My brother's messed up for sure, man,' Conor said worriedly. But I wasn't overly concerned. Luke had just come back from a war, which was bound to make anyone act weird. Besides, real summer hadn't started yet; it wasn't even the end of June, and he had to come out sometime. At night, smoking my last cigarette in front of the mirror, I'd practice the things I would say when I saw him. Words that would make him take notice, wonder where I'd been all these years.

Then I thought about Maggie, of how peaceful she looked, sitting there on the steps, as though she didn't want for anything in the world. I wondered how it would be to carry Luke's baby inside me, to have that weight against my skin, beneath my heart.

'God, can you believe it, we're finally getting out of this dump?' Nanny said.

'Really,' I said, though walking the halls of Elephant Beach High School made me feel like crying. I hadn't loved school since I graduated from sixth grade, but every morning when my alarm clock went off at seven, at least I knew what to expect.

'I can already hear my mother, when they give out the awards and all that shit,' Liz said. '"Look, Dick, none of Liz's friends won the Regents scholarship. None of Liz's friends were named Athlete of the Year."'

We arrived at the main office and walked underneath the banner that stretched across the doorway and read 'Best of Luck, Class of '72.' Mrs. Cathaway was handing out boxes and crossing names off a sheet of yellow lined paper. 'Here you go,' she said, handing Nanny the box that held her cap and gown. She ran a red pencil through Nanny's name with a flourish.

'Gonna miss us, Mrs. Cathe – Cathaway?' Liz asked sweetly. We smothered our smiles; she'd almost slipped and called her Mrs. Catheter, which everyone called her behind her back. Mrs. Cathaway was the secretary to the principal, Dr. Steadman, and sat sentry outside his office like a guard dog. Whenever she said, 'Dr. Steadman will see you now,' it always sounded as though you were getting an audience with God and should consider yourself blessed.

'Good luck, girls,' Mrs. Cathaway told us, then clamped her lips shut tight as a purse.

We left the office and walked down the hall to the South Wing bathroom, where all the Trunk kids hung out. It was in this very bathroom that Liz and I had first become friends. Nanny came later, when Liz started bringing me around and she saw that it was safe for us to be friends. It was back in the fall of our sophomore year, right before third period when Barbara Malone had started pulling the hair right out of my head because she thought her boyfriend had winked at me in study hall. Liz had jumped on Barbara's back and rode

14

her around the bathroom, threatening to dunk her in the toilet bowl if she didn't leave me the fuck alone. I was surprised, because Liz and I had only ever spoken in the one class we had together, World History, or to bum cigarettes from each other in the bathroom. I had no idea why she'd plucked me from the shadows to come to my defense. But I was excited when she extended the invitation to come hang out on Comanche Street. The Trunk was an exotic, forbidden place, older and rougher than other neighborhoods in town, where kids stood on street corners doing secret, forbidden things out in the open. Whenever we drove through there on the way back from my grandmother's house in Brooklyn, I'd watch them from the windows of my parents' car, wondering at the ease with which they slouched against the walls of the shabby bars and candy stores that lined the dark, narrow streets. I wanted that for myself. I wanted to feel sure of something that no one could take away from me. Besides, it was a lonely time for me; Marcel, my best friend since junior high school, wasn't around much because of family troubles and I didn't know where I belonged anymore.

'Shit,' Nanny said, looking at herself in the smeared mirror. The blue graduation gown was billowing around her like a tent. 'You could fit two of me in here, it's so friggin' big. Ginger could have worn this and no one would've ever suspected she was pregnant.'

'She wasn't going to graduate, baby or no baby,' Liz said, stuffing her gown carelessly back into the box. 'She cut out so much in junior year that when she came up to withdraw, they didn't even have her name on the list, man. They didn't even know who she *was*.'

15

Nanny was tearing the cellophane off a fresh pack of Marlboros. 'What do you think?' she asked. 'One for the road? I mean, what are they gonna do three days before graduation, suspend us?'

'Suspend us, right,' Liz said, taking out her own pack. 'You think they want us back here next year?'

'Fuck 'em if they can't take a joke,' I said, lighting up. I looked around at the puke-green walls and faded green-and-black tiles. Would I miss this? Any of it?

Nanny started to say something, but Liz held up her hand for silence. She closed the door to the bathroom, then turned back to us. 'I got something to tell you guys and I don't want any interruptions,' she said. 'And you have to swear on your mother's life you won't breathe a word to anyone, ever. No shit.'

Nanny and I nodded, trying to keep our faces straight. It was Liz who had the big mouth; she couldn't keep a secret to save her life.

Liz sat back down on the edge of the sink, lit a cigarette. The smoke streamed into the filtered sunlight coming through the window. She smiled in a way I'd never seen her smile before.

'Me and Cory did it last night,' she said.

We looked at her. In the mirror I could see Nanny's eyes bugging out. Cory McGill was a couple years older than us and worked at Liz's father's dealership on Merrick Road, where Liz was working for the summer. They did a lot of wisecracking at work and had made out a couple of times in the parking lot when Liz's father wasn't around, but he'd never even asked her out.

'So, you mean, like—'

'Yep,' Liz said, nodding smugly. 'That's exactly what I mean.' She leaned back against the tiles and closed her eyes, smiling.

'But when?' I asked. 'How did it—'

She opened her eyes and turned toward us, waving her cigarette like a wand. 'I went to work yesterday, right, and I looked really hot even though I can't wear halters and shit because of my father, and I had on my new Maidenform, the off-white one with the cream lace. So we were kidding around, and he kept looking for excuses to get close to me, you know, hanging around the reception desk, the kitchen whenever I went in to make fresh coffee, like that. You know Thursday's our late night, we close at nine thirty, so he comes up to me, he says, "I'm taking the Dodge out for a test run up Sunrise Highway, you wanna come for the ride?" And I'm like, "Yeah, sure," he never asked me to come out on a run before, right? In the Dodge Challenger, forest green, my lucky color. So I'm like, there, man, I'm totally psyched.

'So we barely pull out of the lot and he turns into a friggin' octopus, he's like all over me at the red lights, and then all of a sudden he pulls up behind this boarded-up White Castle on Sunrise Highway, and he says, "Let's get in back." So now we're in the backseat, and it's getting, it's getting really hot, I mean, like the windows are fogging, and I tell him, I say, "Cory, Cory, man, I'm a virgin," and he says, "Liz, I swear on my mother's life I'll handle you with kid gloves. I'll make it the most beautiful night of your life," and then it's, like, it all happened at once, man. Like, everything.'

'You are blowing my freakin' mind,' Nanny said.

17

'Wait a minute,' I said. 'What about your father? Where was he?'

Liz made a face. 'Thursday night's his poker night, he lets Cory close up,' she said. 'Where'd you think he was, man? In the car with us?' She laughed. 'Not that it would matter, you know he never pays me any attention.'

'What did it feel like?' Nanny whispered.

Liz leaned forward. 'I don't know where all the hearts and flowers and violins come in,' she whispered back. 'All that bullshit they tell you. Because it hurt like hell. I was in brutal, brutal pain, it's like I got welts and bruises all up and down my back, on my ass.'

'What about – I mean, did you use something? Did he—'

'"I got rhythm, I got music,"' she started singing.

'Liz, man—'

'You don't know what it's like,' she whispered, closing her eyes again. 'When I felt him come inside me. It's like this – this total rush, when you make a guy come.' She started rocking, gently, against the wall behind the sink, that smile playing on her lips. 'That was the best part of the whole thing. It's like – it's so intense, man, it's like you're living and dying, all at once.' A slight shudder went through her body, and then she opened her eyes wide and looked around the bathroom as though she'd never seen it before.

'But Liz,' I said. 'I mean, shit—'

'And he said the most romantic thing,' she said, her eyes shining. 'After, he said, "Baby, if I knew it was going to be your first time, I would have taken out the Cadillac Sedan instead of the Dodge."'

'Liz—'

18

Liz leaned over and patted my thigh. 'That's okay,' she said. 'You just don't understand the way passion works. Anyway, it's safe, my period's due in a couple days, I can feel it. My tits are killing me, man, it's like they're gonna pop off and hit the fucking ceiling any minute.'

Nanny snorted. 'That's what my cousin Maggie thought and look what happened,' she said. 'That's what everyone thinks. I mean, look at Ginger, man. If you're going to see him again, you should—'

'What do you mean, if I'm going to see him again?' Liz said, staring hard at Nanny. 'Guy just took my virginity and I'm not going to see him again?'

'If you're going to see him again,' Nanny said patiently, 'you should think about going on the Pill.'

Liz shook her head. 'Uh-uh,' she said. She cupped her breasts in her hands. 'No way. I don't want these babies getting any bigger.'

'Well, what are you going to do?' Nanny asked, exasperated. 'You gotta do something.'

'I don't have to do anything,' Liz said, smiling. 'I don't have to do a fucking thing.'

Nanny and I stayed silent. When Liz got this way over a guy, it was like she was high on angel dust or something, her brain riffing bullshit. 'Delusional' didn't even begin to cover it.

'So when are you going to see him again?' I asked, finally.

'Tonight,' she said, smiling her new smile. 'I'll see him tonight at work.'

'I mean,' I said, 'I mean, are you going to – did he say anything, like—'

'Oh, grow up,' Liz snapped. 'The whole thing just happened, what's he going to say? I mean, he had to get the car cleaned after, he probably paid for it out of his own pocket. He put his job in jeopardy for me, what more does he have to say?'

I looked at Nanny and shrugged: *I give up.*

'And besides,' Liz said, sounding suddenly aggrieved, 'you guys, you're like freaking me out, man, all these questions, I mean, you should be happy for me, being with Cory, knowing how I feel about him, after all this time—' She jumped off the sink, started walking toward the door.

'It's not like we're not happy for you,' Nanny said.

'It's just, we don't want you to get hurt, is all,' I finished lamely.

But Liz wasn't listening. She had stopped in front of the mirror, staring at her reflection.

'Do I look different?' she asked. 'I feel different.' She ran her hands down her breasts, over her stomach. 'What if I'm pregnant?' she whispered.

Nanny's eyes grew huge with alarm. She looked at me. Suddenly I felt depressed and I didn't know why.

'Is that what you want?' I asked.

Liz just smiled her new smile, her eyes staring at us backward through the mirror. 'Wouldn't that be a trip, man? Walking down the aisle at graduation with Cory's baby inside me?' She turned sideways, her hands clasped over her womb. 'Wouldn't that just be something else?'

It seemed as though the car was flying, but we were only doing around sixty, and that was safe on the Meadowbrook Parkway.

'Ginger called me,' Nanny said from the backseat. 'I wanted to go with her, but she said the cab was already honking in the street and she had to run.'

'She took a *cab*? To the *hospital*? Where was her mother?' I asked.

'Oh, Mrs. Shea, mother of the year?' Nanny said. 'She wasn't around, surprise, surprise. You got that lighter, or should I start rubbing two sticks together?'

Liz cruised into the right lane, cutting off a white Mustang. The driver began honking frantically. 'Your horn blows good, how about your mother?' Liz yelled back at him.

'God, it's so lonely even thinking about taking a cab to have your baby,' I said, passing the lighter back to Nanny. And it must have cost a fortune, since Ginger was going to County instead of Elephant Beach Hospital. She had to have the baby there because she didn't have any money or health insurance and she was only seventeen years old.

Liz patted my thigh. 'That's why we're here, sweetie,' she said. 'For moral support. It's too bad we couldn't have taken her there ourselves, but—' Liz shrugged. She'd been just getting off work when Nanny called, and she was the only one of us with a car.

'Jesus, what if she had the baby in the cab?' Nanny said. 'You think that could have happened? I saw a movie once, the woman was stuck in traffic, right, and her water broke—'

'This isn't a fucking movie,' Liz said, racing a blue Volkswagen bug to get into the exit lane. 'Things like that

21

don't happen in real life. She's probably still in labor, won't have the baby for hours.'

But Ginger's baby had already been born, so quickly it was like he was sliding down the water chute at Coney Island, out and about in less than an hour after she arrived at the hospital. 'That's the way it always is with your kind,' the nurse told her, before she scooped the baby up and took him away. Now Ginger was sitting up in bed, her breasts hanging over her belly inside the thin cotton smock, looking wiped out. A strange woman was sitting at her bedside, talking in low, serious tones and trying to push some papers into her hand.

'Anyone got a cigarette?' Ginger greeted us. We all started shoving packs at her, and the strange woman said, 'You really shouldn't be smoking so soon afterward.'

'The baby's born,' Ginger said, her voice weary. 'And this cigarette isn't going to do anything to me the last six thousand haven't done.'

'If you'd only see your child, I'm sure you'd—'

'Who is she?' Liz asked.

'Who are you again?' Ginger asked the woman.

'My organization represents young girls like yourself, who get in the family way and can't care for their children,' the woman said, facing Ginger. 'We help them to—'

'How long since you gave birth, Ginger?' Liz asked.

Ginger shrugged tiredly. 'About an hour. Doc said it was like dropping kittens, and I told you what the nurse said, the bitch.'

'So the labor took about an hour, and now you're here – let's make it two hours,' Liz said, checking her watch.

'Yeah, about that,' Ginger said, sinking back against the pillows, her eyes closed.

'And you come around, bugging her about mistakes?' Liz asked the woman. 'What were you, waiting outside the delivery room?'

The woman flushed over her stiff mouth up to her veiled eyes, but she still didn't move off the bed. 'My organization wants to help girls like – er – what did you say your name was?' She riffled through the papers she was holding, frowning, impatient.

'You want to help her so much, you don't even know her name?' Nanny asked. 'I think it's time for you to hit the road, Jackie.'

'I don't think—' the woman started, but we moved in on her, practically crushing her off the bed as we sat down.

'Right. Don't think,' Liz said. 'Just make like an egg and beat it. Before we beat you.'

In a flash, the woman was off the bed and out the door.

'Thanks,' Ginger said, opening her eyes. 'I thought she'd never leave. I mean, I told her I was giving the kid up, what more does she want?'

'Screw her,' Liz said, lighting a cigarette. She handed it to Ginger. 'How you feeling?'

'You want anything, Ginge?' Nanny asked gently. 'Something to eat? A Tab, maybe?'

'Here's some water,' I said, pouring from the pitcher on the side table into a plastic cup. I held it close to Ginger's lips while she sipped, and put my other arm around her. She leaned against me. 'Thanks,' she whispered, and closed her eyes again.

On the way out of the hospital, we stopped to see the baby. He was in a glass cubicle, a big baby boy, fast asleep, like his mother had been when we left her.

'He's a bruiser,' Nanny said, peering through the glass. 'You think he looks like anyone we know?'

'He was just born, for chrissake,' Liz said. 'They don't look like anybody then, and the eyes change color after a few weeks.'

Rumor had it that Allie D'Amore was the father; he and Ginger had been together on and off since eighth grade. But after they'd broken up the last time, she started hanging out with a lot of guys, and Allie wouldn't even look at her when she came around Comanche Street, barefoot, wearing a man's oversized white tee shirt that strained against her belly. Then he flipped out after doing some beat acid and now he was in a psych ward somewhere out on the Island and no one had seen him for weeks.

'I'm glad she didn't see him,' Nanny said. 'The baby, I mean. She might have changed her mind and kept him.'

'That might not have been such a bad thing,' Liz said. 'Maybe then Miss Ginger would have to do something else besides get high and fuck the world.'

'Don't talk about her that way,' Nanny said, her hazel eyes huge with tears. She and Ginger had grown up together, when their families only came down to Elephant Beach for the summer and they used to buy cough syrup at Coffey's Drugs and drink it to get high behind the old umbrella factory. Liz shrugged and lit a cigarette directly beneath the 'No Smoking' sign in the hallway.

Ginger told me she'd thought about keeping it, one night

24

when we were going to the bathroom behind the dunes on the beach. That's where all the girls had to go, since the public restrooms closed after six o'clock. We called it the Elephant Hole. She said she was afraid she'd be like her mother and her sisters, who'd all had babies out of wedlock. 'It's in the blood, Kate,' she said, zipping her jeans only halfway over her ballooning belly. 'You can't escape what's in the blood.' I wondered if that was true. I thought of my own mother, the one who'd given me up for adoption. Did she decide one night, while zipping up her jeans at an Elephant Hole of her own? Had she been like Ginger, who never stopped getting high, or smoking, or any of the things you hear expectant mothers shouldn't do? Though she did drink a lot of chocolate malteds at the counter at Eddy's. 'Good for the baby,' she'd say, patting her stomach, while Desi shook his head, ringing up the cash register.

The ride home was quieter. I was sitting in the backseat, smoking, listening to Rod Stewart belt out 'Maggie May' on the radio, thinking about Luke. Conor said he was still hanging out in his bedroom, taking walks late at night, sitting up smoking when he should have been sleeping. Conor said he was quiet, still, more quiet than before he went away. Even when Ray Mackey, his best friend, came over to see him. 'It was way weird, man,' Conor said. 'I mean, Luke and Ray were like brothers, tighter than him and me, being the same age and all. I could tell Ray was, like, hurt, man. He pulled me aside after, asked me if Luke was like this with everyone since he got back.'

I thought about Luke sitting by his window, staring out at the ocean, as if he was seeing new worlds across the water.

I wanted him in this world. I wanted him in Elephant Beach, living with me in one of the bungalows that lined Comanche Street. I thought about standing in front of our bungalow, waiting for him to come home at night, rocking our daughter in the misty twilight until she slept. She would have eyes like mine and Luke's, and honey-colored hair as silky fine as beach grass when it first starts growing, slender stalks that bend slightly in the wind. She would look like the best of us and grow up laughing. Her laugh would sound like silver bells when we lifted her in and out of the shallow waves at the shoreline.

~⌇~

Maggie Mayhew was having her baby at last. There would be no interference of relatives or hospitals where everything was white and sterile. Beth Fagan, Maggie's best friend, was the midwife; she'd just completed her first year of nursing school. If the baby was a girl, they were naming it Joni; if it was a boy, Donovan.

We were all crowded in front of the bungalow, inside the chain-link fence, where we could see the glow of white candles through the windows. It was after supper but still light out and everyone was milling around. It was what we did every night, but now there was a purpose. I searched the crowd of faces for Luke's, but he wasn't there.

Inside the bungalow, Maggie let out a scream. 'What are they, beating her with chains in there?' Mr. Connelly called over the fence. He was sitting on his front steps, drinking a Budweiser. You couldn't hide anything on Comanche Street;

26

the houses were so close together, the neighbors could hear every cough, every moan during the night. They often ended up in one another's dreams by mistake.

'Really, man,' Mitch said. 'I mean, giving birth's a trip all right, but it's not like she's in a fucking rice paddy in the middle of the Mekong Delta, for chrissake.'

'Yeah, like you'd know what giving birth is like,' Liz said.

Nanny banged out of the bungalow, slamming the screen door behind her. 'Fuck it, I'm calling Aunt Francie,' she said, heading to the pay phone by the entrance to the beach.

'I feel like we should go to church, light a candle,' Liz said.

'Fuck that,' Billy Mackey said. He lit a match and held it high. 'Here's our church, man. Right here. It's the church of life, man! Light your matches. Lift your matches to the sky for the baby.' He was so stoned his eyes looked like they were about to fall out of his face.

Everyone took it up. It was a clear night, no wind coming off the ocean. The sunset fell in ribbons across the sky. Soon the air was filled with matchsticks and lighters; when the matches went out, we lit others to take their place. People held cigarettes to the sky until they glowed down to stubs.

'It's like a Dead concert, man,' Timmy Jones said, ecstatic. He was a real Dead Head and followed them around the country, hitchhiking to wherever they were playing.

'No, man,' Billy said solemnly. 'It's like the concert of life.'

Mrs. Connelly came out of her bungalow next door with a large plastic bag in her hand. She looked over at us, and then shook her head pityingly. 'Assholes,' she said. She put the bag in the trash can near the fence, waddled back inside and slammed the door behind her.

27

We heard the sirens come screaming up the street. Aunt Francie pulled up behind the ambulance in her silver Toyota. She didn't look at us as she ran into the house behind the ambulance crew. Nanny followed her inside.

Minutes later, everyone emerged. The medics carried Maggie on a stretcher, her eyes closed. Matty and Beth were on either side of her, and Beth was leaning down, whispering. Nanny came behind them, shaking her head. 'No show, yet,' she said. Raven and Cha-Cha followed, with Aunt Francie bringing up the rear, beating them around their heads and shoulders with her handbag. 'You were breathing with her?' she screamed, swatting at Raven. 'What the hell were you going to do if she stopped breathing, stop with her?' She marched to the ambulance and jumped in back with Maggie, then looked out at her sons one last time, shaking her head. 'If youse had two brains, you'd both be half-wits,' she said. The medic closed the doors and the ambulance raced up the block.

Everyone on Comanche Street applauded as the ambulance pulled away. Once it turned the corner, we all started drifting toward the lounge at The Starlight Hotel. I thought of Maggie, so sure she would have a daughter. I thought about Luke, staring out his bedroom window, looking sad enough to cry. You had to be prepared for anything in this life. I wanted him to stay here, but if he couldn't, then I would go with him. Maybe we would live in the mountains for a while. Maybe our baby would be born in the mountains. The beach had been my life, but I was growing tired of Comanche Street, the drinking, the drugs, everyone falling asleep in the sand with lit cigarettes between their fingers. Waiting for something to happen, night after night.

I decided that if he wanted to, Luke and I would leave Elephant Beach together. We would find a cabin at the foot of a mountain and at night we would sit by the firelight. Our daughter would lie at our feet, swaddled in a brightly colored quilt, and the sound of her laughter would run over us like a clear, bright stream.

THREE

sex and drugs and rock 'n' roll

On those summer nights, after I finished my shift at the A&P and showered, I would look in the bathroom mirror and it seemed to me that my eyes had never been brighter, my hair never shinier, my tan never more even. My peasant shirts hung perfectly off my shoulders and my jeans settled on my hips as though they lived there. Even my teeth seemed straighter. I looked exactly as I had always wanted to look, and sometimes I'd close my eyes and feel so good about it I knew I could never tell anyone because they'd think I was too crazy to live.

On those nights, while I was getting ready to walk down to Comanche Street, my mother would lean against the door-jamb of the bathroom, watching me put on my mascara, smelling my perfume. Her eyes would narrow and her lips would purse into a thin, pinched line. I wouldn't say anything, but my hands would start shaking a little, so that the mascara brush would slip and smear my eyelid closer to the brow. I'd reach across the sink to tear off a piece of toilet paper, dab it with cold water, and wipe my eyelid until the black stain disappeared. Then I'd steady my hand so that the brush washed lightly over my lashes, careful not to leave clumps.

'Again?' my mother would say from the doorway. And then we were off. She always started out as though trying to be reasonable, but once I heard the sharpness edging into her voice, I moved faster and sometimes I wasn't really listening at all and other times I ran out of the house with her voice chasing me, like a wayward knife, stopping short of the front door only so the neighbors wouldn't hear. What she said was never the same yet always the same, usually about hanging around street corners, how she'd driven past Comanche Street on her way home from Top Banana, the discount vegetable store, and saw them all standing in front of Eddy's, my God that hair! Those clothes! They looked like a bunch of circus freaks. No wonder I had failed Regents geometry and now look, I'd gotten accepted only to Carver Community College, how did I expect to get up in the world? Here we lived on a tree-lined street with a lawn instead of farther down the Trunk where there was only sky and concrete and people living lives that were going nowhere. By the end of June, she was lamenting the prom, or the fact that I hadn't had one. 'I always wanted to have a daughter,' she said, 'so that on prom night I could watch her walking down the stairs to meet her date and put on her corsage and then wait up so that when she came home, we could have tea together and she'd tell me all about it.' But we didn't have a staircase, our house was all on one level, and the senior class at Elephant Beach High School had voted not to have a prom; we'd voted

31

instead to have a camping trip at Tully State Park, but in the end nobody signed up because there would be too many chaperones and mosquitoes.

On the Friday night that Luke was finally supposed to come out to the lounge at The Starlight Hotel, my mother never said a word. She just kept watching me until I turned out the light in the bathroom and brushed past her on my way to the front door, mumbling good-bye, waiting for her to say something, to start screaming that I was wasting time, why couldn't I just give myself a chance, that these years would never come back, why couldn't I understand that? It was always hard to tell with my mother. When she wasn't yelling at me about something, I longed for her touch, for the way she would sit on my bed some nights, holding my hand, talking in the darkness as though we were the closest of friends; telling me how badly she'd wanted a daughter, how thrilled she was when they received the call from the adoption agency, how the day they'd brought me home from St. Joseph's had been the happiest day of her life. At those times, I thought she loved me more than anyone, even my father and brother. But then it would start all over again, that hectic, hazardous edge in her voice that made my throat tighten, that had me feeling so relieved when I shut the door behind me and walked out into the night, where anything could happen.

On that Thursday night, though, when I reached the door, I heard only silence behind me. My brother was out playing stickball with the neighborhood boys and my father was still at work. I turned back and saw my mother standing in the archway of our living room, watching me leave. Her eyes were smudged with sadness. 'You look so pretty,' was all she said, and then she turned away, as if the sight of me was more than she could bear.

～ᵧ～

It was barely July, still the earliest thrush of summer, and ever since graduation, hands had been coming at me like a swarm of three-headed flies; arms hooking around me, tugging at the fringes of my suede belt, trying to lure me for a walk on the beach, or to sit on the abandoned lifeguard chair, where everyone went to ball. Boys I'd gone to school with, known forever, groping, sniffing, sliding around me, everyone high on acid or THC, thinking I was just as stoned as they were and it would be easy. Another time, I might have been more moved by the attention, because it had taken me so long to be accepted, not having gone to St. Timothy's Grammar like everyone else and my father wasn't a cop or a carpenter or a fireman; he wore a suit and tie to work and had gone to college. It had taken ages for me to belong, until shouts of greeting would go up when I approached Comanche Street, until I'd walk into Eddy's and Desi would point to me and say, 'Wait here, Liz and them went up to Coffey's Drugs and then they're picking you up to go to the church bazaar.' At night, when I walked down the block of close-knit bungalows, past freckle-faced children playing stickball in the street and mothers standing inside their chain-link fences smoking after-dishes cigarettes, and men sitting on their stoops, scratching, belching, watching the sunset, at the end of the block I'd see the crowd milling around the entrance to the beach, hear the

33

catcalls, the dogs barking, see ten-speeds flying, surfboards leaning against the seawall, cigarettes glowing like fireflies in the dusky heat, and my heart would beat harder, faster inside me, and I'd think to myself: *These are my people.*

But this summer, I didn't care about any of those boys, even the older ones who tried paying for my egg creams at Eddy's and buying me whiskey sours at the lounge at The Starlight Hotel. All that mattered was that Luke was home, and after years of watching him from street corners and car windows he was finally going to come to me, and I wanted to be alert, awake when it happened. After all these years of silent worship, I wanted to be *ready*.

On the way, walking down to Comanche Street, I passed the Brennans' house, where my best friend, Marcel, used to live. Now she was living up on Cape Cod with her husband, James, trying to figure out if she still loved him. I thought about stopping in briefly, asking Claudine, her mother, for a quick reading; nothing dramatic, just a seven-card shuffle, where I'd ask a question, and then Claudine would lay the cards in a semicircle on the kitchen table and tell me what I could expect when I finally saw Luke that night. But there really wasn't any such thing as a quick visit to the Brennans', even with Marcel gone, and I was supposed to pick Nanny up at her house by seven o'clock and it was already ten minutes after. So I hurried past, hoping Claudine hadn't been looking out the window and seen me hesitate. Part of me didn't want to know what the cards had to say. Now that Luke was back for real, it was up to me to find my fortune.

Nanny signaled me to step outside. We were in the lounge at The Starlight Hotel and I didn't want to step outside, because Luke was finally here and I wanted to be wherever he was. When he walked into the lounge with Ray and Raven and Cha-Cha, it was like he was some kind of celebrity. 'El Exigente,' Billy said, bowing in front of him, handing him a cold one. Christa Cutler, another of Nanny's city cousins who no one liked because she thought who the hell she was, shimmied over and threw her arms around Luke, kissed him on the lips.

Luke's honey-colored hair was longer, shaggier, cut ragged across his forehead. His eyes looked tired and he was thinner than before he'd gone away and had lost his surfing muscles. He was wearing a plaid flannel shirt over a white tee shirt and faded jeans and flip-flops. He was wearing what pretty much everyone wore but he looked more beautiful than anyone else. I was wondering whether I should go over and throw my arms around him and kiss him longer than Christa had. I was watching myself in my mind's eye, wondering if my breath smelled good enough to do it. But right then Nanny came over and tugged at my arm and said, 'Katie, man, come on, come out to the alley with me. I have to talk to you. I *need* to talk to you.'

I began walking with her and turned back once to see Luke standing at the end of the bar near the patio, surrounded by people. It would have been easy enough to join the crowd, sidle toward the center at some point and catch his eye. I saw them all raise their mugs of beer and heard Raven say, 'Welcome back, man. We missed the shit out of you.' Luke didn't smile. He seemed wiry and edgy, like he was coiled inside himself, away from everyone. He raised his glass but didn't drink.

I followed Nanny into the alley between the hotel and the summer apartments on the corner. Over Nanny's shoulder the moon hung low, slinging a white path across the ocean. Nanny put her hand on my arm and tried looking up at me. Whenever she was fucked up, her eyes looked like crooked stars.

'I have to tell you something and you can't tell anyone, not even Liz,' she said, her voice soft and slurry. 'Especially not Liz.'

'My sisters,' we heard, and there was Ginger, coming out of the alley.

'Shit,' Nanny murmured.

Ginger was wearing cutoffs and a tight tee shirt that hugged the weight she hadn't lost since the baby. She smelled of stale smoke and Boone's Farm Apple Wine.

'I missed you guys so much,' she said, putting her arms around us. 'Soooo much, man. Missed trucking with yas.' She backed up and looked at us, her eyes woozy. 'I really love you guys,' she said. 'You know, like when you came and visited me and the baby? That was, that was so far out, man. Like, far fucking out. I mean, I'm just glad it's over, you know? I mean, dig it, can you picture me with a kid?'

'Love you, too, Ginge,' I said, kissing her cheek, while Nanny swayed on her flip-flops, silent as stone.

'What's a matter, bitch, you don't love me anymore?' Ginger turned to Nanny, who she'd known for the longest.

'You know it,' Nanny said. 'You know I do, man. I'm just, I'm really stoned, Ginge. Really, really stoned. Even my tongue's like, tired, man.'

Ginger laughed. 'The tired tongue,' she said. 'Outasight.' She kissed each of us wetly on the cheek and walked around the corner, into the lounge. We watched the door swing open and then close. I turned back to Nanny.

'So what's the big secret I can't tell Liz?' I asked.

'Me and Voodoo did it the other night.'

'Wow,' I said. I meant it; it wasn't just something to say.

'He saw the hickeys,' she said, her voice dipping. 'We were fooling around, you know, bullshitting in the sand, and I turned my head the wrong way. I forgot to put on foundation and he saw them.'

Nanny really liked Voodoo. We all liked Voodoo because he was kind and easygoing and fun and affectionate. His real name was Dennis Kelly, but he was a Jimi Hendrix freak whose favorite song was 'Voodoo Chile,' which he listened to every morning before leaving the house and when he smoked a joint before going to bed. He wanted Len, the bartender, to put it in the jukebox, but Len refused; he thought Hendrix was nothing but empty noise. Voodoo wore a blue bandanna around his albino curls, which he'd trained into a white-boy Afro. It was a hard thing to pull off, but somehow he did it. Nanny really liked him, but she was crazy about Tony Furimonte – we called him Tony Fury – who was not kind or easygoing or fun and had a temper that stretched and snapped equally over big and little things. He'd been thrown out of school three weeks before graduation for punching Mr. Diamond, the history teacher, for giving him a failing grade for the quarter, even though he rarely went to class and frankly wasn't the brightest bulb in the chandelier. To punish him, his parents had sent him to live with his aunt and uncle in Providence, Rhode Island, to work construction and finish his senior year. They thought his chances were better in a place where nobody knew him. The night before Tony left, he and Nanny did everything-but in the attic of his parents' house, and still he wouldn't call her his girlfriend. He'd been home the first week in July because his grandmother had died, hence the hickeys on Nanny's neck. It was like he had to leave his mark on Nanny for Voodoo and everyone to see. Since Tony left, she'd been covering the hickeys with Max Factor makeup.

'So did he, like, freak out?' I asked.

Nanny tried to widen her eyes but her lids were like little logs, rolling downward. She stood there for a minute, nodding, her eyes closed. 'No,' she said. Her voice sounded broken. 'He just turned my head this way and that, and then he dropped his hand and he looked at me with those big, droopy eyes. And then he said, "You know, you are one sweet little heart-breaker, foxy lady." Made me feel like shit.'

I could hear laughter from inside The Starlight Hotel. The jukebox was playing 'Layla' by Derek and the Dominos. It was the song I listened to under my headphones late at night when I got home from Comanche Street. It was the song I'd always imagined would be playing while Luke and I made love.

'What was it like?' I asked her. I wanted to know what it was like to make love to someone you weren't in love with.

Nanny kept swaying. She put a hand on my arm to steady herself. 'Katie, man, swear to God, it was about as exciting as drinking an ice-cream soda,' she said. She had always loved kissing Voodoo. She said he was a great kisser. They liked walking with their arms around each other, Voodoo's

38

arm hooked around Nanny's neck, hugging her close. They'd be walking down Comanche Street, bumping into people coming from the other direction, because they were too busy laughing into each other's eyes to notice.

'Like maybe a strawberry ice-cream soda, not even a black-and-white,' she added. 'With no whipped cream.'

'Were you high?' I asked.

Nanny tried rolling her eyes but they were too heavy, so she closed them again. It *was* a pretty stupid question. 'What do you think?' she said. 'We were in his room, no one was home. The sheets were dirty, I could smell them. I didn't think my first time would be on dirty sheets.'

She hiccupped a sob. 'What am I going to do, Katie? What am I going to tell Tony? What if Voodoo tells him first?'

'Didn't you feel anything? With Voodoo, like, didn't you—'

'I just told you,' she said, frowning, impatient. 'Nothing. Nothing, nothing, nothing. I'm talking about Tony now.'

'You think Tony hasn't been with other girls?'

'It's different with guys,' she said. 'You know it is.'

'Besides,' I said, picking my words delicately, 'it's not like Tony – like you and Tony—'

'I love him, Katie,' she whimpered. 'The night before he went back, he stood outside my house throwing little rocks at my window. Like we were kids, right? And when I opened the window, he just looked up at me. Didn't say a word. Just kept looking up at me. Then he went back to his car, and he turned around and lifted his hand in this, like, wave. It was so romantic.' She closed her eyes again and began nodding. 'He never said, "I love you." But I know what was in his heart.'

'Let's go back inside,' I said, taking her arm. But Nanny

stayed surprisingly firm against my grip. 'Wait a minute,' she said. 'Wait one fucking minute. Just tell me the truth, Katie, that's all I want. Do you think Tony will think I'm a slut if he finds out?'

I'd seen Tony go ballistic when someone sat in the seat he wanted on the early bus going home from school. He would have beaten Porter Jacobs, the poor kid sitting in it, to a pulp if the bus driver hadn't pulled over and thrown Tony off the bus. They didn't call him Tony Fury for nothing.

'How is Tony going to find out?' I asked, making my voice strong. 'You aren't going to tell him—'

'I have to tell him,' Nanny said, sounding sorrowful, like someone had died.

'You don't have to do anything,' I said. 'You don't have to tell him a thing. Voodoo isn't going to say anything. I mean, what, you think he's going to write him a letter? And Tony won't be home until Christmas, right? Leave it alone till then, man. Leave it alone, Nanny babe.' That was what her mother called her. Nanny babe.

Suddenly her eyes swung open, like rolled-up shades that snapped. 'Should I confess?' she whispered. 'Maybe I should go to confession. Not with Father Donnelly, but maybe Father Tom—'

'Nanny,' I said. Confession was supposed to be anonymous, but the priests at St. Timothy's had known most of us since birth and now knew even our footfalls by heart.

'I'm so scared,' Nanny said. 'Katie, I'm so fucking scared. What if I'm pregnant? All he did was pull out, he always says he's sterile because he never knocked anybody up, but what if I'm—'

'It's not time to worry yet,' I said, firmly. That's what Atticus Finch used to tell Jem and Scout in *To Kill a Mockingbird*. Sometimes I said it to myself, inside. I found the words comforting.

'I wish,' she said haltingly. 'I wish . . .' Nanny's eyes closed again. She began rocking on the heels of her flip-flops. I looked toward the lighted windows of the lounge at The Starlight Hotel. The door was open and I could hear Bobby Darin singing 'Mack the Knife.'

'I'm going back inside,' I said. It was making me too sad, standing in the alley with Nanny. Luke barely knew I was alive, Tony Fury had never even bought Nanny a Coke. It felt like we were living in some kind of half-love twilight where everything was possible but nothing ever happened. I wanted to get back inside where there was light and music and Luke. By now, maybe the crowd around him had dispersed to play the jukebox or go out on the piazza to get high, and I could catch him alone, maybe grab the seat next to him at the bar and start a conversation that didn't sound stupid.

'Am I a slut, Katie?' Nanny asked again, her eyelids flinching. 'Tell me the truth. Do you think I am?'

'No,' I said quickly.

'Don't tell Liz,' she said again. 'She has a big fucking mouth, you know she does.'

'I won't,' I promised. Liz was at work, probably waiting for Cory to take her for another Thursday-night test drive. So far, they'd done it in a Chevy Monte Carlo, a Ford Mustang and a Cadillac Sedan DeVille. But he'd still never taken her to the movies or to the Sunrise Diner for coffee, or for a ride in his own car, a Triumph TR6 that he'd bought secondhand.

41

Liz wanted to marry him, even though she said it still hurt sometimes when he balled her, that she'd lie awake all night, throbbing, afterward. Even when there was love involved, something always seemed to hurt.

'Come on, man,' I said, growing impatient. It was late now. I took Nanny's arm again and guided her through the moonlit alley. Once, she missed a step and caused us both to stumble in the darkness.

When we got back inside, Luke and Mitch were sitting in the far corner of the bar near the jukebox, both of them smoking like chimneys, talking so intently I didn't dare go over. I went to play the jukebox instead, which was already buzzing with quarters, so I could listen to what they were saying. But between the music and the stoned babble all around me, it was hard to hear anything. I was turning to leave when I heard Mitch say, 'You know how it is over there, the flowers?' I stopped to listen. He went on: 'How sometimes you'd be walking and you'd forget for a minute why you were there? Because all around, man, so much damned beauty! All these exotic blooms, growing on top of each other! Orchids, right? You'd touch the petals and they gave off this scent, different from the flowers here, more delicate, but . . . pungent, that's the word. Delicately pungent. Like a – a psychedelic garden. But it never lasted because of all the, you know, the smoke, the . . . you know, right? Yeah . . . so we're walking, marching, by the river . . . the Mekong River . . . and we're stoned out of our tits, man, the weed was, like, tripping weed over there,

42

un-fucking-believable. Like the dope, man, everything so pure . . . and I see this, like . . . this giant . . . blossom, the biggest blossom I've ever seen, right on the river, like this unbeliev- ably beautiful flower just floating on the river, getting bigger and bigger, like it was taking over the river, right? Like the river was a big, fucking, flowing flower! I was just blown away, man. Blown the fuck away. So I went down by the riverbank, so I can, like, touch it, pick a piece of it to take with me, for, I don't know, luck or something, maybe give it to one of the girls to put in her hair or something. So . . . I start leaning in, to, like, pick a part of this river flower, and my buddy, Tang, he comes over and pulls me back, he's like, "What the fuck you doing, man?" And I'm like, "Get off me, man, I want to pick part of this flower, you ever seen anything so beautiful? You ever seen anything like it in your life?" And he looks at me, and he says, "Asshole, that ain't no flower." And I say, "Sure it is, just look at it, motherfucker! If that's not a flower, then what the fuck is it?" And he gets pissed, right, he shoves me so I'm almost in the river, and he says, "*You* look at it, motherfucker." And I turn and I put my hands on it, I plunge my hands right *in* it, and he's right, man. It ain't no fucking flower. It's blood. Blood on the water. Spreading as far as the eye could see.' Mitch laughed. He laughed like he'd heard a really funny joke. I didn't want to turn around, to seem as though I was eavesdropping. I didn't hear Luke laughing. I hadn't heard him say a word the entire time I'd been standing at the jukebox. I saw from the corner of my eye Len putting a twin set of shots in front of Mitch and Luke. Mitch downed his right away. 'Anytime anyone asks me, "What was it like over in Nam?" I tell them that story.

Whole country full of flowers, everywhere you look. All those flowers, drowning in blood. Hey, little darling!'

I looked up. I felt Mitch's hand on my arm. He pulled me so close I could smell how fucked up he was. His eyes were squinty and filled with light.

'*Mmm-mmm*, you look good enough to eat,' he crooned, looking me up and down. I was wearing the new brown cotton peasant shirt with the hand-sewn blue silk roses at the collar that I'd bought at Heads Up, the local hippie head shop. I'd bought it thinking of Luke, thinking it would be the perfect thing to wear when I saw him. But then Mitch kissed the side of my face and hugged me tight so that my back was to Luke and I couldn't see his face. I wondered what he was thinking.

When I turned around again, his seat was empty.

Mitch still had his arm around me and was banging on the bar with his other hand. 'Service! Service!' he cried over Pat Whalen and the Country Whalers singing 'The Wearin' of the Green.' 'A little service for the servicemen, Goddamnit!' I gently twisted out from under his arm and Mitch barely noticed, he just kept banging on the bar to get Len's attention. I thought maybe Luke was in the bathroom and would be coming back. I glanced toward the men's room, but when Billy came out and swung the door behind him, it looked empty. I waited a little longer, for the song to end, and then I was tired of waiting. I was ready to leave. I was out of cigarettes and I had to be at work early the next morning.

I walked away from Mitch and his clamoring for a drink he didn't need, looking around for Luke and not seeing him anywhere. I looked around for Nanny but couldn't find her, either. I felt my blood quicken with this new impatience that had been stalking me lately, at home, standing on the corner by Eddy's, at work, ringing things up on the cash register. Everything, everyone was moving too slowly for me. I was tired of waiting on people, on things to happen. That seemed like all I'd done for the past three years, since I'd first seen Luke coming off Comanche Street beach, carrying his surfboard, dripping and grinning and golden. And now I couldn't escape the feeling that everyone had been at the party for a while but I was just getting there, in danger of being left behind. Even now it was later than I thought, too late to walk home alone, so I started up Comanche Street to catch the bus on Lighthouse Avenue. I heard someone call my name and turned around. It was Bennie Esposito. He was walking instead of stumbling, and his eyes were wide and clear.

'Where you going so early, man?' And yet another surprise, he wasn't slurring his words. 'The night is young.'

'You okay, Bennie?' I asked.

He slipped a sly arm around me and pulled me close. 'I'd be better if you was to, say, take a little walk on the beach with me, maybe search for starfish, you know, it's an outasight night, man.' He winked at me and I laughed. Bennie was one of the city boys. I liked him. I used to have a crush on him, when he first moved to the Beach. When he wasn't on downs and his eyes were open, you could see how beautiful they really were.

'Well, it would be too obvious if I asked you over to see my etchings,' he said. 'Besides, my room's a fucking mess.'

'It's late,' I said. 'I have to be to work at nine tomorrow.'

'Ouch,' he said, wincing. 'That's like the middle of the night

45

for me, man.' His hands were working upward, resting on my rib cage. They felt hot against my skin. I looked up at the sky, crowded with stars, a fat, full moon staring down at us. I looked back at The Starlight Hotel. I wished I could have seen Luke's face when Mitch was talking about the blood flowers. I wished I could see him now, just to know where he was. I wondered if he was walking the beach, or maybe hanging out with Christa Cutler on the lifeguard chair. The thought made my insides twist, as though my heart was lined with bruises.

I looked back at Bennie for a long minute. Then I put my arms around his neck and kissed him, full on the lips. His eyes widened and then he laughed. 'Man, this night's just getting better and better,' he said. He held out his hand and turned toward the Comanche Beach entrance. I looked back one last time before twining Bennie's outstretched fingers with my own. We crossed the entrance threshold and walked toward the abandoned lifeguard chair down by the water, the sand wet and cool as crushed flowers beneath my feet.

FOUR

adventures in zombie land

Elephant Beach was sinking; it had been for years. In 1928, Dolphus Rugby, the millionaire, commissioned circus elephants to build the boardwalk for Sally Stewart, his child bride, who wanted to live by the ocean. He built her Moonlight Manor, a sparkling palace with one hundred rooms facing the water; even the servants' quarters had seaside views. There were ballrooms for dining and dancing and a rooftop garden with an orchestra, and at night, boats filled with liquor would pull up to the shoreline, and soon the town was filled with bootleggers and film stars and Broadway producers who came down from the city to savor the sea air. Before dinner, everyone would promenade the boardwalk, dressed in Mainbocher and Schiaparelli, sipping from their sterling silver flasks as they gazed restively at the sunset, waiting for the night to begin. Those were the days when the grand old hotels like the Prince Albert and the Sea Lion were filled to capacity. Florenz Ziegfeld and his Folly girls would come down after their show for a late supper; Fanny Brice held dinner parties in her rented mansion on the bay. Cab Calloway, the famed bandleader, built a house in the Dunes, where all the rich people lived, and each morning tipped the boy who delivered his newspapers five dollars for bringing them right up to his front door.

Nobody promenaded the boardwalk anymore because you could trip on a rotting board and break your leg during an after-dinner stroll. The wonderful old hotels were now crumbling castles, left to dust after the film stars and bootleggers discovered air travel. Elephant Beach might have been only fifty-two minutes from the city by car or rail, but if you could fly to Santa Barbara or Cuba or the French Riviera, why would you spend your summers here? The hotels and the great mansions by the bay, with their glorious floor-to-ceiling windows broken and boarded up, went on the market at severely reduced prices. But the taxes were monstrous and nobody could afford the upkeep of so many rooms; they were taken over by squatters or converted into housing for welfare recipients.

After everyone deserted Elephant Beach, stores went out of business and the once prosperous Buoy Boulevard became shabby and mean. People blamed the Negroes who'd come up from Georgia and Alabama to work as chambermaids and butlers and drivers at the hotels and now had nothing to do but loaf in front of Brown's Liquor Store, right across the street from the railroad station. People said it didn't look good, black faces the first thing you saw when coming off the train or driving in from the Meadowbrook Parkway, and the town's seedy glamour faded even further.

Just when we were running out of people to blame for Elephant Beach's slide from a playland paradise to just another seaside town on the skids, the County Asylum let all the patients out for some kind of experiment in community living and it was decided that the abandoned hotels on the board-walk would make wonderful communal residencies. There would be on-site psychiatrists and doctors and medical workers, and medicine and jobs, and families who lived nearby to help take care of the mental patients and streamline them back into society. But whoever was in charge of the experi-ment dumped them in Elephant Beach before figuring out schedules and staffing and meals and all the things that might make the experiment a success. What followed caused an uproar that lasted through the fall and winter until the spring thaw, when the sweet scent of melting snow sifted through the air and the streets filled with water and rainbows.

At first, it seemed that a lot of the mental patients ran out of medication or simply stopped taking it, to the baffle-ment of everyone we hung around with. ('Free drugs, man! Free drugs and they're turning them down? Shit, they really must be crazy.') Or they forgot where the clinic was where they were supposed to refill their prescriptions. Or they couldn't remember the names of the medications. Or the whole thing about family proximity had been greatly exaggerated and there were no family members living close enough to help take care of them. Or the family members got fed up and didn't want to deal with them. Or there wasn't sufficient on-site medical staff at the new residencies to supervise them or see to their well-being. Or the staff that was there didn't really want to be, and instead of taking care of the patients, they got drunk or ran card games out of the residencies in rooms with the doors locked, playing loud music to drown out any requests and outright pleas for assistance. Or it was all of the above combined, and so, not getting any cooperation or compassion or any of the things they should have received under the circumstances, the ghost people took to the streets.

We called them the ghost people because their eyes always looked haunted. They wandered into traffic, dazed and confused, smiling or sobbing hysterically, or laughing maniacally at the top of their lungs. Or they sat in Leo's Luncheonette mumbling over cups of tea, stuffing packets of Sweet'N Low into their pockets, spilling them onto the tables. Sometimes Leo himself would come out from behind the counter and say sternly, 'Okay, all right now, move it along, you can't just sit here all day playing with the sugar, go, *go*,' and they'd just look up at him and ask numbly, 'Where?' as if they really wanted to know. Then Leo would sigh and shake his head and go back behind the counter, muttering. When they forgot where they lived, they'd stop us on the street and ask, or they'd spend the night on the beach, or in empty swimming pools, or in back of Jackson's Lumber Yard, down by the bay. Suddenly, the town seemed overrun with stray, scary strangers, and it wasn't as if these were our own local lunatics, like the ones who lived in The Starlight Hotel and were as harmless and familiar as the children who ran laughing through puddles after the rain. Adults tried to avoid the ghost people whenever possible, and when children looked up into their faces, they began crying. It seemed you couldn't turn a corner in town without running up against their great haunted eyes.

Raven loved it; he thought the ghost people were the coolest thing on earth. 'Man, it's like living in a Fellini movie,' he marveled. He wanted to make them his portfolio project at the Photography Institute in the city, where he was taking classes. He wanted to call the project 'Adventures in Zombie Land,' and thought it could win an award or at least a scholarship to cover his next year's tuition. He tried hanging out with some of them, but it was difficult. He spoke to a man wearing a crown made of newspapers who said the crown kept his thoughts inside his head. 'I wouldn't want them getting out and about,' he told Raven gravely. He tried speaking to a small woman with a button mouth and pearl-gray eyes, who scolded him, 'Quiet! I'm listening.' When Raven asked if she was hearing voices, the woman threw back her head and barked a laugh. But then she turned wistful. 'I wish,' she said, gazing out toward the ocean. He watched a man burning dollar bills, frantically lighting match after match as the wind blew them out. 'Burn, baby, burn,' the man cried ecstatically when a bill caught fire, his eyes rolling upward. He told Raven burning the money made him feel prosperous. But mostly, the ghost people shielded their faces and ran away when they saw Raven coming, frightened by his camera. He begged his girlfriend, Rita, who got along with everyone and could talk to anybody, to come with him and help crack the ice, but she said no, shaking her head so hard that her long, blond curls bounced off her shoulders. 'I got enough of that in the city, man,' she told him. 'We moved down here to escape the nut jobs, remember?' He tried enlisting Mitch, because some of the ghost people were war veterans who had flipped out in the jungle. But when he asked, Mitch's eyes turned cold, and his voice sounded the way it must have when he was barking orders at the men in his platoon as they stumbled over mine-fields and bodies. 'Give it a rest, hippie boy,' he said. 'This ain't no fucking freak show. It's their lives, man. Their *lives*.'

Still, Raven kept trying. He ate his entire stash of black beauties and started hanging around the boardwalk at night, watching the residencies. He kept his pockets full of Jolly Ranchers and miniature Chunky chocolates but the ghost people never came close enough to take anything from his outstretched hand. 'It's like they think I'm the crazy one,' he said. 'They sit out on those big porches under those tattered awnings or drape themselves over the stone lions at the old Sea Lion Inn, and sometimes nobody says a word for hours. And then when it starts getting dark, the workers or whoever they are come out and kind of corral them all in at the same time, and you see the lights go on in their rooms and this, like, moan goes up, right, this, like, raging, righteous moan. Man, I wish I could photograph it. I wish I could get a picture of that moan.' The words danced out of his mouth as though they were jitterbugging. 'Shit, I wish I could afford a new flash, the one where the light doesn't burst so much and wouldn't scare them away. I bet I could get them on the cover of *Life* magazine.'

But the ghost people were already famous. They were regu-lars on the front page of the *Elephant Beach Gazette*, and had been in *Newsday* and even *The New York Times*. Words like 'outrage' and 'unsightly' and 'Goddamned dumping ground' were used to describe the situation; you couldn't go anywhere in town without hearing people talk about it. At Nanny's house, her mother would be screaming into the phone, 'I spent my honeymoon at the Prince Albert, and now look; you can't even go up there between the spics and the psychos.' Our neighbor Mr. Zinc almost ran one of them down on his way home from buying milk at the Dairy Barn. 'Goddamned zombies, go back where you came from!' he yelled out the window.

Once, after I got my license, my brother and I were driving aimlessly through the side streets, listening to Cousin Brucie, when we stopped at a light on Filmore Avenue. An elderly man with stringy white hair began crossing the street, then suddenly dropped his pants, squatted down and began defecating. When he couldn't get up again, he began weeping, his face crumpling like a wrinkled magazine. He knelt in the middle of the street, naked from the waist down, huge tears making dirty tracks down his weathered face. My brother jumped out of the car, helped him pull up his trousers, and walked him across the street. The man insisted on shaking my brother's hand, and when he got back in the car, my brother rode the rest of the way with his arms stretched straight out in front of him, careful not to touch anything until he got home and was able to wash.

'If you could have seen this town when we first moved here,' my mother said, sighing and staring out the car window at a young woman twirling on the corner of Buoy Boulevard as though she were on top of a music box. My parents had our house appraised because everyone on our block was looking to sell and flee Elephant Beach, even the McIvers, who had a grape arbor and nineteen grandchildren and had been there forever. The appraisal hadn't gone well; after the real estate lady left, my mother locked herself in the bathroom and cried.

I was happy, though; I didn't want to move away, to an anonymous town with malls and split-level houses and no beach, no Comanche Street.

But everyone else was freaking out. They felt that Elephant Beach had been invaded and that it wasn't fair, really, the best ocean views in town going to mental patients who were too crazy to know their value or appreciate them. The people who lived farther uptown, near the residencies, started complaining about the sound of that same moan Raven had described, saying that it swelled and carried out over the water and across town toward the bay. They said it was unbearable, keeping them up at night, like a foghorn that just wouldn't quit. The cops tried locking some of the ghost people up for disturbing the peace, but once they put them in cells, Sergeant Ray Duffy told my father, the moan was an awful, terrible thing to hear. 'Like they have the D.T.'s and someone's eating them alive at the same time,' he said, shuddering. 'Hell with disturbing the peace; I had to let 'em go before I went on a bender and got the D.T.'s myself.' At town meetings, our parents and their friends and the few merchants left raved on about plummeting property values and safety, but so far the most dangerous thing that happened was that a woman wearing a shawl made of wet panty-hose jumped into Bertha Levine the librarian's car when she forgot to lock the doors and wouldn't leave, just sat there with her arms folded across her chest, staring out the window and speaking in a wheedling tone that drove Bertha nuts. 'Just take me for a little spin, someplace nice,' she begged Bertha, who drove straight to the police station and honked her horn for someone to come out and take the woman away. During a slight scuffle, the woman's panty-hose shawl fell on the floor of Bertha's Toyota, where Bertha said it looked like a nest of dead snakes. She kicked the coiled mess out of the car, locked all the doors, then laid her head down on the steering wheel and wept.

Just when things were reaching a fever pitch and people seemed ready to storm the boardwalk with blazing torches, something happened. One of the ghost people died. He was a young man, believed to be in his twenties, dressed in an overcoat that was too big and didn't keep him warm enough because he froze to death under the boardwalk one bitter night, beneath the icicles that hung down from the splintered wood. His body was frozen in the shape of a human question mark, and his eyes were open wide, as if focused on some distant dream. He carried no identification and, after the police asked around, it was determined that his name might have been Chuck.

Hunker Moran, editor of the *Elephant Beach Gazette*, wrote an editorial about it. He said that Chuck's death put a face to the whole issue of criminalizing craziness. 'Lock them away! Out of our sight!' he wrote in the paper. 'Until one of them dies on a cold night in February, alone, thrown into an anonymous grave in Potter's Field, unmarked because nobody knows his real name. Where is our compassion? Buried beneath fear and worry over property values? What about the real values, the ones that matter?' The *Nassau County Press* and the *Long Island Reader* picked up the story, as well as *Newsday* and the *Times*. People turned it over in their minds and decided that Hunker was right. After all, it wasn't the fault of the ghost people that they were too crazy to fend for themselves; the politicians and professionals who released them should have known better. And property values had been in the toilet long before they'd come to town; why take it out on them? In fact, you could even say they were the real victims of the whole situation but were too messed up to know it. Or maybe they did, and that was what all the crying and singing and moaning were about.

So they became ours, the way the stray dogs and cats became ours after the summer people left them behind and moved back to the city. Now when the man wearing the safari helmet stood in front of the Episcopal church, screaming, 'Jesus didn't tell you dick, motherfucker,' over and over, instead of calling the cops, Reverend Denton led him inside the rectory and had the housekeeper serve him hot chocolate and Entenmann's donuts. When our neighbor Mr. Zinc passed one of them crying in the rain, he offered her a ride and brought her right inside the old Prince Albert Hotel to make sure she was in the right place. When the woman with jelly rolls of fat dripping from her body performed a frenzied frug in front of Leo's Luncheonette, instead of pointing and laughing, people applauded. And when Raven and Rita found a young guy wandering down Starfish Avenue, crying, they brought him back to Comanche Street, where they made him smoke a joint to calm down, then fed him scrambled eggs with Wonder Bread toast. They put him to sleep on the enclosed porch, and in the morning he left a note on a paper napkin that read 'What wisdom can you find that is greater than kindness?' and signed it Jean-Jacques Rousseau.

Because of Hunker Moran's editorial, things began improving at the residencies as well. They were quickly staffed

56

with shrinks and doctors and health aides who made sure the ghost people took their medication and ate regular meals and went to sleep on time. There was less mumbling, less weeping, less of them wandering around town looking lost and bewildered. The drugs took the great haunted staring out of their eyes so that now, if you passed them on the street, you'd think they were just like everyone else. Oh, there were still some standouts among them, but they were harmless, like the characters you find in fading small towns everywhere: the wizened old woman in the sky-blue ski hat, who sailed down Buoy Boulevard telling anyone who would listen, 'Anita D'Arcy is my name, perhaps you've heard of me? I was a star of the stage and screen, you know'; the tall, distinguished-looking black man with salt-and-pepper hair who stood in front of the Elephant Beach Savings and Loan, tipping his chauffeur's cap and saying, 'Where to, Captain?' while opening an imaginary car door; the coffee-colored woman with the most startling sea-green eyes who met all the trains at the railroad station, asking passengers, 'Are you from New York? Do you know my husband?' And there was Ruby, who wasn't really crazy, just old and down on her luck.

Ruby was short and wide and wore lavender lipstick and rouge to match, and would come into the A&P where I worked, every Saturday night before closing, the hem of her flowered housedress dragging beneath her long wool coat, her stockings sagging around her ankles. She took forever to pay for her groceries, because she always had a hundred coupons and her money was hidden all over her body: a dollar in her coat pocket. Fifty cents in a change purse pinned to her brassiere. A half-dollar in the heel of her stout, stubby shoe.

57

'Please, Ruby, can't you see there's a line behind you,' we'd beg her, watching the big clock above the glass windows, knowing it would be past closing when we finally cashed out. Sometimes we were sharp with her, sometimes downright rude, but how rude could you be to a woman who was like your grandmother would be if your mother and aunts weren't around to look after her? Nothing rattled her; no matter what we said, she just kept smiling, digging, turning herself inside out until she found every last cent. Then she'd sigh and say brightly, 'There! That's done. Darling, give me double bags, will you, so they don't break on my way home?' And she'd put the bags in her old lady cart and go sit on the ledge by the windows facing the street, with her old lady scarf tied in a knot under her chin, take a blurry compact from her handbag and freshen her lipstick, lean her head against the glass and rest until the bus came. At Christmas time, she'd come in with a brand-new roll of freshly minted pennies from the Elephant Beach Savings and Loan and hand them out to all the checkout girls and stock boys and managers. 'Please, darling, take it,' she'd say, curling our fingers around the shiny new pennies with her own. You'd think her hands would be gnarled and rough and covered with spots, but they were soft and smooth, as if she applied lotion every night from a bottle she kept on the windowsill of her room at the Moonlight Manor. 'Take it,' she'd urge us, 'because you never know. You never know.'

FIVE

my country right or wrong

'Step into my office,' Mitch said, slinging the door open wide, so that one minute we were blinded by sunlight and the next cratered in darkness. I had never been in the lounge at The Starlight Hotel during daytime, and for a minute I felt disoriented; I wasn't used to seeing the ocean so sparkling blue outside the windows, or the sun spots on the wooden floor made from the same planks they'd used to build the boardwalk. Len, the bartender, looked paler than he did at night, his stubble more pronounced, and even the smell was worse, because the stench of ammonia mixed with beer foam that clung to most bars in Elephant Beach was like smelling an antiseptic hangover. I felt a gag rising at the back of my throat as Len set my ginger ale in front of me. I would have left, but I'd been wanting to talk to Mitch, and had run into him at Eddy's, buying cigarettes, and since he didn't love going to the beach ('Hard to stump around in the sand, man') and he tended to shun bright sunlight for long periods ('The glare! The glare!'), we'd ended up in the lounge at The Starlight Hotel.

Mitch wasn't a local like the rest of us; he was originally from San Francisco. When Billy asked him once why he didn't go back to California, why anyone would choose Elephant Beach over San Francisco, he said, 'Because all that hippie dippy candles-in-the-park, strung-out-in-the-Haight bullshit ruined it for me, that's why. Since when is watching a thirteen-year-old runaway freak out on acid a Goddamned tourist attraction? Peace, love and happiness, my ass. Bunch of con artists is all they are, man, picking your fucking pocket with a smile.'

Mitch was twenty-nine; his beard was threaded with gray and even though he rarely sat in the sun, his face was dark and weathered, which made his eyes all the more startling. They were this really intense blue-green, the color of Caribbean water, and they blazed out of his face like bullets. I wanted to talk to him because he was older and he'd been in the same war as Luke and he knew things that might help me to understand Luke better. I had to talk quickly, though, because once Mitch reached a certain point in his drinking it would be useless to try and get his opinion on anything. The good thing was, the drunker he got, the less likely he would be to remember what we'd talked about and repeat it to anyone else we knew. The trick was to get his wisdom on the subject before he reached 'the click,' 'that place between the last drink you should have had and the last drink you actually drank. You know, the one you're still tasting the next morning, while your head's exploding and you're sitting around waiting for the room to blow up,' he once explained to me.

60

We were sitting in the same corner that he'd been sitting in with Luke when Luke had first come out that night a week ago. Mitch's cane was hooked over the back of the barstool; it was made out of bloodwood, reddish-brown, with a silver dragon's head that fit the curl of his fingers perfectly. He'd bought it at a pawnshop next door to the VA hospital in Manhattan, 'like it was right there waiting for me, right in the fucking window, man,' and the pawnbroker had given him a discount because he was a veteran. Sometimes, when Mitch was really lit, he left the cane in the bar and stumped up the stairs to his room without it, but there was never any danger of it getting lost or stolen. Everyone knew the cane was his, and Len would just keep it behind the bar until Mitch stumbled downstairs the next day or whenever, ready to begin all over again.

Mitch eyed my ginger ale with disgust. 'That all you're having?' he said. 'Bah! C'mon, have a real drink. Disability check came today, so the sky's the limit.'

'No thanks,' I said. 'I have to be at work by three.'

'It's only eleven thirty,' Mitch said. 'Plenty of time to sober up by then.'

'I'm fine,' I said. Sitting in a bar at this hour was bad enough, but drinking at this hour would make me as bad as the women that hung around the boardwalk bars, those women with sunken eyes and sagging faces and puckered cleavage you'd see whenever you went into places like the Shipwreck Tavern to buy cigarettes or use the bathroom.

Mitch shrugged. 'Suit yourself,' he said. He lit a cigarette, then held the match out to me, cupped in his hands. He took a long pull on his drink. Then he leaned forward and I could

61

smell yesterday's sweat and the taste of gin on his breath. I could see the pint bottle of Gordon's sticking out of the brown paper bag in his jacket pocket. His fingernails were dirty, the cuticles crusted. But Liz was right. There was something sexy about Mitch, about the way his fingers cupped the flame, the way he looked at you with those piercing eyes.

He blew out the match and caught me watching him. 'What?' he asked.

'Liz is right,' I said. 'You do have sexy wrists.'

Mitch smiled, then winked at me. 'Yeah,' he drawled. 'But not as sexy as – what's that cat's name? The one just got back from Nam?'

I startled, looking around to make sure nobody had heard him. All I could see were shadows against the bar.

'Relax,' Mitch said. 'I mean, shit, I can't even remember his name.'

'How'd you know that—'

'Happened before the click,' he said. 'I saw you lingering by the jukebox, trying to scope us out. Plus, I saw how you were looking at him when you thought no one else was looking, and besides, I knew you weren't biding your time for Mitchell J. Ronkowski, the one-legged wonder, whose romantic aspirations are confined to the five fingers of love.' He leaned back and laughed uproariously, banging his drink on the bar. He began coughing as if he would choke to death. Len poured a glass of water and came and set it down in front of Mitch. 'Take it easy,' he said. Mitch guzzled the water, then pushed his liquor glass out for a refill. He turned back to me and said, 'As you were saying, my dear.'

I drew a short breath. 'A couple things.'

62

'I'm at your disposal,' Mitch said. 'For as long as you need me, or until the booze renders me unconscious, whichever comes first.'

'First, you think guys really like virgins better?' I asked.

'Better than what?' Mitch said.

'Better than chicks who sleep with other guys,' I said. 'Who sleep around.'

Mitch's face looked pained. 'Not that Madonna-whore crap,' he said. 'Didn't all that free love bullshit put an end to that nonsense?'

'Not around here it didn't,' I said.

'Bah!' Mitch scoffed. 'Around here? I'd say the priority around these parts is catching a buzz. Half the cats around here are too stiff to get stiff, you dig my meaning. They may be thinking about it, and they may be talking about it, but I'd bet my next disability check there's a lot more talk than action.' Above us, we heard Roof Dog howling, the German shepherd that lived on the roof of The Starlight Hotel. 'See there, even that Goddamned dog agrees with me,' he said.

Mitch did have a point. That night that me and Bennie had walked down to the abandoned lifeguard chair, I was after experience; seeing if I could feel something for another guy even while I was so into Luke. We'd climbed up on the chair and had gotten all cozy and I was actually a little turned on. Bennie had a great body for a junkie, and those beautiful eyes. But it turned out he hadn't gotten his stash until late in the evening, so he'd taken his nightly dosage of ludes later than usual, and as a result, it was like his tongue went to sleep in my mouth. I'd left him sprawled and snoring in the moonlight, alerted Voodoo and Billy so they could find him and carry him to his aunt's house on Sister Street, and caught the last bus home. By the time I was in my room smoking my last cigarette before going to sleep, I was more relieved than anything else.

'Some guys are always going to go for that pure-as-the-driven-snow stuff,' Mitch was saying. 'But there are others, more enlightened, shall we say, who prefer someone knows her way around the sheets just a little.' He took another cigarette from the pack of Camels in his shirt pocket, lit it, and exhaled, long and slow. The smoke mingled with the dusty sunlight slanting through the porthole windows behind the bar. 'Six of one, half dozen of the other, really,' he said, squinting through the smoke. 'But Goddamn, where do all these myths come from? Like women being the weaker sex. Bah! That's a good one. Think the Pill liberated you, and that had nothing to do with it.' He took the cigarette from his mouth and pointed it toward me, the ashes falling on the bar. 'Women always got the power, they just don't know how to use it. Too ready to hand over the reins to any asshole with a pecker. Shit, all the scars I carry inside me – and a few on the outside, come to think of it – I got from a woman. Lot of truth to that old saying, "One hair off a pussy can pull a freight train."' He raised his glass and drained it. I stared into Mitch's face. His eyes still looked okay. I was about to ask another question, but then he said, 'Besides, virginity is the least of your problems with that cat – what's his name again?'

'Luke?' I asked.

'Yeah, him,' Mitch said. 'I don't know, darlin'. You might want to shine it on with that enterprise, maybe reconsider.'

I felt cold inside, like a piece of ice was rubbing against my bones. 'Why do you say that?' I asked.

Mitch shrugged. 'At the very least, you got to give it time,' he said. 'He's back, what? A month, maybe?'

'How much time?' I asked, and even I could hear the anxiety in my voice.

Mitch looked at me sharply. 'What's the rush?'

'No rush,' I said. 'It's just that—' I closed up. I didn't want to tell him about the years of waiting, the years of watching Luke like I was watching a movie over and over, hoping the ending would be different.

'Listen, things happen over there,' Mitch said. His voice dipped a shade, as though something was weighing it down. 'War does things to a cat.'

'Like what things?' I asked. 'I mean, I know it must have been horrible, but—'

'Darlin',' Mitch said gently, 'you're a beautiful kid, but you don't know shit. Now, don't take it personally. Because neither does anyone else who hasn't had the pleasure.'

'I read the papers,' I said, though this was only partially true. 'And I saw on TV—'

'Doesn't mean shit,' he said. 'Don't mean shit to a tree. There's shit over there, is what I'm saying. Bad shit. Scary shit. And the Vietcong are the least of it. At least you know they're the enemy.' Mitch drank long and greedily. 'Minefields everywhere you look. Tiny little whores, so beautiful they could make your heart stop, packing razor blades. Vietnamese birth control, cut you right where it hurts. Had a buddy killed one of 'em for what she done to him.'

I shuddered just thinking about it. I had enough trouble

65

shaving my legs, trying not to cut my shinbone to ribbons with the razor. 'But how does that even work?'

'No fucking idea, but the damage is done,' Mitch said. He licked the dregs of his glass and signaled to Len for another.

'And then you come back,' he said. 'To this fucking sinkhole. All that Stars and Stripes forever crap. And instead of a ticker-tape parade – though you ask me, who needs that bullshit – you get some sixteen-year-old twat – sorry, sweetheart, but that's what she was – whose dress doesn't even cover her ass, asking are you proud of yourself, killing all those babies. And nobody wants to hire you because all they remember out of the whole fucking war is the My Lai massacre and they think you're some kind of monster. But no one ever talks about the four-year-olds with dynamite strapped all over 'em, walking at you, waving, "Hey, GI! Okay, GI!" Putting their arms out for you to pick 'em up and hug 'em so you could blow the fuck up.'

I didn't know what to say. I wanted to ask what Luke had told him, but I knew that even if Mitch remembered the conversation, he wouldn't tell me.

'And then, when you can't take it anymore, you turn to Uncle Sam for help, and look at what happens.' Mitch shook his head and made the sign of the cross with his middle finger. 'Those poor bastards.' He was talking about the Veteran's Hospital in St. Cecily's Parish, over in Suffolk County. It had been in all the papers, the news stations, everywhere. They had a weekly support group for Vietnam veterans having a hard time adjusting to life back in the States. The group had nine men in it, plus the psychologist who ran it. On a rainy Thursday, while they were all sitting around talking about whatever people in support groups talk about, one of the veterans took out a .22 pistol and shot up the men in the group. He killed five of them, including the psychologist, and most of the others were critically injured. Afterward, he just sat there until the cops came and arrested him. When they asked him why, he just kept saying, *'Dung lye, dung lye,'* over and over again. *Newsday* said *dung lye* means 'no more' in Vietnamese.

'Excuse me, pal.' A voice came down from the end of the bar, hidden by the dust motes dancing through the streaming sunlight. It came from the group of construction workers sitting at the other end of the bar. 'Some of us don't appreciate hearing this country being referred to as "a fucking sinkhole."'

'Is that so?' Mitch asked, like he was really interested.

'Yeah, it's so,' another voice said.

'What company you fight in?' Mitch asked quietly. 'Where were you, '68, '69? Da Nang? Saigon? Mekong Delta?'

'I was in Korea,' the voice said. It was a fat man's voice. I couldn't make out faces or features in their sunlit silhouettes, but their asses were crowding their barstools, hanging over the sides.

'Korea? You mean that pussy war, lasted about two minutes?' Mitch asked, like he was making polite conversation.

I heard the stools swivel and shift, heard the creaking as someone stood up, his work boots hitting the floor.

'I'd watch my mouth, I was you, pal,' the voice said.

'There's some of us here still believe that America is the greatest country on earth,' someone else said.

'Then some of us must be real fucking assholes,' Mitch said, blowing smoke rings. They rose up to the ceiling.

67

Len was looking back and forth between Mitch and the construction workers. 'Let's take it easy,' he said, his fingers curling around the brass rungs behind the bar.

'You don't like it here, why don't you move to Russia?' one of the construction workers asked.

'Too fucking cold,' Mitch said, shaking his head. 'Listen though, let me ask you something: You love your kids?'

'Leave my kids out of this,' the fat voice said.

'You love 'em?' Mitch asked again.

'I said—'

'Yeah, yeah, I love my kids,' the other voice said. 'So what? What's that got to do with anything?'

'You ever criticize 'em?' Mitch asked. 'Yell at 'em? Hit 'em, maybe?'

There was silence at the other end of the bar. Someone snorted and said, 'This fucking guy—'

'Tell 'em get a haircut, get better grades, turn the music down?' Mitch asked. 'Ground 'em for cutting school? Smack 'em upside the head for sassing their mother? Tell 'em, "You get knocked up, don't bother coming home"?'

Silence, still, at the other end of the bar.

'You ever wish you never had 'em?' Mitch asked.

'Shut it down, now, you son of a bitch,' one of the men said. 'Shut it down right now, or—'

'You still love 'em?' Mitch asked.

More silence. A lighter flared. Someone raised his mug to his lips and took a long drink. I couldn't make out their faces in the dim light. I couldn't tell the color of their eyes.

'Yeah, you still love 'em,' Mitch said, stubbing out his Camel. 'You can talk all that shit about 'em, but you still love 'em.'

'The fuck's he talking about?' one of the men said.

Mitch laughed, and the sound of it was warm and rich. He drained his drink and got up from his stool, leaning against the bar for balance. 'The fuck am I talking about,' he said, shaking his head.

'Go fuck yourself, you commie prick,' the fat voice said loudly.

'If I could've done that, I wouldn't have gotten out of bed this morning,' Mitch said.

Two of the men began moving forward. They were big and pretty bald with beer guts hanging over their tool belts. I didn't recognize them. I was glad they didn't appear to be somebody's father or uncle. Somebody's brother I might have to recognize.

'Let's take it down a notch,' Len said quietly from behind the bar.

'Guy's got a big mouth,' the fat voice said.

Mitch stepped forward, farther into the light. The younger construction worker with more hair looked down at Mitch's stump. He put his hand on the fat man's arm. He nodded toward Mitch's wooden leg. Mitch never covered it up. He wore his pants rolled up to just below his knee, where the wooden leg began. He watched the men looking. He smiled so that his face creased up. His eyes were the brightest thing in the room.

'Don't let that stop you,' he said softly.

'Let's take it down a notch,' Len said. 'Let's everybody relax and have another drink. On the house.' Everybody liked Len. He knew how to run a bar right. He had silver hair but his face was young. He'd been laid off the Sandhogs, which was why he tended bar at the lounge at The Starlight Hotel.

'Sure,' the younger construction worker said. 'Sure.' He turned back to the bar, to the place where the other men were standing. The fat man waited a minute longer before walking back to his place at the bar.

Len served the construction workers first. When he began making Mitch's boilermaker, Mitch put up his hand and shook his head no. He threw some bills on the bar and picked up his jacket with the bottle of Gordon's in the pocket and began walking toward the door that led to the rooms in the hotel. He'd left his cane on the back of his chair, but neither Len nor I called after him to take it. He whistled 'The Star-Spangled Banner' as he walked through the door. You could hear him whistling as he walked up the stairs to his room, one step at a time.

'Guy's got an attitude problem,' the fat voice said.

'Lay off, Jimmy,' one of the men said.

'Hey, he's not the only one, is all I'm saying,' the fat man said. 'He's not the only one came back—'

'Everything all right over there?' Len said sharply. 'Your drinks okay? Taste all right?' He stared down the bar at the men, his arms stretched out behind him. Len kept a bat behind the bar. On the shelf just opposite the taps for the draft beer.

'We're good,' one of the men finally said.

'All right then,' Len said. He stared at the construction workers until they began talking among themselves. Then he came down the bar and took my glass and filled it with fresh ice and ginger ale. He nodded toward Mitch's cane, and I handed it over the bar to him. Len put it on the shelf where he kept the baseball bat. The younger construction worker walked over to the jukebox and put money in. Tony Bennett started singing 'Fly Me to the Moon.' The construction worker stood over the jukebox, his eyes closed, snapping his fingers in time to the music.

Len leaned his elbows on the bar and sighed. 'Sometimes I hear him at night, screaming,' he said. 'After everyone's gone, when I'm closing up. Screaming himself to sleep. And then it's quiet for a while and then he starts back up again.' Len pushed himself off the bar, shaking his head. 'My brother-in-law, same thing,' he said. 'Same damn thing, ever since he got home. My sister sleeps in the kids' room. They're scared to death of him. Of their own father.' The door to the lounge opened and a man and a woman walked in, laughing. I'd never seen them before, just like I'd never seen the construction workers or any of these other daytime people. It was a whole different world, being in the lounge during daylight.

'No one's sleeping in that house,' Len said, watching the couple sit down toward the middle of the bar. 'Walking around like a bunch of zombies. The kids, everybody. They can't get him to stop because he doesn't even know he's doing it. He wakes up in the morning, doesn't remember a thing.' He shook his head and sighed again. He kept his eyes on the couple, waiting until they were fully settled, until the woman flounced her skirt over the barstool for the final time. Then he walked down the bar to serve them.

the fourth feeney sister

Georgie groaned, but the nurse wasn't paying attention. 'I cannot believe girls are still standing around mooning over Luke McCallister,' he said. 'It defies . . . well, I don't know what it defies. I mean, he is beautiful. Can you light me up, please?'

The nurse shook her head and left the room.

'Bitch,' Georgie said.

I put two Marlboros in my mouth, lit them both, and put one between his lips. Georgie sucked the smoke as though it was oxygen. I took the cigarette from his mouth and let him exhale. 'Want me to smoke it for you, too?' I joked.

'My, my, aren't we mouthy now that we're no longer jailbait,' Georgie said.

One time last winter, before she married James and moved away, I brought Marcel over to Georgie's to hang out. It was his day off from the bus company, where he'd gotten a job after graduating two years ago. We were in his room, drinking coffee and smoking our brains out. Georgie's hair was long and stringy and covered his face. He knelt before a poster of Rod Stewart taped to his wall. 'Look at him,' he said, his eyes glowing. He began salaaming and chanting, 'Rod, Rod, you are God.' He couldn't take his eyes off the poster. Marcel had met Georgie before, but after that morning, she didn't want to go over there again. 'Sorry, man,' she apologized. 'But he, like, creeps me out.'

'Sara Pettingill used to have a big thing for Luke,' Georgie said. 'She'd come around Eddy's in her jeans and deck sneakers, and let out this Janis Joplin yell, screaming, "Luke!" at the top of her lungs. Then when Luke came around, she'd go all sugar water and wouldn't open her mouth, just like someone else I know. What's with all you girls, mooning around in silence? You got to sing it out, honey chile. "Oh my man, I love him so,"' Georgie sang from his hospital bed, '"he'll never know . . ."' He had seen *Funny Girl* twelve times and worn out two albums. Barbra Streisand was right up there with Rod Stewart as far as he was concerned. I put the cigarette back in his mouth. He dragged again, then leaned his head back on the pillows.

'Luke went out with Sara, didn't he?' I said, feeling a blade turn under my skin. Sara Pettingill was one of the city people who came down for the summer. It was her arm I'd wanted to cut off when I'd seen it draped across his back at the movies, when I should have been watching *Butch Cassidy and the Sundance Kid*. I had to ask if Butch and Sundance had died at the end and everyone looked at me like I had two heads. 'The scary thing is, she doesn't even do drugs,' Liz had said, rolling her eyes.

73

'Yes, yes, I do seem to remember her stumbling over to him one drunken night,' Georgie said. Georgie knew everything about everyone in the Trunk; that's why I'd wanted to speak to him. We'd made plans to have breakfast at Leo's Luncheonette before I went to work, and then I'd gotten the call from the hospital. His eyes were still purple and swollen. This was the first day that he could actually see. Two black eyes, a broken collarbone, broken ribs, sunset bruises all over his face and neck. But they'd let his mouth alone; no split lips, teeth intact. 'The better to blow you with, my dear,' Georgie said, after making me hold up a mirror so he could see his face. 'And please don't act all shocked and bothered. You're eighteen now, there are things you should know.'

When Georgie was little, his mother left and he hasn't seen her since. She tried to kill him and his brother, Bobby, by feeding them ink instead of milk in their baby bottles. Georgie used to spit it out, throw it up, anything but swallow it, but Bobby was the better baby and he drank it all down and never grew to his full height. They called him the Dwarf, even though he was a really sweet kid with a wonderful smile. He would smile even when people called him names, when they shoved him in the hall or tried to trip him on the bus.

"'You're not a kid anymore,'" Georgie croaked. "'You're not a kid anymore . . .'"

I met Georgie when I was in tenth grade and he was a senior. He pretended to be in love with me and followed me around and teased me when I came looking for him so I could bum a cigarette. 'What'd you do, smell the smoke?' he'd say, hiding behind the chemistry labs. People made fun of him but only behind his back because he hung out with the

Hitters, a group of tough, tough kids who were older than our people and gave new meaning to the phrase, 'They'd just as soon kill you as look at you.' Georgie was not tough but he was best friends with Moira Feeney and her sisters, Deirdre and Fiona, who were Hitter queens, shared a penchant for pissing in wine bottles when they were drunk on the beach, and lived down the block from the house Georgie lived in with Bobby and his father and grandmother, who everyone called Sissie. It was an oddly barren house, sparsely furnished with dingy walls, but cozy somehow because they used the fireplace a lot to save on heat. Sometimes after school I'd go home with Georgie and watch *The 4:30 Movie*, and on Sunday afternoons we'd watch old films like *All About Eve* and *On the Waterfront*. On Sundays, his father would sit in the corduroy recliner, drinking Budweiser and barking, 'Another nail in your coffin!' every time one of us lit a cigarette. He wore white socks with black shoes shined to a high gloss that gleamed under the living room lights. Sissie would serve us tea and chocolate chip cookies baked from a frozen Pillsbury roll. Those private times at Georgie's house were my favorite times with him, because in public he acted in certain ways that embarrassed me, and the people he hung out with made me nervous.

All around Elephant Beach things were changing, but the Hitter kids stayed the same. Even after they graduated and started working in the city or going to secretarial school, they hung out at MarioEstelle's, a hole-in-the-wall luncheonette that looked like it belonged in Florida. It was a short brick building painted pale orange with green trim and had a tiny enclosed space on the side where people could sit and eat.

Mario and Estelle lived in an apartment above the luncheonette that had jalousied windows and a stucco porch and a beach umbrella they kept up all year round. They sold pizzas and pork Parmesan heroes and big, fluffy meatballs served in a napkin for a nickel, ten cents with sauce served in a Styrofoam cup. It was something, on a cold afternoon in January, to feel the steam heat hit you as you walked into the little luncheonette and bit into one of Mario's meatballs. The taste was warm and tangy and filling and made you forget how much people sucked most of the time. Unfortunately, you couldn't go there very often, because you didn't want to stand around waiting for Estelle to ladle your meatball from the big, black cast-iron kettle with twenty pairs of eyes on you, their collective silence freezing you out, or worse, let your eyes wander in the wrong direction for a split second too long and hear Fiona Feeney or one of her sisters say, 'What the fuck you looking at?' Easier instead to cop an egg roll or a Lucky Lunch at Ten Dragons takeout farther up Lighthouse Avenue. It might not taste like home, but at least you could enjoy your food without all that vicious scrutiny.

The Hitters loved two things in life: fighting and dancing. They would fight anyone, anytime, and even though Jimmy Murphy and some of his friends carried switchblades, the girls were worse than the boys. They fought the black kids, they fought the hippies, they fought strangers who stopped at red lights and rolled down their windows to ask for directions. When they weren't kicking someone's ass or getting drunk on the beach or at Dave's Dive farther down the Trunk, they were dancing. Dancing had the same effect on the Hitters as quaaludes had on Billy and Voodoo; it tranquilized that inner coil of violence that lay crouched and ready to spring at the slightest provocation. We used to watch them at the St. Timothy dances, draped over one another like blankets, Jimmy Murphy's hand cupping Deirdre Feeney's ass in ways she never would have allowed on the school bus or at MarioEstelle's. Deirdre was the beautiful one, quieter than her sisters and less inclined to take offense at pretty much anything. Moira was quiet, too, until she had a few drinks; she'd been banned from the dances after Father Tom had had to practically wrestle her out the door when she'd tried doing a striptease to the tune of 'Sherry Baby.' She'd gotten as far as unbuttoning her blouse so you could see the twin cups of her black brassiere. Fiona would be curled into Mickey Fallon's arms, docile as a kitten, so you'd never guess she was capable of screaming, 'Get the nigger bitches!' while leading a charge across the cafeteria that had even Mr. Farnikan, the assistant principal, backed against the wall to get out of her way. Sometimes, at the beach, they'd turn the transistor radio to the oldies station and twirl one another around to Sam Cooke and Frankie Valli and the Four Seasons, standing in a circle while Mickey and Fiona, who were the best dancers, did a solo number. Or they'd slow dance with their eyes closed, their bare ankles sinking into the sand. If people on neighboring beach blankets who didn't know any better asked them to please turn down the music so they could get their kid to sleep or something, one of the Hitters was sure to turn the music all the way up so you could hear it in New Jersey, then say, 'Excuse me? Sorry, can't hear you, what was that again?'

Fiona Feeney had dyed black hair teased into a frothy bubble that cascaded down her back. She wore black eyeliner that winged at the corners, making her eyes look as though they could fly out of her face at a moment's notice. She sometimes came to school drunk, but the teachers were too afraid to suspend her and they knew it wouldn't do any good. Sometimes I'd catch her watching me in the smoking bathroom, a little smile on her face, but the only thing she ever said to me was 'Be good to Georgie. Don't hurt him.' She said it nicely enough, but I felt my heart banging against my spine; I had seen Fiona in action on more than one occasion.

After what happened to Georgie, she had marched up to Jimmy Murphy in front of MarioEstelle's and smacked him right across the face, even though he was engaged to her sister Deirdre. 'Go ahead, Jimmy,' she said. 'Go ahead, hit me. Right here, in front of everybody. Right up your alley, right? How drunk did you have to be? How drunk did all a youse have to be, to do what you did?' It was a funny thing to say, because the Hitter boys never needed liquor to throw anyone a beating. Jimmy was pretty crazy himself, but Fiona was crazy and tough and fearless, and you could see he was scared and trying not to show it.

'Leave it alone, Fiona, you know what's good for you,' he told her.

'You leave him alone,' she said. 'You hear me, Jimmy?'

'Or what?' Jimmy sneered. 'What, he coming after me with the faggot army patrol?'

Fiona's eyes narrowed. She took a step closer to Jimmy until she was almost touching his chest. She looked up into his face and said very quietly, 'He knows who he is. You know who you are, Jimmy?'

'Shut the fuck up, Fiona,' Jimmy said loudly.

'You leave him alone,' she repeated, and it was Jimmy Murphy who turned first and walked away.

Georgie sighed when I told him. 'I wish she hadn't of done that,' he said.

'She's looking out for you,' I said. 'Being a good friend.' I had run into Fiona in the hospital lobby. She was wearing a blue dress with a scoop neck that showed her freckled chest. Behind her sunglasses her eyes were threaded and bloodshot, and when she turned to leave, I caught a whiff of stale sweat and something else, something greasy and unclean. She worked at Donnelly's Insurance Agency on Buoy Boulevard and Georgie had told me she was taking night classes at Carver Community College. At the door she turned and beckoned me with a crooked finger. My throat began closing up, but I followed her out the glass doors into the sunlight. In front of the hospital, she took a can of Schaefer beer from her bag, popped the tab and took a sip. She held it out to me. 'No thanks,' I said politely. It was eleven thirty in the morning and I was going to work at the A&P straight from the hospital. I hoped it was her day off from the insurance agency. I hoped she wasn't going back to work looking like she'd slept on the beach after pulling an all-nighter.

'You know what's going on here?' she asked me suddenly. 'You know what this is about?'

'Kind of,' I said. On those Sunday afternoons at his house, Georgie said some things. 'They can't ask their good little Catholic girlfriends,' he told me. 'So they ask me instead. I mean, let's face it, they don't call me the fourth Feeney sister for nothing.' Some of it I didn't understand, some of it I didn't want to.

Fiona sighed. 'Dimwit probably said something, one of his smart-ass remarks,' she said. 'He doesn't know how to be careful.' She drained the beer, then idly crushed the can with one hand. She pointed a finger at me. 'You be careful,' she said, then turned and walked toward the parking lot.

Georgie tried to sit up, groaned, and sank back down again. 'Well, I guess this little incident brings it all the way home,' he said. 'Time for the Manhattan transfer.' He talked about moving to the city all the time, even had a separate savings account aside from what he gave his grandmother to run the house. She didn't know he was in the hospital. He'd instructed his brother to tell their father and Sissie that he was working double shifts and sleeping at a coworker's apartment that was closer to the bus station. He'd think of something later to explain the bruises. Bobby wept when he saw his brother lying in the hospital bed, huge, leaky tears that threatened to swallow his face. His small shoulders heaved under the weight of his sobs. After he left, Georgie had turned away, his own eyes wet. 'I always wanted to save him,' he sighed. 'But shit, who's going to save me?'

'Everyone else is moving down here to get away from the city,' I said, pouring water from the plastic blue pitcher beside his bed. I lifted the cup to his lips.

'Exactly why I'm moving out, darling,' he said. 'I'll finally be able to use my talents where they'll be appreciated. I can get a walk-up in the Village and decorate the way I've always wanted to without being afraid of giving Daddy a heart attack. Red Chinese screens, thrift-shop flamingos, art deco glass . . . it will be simply fabulous. And after this latest debacle, I'm so looking forward to the kindness of strangers, I can't tell you.' He closed his eyes. His face against the pillows looked very small and white. I put my hand up to push his hair back from his forehead. There was a welt that hadn't been there before, a fragile pink bump that seemed to be getting larger as I watched. When I touched it, Georgie whimpered. 'Does that hurt?' I asked him. He shivered. The bump seemed to be growing bigger, harder, by the second. 'I'm going to call the nurse,' I said, pressing the buzzer by the bed.

Georgie took my hand and kissed it. 'Promise you'll come visit,' he whispered. 'Me and my pretty new apartment in the city.'

'It's expensive, now,' I said. 'Dig it, Cha-Cha was saying apartments in the city are three times what they cost in Elephant Beach for half the space. He said you could rent a whole bungalow on Comanche Street for the price of a one-bedroom apartment in the city.'

Georgie struggled to sit up. '"Don't rain on my parade,"' he sang. '"I got my band out . . ."' His voice wobbled, and he slumped back against the pillows, moaning.

'Georgie,' I said. I rang the nurse's buzzer again. Georgie's mouth twisted, the way it did that time Duncan Cray called from the corner, 'Hey, Georgina, your slip is showing.'

'Promise you'll come,' he whispered weakly.

'Yes,' I said, pressing the buzzer harder, so it sounded angry.

'Promise,' he said again.

'I promise,' I said, abandoning the buzzer and going out in the hall to find someone who would come and make the bump stop growing, make it go away.

SEVEN

running with ramone

We're just driving, Bennie, Voodoo, me and Nanny, in Bennie's white Pontiac that smells so bad we have the windows rolled down even though it's one of those nights that's totally dark, no stars in the sky, dead air outside the windows, and as much as you love summer in your mind, you start thinking that maybe it's time for it to be over. We're driving from one end of Elephant Beach to the other, just to get away from Comanche Street for a couple of hours. It's a Wednesday night and the uptown streets are empty. We're just waiting for the weekend, even though we do pretty much the same thing every night.

'Scumbag!' Bennie yells suddenly out the open window. 'Lady, you're a scumbag and you suck!'

'Great,' Nanny says. 'That's great, man. Can't we go anywhere with you guys without worrying about sirens chasing us all over the place?'

'Did you perchance not see what just happened?' Bennie

asked. 'Did you not see the close call I cleverly avoided by swerving away from that bitch's car that was encroaching my lane?'

'You been reading the dictionary again or what?' Voodoo asked. He had his eyes closed and was playing air guitar, even though the radio in Bennie's car didn't work.

'Trouble with this fucking one-horse town, nothing to do but get into car accidents,' Bennie grumbled.

'Yeah, you must miss the panoramic view of those alleys on a Hundred Thirty-third Street.' Voodoo laughed.

Everyone was in an itchy mood. Nanny was still doing it with Voodoo because she didn't know how to stop. They did it in his bedroom underneath the Jimi Hendrix poster, the one where Jimi was on his knees, burning his guitar. Nanny said the way the flames came up his thighs, it looked like he was burning his own dick. She felt like they were in bed with Jimi Hendrix and his burning penis. It was making her angry. She was also angry at Voodoo for being in love with her and for not being Tony Fury. Bennie and Voodoo were grumpy because there was a drought; there had been a huge bust in Lefferton, the next town over, and all the dealers were diving for cover until the heat lifted. I was antsy because it was almost the middle of July and nothing had happened with Luke yet. Here's what I'd heard: that before leaving for Nam, he'd had a girl in the city who no one knew and he'd come home to find she was shacked up with someone else and he was in a heartbroken rage over it. I didn't believe this story, because I couldn't imagine such a thing. If this know-nothing girl was too stupid to realize how lucky she was – no, I couldn't imagine it. Then I heard that Luke was strung out, that in

83

the jungle he'd developed a heroin habit because the dope there was so pure, so fine, that it took less than a bag to get off, and back here, it took much more to feel even the slightest glimmer. But Conor, Luke's brother, said that was horseshit, man, there were no bent spoons, bloody needles, any of that shit lying around, and, if anything, Luke was speedier than he used to be, pacing back and forth in his room at night, chain-smoking, too jittery to finish a full meal. He rarely slept, and even though he was around, he kept his distance, getting up earlier to surf when it was barely light out, heading to the beach late in the day, when everyone else was leaving. I ached with love for Luke, but sometimes it felt like loving a ghost.

Now we were stopped at a green light at Buoy and Crescent when Bennie pulled a sudden U-turn and the Pontiac began choking toward the abandoned mall across the street from the train station.

'What the fuck?' Voodoo yelled.

'Really, will you not be happy until we're finally arrested?' Nanny said. Bennie turned sideways and smiled his lopsided smile.

'Lips in a Hole,' he said triumphantly.

'Lips in a Hole!' Voodoo shouted, and they high-fived, happy as though they'd won the lottery.

'Oh, shit,' Nanny groaned.

'Really,' I agreed.

'"Please pass me the peace weed, and take some heed,"' Voodoo sang, beating the air.

Nanny snagged my eyes with her own. 'Drop us back at Eddy's, then you can go do what you want,' she said, but Bennie was already looking for a parking space.

Voodoo stopped playing the air and turned around. He looked into Nanny's eyes, long and level. 'You want to cop the breeze, go ahead,' he said. 'Because for a born and bred city chick, you sure don't act like one.'

Nanny's eyes were startled; she wasn't used to Voodoo talking to her like that. She mumbled something, then turned and stared out the window.

Lips in a Hole was run out of the abandoned mall behind the housing projects, across the way from the railroad tracks. Word on the street was that no matter how dry the terrain, you could always purchase your drug of choice from Lips in a Hole, which was really just a voice behind a small slot carved into the back wall of a half-finished Pancake Heaven. It wasn't the safest place on earth for white people, but it opened only after dark to attract less attention. Sometimes a line would form and straggle outward until it touched the burglar bars on the public houses that ran parallel to the railroad tracks. None of the tenants complained, because they didn't want trouble. If anyone spotted a cruiser, they'd whistle once, sharply, and the line would disperse, shadows creeping swiftly through the darkness. The cops had to have been pretty stupid not to know about Lips in a Hole, but whoever was behind that door must have been very crafty because so far, no one had been caught.

'Wassamatta for you, man, just park already,' Voodoo grumbled.

'Easy for you to say, man,' Bennie said, driving cautiously through one of the parking islands in the middle of Buoy Boulevard. 'This is a dangerous part of town. Don't want my wheels getting stolen.'

We all laughed hysterically. 'What are you, fucking kidding me?' Voodoo said, holding his sides. 'Who would steal this piece of shit?'

'Niggers,' Bennie replied. 'Niggers'll steal anything. Steal your eyeballs, you ain't looking.' He pulled into a space and insisted we lock the doors even though one of the windows was broken and couldn't roll all the way up.

It was a murky, humid night, no breeze anywhere. The air smelled like a moldy sheet left in the hamper too long. We crossed Buoy Boulevard, landing on the side of the street where Buster's Florsheim Shoes used to be. The Krackoff Bakery had been next to it, where you could buy the best raisin coffee-cake rings in the world. My mother would send me there to get a coffee ring for her mah-jongg game and on the way home I'd pick all the raisins out. Then I'd have to turn back and buy another one out of my own money so she wouldn't go nuts. That's how good those coffee rings were. But now Krackoff's was gone, along with Elephant Beach Dry Goods, where we bought all our corduroys and flannel shirts and desert boots. All the stores had been kicked off the block, bought out to make way for the shiny new mall that was supposed to lift Elephant Beach from the skids and bring prosperity back to its center. We heard the builder had gone belly-up because the economy was so bad, but the other rumor was that he'd pulled out because of the black men from the housing projects staggering around drunk at ten o'clock in the morning. We heard he'd known about the projects, but didn't think the people who lived there would be so visible.

'Belly-up, my ass,' Desi said. 'Were they blind or what that they didn't know this from the get-go? It's not like anyone was hiding, they're all out in plain sight, at least when I drive over the bridge from Queens.'

We crossed the street. Nanny was scared, I could tell. She was leaning all over Voodoo, and he had his arm draped protectively around her. I wasn't scared, because I'd lived in Elephant Beach all my life and I hadn't gone to Catholic school like Nanny and Liz and practically everyone else because my father said the nuns were a bunch of bitter old biddies taking their frustrations out on children and he wanted his kids to know there were other people in the world besides Catholics. 'They'll have to get used to it sooner or later,' he told my mother when they argued. It was another of the ways I was different; I had gone to Central District Elementary, on the other side of the train station, and I knew these streets as well as I now knew the Trunk. I knew about the staggering drunk black men and the junkies who hung out in the play-ground at Central District after dark, sitting on the swings, shivering, pumping themselves high in the air to keep warm until their connection showed. I knew all this, but it hadn't always been this way, and because it was familiar I never felt that anything really bad would ever happen to me.

Sure enough, the line for Lips in a Hole snaked down the alley, but it moved quickly, since nobody wanted to linger too long. Bennie, Voodoo and Nanny moved ahead, trying to find the end of the line. I wished I hadn't come, that I was back at the lounge at The Starlight Hotel, watching Luke. He'd be there by now, huddled in a corner with Mitch, or maybe smoking a joint with Cha-Cha and Raven out on the piazza. I didn't love drugs as much as everyone else did; I was always too afraid I'd be the one who put the baby in the oven instead of the turkey, like the Thanksgiving babysitter did while she was tripping. I was on the verge of walking over to the station to catch a bus back down to Comanche Street when I heard behind me 'Katharine?' I paid only half attention because nobody called me Katharine, not even my grandmother, and I was named for her. But then I saw someone coming into the alley from the side panels of the Pancake Heaven. He began walking toward me. 'Katharine, is that you?'

I only recognized him by his eyes, huge and dark and liquid, like they'd been poured into his face. I walked toward him and said, 'Ramone?' When he leaned forward to kiss my cheek, I was surprised. We hadn't spoken in years. When he hugged me, I caught a whiff of something sly and humid.

'Been a long time, man.'

'For sure,' I said, looking down at his feet. In summer, a lot of people went barefoot in Elephant Beach, but not in the center of town, where the pavement was tar-stained and dirty and littered with glass. Ramone's feet were filthy, the toenails yellow, cracked. They looked like the feet of an old man, even though he was only eighteen years old, the same age as me. His once thick, curly black hair was now lank and stringy, tied back from his face with a blue bandanna.

His shirtsleeves were floppy at the wrists. Nobody wore long sleeves in summer, unless they were trying to hide something.

'How's Ophelia?' I asked.

Ramone nodded, smiling. 'Fat,' he said. '*Gordita*. Third kid on the way.' Then he asked, 'What you waiting on?'

'My friends,' I said.

He laughed. 'That's what they all say.'

'No, really, I—' And then it came to me. Ramone walking out of those side panels, into the alley. I whispered, 'So you – you're the—'

'I work for my brother now,' he said. 'You remember Eddie?'

'Sure, I remember Eddie,' I said. Eddie Lopez had at one time been the town track star. So good-looking, everyone was in love with him. My babysitter, Susie Rickman, showed me her yearbook one night when she let me stay up late to watch *Saturday Night at the Movies.* I was around eleven at the time and she was sixteen. She showed me the pages where people were voted Most Congenial, Best Dressed. Then she pointed to the Most Athletic couple and sighed. 'That's Eddie Lopez,' she said. 'He's the first Puerto Rican to ever be voted in for anything. Isn't he gorgeous?'

I stared at the picture. 'That's Ophelia's cousin,' I said. 'He drives us to the kickball games in her uncle Manuel's truck.' Sometimes Uncle Manuel drove us to the games at other elementary schools, but on the days that Eddie drove us, everyone was quiet while he sang along to the radio. When he helped us down from the back of the truck, we demurely murmured, 'Thank you,' afraid to look at him. He always smiled that famous Lopez smile, riddled with dimples. 'Break a leg,' he'd call as we walked toward the playing field. Then he'd honk the horn as he backed out of the parking lot and yell, 'Only kidding! *Buena suerte, chicas!* Good luck!' before driving off to his gardening job.

Susie nodded. 'He was going out with Stephanie Clayborn, they were so cute together. She told her parents he was Italian, you know, he's so light-skinned, she thought they could get away with it, but then they heard him speaking Spanish one day and flipped out. They told her if she didn't stop seeing him, they wouldn't pay for college. What was she gonna do? Then he was supposed to get a scholarship to one of the state schools, Cortland, I think, that's where all the jocks go, but something messed up and he didn't get it.' She closed the yearbook and began rooting around in her purse for her cigarettes.

'What messed up?' I asked.

Susie shrugged, fitting a Herbert Tareyton between her lips. 'Could have been anything,' she said. 'That's just how it is with the spics. It's not like you can expect things to work out for them.'

'How's Eddie doing?' I asked Ramone now.

Ramone jerked his head toward the slot in the door. 'Ask him,' he said. I recognized Hutchy Michaels, a boy from the Dunes, hunched over the slot, earnestly placing an order. I knew Ramone wasn't talking about Hutchy.

'So Eddie is—'

Ramone shrugged. 'We take turns,' he said.

'A Lopez family franchise,' I said, and then I was sorry. That's the trouble with hanging out with the people I hang out with, everyone's a smart-ass and you get into the habit. Ramone only shrugged, but his smile was uncertain, and for a minute I wondered if he knew what a franchise was. I remembered he had either dropped out of high school or gone to BOCES, the vocational program, somewhere out on the Island. Behind him, I heard a slight scraping noise, and Ramone's eyes darted quickly to the loose panel in the wall. 'Just a minute,' he said, and he walked back through the panel and then he was gone.

'Katie.' Nanny and Voodoo were suddenly beside me. Behind them were hundreds of eyes in the night, and the glowing embers of what seemed like a thousand cigarettes. I could see Bennie farther down the line, craning his neck to look at me. I was flattered that he could take his mind off copping drugs for even two seconds.

'You know that guy?' Voodoo asked. In the dark, you couldn't tell that his Afro was blond. You couldn't tell that he was a white boy who wanted to be Jimi Hendrix. In the dark, he looked like one of the junkies who hung out on the playground swings at Central District Elementary.

'Yeah, I know him,' I said.

Voodoo leaned forward and whispered, 'Bennie wants to know can you talk to him, maybe get us a discount?'

~⸙~

I had known Ramone since he was a skinny kid in the fourth grade. He and his cousin, Ophelia, were in my class at Central District Elementary, and my first crystal-clear memory of us all together was when Mrs. Rothman, our teacher, lost patience with Ophelia and slapped her hands because she couldn't understand English. Ophelia burst into tears, tying her two satiny braids across her face in distress. Ramone had drawn his cousin into a sturdy, protective embrace. Mrs. Rothman's face was sweating, like it always did when she was angry. I walked over and took the two of them by their hands and began leading them out of the room.

'Where do you think you are going, Katharine?' Mrs. Rothman cried; she deplored nicknames and always called us by our formal names. But there was no heat to her words and she made no move to stop us. She knew she should never have slapped Ophelia. She would never have hit a white kid. 'I have the pass,' I said, holding up the beaten piece of cardboard with the word 'Pass' written across it in big, black letters. As the frosted glass door closed behind us, we could hear her droning on about the importance of diagramming sentences.

Once in the hall, I walked in front of them, leading the way to Mrs. Myer's sixth-grade classroom down the stairs, on the first floor.

'Where are we going?' Ramone asked.

'I'm taking you to your sister,' I said. I honestly felt bad about the way Mrs. Rothman had treated Ophelia, but I had an ulterior motive. I actually couldn't wait. I couldn't wait to get to Mrs. Myer's room and ask permission for Olga to come out in the hall. To say, 'It's a family matter.' I had heard Jody Klein's older sister say that when she came to get him from our class the day his grandfather died, and I'd thought it impressive. And I had the pass, so Mrs. Myer would think I had permission from my teacher.

The truth was, I was fascinated with the Lopez family, with all the Puerto Ricans in our school. They were always walking together, chattering in Spanish, and they all seemed related somehow. They sat together at one long table in the cafeteria during lunchtime, eating baloney sandwiches, their milk mustaches more pronounced against their dark skin. At recess, they ran over the playground like a flock of colorful birds, their thin legs pumping like pistons. Olga, Ramone's sister, was the oldest, a sixth grader, and reportedly excellent in math, my worst subject. I'd overheard Mrs. Myer telling Mrs. Rothman, 'She's a whiz at numbers, but so what? She'll be pregnant and married by the time she's fifteen. Better she should learn how to budget her food stamps and care for a family.' I thought if Olga had heard Mrs. Myer say that, she would have kicked her in the shin. She was a tough girl, with a wide mouth and big teeth, and she wore dangling earrings and a beige ski jacket and black flats with no stockings that made her seem wickedly grown-up. She presided over the younger children, scolding them, hugging them, counting them when she rounded everyone up to go home at dismissal time. *'Mira, mami!'* she'd call. *'Ándale!'* Sometimes she'd let out a bloodcurdling whistle. I thought she was beautiful and wished she was my sister. My brother was too young to come to school yet, and though I had friends to eat lunch with and walk home with, I longed to be part of a big, jostling crowd like the Lopezes, standing next to Olga, having her arm around me as she threw back her head and laughed her huge, hearty laugh.

Everything went exactly as planned. We arrived at Olga's classroom, and I knocked at the door. Mrs. Myer opened it. 'Yes, Katie?' she said. I asked to see Olga Lopez, indicating Ramone and Ophelia standing behind me. 'It's a family matter,' I whispered. She pursed her lips and stared at them for several seconds and then closed the door. Olga came out. She was wearing the beige ski jacket over a frilly black-and-white dress that came only to above her knees, which were discolored with faded bruises. She walked right past me to where Ophelia was huddled against the lockers, Ramone beside her. She and Ramone began speaking in rapid Spanish, then Olga asked

Ophelia something and Ophelia began crying again. Olga drew Ophelia against her, caressing her braids, whispering soothing words in Spanish. At least they sounded soothing. I stood there, watching.

Olga finally turned toward me. 'What you looking at, little white girl?' she asked contemptuously. Her eyes were cold as stone. Ramone looked at me and then began speaking in Spanish. I thought he was telling her how I had led them to safety. She looked back over at me. I thought her eyes would change, but they didn't. 'You better get back,' she said. 'Go on, get back to class.'

'But I have the pass,' I said.

Olga gently disengaged Ophelia's hands from around her waist. She walked over to me and snatched the pass from my hand, then stood there, her mouth stretched into a cruel smile. 'Not anymore,' she said. Ramone looked down at his sneakers. There were tears in my eyes, but I was afraid if I started crying, Olga would only laugh, or yell at me the way the teachers yelled whenever the Spanish kids began crying in class, which was often. The teachers didn't like them because they were too emotional and couldn't speak English properly. They became sleepy after lunch and had to be roused from putting their heads in their arms on their desks. They couldn't understand the simplest directions. Like the time Ava and Marisol Ortiz, beautiful twins in the fifth grade, brought their father's goat to school for show-and-tell. His name was Gabriel, and he caused quite a commotion. The principal, Mr. Weissman, wanted to call their parents to come take the goat home, but they didn't have a phone. Gabriel ended up grazing the lonely weeds shooting up between the cracks in the school playground until dismissal time.

The only teacher who was warm to the Spanish kids was Mr. Farnsworth, the gym teacher. He liked them for the same reason he liked the Negro kids, because they were fast and could outrun everybody else, including the track teams at the three other Elephant Beach elementary schools. 'It's in their blood,' we heard him explaining to Mr. Dillard, the art teacher, whose classroom was next door to the gym. It was true; their light, lithe bodies seemed weightless as they ran the inside track, their sneakers barely touching the varnished floor. Ophelia was a somewhat indifferent athlete, but Ramone was gifted, 'fleet of foot, a wonder to behold,' Mr. Farnsworth would say, beaming, eyes on his stopwatch. Ramone's coordination was superior, and it wasn't just his legs, his feet; you could see it in his eyes. When he ran, he would lift his face to the sky like a flower to the sun. Sometimes he'd laugh aloud from sheer joy.

Olga may not have taken to me, but Ramone and Ophelia and I became friends. We played together during recess and in gym class. Ramone and I coached Ophelia in English, so that she gradually began picking up words and phrases, speaking in lyrical bursts. I was overjoyed when she asked me to come over after school; I told her I had to go home first and would be there by four o'clock. At home, my mother's nose came up sharply when I told her where I was going. She questioned me about 'this Ophelia Lopez' and when I told her where Ophelia lived, she put down her crossword puzzle and put on her shoes and said she'd walk me over there. When we arrived in front of Ophelia's building, a three-story, salmon-colored affair, my mother looked up at the broken windows – the colorful sheets being used instead of blinds or curtains (which I thought wildly gay and inventive), the front door hanging off one hinge – heard the foreign shouts from the narrow hallway, and grabbed my hand and did a rapid about-face.

'You'll call her from home and ask her to come to your house,' she said, walking quickly.

'But she doesn't have a phone,' I said. 'Why can't we just get her now and bring her with us?' We were less than a block away.

'You're not setting foot in that building,' my mother said firmly. She ignored my questions and steered me into Leo's Luncheonette for a black-and-white ice-cream soda. Then we stopped by her friend Harriet's, who had a huge color television in her den. I watched *From Here to Eternity* on *The 4:30 Movie* while they had coffee in the kitchen, and when I ran in to ask if I could have a cold drink, Harriet was shaking her head, saying, 'They're everywhere now, they have their own grocery store for chrissake. How the hell did that get by the council? I mean, where do they think we are, San Juan?'

'What grocery store?' I asked, and my mother, shaking a packet of Sweet'N Low into her coffee, said firmly, 'Go inside, sweetie, we're talking,' and their conversation didn't resume until I turned the television volume up again.

The next day at school I told Ophelia I had developed a nosebleed when I got home, and had to spend two hours sitting up with small ice packs up my nose to stop the bleeding. I didn't consider it a total lie because this had actually happened when I was seven and had the measles. Ophelia exclaimed in Spanish, then stroked my arm in commiseration. I felt guilty that I'd been so distracted by ice cream and TV, and felt worse at recess when Ramone handed me the yellow tulip he'd picked from someone's garden across the street from our school. He presented the tulip, then bowed, so that his too-big shirt billowed out and touched the ground. I curtsied and we giggled, and then the three of us began climbing to the top of the jungle gym.

But that wasn't my best memory of Ramone. That came later, after Olga had graduated and we were sixth graders ourselves. That was the year we were competing for the John F. Kennedy Memorial Trophy against the three other Elephant Beach elementary schools. The trophy was brought to each school so that we could all see what was at stake. It was huge, with two streams of gold plating down the sides, and Mr. Farnsworth told us that the winning team would have their names engraved on the sides of the trophy. Then he bowed his head and nodded three times, which he always did when he had something important to say. 'President John F. Kennedy came from a family of athletes. Who knew what healthy competition was. Who knew what it meant to win. President Kennedy was a winner, all right. He was the first Irish American to be elected president of these United States. He opened the door. The door is now open for anyone to be president. For anyone to win.'

We all nodded solemnly. President Kennedy had died two years earlier. We'd had a moment of silence and then they let us out of school early. We felt a personal connection to the president because during his campaign, he'd come to Elephant Beach, which was one of the few Democratic towns on Long Island. My father had taken me to see him, had lifted me up high so that I could see him through the crowds. He was riding down Buoy Boulevard, standing in the back of a convertible in his shirtsleeves, smiling and waving at everyone. His teeth were very white. Against the sunlight, he looked more like a god than a regular man. Among us, we agreed it would be an honor to win the trophy named after the president. It would be like having a little piece of him for ourselves forever.

The trophy was all anyone talked about for days, even kids who weren't on the track team. Those of us who were reached an exalted status that surpassed making the Principal's Honor Roll or being a hall monitor and wearing a silver badge, both of which I'd achieved, but neither of which had been this exciting. I had been running track since fourth grade because I was tall and had long legs and was fast, and it brought me closer to the Lopezes. I used to leave the house to walk to school while it was still dark out, eager to get to Stein's candy store and split a Yoo-hoo and cheese Danish with Ophelia and Ramone and whoever else showed up early, mostly the Negro kids who lived near the railroad tracks, who would sometimes bring their little brothers and sisters with them while their mothers went to work. Sometimes Kenny the janitor would let us into the gymnasium before homeroom, where we'd practice running relays, using an old ruler from one of the classrooms to pass off to one another. Sometimes we'd just run wildly through the school yard, watching our breath come out in white puffs as the sun rose higher over the bay. But now we had a goal and a purpose, and the whole school was cheering for us, especially for Ramone. His nickname was Rocket. 'Hey, Rocket,' white kids who never talked to the Spanish kids would hail him in the hallways. Even the teachers smiled at Ramone now, responding to his inner light. None of them yelled at him or made sarcastic remarks when he didn't know an answer to a question in class. Everyone loved his rhythm, the way his feet skimmed the earth.

The day of the meet, I was up at dawn. The meet was scheduled for ten o'clock and the bus was picking the team up at nine twenty in front of Central District Elementary. My father wouldn't let me leave until it was light out and offered to drive me, but then discovered the car had a flat tire from a bent nail. My mother insisted I eat something before leaving the house, but then my younger brother threw up all over the kitchen table from a virus nobody knew he had and the house was in an uproar and I couldn't get into the bathroom on time. I ended up running the three long blocks to school with tears streaming down my face because I was using up valuable energy that should have been saved for the race. I didn't want to let the team down. By the time I got there, the bus had already departed and now I was crying in earnest. I heard somebody shout my name and looked up to see Ramone, Ophelia and their cousin Julio coming toward me, all wearing black shorts, white tee shirts, and high, white ribbed socks with black piping around the top, the kind you could buy at Irv's Bargain Center, three for a dollar fifty. They, too, had missed the bus. 'Eddie was supposed to drive us, but he never showed up,' Ramone explained, panting. Ophelia's eyes filled with tears. Julio shook his head; he was short and stocky with slicked-back hair and a low forehead. 'Girls always making things worse,' he said disgustedly. 'Fuck it, it's not like they giving us money or nothing.' He rolled saliva in his mouth and spat it out on the sidewalk.

Ramone looked like he was searching the air for solutions. He felt around in his pockets and came up with two dimes. 'How much money you got?' he demanded. 'Quick!' Ophelia brought forth seven cents. Julio just laughed until Ramone spoke to him sharply in Spanish; I'd never heard him speak so sharply before. Julio narrowed his eyes but he flipped a quarter out of his pocket into the air so it would fall to the sidewalk. Ramone caught it in mid-flight. He looked at me. I hung my head, feeling more tears coming up in my throat. 'I don't have any money,' I said. I'd been in such a hurry leaving the house that I'd forgotten to take my change purse. 'White people always got money,' Julio said, but Ramone was already pulling my hand, coaxing me to run with him toward the taxi stand at the train station.

At the taxi stand, we found one lone green-and-white-checkered cab; the driver was an older man with silvery hair, sitting with the window open, reading the paper. We climbed into the cab, shouting instructions. The inside of all the Elephant Beach taxis smelled of cigar smoke. The driver was unperturbed; he didn't even lift his eyes from his newspaper as he said, 'Fifty cents a head, my friends.'

'We have fifty-two cents,' Ramone said. The driver shrugged and kept reading. 'I'll leave,' I said, feeling it was only fair, since I didn't have any money, but Ramone held my hand fast and hard. Everyone began clamoring, about the track meet, how they were waiting for us, how a photographer from the *Elephant Beach Gazette* would be there. Ophelia was pulling on her hair, shouting in Spanish. I was crying and yelling at the same time. Julio just looked out the window, snapping his gum. Finally, Ramone tugged at the driver's elbow until he looked up. 'It's the John F. Kennedy Memorial Trophy,' he said patiently. 'They'll print our names on the sides in gold. The trophy will go in the glass case next to the principal's office for all to see. If we win, we'll bring glory to our families, to the school, to the entire town.' He spoke solemnly, with great dignity. I realized that he had made this speech before, somewhere, to someone, or perhaps just in front of the mirror. Perhaps that was what he did while combing the curl that fell forward onto his forehead.

The driver looked at Ramone. He turned and looked at all of us. Then he sighed, put down his paper, and started the engine.

'Please drive quickly,' Ramone said. 'The meet starts at ten o'clock, and my race is first. I'm the fastest runner.'

'It's true,' I said, in case the driver thought he was just conceited. 'We can't win without him.'

'Don't push your luck, kids,' the driver said, but the taxi picked up speed. When we passed the steepled clock at City Hall, it was seven minutes to ten. We squirmed on the seat. Ramone hung his head between his knees. Ophelia put her lips to her fingertips and then crossed herself. Julio turned around and looked at me with a twisted smile. 'White girl rides for free,' he said. I wanted to tell him to shut up, but I didn't. I wished he wasn't there. He had squinty eyes and during recess he stood against the wire fence, watching everyone run with a sneering expression on his face. He had none of the grace or beauty of the rest of the Lopez clan. I didn't understand how he'd gotten into that family in the first place.

The meet was at Rum Hill Elementary School, up in the Dunes. It was the silk stocking district of Elephant Beach, set slightly apart from the rest of the town. Whenever Uncle Manuel drove the kickball team to games there in his truck, the Rum Hill kids laughed at us, called us the nigger school, but never right in front of the Negro girls, because they were afraid of getting beat up. They were sly and wily and our sworn enemies. At the last practice before the track meet, Ramone said, 'When you run against them, put in your mind that if you don't win the race, your mother will die.' There was a collective gasp among us, and Raynelle Johnson started jumping from side to side, saying, 'Don't you be putting no bad mouth on my mama!' Ramone smiled, his dimples shining. He said patiently, 'Think how afraid it makes you to think of it. That's what will make you win the race.'

The cab driver made the turn up the long driveway to Rum Hill Elementary. He drove the length and then curved around back to the parking lot. We could see the crowds in the bleachers, see Mr. Farnsworth in his striped gym pants and lucky red bow tie pacing the field, looking at his watch. He was waiting for Ramone. The first race was the boys' hundred-yard dash; the relay would follow. From the windows of the cab, we saw Mr. Farnsworth shake his head and throw up his hands. We saw the runners for the hundred-yard dash line up at the starting line. From the distance they looked

102

like toy soldiers waiting to get shot. 'Pull up!' Ramone shouted. 'Pull up to the line! You can go through the grass, that way, pull up, *pull up!*' Caught by the urgency in his voice, the driver obeyed. Before the cab had even rolled to a complete stop, Ramone shot out of the seat so quickly it was as though he vaporized. 'Jesus,' the driver said, getting out of the cab. The other runners had just taken off in their lanes when Ramone came up behind them. The photographer from the *Elephant Beach Gazette* said he had never seen anything like it in his life. 'The kid comes out of nowhere,' he said, afterward, 'nowhere! And the race already started! And he's running like the furies of hell are chasing him, right? And there's one point, one instant, where I swear on my mother's life, he was airborne. He was running so fast, his feet weren't touching the ground. I tried, but the camera couldn't catch it. I wanted everyone to see it, but – Jesus! Would that have made a great front page, or what?' Still, Ramone made the paper; we all did. The *Gazette* dedicated an entire page to Central District Elementary, a photomontage with Ramone at the center, smiling, his arms around the John F. Kennedy Memorial Trophy.

Ramone never came back out of the forsaken Pancake Heaven. He disappeared, just like in junior high school, where we all got swallowed up whole and spit back out again. That first year, in seventh grade, I was rudderless; all the things that had served me well at Central District Elementary went down the toilet. There were cliques and hierarchies that I didn't understand. Suddenly, it mattered where you lived, where you bought your clothes, how you wore your hair. In gym class, there were too many sniggering girls waiting to laugh at the way your legs looked in your gym uniform. I became self-conscious about things that had never occurred to me before. I would walk to school with my stomach clenched and knotted with dread, homesick for the mornings at Central District Elementary when we would run with abandon around the school playground before the first bell. My mother saw how it was with me; she was concerned, but distracted. That fall, my brother had contracted pneumonia, running such a high fever he'd become delirious, and on the way to the doctor's office we thought we'd lost him. He was hospitalized for several weeks and couldn't go to school for a month afterward, so the household revolved around him and his weekly blood tests and trying to keep him quietly entertained. My mother would sit by his bed while he slept, watching him breathe, and if I asked her something as simple as if she'd ironed my navy blue skirt, she either didn't answer or snapped at me impatiently. I missed the times she'd come into my room to say good night, and we'd end up talking until my father called for her to turn out the lights. Now at night, I would lie in bed, staring into darkness, wondering what was to become of me.

I had not seen any of the Lopez clan in junior high. The building was huge, resting on the bay in a more secluded part of town, and instead of six classes to one grade, there were eighteen. There was also tracking that kept us separated from one another: Academic, Vocational, Industrial. I looked for Ophelia's shiny tresses, for Ramone's raging dimples, but could never seem to find them in the carefully monitored hallways. I was afraid to go searching for them, because like everyone else at Elephant Beach Junior High School, I lived in fear of walking down the wrong corridor and meeting up with the principal, Miss Sullivan, who had a glass eye and walked the halls with a wooden stick she used to whack kids who misbehaved. She was rumored to have the ability to make ninth-grade boys cry.

Finally, in November of that horrible year, while walking down the school steps at the end of the day, I saw them, clustered in the corner of a sealed-off entrance that nobody used. It was a cold, sunny day, blue skies, waves lapping gently against the stained seawall. The Spanish kids were standing in the darkened shade, waiting for their bus. My heart leaped a little in my chest; I began walking toward them, a big smile blooming on my face, the first smile I could feel with my body since arriving at this dismal place in September. I got closer and saw Ramone and Julio and another boy I didn't know huddled together, wearing white socks with pointy black shoes and dark pants that didn't quite cover their ankles. They wore thin black jackets with the collars turned up and their hair was slick with oil. Ophelia looked different now; maybe it was her tight skirt, or the long silver hoops dangling from her ears. They all looked much older than the last time I'd seen them. Olga was standing at the top of the steps, her eyes narrowed with black eyeliner, her lips purple, her legs bare despite the temperature. I wondered if she'd recognize me, but she was draped all over some boy wearing a battered leather jacket, smoking a cigarette.

Ramone had his back to me, but just then, Ophelia turned

around. I started moving toward her, but stopped when I saw the look on her face. Her eyes had the same coldness as her cousin Olga's had on that day so long ago, when we'd stood in the hallway outside Mrs. Myer's classroom. Just then, Julio spotted me, and Ramone turned around as well. I caught the tail end of a dimple, but Ramone didn't speak. He made no move toward me. It was Julio, Julio of the squinty, shifting eyes and sneering smile, who looked at me and laughed. 'White girl rides for free, right?' he said. I wanted to remind him that we'd all ended up riding for free that day, that the cab driver had been cheering so hard for Ramone to win the race that he'd forgotten to collect the fifty-two cents we owed for his fare. But I didn't say anything. I turned around quickly so that no one could see my face. I could hear Julio still laughing behind me. 'Yeah,' he said. 'White girl always rides for free.'

∽〇∽

'Katie, man. You ready?' Bennie, Voodoo and Nanny were behind me. I looked one last time toward the loose panels, where I had watched Ramone disappear.

'Yeah,' I said. We walked out of the alley, onto the street, past the rotting boards of abandoned construction, where a tall, thin man stood with one foot propped against a crumbling wall. In the flare of the match he was using to light his cigarette, I saw his face for a split second. He looked old to be Eddie Lopez, but it could have been. It probably was. I watched him lean his head back against the building and blow smoke up toward the sky. I thought about going over to say something, but he would never remember me. I hadn't stood out from any of the other little girls crowded into the back of his father's truck, subdued into silence by his impossible beauty. He had loved the song 'Brown Eyed Girl.' Whenever it came on the radio, he'd yell back to us, '*Chicas!* Come on, sing along with me!' But none of us ever did.

When we got back to the car, Bennie fumbled with his keys. 'Now everybody be cool,' he said. 'I'm heavy.' We laughed again. Bennie always said that. He was the only one of us who was always either high or heavy or both.

'"Be cool, I'm heavy,"' Voodoo mimicked. 'We get busted, it's gonna be on you, not anyone else. You and this fucking car. Christ, you could hear that muffler in New Jersey. Let Katie drive. She's clean, the least likely to attract attention.' He turned to me. 'Katie, you cool with that?'

'Yeah,' I said. I usually ended up driving, wherever we were. I liked driving on the parkway at night and thought about taking us for a spin. No lights to stop at, just pure road and beach grass lining the lanes. Nanny was nodding, her head resting on Voodoo's shoulder. Voodoo's eyes were closed, his hands still. A slight smile played on his lips. Bennie was sitting beside me, his eyelids practically dragging down to his cheekbones. He turned his stoned, sorrowful gaze on me. 'So what, you couldn't ask your buddy back there for a discount?' he slurred.

I snorted, lit a cigarette, and rolled down the window. A slight breeze was finally stirring, lifting the smell of the ocean into the air. I pulled out of the parking space and took off in the direction of the parkway. Everyone was too stoned to notice we were driving away from the Trunk and by the time they did we'd probably be on our way back.

'Katie, man, where'd you know that guy from again?' Voodoo asked, his voice drowsy. Bennie was trying to light a cigarette. When it dropped to the floor, he left it there. He leaned back against the seat and closed his eyes. 'Yeah, what was that about, man? How the fuck does someone like you know someone like him?'

'We used to run together,' I said. 'When we were kids in elementary school.' When Ramone would run like his feet had wings.

EIGHT

for better or worse

Maggie all but tore the paisley gown off the hanger and thrust it into Nanny's hands. 'Here,' she said. 'You can cut it down, wear it to school, to work, wear it to hang out at Eddy's for all I care.' The rusted lily stains on the bodice of the dress were faded, but still noticeable.

'That's your wedding dress,' Nanny said, appalled.

'Not any more, cuz,' Maggie said, whipping through her closet. 'Doesn't fit since I had the baby. And I don't ever plan on getting married again. Once was enough.'

We were at Maggie's because Nanny needed something to wear to the formal orientation tea at Sacred Heart Secretarial School, which she'd be attending in the fall, and Maggie said she was welcome to stop by and browse her closet. The paisley gown had a yellow silk sash that tied in the back and matched the streamers in the bouquet that Maggie had carried down the aisle at St. Timothy's Church on her wedding day.

'Shit!' Maggie stomped over to the crib, where the baby

was crying. She picked him up and cradled him and walked into the living room. 'Let's split,' Liz mouthed, as Nanny carefully folded the dress and put it in the Macy's shopping bag she'd brought from home. We walked past Maggie, who had the baby at her breast, rocking him. Ringlets of hair rushed down her back like greasy waterfalls; she smelled faintly of milk and perspiration. She gave us a tight-lipped smile as Nanny kissed her cheek and whispered, 'Thank you.'

'You think Matty's stepping out on her?' Liz asked, her eyes narrowed with interest, as we walked up the block to Eddy's. I looked at her. It was inconceivable to me that Matty would be cheating on Maggie; they'd just gotten married last year and he'd always seemed so crazy about her.

Nanny shook her head. 'I don't think that's his thing,' she said. 'Besides, if it was someone around here we would have heard about it by now.' Nanny was big on family loyalty, but she'd told me in private that a couple weeks back Matty had stayed out all night and came stumbling home just as the streetlights went off. She'd sworn me to secrecy, especially in front of Liz, who would tell the earth if she knew.

'Still, he's out a lot without her—'

'With the guys,' Nanny said, a light sharpness to her tone. 'My mother says it's the way with Irish men, always in the bars, no women around. She says you didn't know any better, you'd think they were all a bunch of fags.'

'That's what Mitch says, all talk and no action,' I said. I imitated Mitch's lazy drawl. '"Half the cats around here are too stiff to get stiff, you dig my meaning."' Me and Nanny laughed, but Liz said, in a mimicking voice, 'Mitch says, Mitch says. You and ol' Mitch seem pretty tight lately. Pretty chummy with a rummy.'

'Don't call him that,' I said.

'Why the hell not?' Liz asked. 'It's not like he's hiding it.'

'Nobody's ever only one thing, man,' I said, and even in my own ears I sounded solemn and priggish.

'Wow, Katie, man. That's intense,' Nanny said.

'What are you, into him?' Liz asked. She laughed and shook her head. 'That would be just like you, Katie. Digging a one-legged drunk.'

'What's that supposed to mean?' I asked. Usually I shut up when Liz got this way, but she'd been this way a lot lately and it was working my nerves.

'The Katie Hanson sick puppy syndrome,' Liz said. 'Bennie Esposito, too stoned to walk, Georgie the faggot—'

'At least I see them,' I said. 'Maybe if you spent more time with Cory, you wouldn't be such a bitch.'

Even Nanny turned to look at me. I was surprised myself; usually I kept still and waited until Liz ran down on one of her moods, but it was hot and I was frustrated over Luke and the way the summer was going. Besides, Mitch and Georgie were my friends.

Liz didn't say anything. She just waved her hand, as if pushing me backward, and turned and walked in the opposite direction.

'Do you, Katie?' Nanny said softly. 'Dig Mitch?'

'No,' I said. 'No, man, we're just – he's a good friend. Just don't tell Liz, she's always on me about being friends with guys instead of—'

'I know, I know,' Nanny said wearily. 'Maybe you're just

111

smarter than the rest of us, not losing your shit over some asshole.' I knew she was talking about Tony Fury; she hadn't heard from him since the night he'd stood outside her window, throwing rocks.

'Maybe not,' I said. I had that hollow feeling inside I got whenever I had words with someone, which wasn't often. I usually backed out of fights; I didn't like for people to be mad at me. Suddenly, I missed Marcel, even though I'd gone up to Cape Cod to visit right before Fourth of July. I missed how it had been when it was just the two of us, before she met James and I started hanging out in the Trunk. Marcel was like me, she didn't like harsh words and never saw the need for them. We'd been friends since seventh grade and had never had one fight. 'I feel bad,' I said now, holding my arms across my stomach.

Nanny snorted. 'Don't start kicking your own ass,' she said. 'She had it coming.'

'Drunk, drunk, drunk!' Maggie railed, whipping around the small living room of the bungalow, waving her arms. 'Matty! My brothers! Just like my father, just like him! Jesus!' From the crib in the corner, the baby began squalling.

'Christ,' Maggie whispered wearily. There were violet stains under her eyes. Her breasts were bursting out of her tee shirt. She picked up the baby, hoisted him on her shoulder. His whimpering tapered to a low mewling, sounding like a lost kitten.

It was my day off from the A&P. Me and Nanny were

heading for the beach, and she wanted to stop in and see how Maggie was doing, since it was right on the way. It had been several days since we'd last seen her, but it seemed like we had never left.

'You know, sometimes I forget,' she whispered, her eyes closed. 'I forget he's here, you know? When he's sleeping . . . the other day, right, I actually started getting dressed to go to the beach. You know, Thursday, it was one of those days, makes you feel like – like someone gave you a present, right? So pretty – and I swear to God, I was almost out the door, man, with my towel and the baby oil . . . If he hadn't woken up just then, if I hadn't heard him crying, I would have been, like, gone, man. And he would have been . . .' She trailed off. Tears started leaking from her eyes, running down her face.

'Maggie.' Nanny walked over, patted her arm in sympathy.

I felt awkward, standing there watching, not knowing what to do. I wasn't close to Maggie; our association was through Nanny, but I'd always envied her, so sure, so secure, with her cool, good-looking brothers, and Matty Mayhew, with his killer blue eyes, who she'd been with forever. I had a sudden flashback of a hot day several summers ago, watching Matty riding her on the handlebars of a Sting-Ray bicycle, Maggie squealing as he circled curbs and cars, the two of them laughing in the late afternoon sunlight.

The baby was almost quiet now, rocking gently against Maggie's skin.

'It's all right,' Maggie whispered. 'Shhh, shhh. It's all right.'

By the first week in August they were gone, headed to Colorado in the blue-and-white Volkswagen van that Matty had purchased secondhand from the Sunoco station on Buoy Boulevard. Nanny told us how it had come about, what she'd pieced together from overheard phone conversations between her mother and Aunt Francie, and what Maggie had told her. What happened was, one night, 'fed up to the teeth and sick to death of this shit,' Maggie had wrapped Donovan in his blue-and-white blanket and gone to stay at her mother's. The next day, when Matty came around demanding to see Maggie and the baby, Aunt Francie met him at the door with her arms folded over her chest, refusing to let him in. The second day he stayed away, figuring Maggie would come around in good time, call him to come get her, or just show up at home, recovered from her snit. 'Just wait it out, man,' Raven advised him. 'She'll get sick of listening to my mother run you down sooner or later.' The fourth day he went over to Aunt Francie's house and became belligerent. 'I got a right to see my own kid,' he said. 'Maybe when you start acting like a father,' Aunt Francie said, slamming the door in his face. He went out and got drunk that night, tried calling Maggie at her mother's house from the pay phone at The Starlight Lounge, but either or both of them hung up on him every time. By the end of the week he was a wreck, too upset to even get high. When he showed up at Aunt Francie's, meek and sober, she barred the doorway. Behind her, he could see Donovan's playpen in the middle of the living room. Tears came to his eyes.

'You ready to cut the shit?' Aunt Francie asked, fixing him with that steely look that had made her husband quit drinking during the last years they were together.

'Please let me see them, Francie,' he said humbly, and only when Maggie called from the living room, 'Let him in, Ma,' did Aunt Francie finally step aside.

Maggie had her own arms folded, though, and the Scully steel was in her voice as she told him she wasn't going back to the way things had been. 'I'm done with that bullshit,' she said, and Matty heard the steel and knew that he'd better start listening if he wanted to see his son again. She said she'd thought it out and the only way that made sense was for them to leave Elephant Beach and start someplace new, 'away from the Beach and the bars and my asshole brothers.' She thought even the city was too close, because folks were always breezing in and out on the Long Island Rail Road and besides, it was no place to raise a kid nowadays.

'No arguments there,' said Matty, whose grandparents had been among the first residents of Elephant Beach, back when the boardwalk was being built and Buoy Boulevard was mostly sand.

'Matty,' Maggie said gently, with no trace of anger, 'I love you, but let's face it. We had to get married. We don't have to stay married.'

They ended up talking all night and, by mid-morning of the next day, they'd decided to move to Boulder, Colorado, where Matty's cousin Kevin worked in construction and had told Matty that any time he wanted to come out, he'd have a job and a place to stay; that the people were beautiful and the mountains 'magnificent, man, like un-fucking-real.' It was worth a shot, they agreed, and within weeks they were packed and ready to depart. Nanny's mother, Mrs. Devlin, threw the first of the farewell parties for the Scully side of the family, which was big and so different from my own; Liz and I were invited because we were over there so much, Nanny's parents called us their other daughters. When we turned eighteen in our senior year, Mrs. Devlin included us in the cocktail hour, mixing up a blender full of Kahlúa sombreros made with vodka and real cream. I'd always gargle with Listerine before I went home, because my mother still hadn't gotten over that Mrs. Devlin served us all a glass of champagne before going to midnight mass two Christmases ago.

We were upstairs on the tiny sunporch outside Nanny's bedroom, smoking a joint with her cousin Cha-Cha. We could hear the laughing babble downstairs almost as if it was in the next room. A glass broke, a baby cried. We had drinks and cigarettes and the air smelled of ocean and sunshine.

'I'm sure gonna miss my little sis,' Cha-Cha said, tapping the joint. 'But hey, it's what she wants, man. Since she was a little girl, right? She always wanted her own family, took my old man's leaving harder than the rest of us. Even my mother.' He laughed, his voice scratchy and shuddering from the smoke. I liked Cha-Cha; he was long-haired and lanky and fine in his flannel shirts and jeans, not as wired as Raven or as vivacious as Maggie, but funny and friendly and a terrible flirt. All the city people had a kind of wildness about them though, something smoky and sinister that made you pause before moving forward.

'I can see that, man,' Liz said in her all-knowing voice. Behind her back, me and Nanny covered our mouths to keep from laughing. 'I can, like, definitely see Maggie as a daddy's little girl.'

'When he was around,' Cha-Cha said, laughing. 'When he

quit drinking, everything was cool for a while, until one day he just, like, vanished, man. Went to the hardware store for some lightbulbs and never came back.'

'I remember,' Nanny said. 'That's when you all came to stay with us at the Beach.'

'And my mother was wailing, wailing, man, the whole way down here on the train,' Cha-Cha recalled. 'And then we got to your house and your mother was all, "Good riddance to bad rubbish. Lie down with dogs, you get up with fleas."' He laughed again. 'But Maggie, she was always waiting on him to come home. Used to sit by the window, watching for him to come walking up Dyckman Street. Even at the wedding. I mean, dig it, man, we don't even know if he's still alive, right? But she thought he'd like, magically appear to walk her down the aisle.' It was Raven who'd walked her down the aisle instead, being the oldest. I thought about Maggie, sitting in the apartment in Washington Heights, waiting for her father to come through the door. I'd never thought of her as someone with her face pressed against a window. She'd always seemed to be one of those girls to whom gifts came quickly, in abundance.

'But it'll be cool, man,' Cha-Cha said. 'Boulder's very cool. All those fucking mountains, man! It's a far-out place to start a new life.' Suddenly he turned to me, grinning, and said, 'You want to ride shotgun?' I was so startled that I nodded, yes, and he hit heavily on the joint, sucking the smoke all the way in like it was oxygen. Then his lips were on mine and the smoke dipped and curled around my tongue to the back of my throat, and I held it as though I was underwater, seeing how long I could go before my lungs exploded. Then my breath burst from me, the sweet stench of weed filling the air.

'Nice,' Cha-Cha said approvingly. 'Very nice.' Then he patted his stomach. 'I'm going back down, get some more of your mother's baked ziti,' he told Nanny. 'Damn, the woman can cook! She got all the cooking genes in this family. I love my mother, man, but she can barely open a can of Spam. You coming, cuz?'

'In a bit,' Nanny said dreamily. She was staring across the bungalow roofs that lined the street below. I knew she was thinking about Tony Fury. I could hear it in her voice.

'Okay, be that way,' Cha-Cha said, then winked and slammed through the screen door that led to the staircase.

'He is such a fox,' Liz said.

'For real, if he wasn't my cousin,' Nanny said. 'Katie, man, we could be cousin-in-laws! But you know how he is, right?'

'How did it feel?' Liz whispered to me. 'How did he taste?'

'How did he taste? What is he, a friggin' lollipop?' Nanny asked, and she and Liz started laughing hysterically.

'Good,' I said, 'he tasted good,' but they barely heard me over the sound of their laughter. It was just as well. I wasn't going to tell them that the feel of his lips on mine made me ache for something real that lived in the world and not in my head, for flesh and touch and kisses that mattered. I was tired of renting other people's dreams.

～∂～

'I still can't believe she got Matty to move his ass out of the Beach,' Liz said. We were back in Nanny's bedroom, lying

118

across her bed, watching the sun shadows on the ceiling. It seemed to me they had never been so interesting, resembling clouds and balloon-shaped animals.

Downstairs, Mrs. Devlin was playing her Rosemary Clooney records; 'Come On-a My House' floated up the stairs and made me think of Bing Crosby singing 'White Christmas' in that movie they were in together.

Nanny sighed. 'Maggie gets to go to Colorado, I get to go to fucking Sacred Heart Secretarial School.' She had wanted to go to Carver Community College and take an associate's degree in Secretarial Studies and Administration; she'd pleaded with her mother that the bus to Hempstead was cheaper than the Long Island Rail Road and subway fare combined into Manhattan, but Mrs. Devlin had stood firm. All the girls in the Scully clan went to Sacred Heart Secretarial and that was the end of it.

'Still a change of scenery,' Liz said. She was going to keep working in her father's car dealership and take classes at Mary the Immaculate College for Catholic Women in Garden City. Her grades had been too terrible to get in as a full-time student, so her parents were making her take classes at night until she could begin matriculating.

'She thinks I'll get a job in some insurance company and marry a rich boss, like my cousin Clare,' Nanny said. 'No, what my mother really thinks is I'm going to marry John-John Kennedy when he grows up.'

'Where does she think you're going to meet him, hanging around Eddy's?' Liz asked. 'Or going to an all-girls Catholic school taught by nuns, for chrissake?' She curled her lip in disgust.

119

'Really, man,' I said, sucking on a cocktail cherry. 'It's like, if they wanted us to marry the Kennedys, they should have moved to fucking Hyannis Port instead of Elephant Beach.'

'Katie, man, you lucked out, though,' Nanny said. 'Going to Carver in the fall.'

'Well, Katie always was a heathen,' Liz said. 'Never had the pleasure of feeling Sister Ursula's paddle on her ass in fifth grade. Still, though, you think getting out of Dodge is going to make a difference for them? Like Matty'll take the pledge, stay home every night, be the perfect old man?'

'She's nervous about it, she told me,' Nanny said. 'Before everyone got here, while she was nursing the baby. You know, much as she fights with Aunt Francie, they're close, in their way.' Nanny drained the dregs of her drink. 'Nobody in our family ever moved so far away, to another state, even. Except for New Jersey, and that doesn't really count. Still,' she said reflectively, 'it's like all our parents, thinking if they left the city then everything would be all right, outasight, you know? Like once they got to the Beach everything would be sunshine and blue skies.'

'And look how well that turned out,' I said, thinking of Raven's tongue dancing from all the speed, the track marks on the back of Bennie Esposito's legs. Bennie shot up in his calves because his mother always checked his arms and he didn't want her to know he was still using.

'You hear anything from Marcel lately?' Liz asked suddenly. I looked at her in surprise. She had never been crazy about Marcel; even when Marcel had gone blind for several months, Liz had barely any sympathy. It was weird because Liz was always so funny and popular and Marcel was quieter, more

120

apt to hang back in the shadows; it was like Liz was jealous or something, even though Marcel wasn't around and hadn't been for a while. She hadn't even expressed much interest when I'd told her that Marcel had eloped and left Elephant Beach to live with James. It was Nanny who had asked questions, who'd told me to wish Marcel good luck and give her a hug when I'd gone to visit after graduation.

'Yeah, I talked to her last week,' I said. 'She's cool. She's doing good.' I didn't tell Liz that Marcel had been crying, that she wanted to come home to visit but she didn't have the money and she didn't know if James would let her travel alone.

'Another one who got away,' Liz said, sounding wistful, but then she yawned and stretched her arms high over her head. 'But you know what they say. You can move out of the Beach, but you can never escape.'

～૧～

The party lasted until late. At the end of the night, Aunt Francie, weepy from too many gin rickeys, handed Maggie an envelope with two hundred dollars in it. 'You're doing the right thing, doll,' she said, hugging her. 'Just make sure your numbskull brothers don't follow you out there.'

'No danger of that,' Maggie said, a new light in her eyes. Later that week, at the good-bye party at The Starlight Lounge, she reigned as queen of the scene once again, looking radiant with Matty at her side and the baby in her arms, like families were supposed to look before they got all fucked up. Beth Fagan, Maggie's best friend, cried and swore she'd be out in a month to visit. Everyone took turns giving good-luck toasts. 'Happy trails, motherfuckers,' Raven said, raising his glass, weaving; he'd been partying with Conor and Billy all day and could barely stand up. Maggie said it was a good thing the baby was sleeping and let him ask her again why she was leaving. Cha-Cha got choked up during his toast and gave Maggie a one-armed, bone-crushing hug; the other arm was slung around Christa Cutler's shoulders. He had barely looked at me since the night began, and I was glad I'd had nothing invested in him, that the shotgun sensation his mouth had caused made me think only of Luke. Luke looked more like his old self than he had since he'd been back, his golden-brown hair damp and tied back in a ponytail, his face bronzed from the sun. When it was his turn, he raised his glass and said, 'Go well,' and I thought it was perfect and poignant, but I saw Billy exchange looks with Voodoo and then I saw Luke drain his beer mug and set it down on the wetly ringed bar and walk outside to the old patio table, away from everyone. I walked over to a dark corner of the bar, near a half-boarded exit that nobody used anymore, which overlooked the patio. Luke sat in one of the rusted, rickety chairs and laid his head down in his arms and stared straight out at the night carnival that was Comanche Street.

'Lone wolf rides again,' I heard behind me, and turned to see Mitch, holding the inevitable glass in his other hand. We stood together, watching Luke.

'How long did it take you?' I asked Mitch.

'How long did what take me, angel face?'

'When you got out – came home – you know, before you were, like—' I was going to say 'normal,' but that wasn't the

jesus saves

When Ginger fell in love with Jesus, it wasn't exactly a surprise, but it was something. 'Last person I would have thought to become a fucking Jesus freak,' Billy said, but when you really thought about it, she was the first person who might let Jesus into her heart.

'People find Jesus when there's nothing left, man,' Mitch said. His voice sounded dreamy and distant. 'When the bottle's empty, when there's no more drugs, no one left to fuck, no one to hold your hand and tell you that all the bad, sinful things you've done don't matter and Jesus will love you no matter what. Jesus isn't the first thing you turn to, man. He's the last.'

'Did you find Jesus?' I asked Mitch, curious. He had a faraway look in his eyes, like what he'd just said had come from someplace deep inside him.

Mitch looked at me, then shook his head as if to clear it. He smiled. 'He found me, once or twice, darlin',' he said. 'Then

I lost him along the way. As you can see,' he said, holding his drink up to the light, 'my bottle's never empty.'

What happened was this: After giving the baby away, Ginger started running amok. She had always been a little crazier than the rest of us, but now she was constantly stoned or drunk on Boone's Farm Apple Wine or Old Grand-Dad, stumbling down Comanche Street like one of the rummies who lived on the top floor of The Starlight Hotel. When she came up close and flung her arms around you, the sweet, sweaty liquor smell would seep out of her pores, and underneath her tan, her skin was tinged with gray.

'You think she misses Allie?' I asked Nanny. 'I mean, she hasn't said anything, but they were so tight for so long.'

Nanny sighed. She had always been closer to Ginger, from their childhood city days, and had tried to talk to her, get her to go shopping, take her to the movies, anything to get her away from herself. 'I don't know, man,' she said. 'She won't talk about him. You know, they broke up hard, it wasn't like, "Let's always be friends, peace, love and happiness." And she was pretty faithful while they were together; he was the one screwing around.'

But Ginger wasn't faithful to anyone now, or particular. Once she'd reach the stumbling stage, she'd fling herself at any of the boys we hung out with, drape herself around their necks like a clamshell necklace.

'Ginger, honey, easy,' Billy or someone would say, gently removing her arms. She never seemed hurt or wounded, and her eyes had a vacant look as if she didn't know where she was.

We worried, though, that someday she'd drape herself

126

around some guy who wasn't somebody she'd known forever, who wouldn't walk her home or at least to the counter at Eddy's and order her a Coke or a cup of coffee. Sure enough, one night, after drinking on the beach, she threw herself at a stranger, one of the straggly, sleazy people who showed up on Comanche Street from time to time, usually stray dealers from other towns looking to drum up business.

'What the fuck?' the stranger said, laughing meanly. He pushed her away so that she spun around and almost fell into Mitch just as he was walking out of the lounge. The stranger, still laughing, walked away, in the direction of Eddy's.

'Whoa, baby, whoa,' Mitch said when she almost knocked him to the sidewalk. 'Easy there, darlin', balance isn't one of my strongest suits.' Ginger looked up into Mitch's face, her eyes clearing for a minute, and then she started to cry. She leaned into Mitch's chest and rested her head against his tee shirt and made soft sounds somewhere between a moan and a hiccup.

'Hell, if I'd known, I would have put on deodorant,' Mitch tried to joke, but then he sighed and put an arm around her and held her close. 'It's okay, darlin',' he said softly into her hair. 'We're all lost children at some point in time.'

～჻～

Ginger's sister, Salina, came to town. She was visiting from Port Richey, Florida. 'Came to check up on my little sis, see if she's okay,' she said, watching Ginger from across the living room of their mother's apartment on Gull Lane. Mrs. Shea was never home; she was either working or 'out catting,'

127

Ginger would say. I'd seen her only once, last summer, standing in front of the apartment building wearing sequined sunglasses and high heels and a short blue dress that barely covered her thick thighs. Her hair was freshly curled and combed as though she'd spent the afternoon at the beauty parlor. A man had been helping her into a car. He was bald, with sideburns down to his chin, and wore a powder-blue sports coat that looked like the kind of tuxedo jacket men wore with ruffled shirts in the wedding parties at the Knights of Columbus.

'Is that your mom's new boyfriend?' I'd asked Ginger.

She'd made a face. 'Some guy she met somewhere,' she said, her voice flat and disinterested.

Now Salina sat on the sagging couch, rolling a joint.

'This weed better not be beat,' she mumbled, spitting into the ashtray. 'All these fucking twigs, man, it's like Christmas tree smoke.' She wanted to go out, but Ginger wanted to stay in the apartment.

'Come on, man, don't be a drag,' Salina said, pulling on the joint. She didn't offer it to anyone else. She sounded more annoyed than concerned.

'I'm tired,' Ginger said, in her new, dead voice. 'I'm staying in.'

'You want some company?' I asked. It was one of those muggy gray nights that came in July and made tempers short, and everyone was cranky. I'd heard from Conor that Luke and Ray and Raven and Cha-Cha were heading into Manhattan for a boys' night out; they had tickets for a blues concert in the Village and they were going to crash at someone's apartment. If Luke wasn't around, there seemed no purpose in hanging out, smoking endless cigarettes, drinking beers I didn't want. Besides, I didn't like Salina; I didn't like the way she talked to Ginger, the way she looked at me. I never got along well with girls who looked like her, with their narrow fox faces and rabbity jaws.

I caught Liz looking at me with an 'Oh, no you don't' expression and Ginger patted my leg and said, 'Thanks, man, but dig it, I really, really want to be alone right now.'

Salina stood up, swinging her ratty shoulder bag like she was ready to slug someone with it. 'Oh, fuck you, man, with this Greta Garbo shit,' she said, walking to the door. 'You want to be alone? We'll leave you the fuck alone. Don't wait up.' She opened the door and we could hear her platform heels clunking down the stairs. We looked at Ginger. 'Have fun,' she said, staring at the door her sister hadn't bothered to close.

'We're worried about your sister,' Nanny told Salina, once we were in the car. 'She hasn't been herself lately, since the baby.'

Salina lit a cigarette and laughed. 'She's lucky, man,' she said. 'She doesn't know the half of it. I got two squalling brats at home and an old man out of work. Wish I'd known then what I know now.'

'Maybe the doting mother will take out some Polaroids to show us,' Liz whispered to me in the front seat.

Salina rummaged in her bag, brought out a vial, took out two small tablets, popped them into her mouth, and asked, 'Anyone got anything to drink?'

Liz reached behind the driver's seat and handed her a bottle of warm Tab. Salina took a swig, then guzzled the rest and wiped her mouth with the back of her hand. 'Ahhh,' she said, and let out a belch. 'That's way better. Now I'm ready to party.'

Nanny wasn't giving up so easily. 'Salina, does she talk to you? I've tried, but it's like she's – like part of her disappeared or something, man. She's been acting really weird lately.'

Salina threw her cigarette butt out the open car window. Sparks flew into the backseat, embers cascading to the floor. She leaned her head back and closed her eyes. 'She's a big girl,' she said, her voice beginning to slide. 'She can take care of herself.'

—⟡—

It was after two in the morning when Liz pulled back up to the apartment building on Gull Lane. She killed the motor and looked into the backseat, where Salina was sprawled, snoring, her mouth open, the fly to her jeans unzipped. 'Okay, sleeping beauty,' she said. 'We're home.' The mean part of me wished I had a camera so I could take her picture and leave it by the side of the couch so it would be there when she woke up. I looked up at the third floor, where Ginger's apartment was. The windows were dark.

Liz sighed. We got out of the car, opened the door, and helped Salina out.

'Wha the fuck,' she mumbled. 'Wha the – whoa! Whoa! Where we going, man? Where you takin' me? The night's young!' She looked at me, her gaze loose on ludes and tequila, and smiled, revealing a gold tooth I hadn't noticed before. 'C'mon, man. C'mon! I want to truck with yas, man. C'mon! Let's party. I still got – we could—'

'Yeah, yeah,' Liz said, shoving her up the dark pathway. Salina had been a pain in the ass all night; ordering shots at the lounge at The Starlight Hotel and then not paying for them so that Len became pissed; stumbling around between a barstool and the jukebox, too stoned to read the titles of the songs, spilling change from her purse all over the floor. Finally, Liz, Nanny and I had to drag her out of the bathroom where a long line had formed because she'd fallen asleep on the toilet seat. Thankfully, she hadn't locked the door to the stall.

We opened the front door to the apartment house, where a naked bulb burned above us on the second-story landing. 'Nighty-night,' Liz said, and shut the door. We walked to the curb where the car was parked, but I turned back once.

'Should we make sure she gets in okay?' I asked. 'Those stairs—'

'"She's a big girl,"' Liz mimicked, putting the car key in the lock. 'She can take care of herself.' She opened the car door, then slammed it shut again, locking it. 'Fuck it,' she said wearily. 'Let's go for a walk on the beach.'

It was darker down here by the Lanes, more deserted; I was used to Comanche Street and the streetlights near the ticket booth and the lights of The Starlight Hotel. The night air was cooler but still suppressed, as though waiting to release a secret. Above us, the sky was blue-black, the fingernail moon hanging from a cloud. We left our thongs by the ticket booth at the entrance to the beach and walked barefoot down to the water. The waves licked the hem of the shoreline, tickling our ankles.

I liked it best with Liz when we were alone together. It's

not like I'm a lezzie or anything, it's just the times when I trust her most. She's different in front of people, like: for my birthday she bought me a silver bracelet from Drury's Jewelers in town, engraved 'Friends forever,' with the date. It made me cry, it was so beautiful. But a couple weeks later, when we were hanging by the trash cans at Eddy's, she announced, 'Did everyone see Katie's piece-of-shit sweater, looks like it was made by refugees from the School for the Blind?' It's the way she is, and I know in her heart, Liz loves me. But sometimes, when we're with other people, it's like she left me for dead.

'You ever think of getting away?' Liz asked. We were walking fast, splashing through the foamy water. This end of the beach was empty, silent, except for the sound of the crashing waves.

'Sometimes, sure,' I said.

'I don't mean, like, a vacation,' she said. 'I mean, like, forever, man. Permanently.'

'Sometimes, yeah,' I said. 'I just don't know where to go, you know?' I thought of finally telling her about Luke, about leaving Elephant Beach if we had to, but I wasn't stoned enough to forget who she was.

'Wyoming, man,' she said. I looked up startled, but Liz didn't notice. 'You know, I saw this spread the other day, one of my mother's magazines, this whole, like, ranch spread in Wyoming, it looked so cool, so – it was just the sky, right, and these beautiful horses. I don't know, man, I never felt that way before, looking at pictures of other places, you know, like I just wanted to jump into the picture, just be there right now. Something different, different from – from here, this life. I mean, don't you ever get, like, fed up? Like, sick of everything?'

'Yeah,' I said. 'I do. Lately more than—'

'But you were always the lucky one,' she said, and this time I was beyond startled. Liz was the personality, the one everyone wanted to be with. 'It's like you don't know where you come from, right? It's like a – a total mystery, man. You don't know what's in your blood. You could turn out to be anything. Anything on earth.'

I laughed. 'So could you,' I said. 'So could anyone.'

Liz sighed sharply. Even over the lapping waves, I could hear her intake of breath, sounding like it hurt.

'You okay?' I asked.

She lit a cigarette, staring into the darkness. There weren't any stars out. Above us, the moon fell in the sky.

Liz turned, abruptly, in the opposite direction. 'Let's go back,' she said over her shoulder. 'It's late, it's dark, I have to be in early tomorrow.'

———◊———

We went to see Ginger a couple days later, to make sure Salina had gotten up the stairs alive, but she had already split back to Port Richey, cutting her stay short. Ginger didn't seem too upset about it.

'You're sister's a pisser,' Liz said, crossing her eyes to show she wasn't serious.

Ginger smiled bitterly. 'Yeah, man, she's a gas. Did she tell you about the time she and Del, my oldest sister, went up and down the street, knocking on doors, telling people that our parents died and they needed money to bury them so they wouldn't have to lay in Potter's Field?'

133

We looked at her. When she wasn't high or drinking, Ginger looked very young. Younger than seventeen, that's for sure.

'And then they took the money and bought up some glue, just pots of the shit, man, it stunk up the whole apartment, and they went on a sniffing spree,' Ginger continued. 'Yeah, she's a real pisser.' Ginger shook a cigarette out of the package of Kools on the rattan coffee table.

'Since when do you smoke Kools?' Nanny asked.

Ginger struck the match. For a minute, her freckles looked like they were on fire. She dragged very deeply and then gazed out the window, toward the ocean. 'I needed a change,' she said. She didn't say anything else for a while. Liz and Nanny and I looked at one another. I wondered if she was missing the baby, or thinking about him. 'I need a change,' she whispered, still staring out at the ocean.

———∘———

'It's gotta be hard for her,' I said as we walked up Starfish Avenue to Comanche Street. 'You know, first the baby, then Allie flipping out like that.'

'He treated her like shit,' Liz said.

'But he dug her,' I said. 'You could see it, when they hung out together. At least sometimes.'

'Do you always have to be such a fucking Pollyanna?' Liz asked.

Nanny snorted. 'Someone has to, when you're around,' she said. It was true. Liz had always been the lippiest of the three of us, but lately her sarcasm was beyond borderline; it was just plain bitchy.

134

'Ha! Look who's talking,' Liz said.

'What's that supposed to mean?' Nanny asked.

Liz laughed. '"What's that supposed to mean,"' she said. 'You treat Voodoo like shit. You're mad at him all the time because he's not that asshole Tony Fury. Why he puts up with it, I don't know.'

'Oh, that's deep, man,' Nanny said sarcastically. 'That's really intense. You're just jealous because Cory what's-his-face wouldn't know you were alive if you weren't balling him on a road show down Sunrise Highway—' Nanny stopped then, her eyes wide. She realized she'd gone too far.

Liz's face was tomato red; for a minute she looked like she might cry. And then she tossed her hair backward, away from her face. 'At least he knows I'm a woman,' she said. 'Not some stupid little girl who can't—'

'How'd we get here?' I said. 'We were talking about Ginger. Why are we all on each other's cases now? It's too hot for this shit, let's just give it a rest—'

Liz put up her middle finger. 'Give *this* a rest,' she said, and strode away from us, the bow on the back of her halter top bouncing against her skin.

'What is with her?' I asked. I was upset. I never liked the look of a retreating back.

Nanny shrugged. 'Something to do with Cory the great squeeze, I'm sure,' she said. She lifted her hair off the back of her neck, twisting it on top of her head. 'I shouldn't have said what I said. But it's true, Katie, you've said so yourself, and sometime she'll have to know it, too.'

~⸂~

Jesus freaks were few in Elephant Beach. They were a ragtag group that had taken over the abandoned yarn store on Sea Grove Avenue and made it into a church of sorts; the name, Holy Light of Heaven Spiritual Sanctuary, was etched in charcoal above the burglar bars on the broken windows that faced the street. Some of the kids from the Dunes, the rich part of town, dabbled in Jesus during senior year, the ones who weren't following the guru Maharishi and flying to India on their fathers' credit cards. They'd walk the halls at school flaunting their newfound spirituality, dressed all in white, looking like deranged brides with their ethereal gazes that never met yours and their phony smiles that always seemed crooked. There were Jesus freaks working at Nature's Choice, the tiny health-food store on Buoy Boulevard that always smelled of rotting lentils; they'd smile and smile and tell you that Jesus loved you every time they rang up a purchase. (Liz once pointed out that although they worked in a health-food store they always looked pale and sickly and emaciated while at the A&P, where the food was supposedly laden with chemicals and pesticides, everyone looked ruddy and well fed and healthy.) When you walked by the Holy Light of Heaven Spiritual Sanctuary, it was usually dark and you couldn't see in the windows. Sometimes, you could hear singing that was supposed to sound joyous but often sounded flat and toneless because the church couldn't afford an organ or even a beat-up piano to accompany the hymns. Around town, every once in a while you'd come upon a sign hanging on a tree or a telephone pole, painted in crooked block letters that read 'Jesus Wants You,' or, simply, 'Jesus.' Members of some of the real churches in town complained at the council

136

meetings that it was a sacrilege, but were told that the police would have to actually catch someone in the act of putting up a sign to take action, and so far, that hadn't happened. When those church people took it upon themselves to take down the signs, others would almost immediately spring up in their places.

The irony was that Ginger was led to Jesus by the skeevy-looking stranger who'd shoved her into Mitch's arms that night in front of The Starlight Hotel. He'd sought her out a couple of days later, when he saw her walking off the beach, her tee shirt and cutoffs plastered to her body after she'd gone swimming fully clothed. Ginger hadn't lost the weight she'd gained when she was pregnant and thought she looked too fat for even a one-piece bathing suit; her peach-colored tee shirt clung to her chest and darkened her nipples. The stringy stranger caught up to her by the ticket booth and began apologizing. Ginger had no idea who he was or what he was talking about. 'It was the night I fell from grace,' he explained, in a voice that sounded surprisingly sweet. 'I had closed my heart to Jesus and opened my mouth to liquor after abstaining for nineteen solid months. Jesus forgave me, all right, but how do I forgive myself?'

'How the fuck should I know?' Ginger asked, moving past him, bumping against his bony shoulder.

'Sister,' he called after her, and later Ginger told us there was something in his voice that made her turn back and really look into his eyes.

'My name is Casey,' he said solemnly, holding out his hand.

'I'm Ginger,' she said, and they stood together, talking, until the sun lowered and the waves relaxed and the beach became almost empty as everyone trailed past them to get home in time for dinner.

They started hanging out together and we realized why Casey looked familiar: he and several other Jesus freaks shared a house at the corner of Skylark Lane, right up the street from Eddy's. The Jesus freak church farther uptown hadn't anything even remotely resembling a rectory, and rents in the Trunk were always cheaper than anywhere else, except where the blacks and Puerto Ricans lived. Casey and the rest of the freaks had moved into a worn and weathered yellow bungalow that badly needed painting; there was a side yard, unusual for the Trunk, enclosed by a chain-link fence, where nothing grew except mud-streaked crab-grass. There were sheets on the windows instead of curtains and the windows were filmy with grime. Counting Casey, there were seven people living in the house, and a baby who would crawl through the yellow grass in the yard seemingly unsuper-vised. You'd rarely see any signs of life during the day, but at night, they'd come out and sit in a circle on the parched patch of lawn, bowing their heads, mumbling things that no one could hear. We'd see them on Sundays, piling into a dirty white van parked in front, on their way to the Holy Light of Heaven Spiritual Sanctuary, where Casey was the new preacher.

Ginger had never met anyone like Casey. He never pres-sured her or preached to her privately, but he asked if she'd like to accompany him to evening prayers some night and, curious, she said yes. She went with Casey and the rest of the Jesus freaks to the deserted barge by the bay, where they made a circle with their hands locked, their eyes closed (though

Ginger said she opened hers when she thought she heard the clamoring of water rats in the hold below). 'It's such a rush, man,' she told us, after, her eyes shining. 'It's like – even the air smells better after, like purer, you know?' Ginger started spending more time at the crumbling yellow bungalow. Sometimes, she and Casey would walk down Lighthouse Avenue and cross the street, licking vanilla fudge ice-cream cones like fifteen-year-olds out on their first date.

'It was the drinking that made him act so ugly,' she defended him, when we started asking skeptical questions.

'Cat was born ugly,' Mitch said out of the side of his mouth, watching Casey come out of Eddy's carrying two sugar cones covered with sprinkles. It wasn't just his broken teeth and pockmarked skin, either; Casey and his disciples didn't look spiritual, like Father Donnelly or the Sisters of Sodality, who lit the incense every morning at St. Timothy's Church. They looked like people you would be scared of if you weren't in a familiar place. They looked like the guys who ran the Ferris wheel on the boardwalk in the center of town, with their pointy studded boots and faded jean jackets, huddled in the abandoned arcades with their heads down and their collars turned up, cigarettes dangling from their lips, managing to look tough and frail at the same time. You could just imagine the needle falling out of their arms. The girls they hung around with were like a flock of fragile birds, hunched and furtive-looking in their thrift-shop dresses, always glancing over their shoulders as though they thought someone was following them. We asked Ginger which one was the mother of the baby, and she said the baby's name was Elijah and he belonged to everyone. 'Isn't that beautiful, man?' she said, her eyes shining. She ignored our smirking, our scornful laughter.

Still, Casey did get Ginger to quit drinking. Drinking and drugging. He did it slowly and skillfully. He'd go over to her mother's apartment on Gull Lane and sit and listen to Ginger talk, nodding thoughtfully, and then very gently take the bottle of Old Grand-Dad from her lips and set it on the coffee table and begin talking to her about quenching her spiritual thirst. The first time he said that, she told us, she laughed in his face, told him he was full of shit, but he just kept nodding and smiling, his eyes locked firmly on her face. She'd never had that kind of attention before, not even when she was balling somebody, or really, especially when she was balling somebody; they weren't looking at her face, then. And he'd ask her questions about herself, her life, like what was it like living in the city when she was little, and did she miss having a father, and one day, she put the bottle down on the coffee table all by herself and began crying. Casey just kept talking in soft, comforting tones, urging her, believing in her. He never put his arm around her, but he would lay his hand on Ginger's and hold it while she cried, a strong and steady presence. He asked her to come to the Holy Light of Heaven Spiritual Sanctuary one Sunday morning in mid-July and she described it to us like she'd been to a Jethro Tull concert and made out with Ian Anderson on the stage. 'That whole thing where you see the light?' she said. 'Like in movies or something, where you're supposed to get hit by a bolt of lightning or some shit? It's not like that at all, man, like you've failed if you don't get the shivers or start foaming at the mouth. It's like, it's gradual, you know? Like you have all this time. Jesus doesn't keep a stopwatch.'

'Maybe it is a good thing,' I said one night, when we were hanging out on Liz's porch before heading out. 'I mean, she does seem happy. Happier than she's been, for sure.'

Liz snorted. 'And you think she's really not balling this guy?'

Nanny shrugged. 'She says no. And why would she lie? She's never lied before.'

I couldn't fathom Ginger wanting to ball him. I thought Casey resembled something sleazy and reptilian; his bones seemed oily, fluid, as though any minute he could sink into the sand and slither away. His eyes were dark and wallowing in salvation that made him appear humble, but I remembered the sound of his laughter the night that Ginger had thrown herself at him, the way he had flung her off and turned his back. For all his talk of light, there seemed to be shadows everywhere.

Ginger begged us to come to the Jesus freak church and hear Casey preach, and though we never did, we heard plenty about his sermons because she couldn't shut up about him. She called him her savior. 'But he says it's really not him, see, he's only Christ's vessel. Jesus used Casey as the vessel to come to me, to take me into his loving arms.' She couldn't understand why we wouldn't give him a chance. 'He's a man of God,' she said in her new serene voice. 'You all go to church, you worship Jesus and his father and Mother Mary. How is it different?'

'Because we're not a bunch of lunatics walking around town all hollow-eyed and shit, putting up signs that look like

141

they were drawn by a second grader,' Liz said. 'Dig it, there's a reason they call them freaks.'

'But why are you so angry?' Ginger asked, wonder in her voice. Her eyes were clear, dedicated. She was sitting on the couch in her mother's apartment with her legs tucked underneath her dress. It was a pretty dress, pink with faded green stripes across the bodice; she'd bought it at the Thrift Shift up on Buoy Boulevard. That's where all the Jesus freaks shopped; they had no money for the other stores in town. 'You shouldn't be so angry,' she continued. 'What Casey's preaching – it's the way it's really supposed to be. Like – in regular church, right, it's all about robes and the gold on the altar and how much everyone gives when they pass the basket. But that's not how it's supposed to be,' she said gently. 'The simple life, the one where you give up – worldliness, when you – live simply, without possessions. That's the life worth living.'

'How can you give up worldliness when you live in the world?' Liz asked. I looked around the living room of Ginger's mother's apartment. That's what the Jesus freaks always talked about, renouncing material possessions, but it was different for the Dunes girls at school, giving up their cashmere sweaters and shag carpeting and Princess telephones. What did Ginger have to renounce besides the rickety staircase in the hallway and a lopsided coffee table?

'You just don't seem to – how can I make you understand?' Ginger spoke sadly, shaking her head. 'I mean – maybe you do have to see it, man. Like I – I've seen all this new stuff lately, things I've never – okay, like last week, right, Casey took me out to this place, all the way out in Suffolk County, and there was this guy, right, this preacher, and all of a sudden, he starts speaking in tongues—'

'Speaking in tongues? What does that mean?' I asked.

'It's like – at first you think it's gibberish, like he's just spouting nonsense, but then you can see – you can tell it's – it's the language of God!' Ginger's eyes shone, but she wasn't looking at any of us. She was looking at some private vision over our heads, out the window. 'He's going to teach us how to listen,' she said. 'How to listen and learn—'

'Oh, for chrissake,' Liz said, disgusted. 'You flunked English and beginners' Spanish, now you're talking in tongues?'

'Shut the fuck up,' Ginger said suddenly, sounding like the old Ginger. 'All of you, just shut the fuck up! How come, yeah, how come when I was drunk and stoned all the time, screwing anything that moved, no one said a Goddamned thing? Stumbling around the corner like a – a – a common tramp? Or when I got pregnant? Or when I dropped out of school? How come none of you had anything to say then?' She was standing up now, glaring at us.

We stared at her, openmouthed.

'Ginge—' Nanny started, but Ginger cut her off.

'Don't fucking "Ginge" me,' she said. 'Just don't, Nanny. Your mother always called you home for dinner. All your mothers. You always had to be home for dinner. That's the difference, that's the whole difference right there.' She sat down again and folded her arms across her breasts.

Liz said, 'What the fuck does that have to do with—'

'Liz,' I said. She stopped. Nanny was wiping tears from her eyes. I remembered the times we'd all head home from Comanche Street, bitching about having to set the table, cut up iceberg lettuce for a salad. Ginger would be sitting in the doorway of Eddy's, smoking. We'd wave good-bye, calling, 'Later, man,' envying her freedom, her not having to be anywhere to straighten the napkins, lay the forks to the left of the plates.

'I asked you home for dinner,' Nanny said. 'Plenty of times, I—'

'It's not the same thing,' Ginger said through clenched teeth. 'It's not the same thing at all.'

Suddenly her face relaxed back into a tranquil mask. Her eyes became hooded and her mouth turned upward at the corners.

'But I don't know what I'm getting so upset about,' she said, her voice filled with false brightness. 'Casey said this would happen. He said this was just what would happen.' She clasped her hands in her lap. Her knuckles looked smooth and strong.

'What did Casey say would happen?' Nanny asked, curious.

'He said my friends would try and talk me away from the light,' she said. 'He said you would try and keep me in a sinful state so you wouldn't feel so bad about yourselves. Ginger, the whore. Ginger, the slut of the earth.'

'Jesus, Ginger—'

'Please don't,' Ginger said quietly.

'Don't what?'

'Take his name in vain,' Ginger said, bowing her head. I could see Liz getting ready to explode.

'Ginger, the guy's a skeeve,' I said, and when everybody turned to look at me, I went on, 'He is, Ginger. Every time he's around I get these vibes – he gives me the creeps, for

144

real, man. I'm sorry, I'm sorry for saying it, but – I think he's a – a false prophet.' I was afraid Liz and Nanny would laugh after I said that, but they just nodded in agreement.

Ginger smiled sweetly. 'Peace, sister, you're allowed to speak your mind. And if that's the way you feel, then it's very, very fortunate for you that you're not the one moving in with him.' She stared straight at us, her smile never wavering.

'Whoa! Say what?' Liz asked, putting her hand up to her ear. 'You're not moving into that—'

'Yeah, I am,' Ginger said firmly, staring Liz down.

'Ginger,' Nanny said softly. 'Why?'

'To be closer to Jesus,' Ginger said. 'Closer than I am in this friggin' apartment, that's for sure.' She stared at us, looking like a mannequin in a storefront window, until we got up and left.

That was really the beginning of the end, though no one wanted to admit it.

'Oh, man, where were we?' Nanny mourned, as we walked back up to Comanche Street. 'Where were we that we didn't see this coming?'

Liz leaned her hand on my arm as she stopped to pick a piece of glass from her foot. 'Where was Jesus?' she asked, throwing the shiny sliver into the gutter.

Nanny kept trying. She even enlisted her mother to call Mrs. Shea and intervene. They weren't friends, but they'd all known each other since they lived in the city and Mrs. Devlin didn't like seeing Nanny so upset.

'So she's moving in with this preaching joker into a – what? One of those communes, is that what it's called?' Mrs. Devlin asked.

145

'It's an unsavory situation, Ma,' Nanny said.

Mrs. Devlin looked hard at Nanny. 'It's a what situation?' she said.

'Ma, I'm telling you,' Nanny said, and Mrs. Devlin went to the telephone in the kitchen and dialed. She and Mrs. Shea chatted awhile and we could hear her saying, 'It's an unsavory situation, Didi,' and finally, she hung up the phone, shaking her head.

'I tried, doll,' she said to Nanny. 'But let's face it. Didi Shea was never the brightest bulb in the chandelier when it came to mothering those pups.'

'What'd she say?' I asked.

'She said Ginger was free, white, and of legal age to do what she wanted. And finding Jesus was better than a lot of other things she'd found these past few years.'

'She is not legal,' Nanny pointed out. 'She won't be eighteen until November.'

'Well, there you go.' Mrs. Devlin sighed.

'Fuck her, that's the way she wants it,' Liz said when Mrs. Devlin left the room. Even Nanny finally gave up, and I thought Ginger moving into the peeling yellow bungalow would make her disappear into a new kind of life we'd never be able to follow.

But even though we rarely saw her after she moved in with Casey, it didn't feel like Ginger was really lost to us until she left Elephant Beach for some Jesus ashram in a place called Lubbock, Texas. The landlord was tossing them out of the yellow bungalow because they hadn't paid the rent in like five months. How could they? No one worked; they just hung around the rocky yard watching the baby toddle

146

across the cracked grass, looking stringy and saved. I'd wondered at first if the baby was one of the attractions, if Ginger wanted to be a part-time mother and atone for giving away her little son. But she never mentioned it, and the few times we saw her in the yard with the other women, she made no move to pick the baby up or play with it. Casey had people in Lubbock, Ginger explained. Family? Other Jesus freaks? We didn't ask and she didn't elaborate. She told us there was a post waiting for him and they could live far more cheaply and apparently Lubbock was closer to Jesus, populated with good, simple folk who were righteous and down-to-earth.

'Not like us sinners,' Liz said, raising her eyes to the sky like she was looking for heaven.

On their last day in Elephant Beach, when they were loading up the truck in full view of everyone at Eddy's, Nanny, Liz and I walked over and begged Ginger to let us buy her a farewell egg cream for old time's sake. She was wearing a faded blue-and-white housedress and scruffy shoes that looked like bedroom slippers. She went over and spoke to Casey, who was tying mattresses to the roof of the van with one of his pale disciples. Casey turned to look at us, then back at Ginger, then back at us.

'He doesn't want her getting too close to the devil worshippers,' Liz whispered. 'He's afraid we'll steal her away.'

Finally, we saw him nod, and Ginger came over and we crossed the street and went into Eddy's and ordered chocolate egg creams all around. At the last minute Ginger ordered a double vanilla fudge ice-cream sugar cone with sprinkles. She laughed nervously, sounding very young. 'What the – I mean, my last cone at Eddy's for who knows how long,' she said. 'How do I know they even have sprinkles in Lubbock, Texas?'

Behind the counter, Desi took a paper toot he used for snow cones and filled it with sprinkles. He handed it to Ginger. 'My going-away present,' he said. 'Knock yourself out.' She leaned forward to kiss him, as she would have in the old days, then caught herself and bowed her head in thanks. Desi sighed and moved to the other end of the counter.

'But what am I worrying over?' Ginger said, sounding like a television housewife. 'We have Jesus on our side. He's always been faithful. He will provide whatever we need, no matter what.'

'Then why didn't he provide the rent money for that rattrap across the street?' Liz snapped, and when we all looked at her, she said, 'Sorry, man, I just – it just seems so sudden, you leaving like this. I mean, summer's not even half over.' She reached over and put her arm around Ginger's neck, pulled her close and kissed her cheek, loud and wet and sloppy.

'What'd your mother say?' Nanny asked. 'When you told her you were going?'

Ginger shrugged. 'She hugged me good-bye and wished me well,' she said, her voice even. 'Actually, she said, "I hope you know what the hell you're doing." Told me to keep in touch.'

Ginger kissed us all good-bye and we stood in front of Eddy's, watching the Jesus freaks load themselves into the white van. Casey was already in the driver's seat, waiting. Ginger turned back and waved to us, once, before disappearing into a small sea of clamoring bodies. As we watched the truck pull away from the house, Liz began crying. Nanny and I looked at each other over her head; Nanny's eyes shrugged. We were the emotional ones, sniffling at movies and sad songs, with Liz usually rolling her eyes, saying, 'And now, for the next performance of the sob sisters.' She loved Ginger like we all did, but they hadn't been tight enough for her to be weeping so bitterly. In the distance, church bells chimed a christening at St. Timothy's, or maybe a midweek wedding. Father Tom said they were popular lately because they were cheaper than on the weekends.

Liz let out a strangled cry. We waited, me and Nanny, for the sound of her tears to stop filling the air. Above us, a flock of seagulls cawed loudly, aligned in a circle of sorrow.

TEN

for catholic girls who have considered going to hell when the guilt was not enough

Today

The woman who answered the door could have been any one of our mothers. She had the kind of ashy blond hair that could have been Clairol Nice 'n Easy, or she might have had it done at a beauty parlor, like Antoine's on Main, where our own mothers went to get dolled up for weddings and holidays. Her skin was sun-washed and creased around her eyes, which made her look older than she wanted to, because she dressed young: faded straight-leg jeans rolled into cuffs above her ankles. A white Indian shirt embroidered with gold thread. Hanging silver earrings. Bare feet, with coppery polish on her toes. I tried to get a good look at her fingernails, because that's the first thing they always tell you: dirty fingernails, after you pass through the dark alley to get to the dirty table in the middle of the night. But she was holding the door halfway open and her hands were hidden.

We were standing in front of a three-story brown wood house with carved white shutters and a wraparound porch with wicker rocking chairs and a widow's watch that looked like the top tier on a wedding cake, at the high end of a road where you looked down at the ocean. Below us, the dunes rose up like small mountains and the sand really did have a silver cast, lighter and finer than the sand we were used to; that was how the town of Silverwood got its name. The houses here were farther apart than the ones in Elephant Beach, and the street was bathed in milky quiet, that special, hot summer afternoon stillness where everyone's either at the beach or huddled up inside with their air-conditioning.

'I'm – I'm here for my two o'clock appointment,' Liz said. That's what Beth had told her to say. No names, no phone calls. No checks or credit cards; cash only, in an unmarked envelope.

'Come in, please,' the woman said, smiling. Her voice had a lilt, like she was singing the words. She held the door open wide. Muted sunlight streamed through the windows; the gauzy curtains lifted in the breeze. In the foyer we glimpsed the living room, which had a fireplace that took up almost a whole wall, filled with egg-shaped urns of flowers. Bunches of dried starfish hung from the walls. There were window boxes on the porch as well, filled with red and purple pansies. There were candles on the mantel, on the coffee table; votives, tapers, tea lights, covered in glass and pewter.

151

The woman closed the door behind us, turned the lock, shot the bolt. She then opened a door on the left side of the hall and motioned us to go in. It was an office with a big desk, bookcases lining the walls, dark, slanted shades at the windows. A cushiony red love seat and chairs clustered around a small table covered with seashells of all sizes.

'Sit down, please,' the woman said, sitting in the fat red chair that faced the windows. Liz sank into a corner of the love seat and I sat down next to her.

'This house, it's like spectacular, man,' Liz said in some new bright voice that didn't sound like her own.

'Except for the mice in the walls,' the woman said, smiling. 'Who come out at night and keep us awake.'

'This house is too beautiful to have mice,' Liz said loudly. 'This town is too beautiful to have mice running around.' I turned to look at Liz. I had never heard her use this fawning, kiss-ass tone before, not to her parents or teachers or even Dr. Steadman, our high school principal, that time she was caught cutting so many classes that she almost didn't graduate.

'Maybe that's what attracts them,' the woman said.

'Who?' Liz asked wildly.

'The mice,' the woman said gently. Then she asked, 'You have something for me, yes?'

Liz stared at her blankly.

'I said, you have something for me, yes?' the woman asked again, still smiling.

I nudged Liz, tapped her purse. 'Oh!' she said. 'Oh! I'm so . . . sorry, man, really, I'm . . .' She rummaged in her purse and came out with an envelope. She held it out to the woman with a shaky hand. Her voice was making me sick. I wanted her to lose that fake, fawning tone and sound like Liz again.

The woman didn't take the envelope. She sat gazing at Liz. She had the calmest eyes I'd ever seen, green or gray, it was hard to tell. The light in the office was dimmer than it had been outside in the foyer, which was fine. All that streaming sunlight made me nervous. It was a perfect beach day, not a cloud in the sky. It was like a painting you could have named *July*. The breeze through the window carried the scent of the ocean. Wind chimes tinkled on the porch. The whole thing was giving me the creeps, everything so white and bright and airy. It should have been raining. The curtains should have had dirty edges, filthy hems from sweeping against a sooty windowsill. A body should have been falling out of the closet, bathed in blood. We should have come at night, in the dark, when children were asleep. But Beth had told us two o'clock on Thursday afternoon, so here we were.

The woman said, 'Before we go upstairs, I'm only going to ask you once, yes? Do you want to go through with this?'

Liz took out her Marlboros, lit two, and handed me one. She began flicking ashes in the largest seashell, the kind we picked up on the beach at home all the time and used for ashtrays in our bedrooms.

'Because if you don't, you can walk back out that door right now and that's the end of it,' the woman said. She didn't sound mad. She didn't look like she cared one way or the other.

Liz blew smoke up at the ceiling fan. Beneath the huge frames of her sunglasses, her cheeks were still stained and splotchy from crying on the bus.

153

'I can tell you this is safer and less painful than childbirth, and will take far less time than a root canal,' the woman said. I could see the corners of Liz's mouth turn down, her lips begin to tremble.

The woman focused on me. 'And you are her good friend, yes?' I nodded.

'And no matter what goes down in the next few minutes, you both know that whatever happens here is confidential, not to be talked about outside of this house, or I could lose my medical license and that's one less option for women to be safe.'

The word 'safe' echoed through the cool room. I thought it was a strange choice of words. It was not a word I would have chosen. It was only after she'd spoken those words that I realized the woman was the doctor. I had thought she was a nurse, an assistant, someone who took care of the preliminaries. I thought the doctor would be short and mannish-looking, with pinched lips and close-cropped dark hair and lines in her forehead, wearing a dirty white coat. I wondered if the woman had children herself, if she sent them to day camp or to the beach with a babysitter, with strict instructions not to come home before a certain time. Or if they were grown, our age, and suspected but weren't sure what was going on in their own house. I tried to imagine how I would feel if I suddenly found out my mother was performing abortions in the basement or out in the backyard shed. I couldn't imagine it. I couldn't get my mind around such a thing. There were no family pictures on the doctor's desk, in the office room. There were no pictures of real people anywhere around.

The woman put her elbows on her knees, rested her chin

in her hands. Liz crushed her cigarette in the shell on the coffee table. A single spark refused to die. She took a deep breath.

'Okay, man,' she said. 'Let's do it. Let's do it now.' She sounded like Liz again. She stood up and held the envelope out again. This time the woman took it. She went to the desk, opened a drawer, and the envelope disappeared. She walked to the door and opened it, then beckoned us through with a graceful finger. I'd been so engrossed in looking around that until now I'd forgotten to look at her hands. She wasn't wearing polish on her fingernails. They were cut short and square. They looked short and square and strong and clean.

Last Monday

'You swear on your mother's life you didn't tell Beth it was me?' Liz asked Nanny for like the ninetieth time.

We were sitting in the Shot Glass Saloon up in the Point, at the other end of Elephant Beach. It was dark and dim and everyone looked familiar even though we didn't know them. We'd purposely come here because it was several miles from the Trunk and anyone we would run into. Even so, Liz had insisted on us wearing dark sunglasses and black jeans and tee shirts and bandannas so that no one would recognize us. It was four thirty in the afternoon and we were sitting at a table in the corner, drinking whiskey sours on the rocks and planning Liz's abortion. She'd gotten pregnant after balling Cory in an AMC Gremlin, her least favorite car on her father's lot, but the only one that had been available. It had been a cramped and hurried encounter; she said she wished it had happened in the Pontiac Bonneville, classically restored and big and roomy as a bed, but it was a premium seller and Cory was afraid her father might notice something was amiss. When she'd told Cory she was late, he'd just nodded and said, 'Bummer.' The next day he gave her two hundred dollars and told her, 'More where that came from if you need it, just get it taken care of. I don't want to know the details.'

Nanny shook her head. 'I told you,' she said patiently. 'Beth doesn't want to know. She says the less people know, the better. She'll make the call and set up the appointment. Then she'll get back to me with the day and time.'

'How does Beth know her again?' I asked. Beth Fagan was in her last year of nursing school at Joshua Stern Medical Center in Manhattan; she'd been the midwife at Maggie Mayhew's home birth. She said it was a deep and life-changing experience, even though everything had gone wrong and Aunt Francie said it was a miracle the baby had been born at all.

'From Joshua Stern,' Nanny said. 'It's kind of like an underground thing, but all the nurses know about it.'

'If it's so underground, what's she doing living in Silverwood?' Liz asked.

Nanny snorted. 'Would you think to go looking for an abortion doctor in Silverwood?'

'So, what, I just knock on the door and say, "Hey man, I'm, like, here for my abortion"?'

'Pretty much, yeah. Beth will tell us everything we need to do.'

'And she doesn't have to know my name or anything?' Liz squinted through the cigarette smoke.

'She doesn't want to know your name,' Nanny whispered.

'Because if anything happens, she could lose her license, go to jail—'

Liz was staring hard at Nanny. 'What is this "if anything happens"? What's going to happen? If nobody's looking in Silverwood for this abortion doctor, then please, somebody tell me, what the fuck is going to happen?'

'Lower your voice,' Nanny hissed. Heads at the bar were beginning to lift and look us over.

Sure enough, the cocktail waitress came by. Her face had that creased look of too many cigarettes and her voice was chipped and hoarse. 'Everything all right over here?' she asked, and Liz burst into tears. Nanny and I looked at each other helplessly. The waitress peeled off some cocktail napkins from the stack on her tray and handed them to Liz. The napkins had 'The Shot Glass Saloon' written in bold red script, and beneath the letters, a cowboy brandishing a six-shooter, standing next to an old-timey saloon with swinging doors. There were no cowboys in the Shot Glass, only drunks with nothing better to do than sit at the bar drinking boilermakers, listening to Frank Sinatra's voice from the jukebox singing 'It Was a Very Good Year' forty-seven times.

The waitress looked at me and Nanny. 'Boyfriend problems?' she asked. She lit a cigarette and laid it on her tray with the smoking end outward.

Nanny looked at me. 'Kind of,' I told her. The minute she'd missed her period, Liz had started planning her wedding. The ceremony would be on Comanche Beach at sunset, and the reception would take place at the new Knights of Columbus catering hall, right on the bay. Liz would wear a red velvet granny dress with a matching crown of roses in her hair.

We'd all be bridesmaids and wear any shade of velvet we wanted, except green, so it didn't look like Christmas. Cory would get promoted to manager of her father's dealership and they'd buy the house that had been for sale forever on Weber Avenue, by the bay, where all the bedrooms faced the water. Even though Cory McGill had never taken Liz to dinner, met her mother, or hung out with any of her friends.

The waitress looked at Liz and nodded. Her eyes were winged with eyeliner at the corners and her roots were showing through at the crown, at her temples. She dragged heavily on her cigarette, placed it back on the rim of her cocktail tray, laid the tray down and put her hands on our table.

'Let me tell you girls something about men,' she said. 'They're all a hundred years out of the trees, and there's not a Goddamned thing you can do about it.'

Last Night

The night before, Liz and Nanny were supposed to come to my house so we could go over our plans for the hundredth time. We were going to take the bus; Liz didn't want to drive in case anyone recognized her car, even though Silverwood was at the other end of Long Island and no one we knew ever hung out there. After it was over, we'd be staying overnight at the Dancing Dolphin Motel; Nanny had the good idea to call the Chamber of Commerce and get a recommendation. It sounded funky and cheerful, and we told our parents we were taking the train to the city to shop at Macy's and see a movie, maybe *The Godfather*, and stay overnight at Nanny's grandmother's apartment in Washington Heights.

Liz still insisted on us wearing our incognito outfits, even though I tried telling her we'd only draw attention to ourselves since nobody in Elephant Beach wore black in summer unless they were going to a funeral. Liz thought that if we wore our black bandannas and shades either no one would recognize us or they'd think we were too crazy to deal with and leave us alone.

We usually didn't hang out at my house, because I lived farther away from Comanche Beach and Eddy's and all our other hangouts. But Liz didn't want to talk at her house, and Nanny was terrified of her mother overhearing us, since the walls of their bungalow were thin. Wednesday was my mother's mah-jongg night so she and her friends would be playing in the kitchen and wouldn't have heard a bomb go off once they got going. We would have the back porch to ourselves. I waited out there, lying on the chaise lounge, munching on mah-jongg food, nonpareils and M&M's, reading a book about growing up in the 1950s when life was simpler with happier endings.

'What, no street corner tonight?' My mother came out on the back porch, shaking the dry mop over the porch railing.

'Nope,' I said, chomping on a nonpareil. I felt safe, knowing she wouldn't start in on me with her friends due to arrive any minute. 'Liz is coming over, we're gonna just hang out, take it easy.'

'Let me have a cigarette,' she said, leaning against the railing. On my eighteenth birthday she had given me permission to smoke because she was tired of me stinking up the bathroom with hair spray to hide the smell; that drove my father crazy. She didn't smoke much herself, only when she

159

played mah-jongg or canasta. But sometimes, when I came home late and she was sitting in the kitchen doing the cross-word puzzle, we'd have a cigarette together and talk about things. Her voice always sounded younger then, especially when she put her hands over her mouth so that the sound of her laughter wouldn't wake my brother or my father.

My mother lit the cigarette and inhaled deeply, leaning against the porch railing, gazing up at the sky. I lit one, too, to be sociable, even though I'd just had one.

'What's with Liz lately?' she asked me. 'She sounded upset when she called before. What is she, having boyfriend trouble?'

I sighed. 'Kind of,' I said.

'The trouble with you girls is, you make everything too easy for these boys,' she said. 'Make them work a little, then they won't treat you like a pair of old shoes.'

'Mom—'

'I know, I know, the mothers, we never know anything,' she said. 'You wonder why I get so upset with you running down to that corner every night. I want you to expect more out of life, not less. But who knows,' she said, the smoke from her cigarette curling above her head like a gauzy crown, 'maybe it's our fault as much as yours. If we had more to give you, you'd expect more. You do the best you can, but sometimes it's not enough.'

I looked at my mother, surprised. She always talked like we were better than other people we knew, certainly than the people I hung out with. But there were things we didn't have; my father refused to buy anything on credit because he'd grown up poor and seen too many repossessions. Our television was black-and-white, and we had a washing

160

machine, but not a dryer. I liked hanging my jeans over the porch railing and letting them dry there; they always smelled like the sun. Billy once told me that I had the best-smelling clothes of any girl he knew. But if I told that to my mother, she'd only ask me why Billy knew that in the first place, and how close was he getting to my clothes anyway, that he could smell them so good.

'Where are you?' my mother asked. She sounded annoyed. 'Have you even heard one word I've said?'

'I was just thinking how I like the way my jeans smell from hanging on the porch in the sun,' I told her.

'What on earth made you think of that?' she asked.

'Only that if we had a clothes dryer they wouldn't smell as good,' I said. 'I'd kind of miss it.'

My mother looked at me for a long moment. Then she smiled. 'Next you'll want me to hunt up Grandma's old washboard and do the washing out here instead of throwing the clothes in the machine,' she said, laughing. She came over and hugged me close, something she rarely did anymore. I hugged her back, and felt tears pushing up against my eyelids.

'You're such a good girl, such a good kid,' she whispered against my hair. 'I only want the best for you, can you see that? You think all I do is carp and criticize, but I only want the best.'

'I know,' I whispered back. My mother held me for a moment longer, then kissed the side of my head and pushed herself away. 'Go back to your book,' she said, and went into the house, closing the screen door softly behind her.

About twenty minutes later, I heard the doorbell over the sound of my mother and her friends chattering. Then Liz came banging through the screen door, her mouth stuffed with Almond Joy miniatures. The air was filled with the sound of cicadas and the voices of some kids playing stickball in the street.

Liz said, around a mouthful of chocolate, 'Man, you know I love your mother, but why does she always sound, like, angry?'

'You're just feeling sensitive,' I said, but I knew it was true. My mother was the youngest of four kids. My grandparents hadn't wanted her; they were poor and lived in one of those old-timey tenements on the Lower East Side and my grandfather worked three jobs and was going to night school to learn English when he could fit it in. In those days, they believed that a bumpy trolley-car ride would bring on a miscarriage; my grandmother rode the trolley as much as she could afford to, but it didn't work. For her first year, my mother slept in the bottom drawer of my grandparents' dresser as there was no room or money for more beds. Maybe the reason she yelled at us so much was because, despite the odds, she'd managed to make her way into the world, and she wanted everyone to know she was here to stay.

'Where's Nanny?' I asked Liz.

Liz sat down in the beach chair opposite me. 'Nanny bailed because she thinks I'm going to hell and she will, too, if she comes along for the ride.'

'Oh, she did not—'

'Yeah, she did.' Liz sighed. 'She said there's some christening she has to go to tomorrow, her mother's dragging them all into the city.'

I wondered about this. I'd thought it odd that Nanny hadn't returned my call from yesterday, because we usually spoke daily and now there was all this going on. I guessed she was thinking she'd see me tonight and we'd talk then.

'Well, you know how it is with family stuff, and Mrs. Devlin—'

'Katie.' Liz shook her head like I was an idiot. 'Tomorrow's Thursday. You ever hear of a christening taking place on a Thursday? You ever hear of a christening that gave everyone, like, one day's notice?'

The night smelled heavily of honeysuckle. Liz got up and walked over to the porch railing. She stood there, gazing down at my mother's tomato plants. She was quiet for a long time. Finally, she said, 'I think – I think there's something wrong with me, man. I mean, really, I—' She broke off, looked up at the darkening sky. 'I mean, when I found out, when I knew for sure? Before I told anyone? I was, like, so happy. I – I really thought, right, I really thought that we'd have a wedding on the beach, that he'd be the manager of my father's dealership. That I'd be buying hanging crystals from Heads Up for the baby's room, all that shit.' She shook her head. 'We call you the space shot, you live in your head so much, but I'm the one living on cloud fucking nine.'

The light of day was dying, slowly, leaving inky smudges in the sky. I wanted to walk over and put my arms around her, but Liz never liked being touched; she shrugged off embraces, even on her birthday, was the first to scream, 'Lezzie!' if you even laid a hand on her arm. I leaned back and lit a cigarette.

'I thought maybe if I told my mother,' Liz said. I sat up

163

and stared at her. Mrs. McGann was the same age as the rest of our parents but she seemed older. Her hair was iron gray and she never visited Antoine's on Main because, she said, if God had meant for your hair to stay the same color all your life, he would have made it so. Mr. and Mrs. McGann went to mass every morning, not just on Sundays. They believed in everything the Church said. They believed that the Holy Communion wafer was the body of Jesus. I saw Mrs. McGann's face one Sunday as she walked back from taking Communion up on the altar. I had never seen her smile that way before. She looked – transported. She looked like she was in a much better world than the one the rest of us lived in.

'I thought maybe if I told my mother,' Liz said, 'she'd see it my way, you know, help me have the baby. I mean, let's face it, she'd much rather I had the baby than – than this.' She blew ragged smoke rings out over the garden. 'And then I thought, what am I, nuts? She'd rather I was dead. She'd rather I was dead than having a baby with no husband, than – than any of it.'

'Liz,' I said.

'Don't "Liz" me, you know it's true.' Liz leaned forward on the railing, away from me. I couldn't see her face. 'She'd ship me off someplace for sure, some home for unwed mothers in fucking Nebraska or someplace, as far away as possible, make me put it up for adoption, then make me come home and go to church with her every morning and wear a big scarlet "A" for asshole every day around the house. I'd never hear the end of it.' She lit another cigarette, and, even from where I was sitting, I could see her hands shaking. She threw the match into the air so that it would land below us, in the tomatoes and lettuce and green peppers. Every night before dinner, I would go down to the garden and pick vegetables for the salad. I liked the smell of things growing in the earth.

'That's what would happen, all right,' Liz was saying, her voice bitter. 'My parents would love Jesus no matter what he did, but they would never love me again. They send money to save the innocent babies in the Congo, but they would never love their unmarried daughter's baby.' She shook her head back and forth. I didn't say anything. I knew Liz's parents. I knew what she said was true. 'I can just see my mother's face. My father – hey, he hardly knows I'm around now, right? I mean, if I told him? Like, tried to force Cory into a – a shotgun situation, some shit like that?' She snorted. 'My father would blame me. I bet you my next paycheck that's what would happen. And Cory, it's like he wasn't even worried about that. Wasn't even worried that I might tell my father, that he would – because he knows, right? He sees it every day, the way my father treats me. You've seen him, the way he acts. And once this happened, it's like I wouldn't even exist. And my mother, that look on her face—'

'Liz,' I said. 'Liz, come on, man. You didn't do anything wrong, okay? You loved someone, you didn't do anything wrong.'

'Says the virgin,' she said, sighing. She came over and sat down next to me on the chaise. We sat like that for a while, listening to my mother's friends laughing, the clink of coffee cups, forks scraping the last little bits of Sara Lee chocolate layer cake from their plates. Liz's head was bent so far down it was almost touching the floor. I had to lean forward to hear what she was saying.

165

'I need to know you're with me, Katie,' she said. 'I mean, I thought you were going to be the one to bag out in the first place.'

'Liz—'

'I've heard you say it! "If abortion was around, I wouldn't be here today." I've heard you say it a hundred times.'

'I never said it a hundred—'

'Katie, I know you,' she whispered fiercely. 'You're so fucking dramatic—'

'I'm so fucking dramatic?' I said, thinking of the crown of roses, the red velvet wedding dress.

'In your head, you're more dramatic than the rest of us,' she whispered. 'What happens when we get there? What if you're sitting around waiting and you start thinking it's you I'm killing and not—'

'Stop it!' I whispered, just as fierce. 'Shut the fuck up right now or I'll—'

'I need to know,' she said savagely. 'I need to know if you're with me, because if you're not, it's cool, no, really, man, it is; I can do this by myself, but you have to tell me now. I don't want to feel all safe when I go to sleep tonight and then find out that I'm—' Her head dropped lower, her hair spilling over the porch floor.

I lit another cigarette. Wherever my mother was now, the one who'd given me up so I could have a better life, she hadn't been in the smokers' bathroom at school that day when Barbara Malone began yanking the hair from my scalp like a deranged warrior, or jumped on Barbara's back, threatening to dunk her head in a toilet bowl if she didn't leave me alone. But Liz had. It was Liz who lit my first cigarette, brought

166

me down to Comanche Street, gave me a place to belong. I started to say something, but stopped when I saw her face. It was contorted, her lips quivering, her eyes dry but darting wildly, as if seeking shelter. I took hold of her hands, held them hard against my heart.

'I'm here, man,' I said. 'I'm here, I swear. I swear on my mother's life.'

Liz nodded, then gently removed her hands from mine. After a while she whispered, 'To think I wanted him to marry me.' She covered her face with her hands, and the sound of her sobbing was drowned out by the crashing of tiles against the kitchen table, the triumphant cry of 'Mah-jongg!' by one of my mother's friends.

The Next Morning

Liz insisted we take the 7:27 bus; the few of our friends' parents who worked in the city, including my father, took the 7:55 train that left from the same station, so we'd miss having to run into any of them. No one else we knew got up that early except the surfers and they'd be in the ocean, not at the bus station. She wanted to check into the motel and get her bearings before heading over to the doctor's place. We had the address but no phone number; the doctor refused to speak to her clients on the phone. 'We can pretend it's like a vacation,' Liz said. I agreed, even though it wasn't like we were going to Aruba or someplace. Silverwood was only about two hours away, one of the arty beach towns where painters and writers supposedly had summer places.

There was a thin streamer of gold against the sky as we

walked out to the buses after buying our tickets. I paused for a minute to look at the sky, thinking, when you lived by the water, even the bus station could look beautiful in the early morning light.

'Well, well, look who's here,' I heard, and turned to see Mitch, leaning on a trash dumpster while he tried to light a cigarette. He was wearing his military-issue sunglasses.

'What the fuck is he doing here?' Liz whispered, panicked. 'I thought he never left Comanche Street.'

'What are you doing here?' I asked Mitch. My voice sounded loud in my own ears.

He exhaled and began hobbling over to where we were standing. Away from Comanche Street, he looked taller, straighter, his cane making him seem more distinguished, even though the closer he got, you could smell the booze and sweat.

'Had a rough night,' he said, his voice sounding like crunched gravel. 'Couldn't get to sleep even after the bar closed; fucking birds were on the ledge outside, sounded like they were in the room, for chrissake. I'm due for a visit to the VA hospital to stock my meds and make sure I'm still alive, so instead of killing a whole damn day I'll only kill a whole damn morning, can you dig it? At least the Goddamned train is air-conditioned. But the real question is, where are you two fine beauties off to at this time of the morning? And what's with the funereal garb?'

Liz mumbled, 'Later, man,' and began walking to the opposite end of the station, where the buses were parked.

'I better get going,' I said. 'So we don't miss the bus.'

I could feel Mitch's eyes watching me behind his sunglasses.

168

He scratched the stubble on his chin. Finally, he asked, 'There something you want to tell me, baby doll?'

'Like what?' I asked innocently.

'I don't know,' he said. 'That's why I asked. Everything all right with you and Sister Morphine over there?' He jerked his head in Liz's direction. 'Not like her to be so quiet.'

'No, we're cool,' I said. 'She's just not into being up this early. Thing is, we both have to be to work in the afternoon and we have to buy a – a birthday present for one of our friends from school, you wouldn't know her, they're having a surprise party for her next weekend and this was the only time—'

'Shine it on, darlin',' he said softly. 'I get the drift.'

I felt my insides relax a little. 'Listen, don't tell anyone you saw us, okay?'

Mitch nodded, watching me from behind his sunglasses.

'All right, later,' I said, but he pulled me back as I turned to go. He fumbled in his pocket and came up with a twenty-dollar bill and held it out. 'Here,' he said. 'Buy yourselves some lunch or something.'

'C'mon, man, I don't want your money,' I said, but he shoved the bill into my hand, crumpling it between my fingers. 'Take it,' he said, his voice low and steely.

You live over a bar, I wanted to say. *You sleep on torn sheets. You wake up screaming in the night.* 'Thanks,' I whispered instead. I could feel my throat begin to tremble. I kissed his cheek quickly and then turned and began walking toward Liz and the bus that would take us to Silverwood.

⌇

169

Liz hadn't said much on the way to the bus station and she wasn't saying much as we rolled onto the Meadowbrook Parkway. She just kept lighting cigarettes, staring out the window. The bus wasn't very crowded; most of the seats were empty but we were still sitting way in the back. It's funny, but the people I hang out with, we always gravitate to the back of everything: classrooms, movie theaters, buses. There was a young mother with four kids sitting near the middle, all redheads, and two of them looked like twins. They were keeping her pretty busy, climbing all over the seats, clamoring for juice and cookies, hitting each other. But outside of that, it was pretty quiet.

I thought about my own mother, the one who gave me up. I always pictured her brushing her long, black hair, staring out the window, waiting for someone. Sometimes, I pictured her sitting at a scarred brown vanity table, staring into the scratched mirror, dressed only in a bra and girdle with her flesh bulging between the elastic borders, a glass of something amber by her side. She looked sad like that, staring into the mirror. Had she thought about doing something like this? Had she gone for a two-hour bus ride alone or with her best friend and then chickened out halfway there? Or stood in an alley outside the doctor's door and then fled before even knocking? Or made it as far as the table and then gotten so hysterical that the stern-faced, short-haired, thin-lipped doctor had thrown up her hands and said, 'I can't do this, here, take your money and go'? I never thought about my father, except when people told me I looked part Indian, especially in the summer when I tanned very dark. I thought maybe he'd been part of the Shinnecock tribe we'd studied in Local History at school. My mother had been a good Catholic girl. I'd been adopted through St. Joseph's Sanctuary in Fog River, a home for unwed mothers behind a huge brick wall not far from the ferry. I thought about what would have happened if she'd kept me. Would she stand in the doorway of the bathroom while I put on my mascara, screaming that I'd end up living over a bar with six kids if I kept hanging around street corners? Sometimes lately when I looked in the mirror I wondered if she'd recognize me walking down the street, if there was enough of her in me for that to happen. But when I thought about her, it wasn't a burning in my heart, the way it was when I thought about Luke. I wouldn't be thinking about her now if I wasn't on my way to an abortion doctor.

I was so into my thoughts I didn't realize at first that my seat was rocking. I thought something had broken loose and the seat needed adjusting. Then I realized it was Liz. She was shaking so bad that the seats were vibrating.

'Jesus, Liz,' I said. I thought maybe she had a fever and we would have to call the whole thing off. I put my hand on her arm, and she grabbed hold of me.

'Nanny's right, I'm going to hell,' she said, speaking fast, in a low voice. 'After this, it's the only place for me. I'm going to hell and there's nothing, not one Goddamned thing I can do to save myself.'

'Liz—'

'I know I did a lot of bad things in my life, but I always thought I could make it up later, you know, when we got older. But I can never make this up. I can never save my soul after this. Best thing that could happen, I die on the table, right in the middle—'

'Stop it!' I said, grabbing her shoulders. 'Stop it right now! You're not going to die, it's a clean, safe place—'

'Yeah, yeah, so clean, you could eat off it, like my mother says,' she said bitterly. 'Maybe we could have a dinner party after I – WILL YOU SHUT THAT FUCKING KID UP!' she screamed suddenly, jumping out of her seat. 'SHUT HIM UP! SHUT HIM UP, GODDAMNIT!'

One of the red-haired kids had been crying, but now he stopped mid-wail, abruptly and completely. Everyone was looking at us, including the driver in his rearview mirror. Liz sat down, lit another cigarette, and went back to staring out the window. She had stopped shaking.

The mother of the crying kid was coming at us, snorting fire. I ran up the aisle before she could reach Liz, blocking her way.

'Out of my way,' she said, eyes blazing. 'Just who the hell does she think she is, yelling about my kid like that?'

'Look, I'm sorry,' I said, talking fast, 'she's upset. She's upset and—'

'Huh!' the mother said. 'She don't look too upset to me. She—'

'She's – we're on our way to a funeral,' I said. 'It's – it's someone close to her, very close, and she's just – she's really not herself.' Now I was glad we were dressed in black so the funeral story would be more believable.

'I don't care what she is,' the mother said. 'She's got no right—'

'Her nephew,' I whispered. 'It's her favorite nephew. She can't stand even being around – I mean, your kids, they remind her—'

The mother stared at Liz, her eyes narrowed.

'Since it happened, she's been like – she has these outbursts . . .' I trailed off and raised my eyebrows, trying to make it sound like Liz was one step away from the county asylum.

'How old was the nephew?' the mother whispered.

'Four,' I said. 'Only four years old. It was so tragic, it was—'

'My God, how did it happen?' the mother whispered.

But my imagination was suddenly exhausted. 'I can't talk about it,' I said, making my voice sound sorrowful. 'I'm sorry, but it's just too – I just can't—'

'Sure, sure, I understand,' she said, patting my shoulder. 'Well. We all have our days. Had a few myself. You can imagine, with this crowd.' She jerked her head toward the kids, who were watching her, openmouthed. 'Tell your friend I'm sorry for her loss.' She turned and walked toward her children. She took the two smallest ones with the reddest hair on her lap and began talking softly to them. They were all quiet, listening, their eyes wandering back toward Liz, who was staring out the window.

I walked to my seat and sat down. I put my arm around Liz's shoulders. For once, she didn't flinch. She leaned against me and closed her eyes. We rode like that the rest of the way.

Right Now

The room was hidden from the rest of the house. It was the widow's watch at the top, connected to a small staircase behind an oak closet in the bathroom, so small that it seemed made for children, not adults. 'I feel like Anne fucking Frank,' Liz

173

muttered as we climbed into the space. I smiled. I was happy that Liz sounded like Liz again.

Prisms of light danced from the tiny triangular windows. Bottles of colored glass hung from the walls, casting violet shadows against wide, weathered planks that looked like whitewashed driftwood. In the center of the room was a narrow bed dressed in white. And above the bed, something we hadn't been able to see from the street: a skylight.

There was a portable metal table against one wall, covered with a white cloth, and on the shelf above the table, a tape player; strains of Joni Mitchell singing 'California' floated through the air. A woman younger than the doctor was standing by the table, assembling instruments, checking things over. She wore jeans, a white peasant top, and flip-flops. The doctor gestured toward her and said, 'My assistant,' and I remembered: no names. When the woman turned toward us and smiled, my heart sank; she looked almost exactly like Marily Weiss, a girl at Elephant Beach High School who Liz hated with a passion because she had told Mrs. Jacovides, the home ec teacher, that Liz was trying to copy her answers on a quiz when Liz really wasn't. One time, Marily came into the smoking bathroom by mistake – you could tell by looking at her that she'd never smoked a cigarette in her life – and Liz threatened to wrap her tongue around her tonsils for telling lies and started coming toward her, and Marily screamed and ran out of the bathroom without even taking a piss. I was hoping Liz wouldn't notice the resemblance, but now she was lying on the bed while the doctor swabbed her arm with cotton, holding a needle in her hand. 'Valium,' she explained. 'Within five minutes or so it should be taking effect.'

174

Liz was lying very still beneath the white sheet, staring with great interest at the skylight in the ceiling.

The doctor and her assistant slipped white coats on over their clothes, which made me feel better. It was still too quiet.

'Was that skylight always here?' I asked, staring at the slippery light pouring down.

The doctor turned toward me and smiled. 'No, I had that put in when I bought the house. It was much too dark in here because these windows are so small. I wanted natural light.'

I looked around at the colored bottles and the driftwood walls and suddenly I was wildly angry. I wanted to smash all the instruments on the metal table, smack the doctor hard and jolt that serene look out of her face, the calmness out of her eyes. It was great to talk about light and keeping women safe, but just because you covered it all up with candles and wind chimes and skylights didn't mean nothing bad would ever happen. It didn't mean that people wouldn't get hurt or die. I heard a vague sound, like scratching in the walls, and I thought of the mice, mewling, hungry, waiting for everyone to go to bed so they could start scavenging. But maybe it wasn't mice after all. Maybe it was the sound of the babies, little ghost babies huddled together for warmth, having no idea where they were. Frightened, crying for their mothers.

'Are you all right?' the doctor asked me, looking concerned.

'Just jim-fucking-dandy,' I said.

She looked at me for a long moment. Behind us, the assistant folded Liz's clothes carefully and placed them on a shelf. I wondered if Liz noticed her resemblance to Marily Weiss

175

and if she was too stoned to think about punching her in the face.

The doctor sighed, rolling up her sleeves, busying herself with the tray. 'Women,' she said, shaking her head. 'They'd rather you wrap it all up in dirty sheets and ribbons of blood. And we wonder why men treat us like dirt.' She spoke softly, her lips barely moving. But I heard every word. I started to speak, but then I heard Liz's voice.

'Katie, where are you? Are you still here?' Her voice sounded loose, dreamy. The doctor and I walked toward the bed from opposite directions.

'You're staying with me, right, Katie?' Liz turned her eyes on the doctor. 'She can stay, can't she?'

'Do you want to stay here with your friend or wait downstairs?' the doctor asked me. 'There's a small room, right across from the bathroom, with books, magazines. One of us will come and get you when we're done here.'

'She's staying,' Liz said, closing her eyes. 'Katie, man, tell her you're staying here in the room with me. I love this room. I could live in this room. Katie, are you still here? Where are you?' I didn't want to stay. I wanted to go home. I didn't want to be in this room one more minute, but all day Liz had been slipping in and out of herself and I was afraid she might disappear completely if I left her.

'I'm here,' I said, so loudly the assistant looked up. She had almost the exact same snotty look on her face that Marily Weiss did most of the time. I hoped Liz wouldn't open her eyes in the middle and see that look. 'I'm here. What should I do?' I asked the doctor, feeling panicky. There weren't any chairs in the room. I didn't want to just stand there, watching.

I wanted to close my eyes and when I opened them again, I wanted it to be over.

'You can stand behind her and massage her shoulders,' the doctor said briskly, moving down the length of the bed. 'Help her relax, though she seems to be doing fine with the Valium. Yes, just like that. Just like that.'

I stood behind Liz, kneading her shoulders. Her flesh felt soft and light beneath my hands. In the background, Mick Jagger was singing 'Wild Horses.' The first time I'd heard the song was at Liz's house, in her bedroom, after we'd smoked a joint and she put the headphones over my ears and said, 'Just listen, man, it's like – like listening to a waterfall tripping over tiny stones in a stream.' I closed my eyes and started humming along to the music.

After

And then it was over almost before it began. I thought the whole thing would take hours. I thought everything would take hours; when I pictured Luke and me in his bed making love, his honey-colored skin covering mine, it started out with golden light at the windows and ended with sunset colors crowding the sky. But then I remembered Liz telling us about her brief, passionate couplings with Cory McGill and how Nanny said her first time with Voodoo lasted as long as it took to drink an ice-cream soda. How long does it take to drink an ice-cream soda, even if you drag it out with a few cigarettes in between? A new thought occurred to me, that women had all this drama, all this waiting and hoping and crying over things we'd been told, raised on, warned about, these monumental milestones that ended up lasting only minutes in our lives and were never, ever as wonderful or horrible as you thought they would be.

'Beautiful,' the doctor was saying. I thought that, once again, she'd chosen a word that seemed out of place. I opened my eyes but I didn't see anything. I listened for a minute, but there was no sound coming from the walls. The doctor was patting Liz's leg.

'Everything is fine,' she said. 'I want you to rest a bit, then I'll do a final check and you're all done.' She left the room, closing the door behind her. The assistant snapped the sheet off the bed and placed a brighter one over Liz. I saw the bloodstains on the old sheet, like fresh tracks in the snow, before the assistant bunched it up and threw it in a blue wicker hamper in the corner.

For the first time since we came into the room, I looked directly into Liz's face. She looked pale and tired, but her eyes were clear. Later, at the motel, she'd tell me how at one point she'd felt the room grow dark and thought it was raining. She could hear the rain beating down hard on the bed, soaking her skin, her clothes, even though she felt dry. The raindrops sounded like individual bullets, and in her mind she saw herself facing a firing squad in front of Eddy's candy store on Comanche Street. They kept shooting at her from across the street. Even though they were strangers, she could see by their faces they were frustrated because she wouldn't go all the way down. They finally turned around and began walking away. Liz said she could feel herself smiling, proud that she had fooled them. She felt a twinge of pain, but it was only a nick where a bullet had grazed her thigh without breaking the skin. There wouldn't even be a scar.

Up above, the sky seemed gray and overcast, as though it might really rain. We watched the gulls circling the roof, heard their beggarly cries through the tiny windows. I was careful not to touch Liz. I was afraid if I touched her something might break.

'How you doing, man?' I whispered.

She leaned forward and whispered something back. I leaned closer and said, 'Louder.'

Liz put her lips hard against my ear. 'Who invited Marily Weiss's twin fucking sister? Should I wrap her tongue around her tonsils?' We started laughing. We laughed until we became hysterical, leaning into each other, snorting, gasping, until tears poured down our cheeks. The doctor came into the room, smiling. She said to Liz, 'This will only take a minute.' She stood at the foot of the bed, waiting, and even when she stopped smiling, when she finally said in a sharper voice than we'd heard her use all day, 'All right, girls, that's enough,' still we couldn't stop laughing, as the rain finally began to fall and we heard it beating against the light from the sky.

ELEVEN

casualties

I was on my way back from break when someone said, 'Katie,' and I turned and then I realized who it was. Allie. Alphonse D'Amore was back in town.

'Allie, Jesus,' I said as he came toward me. He looked good. His face was heavier, but that was because of the drugs they'd given him at the treatment center. His hair was cut shorter so you could see how high his forehead was. That was supposed to be a sign of intelligence and Allie had always been smart. He'd always made the most money dealing and had never been busted. He gave me a hug that threatened to bust my bones. It surprised me, because Allie and I had never been tight. The truth was, even though everyone thought he was beyond cool, I hadn't liked him all that much, ever since that time he'd hit Ginger when they were still together. Afterward, he walked into Eddy's and ordered a strawberry milk shake as if nothing had happened. As if Ginger wasn't sitting outside, on the steps of Eddy's side door, crying. It wasn't the first time, either; you could tell by the way Ginger's eyes had flinched, as though she'd been expecting it. I didn't like people who were too cool for this earth. There was always a streak of dirt somewhere inside them.

Now Allie put his hands on my shoulders and stared into my face. His eyes were sunken back, but they looked clear. He was smiling deeply, as if his mouth was rolling backward. 'Katie, you know who I am? I'm Eagleton.'

I looked at him and smiled. I didn't know what else to do.

'That's who I am now,' Allie said. 'You know that guy, Eagleton? On the news? That's me. I'm Eagleton.'

I hadn't been there the night Allie flipped out. At first everyone just thought he was high and finally showing it; Allie had the reputation of being an iron head: acid, ludes, angel dust, THC, Allie was always the one who still knew what time it was. He'd never lost control before. They'd had to take him to the emergency room, call his parents. 'Worst call I ever made in my life, man,' Billy had said, a shudder in his voice. 'To see someone you know your whole life, hand-cuffed to the bed like that. Creeped me out, man. Allie, of all people.'

It was creeping me out now, Allie smiling that big, loud smile. He never used to smile that much before.

'They won't let him run, they say he blew it for McGovern, but he'll be back,' Allie said. 'He'll come back, just like I did. Say, Katie,' he said, his voice more urgent. 'You saw my son, right?'

When I didn't answer, he said, 'You were at the hospital, right? When Ginger had the baby? My son? What's he look like? Does he look like me?'

181

I remembered Ginger's baby, in the hospital, Nanny saying, 'You think he looks like anyone we know?' I wondered if Allie remembered that he and Ginger had been in one of their breakup phases when he flipped out and went to the hospital, if he knew that Ginger had been running amok in the months that followed. I wondered if he knew that Ginger had given the baby up for adoption and that she was living on a born-again farm in Lubbock, Texas. She had called Nanny late one night from a pay phone, but Nanny could barely hear her, and when the operator cut in to ask for more money, the connection was broken. Ginger never called back, and none of us had a number to reach her.

'I've got to get back to work, Allie,' I said, gently removing his hands from my shoulders.

'But you saw him, right? In the hospital? I was in the hospital, too.' It was like a light had been snuffed out suddenly. Allie slumped down, his arms dangling at his sides. He was wearing a green velour pullover and work boots, even though it was August and like ninety-five degrees out. He looked at me and his eyes were anxious. 'I was in one hospital, he was in the other. They had me tied down, that's why I never went to see him. You saw him, Katie, right? Does he look like me?' Allie was almost shouting now. People were watching us. All the people in aisle seven were looking at me and Allie. Desmond, the store manager, was walking toward us from the produce department, where he'd been inspecting canta-loupes. Another man I didn't know was coming up behind him. The man came right up and put his arm around Allie. 'It's all right, Allie, everything's okay,' he said, his voice smooth. He wore glasses and had a bristly mustache.

182

'Everything all right over here?' Desmond asked.

'It's fine, it's fine. Miss, I'm sorry, I'm sorry if he – he's not well, he hasn't been well, he—'

'I know him,' I said. 'We're friends.'

The man looked relieved. 'Okay, then,' he said. 'Okay. That's good, that's good, he just got re – he just got home, he hasn't seen too many people yet.' His eyes were blinking nervously behind his glasses. 'Gotta, gotta get back in the swing here, right, Allie? Back in the saddle.'

'I should get back to work,' I said. Desmond nodded and walked toward the manager's booth at the front of the store.

'Oh, you work here?' the man said. 'That's good, that's, that's nice.' He held out his hand. 'I'm Sam D'Amore, Allie's father. Call me Sam, please.'

'I'm Katie,' I said, holding out my hand. He shook it firmly.

'Dad, she knows my son!' Allie said excitedly. 'Katie met him, she was at his hospital. What's he look like, Katie? Does he look like me?'

'He's beautiful, Allie,' I said. Allie beamed. He beamed like a normal, proud father. I turned away and started walking toward the checkout registers at the front of the store. I was on register number four.

Behind me, Allie's father said, 'I heard her, son, yes I did. Come on, now. Let's go home.'

<hr/>

'That kid a friend of yours?' Martha asked. 'Nut job in aisle seven this morning?'

'He's not a nut job. He has some problems,' I said.

183

Martha snorted. 'Drugs, that's his problem,' she said. 'I heard him shouting up at the front of the store. Nut job.'

'Would you stop calling him that,' I said.

'Just calling it like I see it,' Martha said. She took her sandwich out of the brown paper bag. It was wrapped in wax paper. We were allowed half-price sandwiches from the delicatessen department, but every day Martha Muldoon brought her lunch to work in an aluminum lunch box. She was eating her egg salad sandwich with tiny, fastidious bites, which was weird because she was a big, rawboned woman with a high, ruddy color and that insane home permanent, with iron-gray curls that looked like they were waiting to spring free from prison. She was the most senior cashier at the A&P and never let you forget it. She was also a tattletale, always running to Desmond if one of us was a minute late coming back from break. She told on Jerry Tuttle and Terry Noonan for punching each other in on time even when one of them was late. She told on Cathy Strutz for not emptying the ashtrays when it was her turn to clean the break room. She was never late for work, hadn't called in sick once in eighteen years and was always the last one out the door at night. 'I'm a proud representative of the Atlantic and Pacific Tea Company,' she'd tell anyone who would listen, including the customers on her checkout line. None of us could stand her.

Martha had finished her egg salad sandwich and was wiping her mouth with dainty little nips from a napkin. She opened the lunch box and took out a Saran-wrapped package of carrot sticks. Next to that she put a proud red McIntosh. She always insisted on paying for her fruit, whether it was a lone apple or a handful of cherries, even when Gus, the produce manager,

184

said she could have it for free. 'I pay my own way,' she told him firmly, standing at the scale, making sure he charged her to the penny. 'Sex with that broad must be a barrel of laughs,' Gus would say, watching her march up the aisle. 'Probably keeps a meter running in her snatch.'

Everybody hated Martha, but the tide turned somewhat when she got fired for letting Sugar Lady slide for two bags of sugar. It was ironic, because we were always letting customers slide at the register and we lived in fear of Martha finding out and reporting us to Desmond and here she was the one getting fired. It was a silent conspiracy among the checkout girls and bag boys who worked the registers; while waiting on our friends' parents, former teachers, our mothers' canasta partners, we'd push several items onward without ringing them up. Times were hard; you could see it on the checkout lines, when customers would look at the total and ask you to void a few things, or around the meat department, where more people were buying chicken necks and gizzards than ground round or fryers because they were so much cheaper, and little kids kept coming around the butcher's door to beg for soup bones for their dogs. Everyone knew at least one family where there'd been a layoff, and if we were in a position to help out, why not? As long as we didn't get caught. We always warned everyone to act like they didn't know us while we rang up their groceries. To act like complete strangers, as though they'd never seen us before in their lives. This way, the people on line in back of them were less likely to notice that the price we rang up was substantially less than it should have been. Most of the time everyone complied because they didn't want anything to happen to any of us or to get in trouble themselves. Our friends' mothers, our own mothers (on someone else's checkout line, of course) would hold out their folded tens and twenties with quaking hands, collect their change and scurry out of the store with their shopping bags. Every once in a while there were slipups, though, like the time Conor and Billy came in to buy beer for the Labor Day beach party. I rang up a case of Budweiser at a dollar fifty, and Conor cried, 'Whoa, check this out! Katie, man, you are such an outasight chick!' The two of them were trying to hug me and carrying on and I had to practically push them out the door to get rid of them. Thankfully, nothing happened. But most of the time, things went pretty smoothly, because we never talked about it and because Meghan Leary, the head cashier, was extremely careful about who she passed on to Desmond for hiring. 'One wrong person in here could blow the whole thing sky-high,' she'd say.

The day of Martha's firing was cold for summer, with a nagging rain beating on the big windows that looked out over Main Street. It was a Monday and over the weekend the price of sugar had tripled. In all the aisles, you could hear the customers exclaiming over the rising price of practically everything: tomato sauce, Campbell's soup, nectarines, tomatoes. But the price of sugar was extreme, and by the time Sugar Lady came in, we'd been hearing comments on the checkout lines all morning. Sugar Lady was so called because she had twenty-three grandchildren and used to buy two or three bags of sugar at a time because she loved baking cookies for them. They were good cookies, too; she once brought us a huge tin of them at Christmastime, wrapped in aluminum foil and tied with red and silver ribbons. Sugar Lady was a short, stout black woman with tremendous breasts and a behind that looked like she had another person following her. She must have had some of those grandchildren living with her, because her grocery cart was always filled to the brim and on holidays she'd be pushing one cart in front of her and lugging another one in back. She always dressed to the nines, too, in flouncy dresses and stockings with seams and flowered hats that looked like they belonged in church. She wore those stubby old-lady shoes with the crooked heels, black in winter, white in summer. These past few months, though, Sugar Lady had cut back like everybody else and her cart was only half to three-quarters full by the time she reached the checkout line.

She was on Martha's register that Monday when she began unloading her groceries, which included the customary three bags of Domino sugar. She must have taken them off the shelf without looking at the price, though, because when she saw the total, she actually gasped. She looked at everything, turned over cans of stewed prunes and boxes of Kraft Macaroni & Cheese, and when she saw the sticker price on the sugar bags she gasped again, turning one of the bags over and over. 'Oh, my,' she kept saying. 'Oh, my.' Then she told Martha, 'Please, miss, take off two bags of sugar from the bill. Can't afford but one this time.' Freddy, the best-looking bag boy, whose nickname was Good-Looking Freddy, told us she looked stunned, 'like she was coming off a sugar rush herself, you know, all dazed and everything,' he said.

So Martha, straight-arrow Martha, that proud representative of the Atlantic and Pacific Tea Company, put a void slip into the register and subtracted the money, asked Desmond to sign it, which he did, put the slip at the bottom of the cash box, as we were instructed to do, and when Desmond went back to the manager's office, she shoved the other two bags of sugar down the belt for Good-Looking Freddy to bag up with the rest of the groceries. At first, he was confused and looked at Martha, wondering if she'd made a mistake. He said the look she gave him was so murderous and fierce, he just shoved the sugar into a bag. Then Martha handed the change to Sugar Lady, who didn't seem to know what had happened, Freddy said, and just as she was lifting the bagged groceries into her cart, a voice called out, 'I saw that!'

The voice was loud, you couldn't help but hear. You couldn't. We all looked up and saw the red-faced woman in back of Sugar Lady. She was a semi-regular customer who kept her eye on the cash register the entire time you were ringing up her purchases, the kind who snapped, 'Those are two-for-one, go read the sign!' acting like you were intentionally robbing her instead of making an honest mistake. She'd snatch the receipt out of your hands and stand there reviewing it, refusing to budge out of the way so that you could begin ringing up the next customer. When all the prices jibed and no errors had been made, her mouth was still tightened with distrust. She never replied when you told her to have a nice day. We called her Evil Eye.

'Manager!' she called loudly, in the direction of the manager's booth at the front of the store. Sugar Lady, oblivious, was getting ready to wheel her cart outside. Freddy began sweating, he told us later. Evil Eye had probably seen him bagging the illicit merchandise but he didn't want to leave Martha in the lurch, because he thought she'd done a noble

188

thing. 'I mean, really, man, who would have thought the tight-assed bitch had it in her?'

Desmond was trying to ignore Evil Eye, the way he tried to ignore all customer complaints, by hunkering down in the small wooden booth so that the top of his head was barely visible. Desmond didn't like the customers, who he referred to as pain-in-the-ass carping harpies, convinced their sole mission in life was to make his life miserable. But when Evil Eye began bellowing, 'I see you in there! You can't hide from me!' what could he do? Sighing, he walked over to register five, the same one Martha used every day that she worked. 'What seems to be the trouble, ma'am?' he asked, like he really cared.

'Here's the trouble,' Evil Eye said, pointing at Martha. 'This woman gave that woman' – her finger swung in Sugar Lady's direction – 'two free bags of sugar!'

'And exactly how do you—'

'I saw her! I saw her make out one of those little slips they do whenever they overcharge somebody, which happens way too often, in my opinion, and put it in the bottom of that drawer. Go on, look! Look in there and see if I'm right!' Evil Eye's breasts swelled underneath her cotton housedress until the polka dots looked like balloons.

Desmond looked from Martha to Sugar Lady and back to Martha again. Everything else had come to a standstill in the register area; it was only two o'clock in the afternoon and there weren't a great many customers in the store. Everyone was quiet, watching the scene at register five.

'What? What she saying about sugar?' Sugar Lady looked honestly confused.

189

'Look in her grocery bags! Go on, look! What are you waiting for?' Evil Eye was practically foaming at the mouth. 'It's pilfering, plain and simple!'

'Ain't nobody pilfered nothing,' Sugar Lady said firmly, holding out her receipt to Desmond. 'See that right there, says I bought and paid for one bag of sugar. What she making all this fuss about?'

'Look inside her grocery bags!' Evil Eye said sharply, loudly. 'Look inside the cash drawer for that little slip! What on earth are you waiting for?'

Desmond reached past Martha and opened the register drawer. Martha hadn't said a word through the entire encounter. She just stood there, straight as stone, staring out the window. There were two bright spots on both of her cheeks, hectic splotches of color that matched her pink smock. Desmond pulled out the void slip, then stared at Martha. He didn't like her; he thought she was a pain in the ass as well, the way she ran to him with every little thing. Desmond had started out as a bag boy himself; he didn't care if you were a few minutes late coming back from break unless you were stupid enough to do it during the Friday night or Saturday afternoon rush. But now he looked at Martha, concerned, while Evil Eye screamed in exasperated triumph, 'I told you! Now look in this one's grocery bags! Why on earth are you being so slow? I should think you'd be glad to catch a common thief, giving away merchandise that other people pay for!'

'Who you calling a thief, heifer?' Sugar Lady bridled indignantly. She began rustling through her grocery bags, peering into their contents, and then, slowly, her expression changed, and she looked back at Martha, understanding finally flooding her face. She kept looking at Martha and her eyes filled with tears. 'Oh baby,' she said softly, shaking her head. 'You didn't need to do that. I could have waited until it gone on sale.'

～～

Desmond claimed later that he'd had no choice. What was he supposed to do, with that harpy hag screaming in his ear, threatening to call the police, the main office, and she was the type to do it, too. Besides, if he hadn't fired Martha, what kind of message would it send to the rest of the employees, let alone the customers? Should we be giving free sugar away to everyone just because the price had tripled? Letting Martha off the hook would be setting a precedent, and the next thing you knew, customers would be demanding freebies on everything, we'd have no choice but to capitulate, and it was only a matter of time before the main office found out and one way or another, we'd all be out of a job.

'It's not right, man,' Good-Looking Freddy said when we were all out in the alley, smoking, after closing time. 'She was trying to help someone out and—'

'It serves her right,' Cathy said. 'Running to Desmond every time someone takes a damned cherry without paying. What goes around comes around.'

'Come on, Cathy,' Meghan said. 'It could have been any one of us, man. And she's got that mother to support.'

'You come on,' Cathy said, stamping out her cigarette. 'You hated her more than anyone. And how do you know she wasn't cutting down the price for everybody all along?'

Good-Looking Freddy shook his head sadly. He felt guilty

for the part he'd played, though we tried telling him that it had been Martha's decision to give the sugar away. All he'd done was bag it up. He'd been protecting her, really, by keeping quiet. It wasn't his fault that Evil Eye was a crazy bitch who was still threatening to call the main office, even as Martha handed Desmond her pink smock and employee ID card and walked out the door, clutching her purse in one hand, her aluminum lunch box in the other.

'I don't know, man,' Freddy mourned. 'She should have gotten a warning or something. I mean, eighteen years in and you're out just like that?' He snapped his fingers. 'And that health insurance carried her mother, too. I think we should protest, man. Threaten Desmond with a work stoppage or something.'

But in the end, we did nothing. It wasn't just that Martha failed to arouse sufficient sympathy, even with tears streaming down her cheeks as she'd gathered her things, causing her old-fashioned face powder to crack and crater so that she looked even stiffer and less lovely than usual. Times were hard, see, and nobody wanted to be out of work. Good-Looking Freddy went to see her, though, in the ground-floor apartment she shared with her mother on lower Lighthouse Avenue. She served him tap water and oatmeal cookies. He learned that she'd gotten another job at the Quick 8 Super Market up by the parkway. She had to take two buses to get to work and back, but nobody there knew her or anything about her. They hadn't witnessed her shame. She could make a fresh start. Her secret was safe.

TWELVE

claudine

With her forefinger, Claudine drew a straight line down the center of the kitchen table. 'This,' she said, her finger resting at the table's silver rim, 'is his life, eh? No adventures. No detours. Nothing. Nothing!' She paused to light one of her Kent 100's. 'This is not what I want for my daughter, eh?'

'I don't know about that,' Charlie said mildly, twirling his squat glass filled with ice. 'He's in the service. He's seen things, been around.'

Claudine swung him a withering look. 'He sees nothing,' she said. Charlie shrugged and stood up, holding the glass with the tips of his fingers. After a few minutes, we heard the front door close, the car start. We heard him take off to the Treasure Chest Bar and Grill, right over the bridge. Usually he took a taxi. I sat with Claudine at the table, not knowing what to say. I had stopped by on my way down to Comanche Street to see if Marcel was back from the Cape

193

yet, and found Charlie sitting at the kitchen table, his head in his hands, and Claudine screaming into the telephone receiver, her eyeliner running in black circles down her face.

Marcel had gone and done it. She had married James without telling anyone, not her mother or father, not even me, her closest friend.

Claudine looked at me accusingly. 'Don't tell me you didn't know about this,' she said. 'She tells you everything. You know everything about us. How does she not tell you this?'

'Well, she didn't,' I said. 'I swear on my mother's life.' Of course I'd known that Marcel was visiting James up on Cape Cod, where he was stationed, but she hadn't said anything about getting married this weekend. ('I couldn't risk it,' Marcel told me later. 'If my mother started crying – if my father started crying! I knew you'd tell them. I knew you'd say something.')

We sat smoking for a while, and then I said, 'Claudine, what is it about James? I mean, he loves her, he's good to her, it's not like he's—'

'When I met Charlie,' she said. 'When I first met Charlie. The medals, the uniform, my God . . . I was seventeen when they came marching. After I brought him home the first time, my mother said, "Claudine, he's a good man. But he is not the man for you. You need physical affection, someone to hold you, and he is not the man to give these things." And I said . . .' Claudine dragged deeply, exhaling through her nostrils. 'I said, "But Ama, I can change that."' She threw her head back and blew smoke up at the ceiling. 'And you see us now, eh? You see how it is with us now.' She shook her head. 'Every day for a month, I used to take a little girl to church with me to light a candle, to make him marry me. It was the custom in my village.' She stubbed out her cigarette and made a small steeple of her fingertips, held them to her lips.

Claudine was beautiful. She had wide black eyes that slanted in the corners and dirty blond hair that turned glamorous when she wound it up in a knot at the top of her head. 'She looks typically European,' my mother said, though how she would know that was a mystery, since she'd never been to Europe. 'But she should learn how to dress,' my mother sniffed. 'Who wears a turban to a PTA meeting? She looks like a – a fortune-teller!' It was true, Claudine didn't look like the typical Elephant Beach mother. And she was a fortune-teller of sorts, not like Madame Rhia on the boardwalk, who had a crystal ball and read palms and had a fifty-cent special during the week. Claudine read regular black and red playing cards at the Formica kitchen table, after school or sometimes when I spent the night. Those times were best because she would light candles all around the kitchen and we would laugh and talk until Charlie yelled from his bedroom at the front of the house, 'Claudine, for chrissake, enough already! Come to bed before you burn the Goddamned house down!' My readings were always about Luke. He was the Jack of Diamonds, sharp and steady, and that card would show up inverted as often as not. Inverted cards meant there would be obstacles. At the last reading, Claudine said he had a troubled heart. It hurt me to think of it. But maybe the war had been the problem. A war was bound to bring on a troubled heart.

It was ironic, though, that Claudine should be so bitter and sad about Marcel's marriage, because James had come

195

to the Brennan household through old friends of hers that lived in New Hampshire. It wasn't like he was some sleazy stranger Marcel picked up in a bar or something. He was in the Coast Guard, and had a job and an apartment on Cape Cod. Marcel said the apartment was really nice, surrounded by trees, and you could glimpse a ragged edge of the bay from the kitchen window. That's where she was living now, instead of here in the bedroom next to the kitchen.

The Brennans had had a difficult time before this. Two years ago, during our first year of high school, I learned that Charlie was a drinker. One night, I was going with Marcel to keep her company babysitting. Charlie was supposed to drive us, but at the last minute Claudine gave us money for a taxi. While we waited outside, Marcel began crying. I asked her what was wrong and she said, 'Katie, don't you realize my father's a drunk?' The thing was, I really hadn't. When I thought of alkies, I thought of Nanny's grandfather, rheumy-eyed, slow-gaited, who once hid all the liquor bottles in the oven so that no one could snatch them away and the house almost blew up when Mrs. Devlin went to cook dinner. Charlie would sit in his leather recliner in the corner of the living room, quietly watching television, or he'd tell stories about growing up in Baltimore, which sounded like an exciting place. He would crack jokes all through dinner, unlike my father, who ate silently and expected us to be quiet at mealtimes. The Brennans ate later than most people, European style, sometimes as late as nine o'clock, even on school nights. True, Charlie's hand was always curled around a glass of clear liquid, but since he never raised his voice, slurred his words or punched anyone in the face, behaviors I associated with drunkards, I never thought to ask what he was drinking. Watching Marcel cry as we waited outside for the taxi, I was about to ask her 'Are you sure?' when I realized how stupid that would sound. I loved Charlie and Claudine, and most of all Marcel, who lived only a block away, closer than any of my other friends, and who knew all my secrets, things I never even told Liz and Nanny. I didn't want there to be trouble.

One day during the winter of that year, Claudine brought home a purebred English cocker spaniel that cost three hundred dollars. They named it Coco. 'Every time I turn my back,' Charlie complained, as the dog knelt by his club chair, tail wagging, trying to charm him. 'What about you?' he asked me. 'Do you have a mutt in your house?'

'Uh-uh,' I replied. 'My father put his foot down.'

'So did I,' Charlie said, rubbing Coco between the ears. 'And I stepped on a dog.' That was the Brennan family, though; three-hundred-dollar dogs and festive dinners that took hours to prepare and featured exotic dishes from the Basque region, where Claudine had lived until she married Charlie and came to America: roast duck with figs, shrimp in hot sauce, white bean stew. Claudine was always picking apart crab legs and lobster tails, simmering something in wine and shallots that filled the house with a rich fragrance so that you didn't really notice the sparsely furnished living room, the mattresses on the floor of Marcel's and her brother John Paul's bedrooms, the lack of wall-to-wall carpeting. I would never have thought of them as poor, even though they rented their house by the month instead of owning like everyone else.

Then in our junior year, John Paul went to jail and Marcel went blind for five months. John Paul was three years older than us and so drop-dead gorgeous his beauty transcended the hierarchies at school; he walked easily between the Trunk kids and the crowd from the Dunes, the snotty part of town. He went out with those tall, silky girls we all hated, but would still drive me and Marcel wherever we wanted to go and take us for rides up the parkway, stopping on the way back to treat us to chocolate cones from Carvel. He always walked me home from their house, even though I lived only one block away, and would kiss me good night on both cheeks, something the Brennans always did without thinking. He was Claudine's favorite, the bond between them a pure, strong thing that existed on its own, separate from the rest of the family. Claudine always pronounced his name 'Jean Paul,' but Charlie insisted on calling him John; 'I don't want my son answering to one of those faggoty French names,' he said.

John Paul was nineteen and the girl was sixteen, a respectable age difference, but because she was underage it was considered statutory rape. The girl was not from Elephant Beach; she and John Paul had met at a party in the Dunes, one of those things that starts out local and ends up attracting hundreds of people. The general feeling was that either she was miffed at John Paul because he wasn't madly in love with her afterward, or her parents had found out they'd been having sex and went nuts. At first, no one who knew John Paul thought him capable of committing such a horrible crime. He'd never flaunted his looks and he genuinely liked women, you could see it in the way his face lit up, his dimples like starbursts in his face. When the police came and cuffed him and dragged him to the squad car, his cries of 'Ama! Ama!' were so bereft that the younger of the two cops passed a hand over his own face in distress. Charlie stood at the curb, weaving, weeping as the car pulled away. 'I told him,' he wept, wiping his eyes with his sleeve, 'I always told him, "Be careful, be careful."'

It was a bad time. Charlie made home deliveries for a local oil company and because of the economy things were slow despite the cold weather. More often than not, when Marcel got home from school, Charlie would be sitting at the kitchen table, the squat glass on one side of him, an ashtray on the other. 'Hi honey,' he'd say tiredly, but then he'd say nothing and after a while there was nothing to say that didn't revolve around John Paul and what was to become of him. Charlie picked up a few nights bartending at the Shipwreck, a divey bar on the boardwalk, but things were slow there, too, and he usually ended up drinking the end of his shift away. It was Claudine who sprang into action, who found an attorney that specialized in these types of cases. Claudine, who loved her sleep, and often resembled a curled-up cat on the couch, now woke at dawn, sometimes earlier, Marcel said, and would sit in the kitchen, poring over papers the lawyer had given her, laying out aces and sevens and queens and kings to see what the day would bring. She visited John Paul at the Nassau County Jail every day, and would come back with mascara stains on her cheeks from crying the whole way home. She wouldn't let Marcel come with her, and Charlie wouldn't go; he said it would kill him to see his son in jail, but he was usually too drunk to drive over during evening visiting hours.

Marcel and I wrote John Paul long letters. 'Keep the faith,' we wrote him. 'We are with you, no matter what.' Both of us believed absolutely in his innocence, but rape wasn't like breaking and entering or even assault. Now there were whispers at school, at Sal's Pizza Parlor in the center of town, at Eddy's in the Trunk, that John Paul had been too good-looking for his own good, that his good looks and sunny demeanor may have covered up some crazed and savage beast within, waiting to spring out at something or someone. It seemed that nobody could be that gorgeous and nice and not have something to hide.

There were no more sumptuous dinners at the Brennans' house and everyone, even Charlie, wept when they had to sell Coco, but they were all too distracted to properly care for her, and now even dog food was something of a luxury. Claudine looked for a job and couldn't find one that would accommodate her schedule. She had frequent appointments with the attorney, whose office was in Devon Place, several exits up the parkway, and she dressed for these appointments in slim black dresses and pencil pants with tunics and high heels and tangerine lipstick. Once, she even got her hair done at Antoine's beforehand. 'Chrissake,' Charlie complained, 'you want this guy to think we're millionaires? You look that good, he'll start raising his rates and we can barely afford him now.' But Claudine was busy checking her makeup, daubing her wrists and throat with White Shoulders perfume. 'At times like these,' she said, rubbing her wrists together, 'it's important to keep up appearances, eh?' The look on her face reminded me of when Marcel and I were in eighth grade, before John Paul went to jail, before I started hanging around Comanche Street with Liz and Nanny. We'd be doing our homework at the dining room table, or playing jacks in the hallway, knowing we were too old to be playing but homesick for being young. Claudine would be hurrying out the front door, dressed in her Persian lamb coat and leather gloves, her high heels clicking against the bare floor. Her perfume was sharp and biting, like a wave hitting you in the face. She'd be jangling her car keys. 'Going to see your boyfriend?' we'd ask her, giggling. She'd smile, checking her lipstick in the hallway mirror. 'Of course,' she'd say.

—⁂—

One morning, in January, two months after John Paul had been arrested, Marcel woke up and couldn't see. She kept blinking and blinking but everything stayed black. She touched her face, her eyelids, her lashes, and blinked a final time before screaming out loud in terror, a scream that brought Claudine and Charlie running from the opposite end of the house. She screamed so loudly that Mrs. Kennelly, their neighbor, came running from across the driveway. The night they'd taken John Paul away, she'd come over with a franks-and-beans casserole, as if he'd died instead of being locked up in Nassau County Jail. John Paul always carried her trash cans back from the curb along with the Brennans'. 'So what,' she said to Claudine. 'Plenty of folks should be locked up that aren't, you can bet on it. Don't tell me that sweet boy had anything to do with this.' She was the one who drove Claudine and Marcel to the hospital. They kept Marcel there for several days. They kept her until she'd been seen by the doctors, the specialists, the psychiatrist. When he asked if Marcel had suffered a recent trauma, Claudine told him yes, it involved her brother, and that they'd been especially close. The psychiatrist thought that was what might be causing the hysterical blindness. That's what he called it, hysterical blindness. 'It's a conversion disorder,' he explained. The doctors could find nothing wrong with Marcel physically and thought that her anguish over John Paul's predicament had manifested itself in this way. They recommended counseling. They sent Claudine and Marcel home with a list of therapists that the insurance wouldn't cover.

During those months, Marcel would lie on the mattress on the floor of her bedroom, her eyes wide open. The winter sunlight would stream through the big open window and rest on her tangled, red-gold curls. Sometimes she would cry, but mostly she seemed oddly peaceful. That's what had attracted me to her in the first place, her peaceful ways. She wasn't always running around crazy like everyone else we knew. She was too quiet for the rest of the Comanche Street girls, who befriended her mainly to get closer to John Paul. Marcel also knew how to listen. She listened to the things I said and let me finish sentences. She understood without my having to explain every little thing. While everyone else made fun of me for not lying to my parents, for not doing drugs or getting drunk on the beach at night, Marcel knew that I was good because I was adopted and I didn't want my parents to give me back. She knew that even though I thought about my real mother and wanted to meet her someday, I didn't want to leave the life I had now. I didn't want to go back to something I'd never known in the first place.

Liz and Nanny resented those weeks I sat by Marcel's bed, holding her hand, reading her excerpts from *Charlotte's Web* and *Old Yeller*. She'd always liked animals better than people.

'She's blind,' I told them, when they complained that I wasn't around enough. Liz sniffed. 'Probably just faking it to get attention,' she said. 'Or maybe she doesn't want to come to school because everyone knows about her jailbird brother.' 'Fuck you,' I said, and felt good when Liz's eyes flew open in surprise. I rarely said 'fuck' unless I was angry, and I was known to never get angry. I was afraid of my anger, of where it would take me. I also felt guilty about Marcel, about abandoning her for Liz and them when the Brennans' real problems first began, and she never wanted to go anywhere, to come over for dinner or go to the church dances on Friday nights. Marcel and I had done everything together since we became friends in junior high, but during those first bad months, she never called me and sometimes wouldn't come to the phone when I called over to her house, even though I knew she was home. 'That's what happens when you depend on one friend too much,' my mother said smugly as I moped around the house, angry and lonely and sad. It was I who'd felt abandoned then, even though I felt bad for Marcel and missed the exotic dinners and Charlie's stories and Claudine's card readings by candlelight. With other friends you always had to share, the way I had to share Liz and Nanny, and I missed the way that Marcel and I had been when we only had each other.

Claudine ran around looking for answers, for solutions to make things right. She went to psychics, to positive-thinking seminars at the Elephant Beach Public Library. All over the

Brennans' house, messages were plastered to the walls, the mirrors: 'John Paul is fine, and all goes well with the case.' 'Marcel can see again. She has perfect vision.' Claudine brought home healers, the type of people who lived over the stores on Calypso Street, who put Celestial Seasonings tea bags over Marcel's eyes and forehead, stuffed her mouth with milk thistle, poured a pomegranate poultice onto her chest. Since all the money coming into the house was going to the lawyer, Claudine repaid these healers by reading their cards. Marcel heard them at night through the walls of her bedroom, the soft drone of their voices. Their cigarette smoke seeped under the crack of her bedroom door, filling the air with scented secrets. But it all came to an end when Charlie put his foot down after one woman with wild hair and rolling eyes sat beside Marcel's bed, chanting in a high-pitched wail until Marcel began crying, pleading, 'Enough! Please! Enough!' After the strange woman left, Claudine, exhausted, stood over Marcel's bed and shouted, 'Enough, Marcel, eh? Enough? You think you've had it? Well, I've had it, too!' And she stomped away, sobbing, slamming the door to her bedroom.

Marcel worried that her mother would stop loving her, that she would end up selling pencils out of a tin cup on the corner of Stardust Alley, where the local bums panhandled. She tried to make a joke out of it, but her voice quivered and her laugh was strangled. 'Don't be ridiculous,' I said, taking her hand. 'Claudine's just upset, man, she's worried about you, about John Paul. Anyway, you'll always have me.' It was true, but my heart felt clammy as I said this. Several weeks before, my mother had come into my room after dinner. She'd had the *Elephant Beach Gazette* folded in her hand, the issue where John Paul's name appeared in the police blotter. 'Your father and I don't want you seeing Marcel anymore,' she said. 'We don't want you going over there.' She spoke quietly instead of screaming, which was unusual. She had always liked Marcel, encouraged her to stay for dinner, spend the night. My mother and I stared at each other for a long time. And then I did something unusual, too. I nodded and said, 'Okay.' We looked at each other for a long moment, and then she left my room, closing the door softly behind her.

When I wasn't with Marcel, her milky blue stare haunted me. One day after school, I was running errands on Buoy Boulevard and coming out of Krackoff's Bakery when I heard a car horn honking and saw Claudine leaning over the steering wheel of her green Karmann Ghia. I went over and got into the car. She was sitting, smoking, with the window cracked open. I lit up as well; Marcel had told her that I had permission to smoke, which was a lie. Winter was outside, carrying the scent of melting snow. Ahead of us, the horizon was gray, subdued. The radio was playing even though it would run down the battery, some antiquated jazz our parents listened to that had nothing to do with us.

I looked at Claudine. Her face was thinner, her lips chapped and dry beneath her lipstick. She had borrowed money from her best friend, Renee, to help pay for John Paul's lawyer. Before all this, John Paul had contributed to the household expenses with the money he made working at Moe's Garage. He loved his mother so much that he would have lain down in a sewer filled with rats if he thought it would help her in some way. He had worked on the Karmann Ghia until it was in pristine condition. Claudine sighed. She stubbed out her cigarette. She stared out the window at the changing traffic light, the people bundled up against the cold, crossing Buoy Boulevard. 'I've just come from the lawyer,' she said. 'He found something, some loophole. He says John Paul could be home by June.' Her voice sounded torn and weary.

'But that's good news, isn't it?' I said. 'June's only three months away.'

Claudine sighed again. She reached for another cigarette from the pack on the console. She lit up, then leaned her head back and exhaled through her nose. 'If we can keep paying him,' she said.

But the lawyer was wrong, because John Paul was home at the end of April. The charges had suddenly been dropped. Nobody knew why and nobody cared. We had never known the girl and now her imprint disappeared from everyone's life but John Paul's. Claudine and Charlie wanted to sue the girl's family for defamation of character but John Paul begged them to let it go. He didn't want things dragging out. He wanted to get on with his life. For his homecoming, Claudine baked a Basque cake with white icing, covered with so many candles their wax melted into the frosting. John Paul sat between Claudine and Marcel, holding their hands, beaming. But it wasn't until the last week in May that Marcel opened her eyes one morning and could see again.

It was in our last year of high school that Claudine began to talk of leaving. She would be moving around the kitchen in that quick way she had and begin muttering. She muttered while preparing breakfast, setting dinner on the table, driving us to the movies, her murmur soft beneath the radio static. While she picked up Charlie's squat glass, filled with straight gin, and wiped the wet rings off the glass coffee table. We overheard her on the phone with her friend Renee. 'Now that John Paul is out, eh?' she said. 'I'm waiting for Marcel to finish school and then we'll see.' She finally found a job as a receptionist at the local law firm of McGonigle & Testa. Her hours were from eight to four but she was seldom home before six. 'Are they paying you overtime?' Charlie asked, sitting in his club chair, one ankle crossed over his knee.

Claudine nodded. 'Time and a half,' she said, her face hidden in the closet as she hung up her coat. Then she'd pad into the kitchen in her panty hose, leaving her high heels upright in the middle of the living room, looking as though they were waiting for someone to step into them and take off into the night.

It was still early in our senior year when Marcel met James. He lived in the same small New England town as Claudine's old friends and they had asked her to have him to lunch or dinner while he was in New York for a training. James was tall and thin and nice-looking in a way you might not remember after he left the room, but when he looked at Marcel his face lit up. He had a wonderful smile.

Marcel liked him. She liked that he was so respectful, so deferential, holding her elbow when they walked down the porch steps to take a walk by the bay after dinner. She liked the nasal twang of his New England accent. I liked him because he made Marcel happy. Claudine liked him for the same reason. 'He's perfect for now,' she said, beaming, spreading a freshly baked apple tart with real cream that she'd begun whipping before dinner. While he was in New York, either he'd take the train down to Elephant Beach or Marcel would take the train to the city and they'd walk around Manhattan, see movies, go to dinner in the Village. Once or twice I went with her, and James was always so well-bred and polite; 'Here's both my girls,' he'd declare, as we walked toward him in the waiting room at Penn Station. But the way his eyes lit on Marcel, the way he'd watch her face as she spoke even the simplest phrase, such as, 'The train was late taking off,' made me feel lonely, so I left the two of them to each other and spent more time around Comanche Street, hoping to overhear some news, maybe catch Conor while he was reading snatches of Luke's infrequent letters home. When James left for another station on Cape Cod, Marcel went to visit him one weekend a month. She loved going up to the Cape. She never felt like she was leaving anything behind.

Claudine's muttering reached full tilt right before New Year's. She would talk of starting a new life someplace and Charlie would either laugh and try to crack a joke or he'd get up and leave the room, carrying his drink with him. If he was home, that is; most nights, he'd take taxis to the Treasure Chest. Marcel said he came home late, after she'd fallen asleep, and that one or two nights he hadn't come home at all, claiming to have slept in the truck in the driveway so he wouldn't wake anyone up coming into the house.

Charlie's absence didn't seem to bother Claudine in the least. She'd work late and come home bright-eyed and breathless when she should have been tired, carrying a rotisserie chicken from the A&P instead of preparing crab stew or shellfish and rice. Some nights she would take Marcel to Essie's Diner beneath the bridge for dinner, saying that since it was just the two of them it didn't pay to fuss, that she would cook something special over the weekend, when John Paul came home. He had moved into the city and was living in a sublet on St. Mark's Place, driving a cab and taking a film course at New York University. Marcel didn't care about a special dinner because those nights at the diner were special times, when she and Claudine were like girlfriends instead of mother and daughter, sitting over their hot turkey sandwiches and cups of coffee, smoking their after-dinner cigarettes. Marcel loved when her mother would put her hand against her cheek, gaze into her eyes, ask her about school, about James. But perhaps the rebellion began on those smoky winter nights at Essie's, when you could barely see out the windows because of the steam heat rising and the fog in the harbor. Claudine would nod and smile, pleased to see Marcel happy again, and say, 'Yes, yes, he's a very nice young man, he's fine for now,' and Marcel, annoyed, finally asked, 'What do you mean, "Fine for now"? Why do you always say that?' Claudine, astute enough to realize her mistake, would laugh and wave her fingers for the waitress. 'Never mind, never mind,' she'd say gaily. 'You're smiling again, that's the main thing.' And she'd order a piece of warm blueberry pie with vanilla ice cream for them to share, and more coffee, if it was fresh. Afterward, Claudine stopped saying that James was fine for now, but Marcel's resentment had already taken root. She felt that her mother, who could read everyone's future in the cards, including her own, was denying her daughter a destiny.

On those nights when Charlie was at the Treasure Chest,

and Marcel was in her room, talking long-distance on the phone to James, Claudine would sit up, reading her own cards, poring over maps that had been stored in the basement, pinpointing destinations. She didn't want to head back to the Basque region, as her memories were war-torn and her family mostly gone, having either died or moved away. She planned to save until she had enough for a plane ticket, and longed for Italy or Paris or the French Riviera, but wanted a place where her money would last until she found a job and an apartment and the great romance that she felt she deserved after so many barren years, a great romance with someone who would become the love of her life, confirmed when the cards turned up the King of Clubs: a kind man, loyal, loving, trustworthy. A king among men.

⁓ᴑ⁓

It was a long winter, filled with black ice and snowdrifts. It snowed a great deal, leaving everyone housebound and getting on one another's nerves. It was during this time that Claudine became snappish, her patience more starched and fragile in the aftermath of the terrible times the Brennan family had endured. 'Inside,' she would yell at Charlie, pointing toward the living room with the knife she was using to mince shallots. 'You go your way, I go mine, at least until dinner is ready.' Or else she would follow Marcel around the room with her eyes until Marcel would blurt out, 'What?' Then Claudine would sigh and shake her head and turn back to her cards or her maps or her travel magazines. And for the first time Marcel could remember, Claudine yelled at John Paul, over the phone.

'What do you mean, you're not coming home?' she screamed into the receiver. 'When you needed me, I was there for you, eh? I lived for you. Now that I need you, you disappear?' John Paul was happy living in the city, where no one knew who he was or what had happened to him. He didn't like coming back to Elephant Beach. He said that every time he got off the train at the station, he could feel his heart sink like a punctured balloon. Every week that he didn't come home, he mailed money to Claudine, to help pay back the lawyer. Claudine would open the envelope, smile wistfully, and tuck the bills into her purse before turning back to a Victoria Holt novel that had been in all the drugstores the previous summer. Romance novels were one of Claudine's new passions, Marcel said; she was always beginning or finishing one. They all had the same pictures of bursting bodices and wild embraces on the front cover.

When she could get through, Marcel would climb over dirty snowdrifts to my house to escape her own. My parents either didn't remember their edict about not wanting me to see her or they didn't care to enforce it, now that John Paul had been acquitted.

'I feel like she blames me for something,' she said, sitting in the rocking chair in my bedroom, watching the snow fall through the window.

'What could she possibly blame you for?' I asked.

She sighed. 'I don't know, being here, I guess,' she said. 'I mean, it's over between her and my father, I know that.' We were silent for a minute.

'Are you sad?' I asked her. I was, even though I knew what she said was true. Charlie never told stories anymore. He never cracked jokes or did more than stumble from room to room. Sometimes when he drank, tears would roll down his face, which no one would acknowledge.

Marcel sighed again. 'I was, but not anymore. It would be worse if I didn't have James.'

I looked at her. 'Do you love him? I mean, are you in love with him?'

She smiled. 'I love him,' she said simply. 'How could I not? No one's ever been this good to me. Not that I've dated that many other guys, but—' She shrugged.

'Do you think it would be different if he lived closer?' I asked. 'I mean, if you saw him all the time and shit?'

'You mean like absence makes the heart grow fonder?' She wrinkled her nose. 'I don't know. He was here that one time for three weeks and I didn't get sick of him. I mean, what about you and Luke? You don't see him ever, and look at how you feel.'

'There is no me and Luke,' I said. 'Yet.' The thought of having Luke around all the time, of having him for myself, was so unreal I couldn't get my mind around it. It seemed too marvelous a thing to ever happen.

Marcel shrugged again. 'I miss him when he's not here,' she said. 'I wish we were together. He talks about later, you know, when I finish school.'

'How is school?' I asked. Marcel had missed a lot of time due to her hysterical blindness, and had been having trouble catching up. When given the option, she'd enrolled in the new alternative high school, which had a reputation as being a haven for kids who were troublemakers. 'Is it bullshit like they say? Not that Elephant Beach High is—'

Marcel laughed. 'What, are you afraid of hurting my feelings?

Yeah, it's bullshit. I mean, we're supposed to be prepping for exit exams and they do things like ask us to write a poem about the beach at midnight. To describe how the moon looks on the water. Shit like that. At this point, it's cool as long as I get my diploma.' She looked at me, turning serious. 'James is – he's like my family now,' she said. 'Like you are, only different. You know I love you, but—'

And suddenly she was weeping, her face crumpling like Christmas tissue paper, and then her head was in her hands, tears leaking through her fingers. I jumped off the bed and went and knelt in front of the rocking chair my parents had given me for my sixteenth birthday. I looked up into her face and put her hands in mine.

'I feel like I'm in the way,' she said, her voice cracking. 'Like, okay, man, I get that she doesn't love my father anymore. And John Paul, he was always her love child and you know I love my brother, man, but he's gone, too.' She stopped crying, wiping her eyes with her hands. 'I feel like she thinks I'm keeping her from going away to lead this whole new life, away from all of us.'

'She wouldn't leave you alone, you know she'd never do that,' I said. But then I thought about the maps, the cards, the working late, and I knew I was only talking about my own life, my own mother. It was something she'd never do, but I couldn't be sure about Claudine.

Marcel sighed. I gave her a handful of Kleenex from the box on my night table, but she already looked clear-eyed again, her face peaceful, serene. She took the tissues and smiled. She took my hand. 'I'll always remember how you sat by my bed and read to me when I couldn't see,' she said.

'Now you're the one who sounds like they're saying good-bye,' I said. 'Are you and James thinking about, like, getting married? Are you—'

'We talk about it,' she said. 'We do. He has two more years in the—'

'Would you move away?' I asked. My stomach was jumping like it always did when I was nervous or frightened.

Marcel gazed out the window. The snow had stopped. Outside, the sky looked hushed and empty. 'Away from what?' she asked, and her voice had a bitter, grown-up quality I had never heard before.

'But your mother,' I started, and then said, 'Claudine, I mean, it's weird that if she wants you out of the way, she's never seemed to – she never talks about James like he's – like he's permanent, you know what I mean?'

Marcel made a face, shook her head. 'Claudine likes to think she's in charge of everyone's future, but she's not,' she said. 'She's certainly not in charge of mine.'

'Marcel—'

'Come on,' she said, standing so quickly that the rocking chair rocked backward into the bookcase. 'Let's walk to the bay if it's not too bad out.' She opened the closet to get her coat. Somewhere inside me, I thought I heard a door close.

Marcel waited until the weekend after graduation to elope with James. When I went to visit, my father insisted on dropping me off at the Port Authority bus station, insisted on coming in with me so that I wouldn't get abducted by a pimp or a pervert. I refused his offer of buying my bus ticket, proud that I could pay for it out of my earnings from the A&P. He looked a little lost then, and I felt sorry for him without knowing why. You'd think he'd be happy to have a daughter who could pay for her own ticket. Right before I got on the bus, he stuffed twenty dollars into the sleeve of my purse, and waved my hand away when I tried to give it back. He hugged me once, very quickly; he wasn't one to show emotion. When the bus pulled away, my father was still standing there, watching. I waved once but he must not have seen me, because he didn't wave back. It reminded me of that morning at the Elephant Beach train station, when Liz and I were taking the bus to Silverwood, and Mitch handed me the bill, told me to buy some lunch. Like they thought that money was the only thing they had to give you that would keep you safe.

Marcel and James were living in Buzzards Bay, near the Coast Guard station. It was a crammed and crazy place, with every fast-food restaurant you could imagine on one strip. But the apartment was cozy, on a residential street, one bedroom and a living room with orange curtains Marcel had made herself and a small kitchen that had only a breakfast bar that we never used because every morning we'd drive to the nearby International House of Pancakes, where we'd order pancake platters and hot apple pie à la mode for dessert. James and Marcel sat together, clowning around, feeding each other bites of pie from the same fork. James insisted on paying, even when I waved my father's twenty-dollar bill in front of them. 'You're our guest,' he said, gallantly, kissing the top of Marcel's curls, throwing change on the table for the tip.

~

They appeared happy, and I was glad, until Saturday night when we went to the Red Parrot Tavern and James got mad when a good-looking guy asked Marcel to dance and accused her of flirting because she smiled when she shook her head no. We left early and they stayed in the parking lot arguing while I used Marcel's keys to get into the apartment. When they came in about a half hour later, Marcel was walking ahead of James, her head down, buried in her sweatshirt. James's lips were curled somewhere between a sneer and a smirk, and for the first time I thought about how his eyes seemed to harden when he drank beer. I felt a flash of coldness then, because how well, really, did any of us know James, including Marcel? He might be less than a complete stranger, but he wasn't one of us. They walked into the bedroom and closed the door without saying good night. I sat up on the pullout couch, smoking, thinking of what a good time I'd had at the Red Parrot until James got angry, drinking whiskey sours in a bar where absolutely nobody knew me, where I could be anything, anyone I wanted. I thought about Luke in places like the Red Parrot, asking strange girls to dance the way men had asked me. One guy, Tony, had politely asked to buy me a drink. 'Just a drink and a dance,' he reassured me. 'I'm engaged to my girl back in Valdosta and I miss her and she wouldn't mind, she knows I'm lonely, and damn, girl, please let me have the pleasure of buying a fine-looking lady like you a drink!' I wondered if Luke said things like that to strange girls in bars. I wished he'd say something like that to me.

The next morning, I heard James leave for the Coast Guard station; he'd said he had to fill out a report and afterward we'd go out for Sunday breakfast, then hit the beach. There was to be a barbecue that night at somebody's house and then I'd be leaving the next day. I looked out the orange-skirted windows. The sky was battleship gray, but summer weather was always tricky; by noon, the sun could be shining. I didn't want to smoke until I'd had my coffee. Marcel came walking out of the bedroom just as I was about to knock. She was wearing loose drawstring pants and one of James's tee shirts. She looked pretty and sleepy and too young to be married.

'You look too young to be married,' I told her. She smiled tightly, then went to the narrow little kitchen and began making coffee. Once it was plugged in and perking, she came and lay down next to me on the pullout couch.

'Sorry about last night,' she said, staring up at the ceiling.

I snorted. 'For what, man? You didn't do anything wrong.'

'I just hope it wasn't too weird for you.'

'Did you forget where we come from? Nothing's too weird after Elephant Beach.' She smiled. 'Did you kiss and make up?' I asked.

She sighed and shook her head quickly, so that her curls covered her face.

'Are you crying?' I asked.

She shook her head again. 'It happens every time we go out,' she said. 'He has three beers and thinks I'm flirting with everyone in the place, or every guy is after me. At home he's fine, it's good, it's just – he doesn't want me to work, he doesn't like me going out by myself, it's hard to make friends. He was still mad this morning. He won't talk to me, sometimes the whole next day, into the night. He says I'm stubborn, but it's him.' She took a cigarette from my pack on the couch. 'I'm just sick of apologizing for shit I didn't do.' She was quiet. We could hear the coffee gurgling in the background. 'Did I make a mistake?' she whispered.

I started to say no, but stopped. 'Everyone has fights,' I said, patting her shoulder. I was glad when she closed her eyes, even when tears started trickling from their corners. Her wide-open stare had taken me back to those terrible months when she couldn't see.

When I returned to Elephant Beach, Claudine had me over to dinner. She made a rice and lamb *sofrito* that was my favorite of her Basque dishes, and afterward Charlie retired to the living room with his drink until it was time to head over to the Treasure Chest. Claudine poured us both a cognac in the tiny crystal shot glasses her mother had given her when she left for America. I felt very grown-up and sophisticated sitting at the kitchen table, with the day's last light painting rainbows on the walls. Claudine was wearing her hair piled on top of her head and had on a scoop-neck black blouse. She looked like she belonged more in a movie that you'd see at the City Cinema, where John Paul had taken me and Marcel to see *Pink Flamingos*. She took a delicate sip of the cognac, turned to me, and said, 'So.'

'"So" what?' I asked, though of course I knew. I knew she wanted to pump me about Marcel and James, and Marcel and I had discussed this and what I would tell her. I described the apartment, the orange curtains Marcel had made herself, how they held hands in the car, how they kissed over break-fast at the International House of Pancakes. I did not tell her about their quarrel, or how James had indeed stayed mad the next day, not talking to either of us until Marcel said we wouldn't go to the barbecue at his friend's house unless he stopped pouting.

'So? You really think she's happy with him?' Claudine asked anxiously.

'I think it's fine for now, Claudine,' I said.

She looked deeply into my eyes and then took my hands in her own. She told me that in October, she would be moving to Montreal. It seemed the perfect cross section of all she was looking for: very cosmopolitan without being intimidating, less expensive than Venice or Paris; she would understand both languages, English and French, which would help her find a job, and she had distant cousins living there that she'd contacted, who'd seemed glad to hear from her and had already extended an invitation to stay with them while she looked for an apartment. By the fall, she'd have enough saved from her job at McGonigle & Testa for a plane ticket and to see her through until she began working. I listened, though I wasn't surprised. It had been in the air for some time now, Claudine's leaving.

'What about Charlie?' I asked her.

Her eyes quickly filled with tears, and then, just as quickly, they disappeared. She sighed. 'That love you feel for your first, eh?' she said. 'You'll always feel it. But love, it's not enough. Time for something new.'

'What will happen to him?' I asked.

'He wants to find a place in the city,' she said. 'John Paul is looking for him, they'll live together, at least for a while. Until John Paul finds a new girl and Charlie finds a new bar to keep him company.' She said this without bitterness, because it was the way of things, really. I wondered that I didn't feel more sadness at losing them, at knowing that in a few months the Brennans would no longer be down the block and some new family would be taking their place. It would be odd to walk by and know that new secrets were breathing behind the door, things I didn't know and would probably never find out. I must have looked sadder than I felt, because suddenly Claudine leaned forward and hugged me, and the smell of her, that biting, ocean smell, made tears come to my own eyes and I hugged her back, hard.

'My dear little girl,' she said softly against my hair, and then pushed forward and took my hands in hers. 'We will still be in touch, eh? You will come visit? When I get settled? You're an adult now. You can come and stay as long as you wish.' She kissed my forehead.

'Thank you,' I said. She laughed, and I was glad that she seemed happy. 'Could you read my cards?' I asked her. 'You know, one for the road?'

'Ach!' Claudine let go of my hands, threw her own up in the air. 'No. No more readings. You're a young girl, everything – everything! – is just beginning for you. Let life surprise you.'

I laughed. 'What about you?' I asked. 'Sitting here night

after night, shuffling away? Marcel said you must have read your own cards a thousand times these past few months.'

Claudine laughed, too, and shook her head vehemently, so that tendrils escaped from her piled-up hair and fell over her forehead. 'Not anymore,' she said. 'Not since I made my decision. When you know what you're doing, you don't need the cards.' She took my hands in hers again. 'No more about this boy, eh? Over and over again, asking the same question. You go up to him and you tell him that you want him. No more waiting. You go out and live life, eh? Remember: You live life or it lives you.'

～ᶜ～

Before it was so many years later and Claudine had finally left the man she'd met in Montreal and would stay with for thirty years, who treated her neither well nor badly but with an indifference that made her flail at him, rage at him, and finally turn from him toward the wine, so that her nightly glass or two became a half carafe and then a full carafe and then out to the cafés if she hadn't yet passed out; before the phlebitis took over and she could barely leave her little apartment above the bakery in Montreal that the owners had let her hold on to all those years out of kindness; before Marcel, now living in Albuquerque, close to her sons, stopped answering the phone when her mother called, weary of the litany of complaints and criticism she had endured for too many years; before everything that was to happen had happened, that day in October, at Kennedy Airport, Claudine looked so radiant that even people running toward their gates, afraid of missing their flights, paused to look at her. I drove over with them, Claudine and Charlie and John Paul and Marcel, who'd taken the bus down from the Cape alone, and met Claudine's best friend, Renee, and Renee's husband, Max, in the boarding lounge. Charlie was red-faced and teary, but Renee and Max had brought champagne and Dixie cups, and we sat at a small constellation of chairs and couches and toasted to Claudine's new life. When it was time to board the plane, Claudine hugged all of us one by one, clinging to us, crying, and when she finally broke away from John Paul, who she of course hugged for the longest, she ran toward her gate, the last one to go through, and when she turned back to blow one last kiss, her face, oh, her face! If you could have seen her!

THIRTEEN

the feeney sisters forever

'I cannot believe this is still dragging on,' Georgie said. He was slowly scrolling the Rod Stewart poster off the wall of his bedroom, careful not to take the paint off with the Scotch tape. 'You should have at least been screwing his brains out by now.'

'It's not that easy.' I sighed.

The room was almost bare. I'd been at Georgie's since eleven that morning, helping him pack for the move into Manhattan. Through Ray Mackey's cousin's girlfriend, he'd found an apartment in Greenwich Village, on Sullivan Street. It was a fourth-floor walk-up with a tiny fireplace and a bathtub in the kitchen, where Georgie couldn't wait to have sex with a tall, dark stranger.

'Darling, nothing's that easy,' Georgie said dramatically, dragging his syllables. 'But life is a banquet, do you want to be a starving sucker for the rest of your life?' He turned toward me and bowed. 'Go to him, dearest; love him. Love him forever and ask nothing in return.'

'Where is that from?' I asked.

Georgie straightened up and shrugged. 'I have no idea,' he said. He looked around at the bare walls, the sagging double bed that he refused to bring with him to the new apartment. Then he looked down at the Rod Stewart poster in his hands. He rolled it up and gently pushed it into a cardboard cylinder. 'I'm thinking of having it framed,' he said.

'So Rod the God will be your new roommate?' I asked.

'I could certainly do worse.' Georgie put the poster into a box that held all the others. 'Hang tight, I have to take a leak,' he said, and went out the door to the bathroom down the hall.

It was better teasing Georgie than concentrating on his leaving; I was afraid I might start crying and then he might and it would start a whole hullabaloo. It wasn't like I hung out with him all the time but I always knew he was there: at his house, at MarioEstelle's, on the East Turn bus, which he drove through the opposite end of town. One night last week, I'd met him at the bus station for the last run of his shift, and we'd each drunk a beer and then shared a joint and ended up singing 'I Only Want to Be with You' at the top of our lungs until he pulled into the station. Walking home through the silent town, the summer air was sweet and clear and smelled of honeysuckle and fresh-cut grass and I wondered why anyone wanted to leave Elephant Beach for the tar-stained streets of the city.

I looked around the bedroom. It badly needed a paint job and the splotches of white left by the posters only made it more obvious. I hadn't thought he'd have that much to pack, but there were boxes and half-filled black plastic garbage bags all over the place. I wanted to hurry up and finish so I'd be gone before Fiona Feeney and her crazy sisters showed up to drive him into the city. They made me nervous. I had once seen Fiona throw Ella Hamilton over a table in the lunchroom during the race riots, the year she was a senior and I was a sophomore. Ella lay on the floor, her body looking bruised and crooked, and Fiona would have still kept going if the cops hadn't come and her sister Moira hadn't pulled her away. I didn't want to drive into the city with them, because I'd have to drive back with them alone, without Georgie's protection, and who knew what might happen.

I looked up. Georgie was standing in the doorway, watching me.

'What?' I asked.

'I was just remembering the first time I saw you on Comanche Beach. It was one of the Christmas tree bonfires, around '69, '70.' He came in and flopped down on his naked bed. In January, we would drag all the discarded Christmas trees left out on the curb for trash pickup down to the beach and try to light a fire; the trees never burned well and usually sizzled out slowly, a smoldering hunk of branches. Still, every year, we'd all chip in for a case of Budweiser and go back down the beach and do the same thing. I wondered what would happen this year, now that we were out of school and people were scattering to the wind.

'That first night you came down with Liz, and you were standing there in that gray coat with the belt in the back that I hated, looking so scared and lost by the firelight—'

'And you came up to me and asked would I like a beer to go with my cigarette,' I said. I was ashamed to remember that night, because I'd wished someone else had come over to offer me a beer, Billy or Conor or one of Nanny's cousins, someone who people didn't roll their eyes about behind his back.

'I recognized a kindred spirit,' Georgie said, and then looked at my face and said, 'Oh for God's sake, I didn't mean it that way. And darling, you needn't look so stricken; being of another persuasion, so to speak, is not exactly a fate worse than death, contrary to popular local opinion. What I meant was—'

'I know what you meant,' I said, and I did. Because even though Georgie had lived in the Trunk all his life and was best friends with the Feeney sisters, he'd always been an outsider, too. It was why we'd become friends in the first place. I went over to the bed and flopped down next to him.

Georgie lit a cigarette, taking an old seashell from under the bed to use as an ashtray. 'You want the truth, I never understood why you were so hot to hang around down here in the first place,' he said. I wanted to tell him how it was; how the Trunk was a place where everyone's footsteps seemed to fit so firmly, but then I thought about Georgie's footsteps and the scar on his forehead, a souvenir from the night when Jimmy Murphy and the Hitter boys had jumped all over his face.

'I'll miss you,' I said, taking his hand, guiding the tip of his cigarette to light my own. I couldn't help it; I was never good at hiding my feelings beyond a certain point.

'I'll miss me, too,' he said in his airy-fairy voice, gazing up at the ceiling. 'I'll always have a great deal of affection for who I was. But now it's time to leave all that behind. Because really,' he said, touching his forehead, 'next time I might not be so lucky.'

I leaned over and kissed his cheek. He put his fingers over mine and said dramatically, 'We'll always have Paris.'

'Here's looking at you, kid,' I said, and before my voice could become more wobbly, we heard a soft stampede up the staircase and Fiona Feeney and her sister Moira were in the room, dressed in cutoffs and beach thongs, Fiona's hair wrapped in huge curlers. 'We ready to get this show on the road or what?' she said, and then laughed her crazy laugh that sounded like machine-gun fire.

Georgie sprang up off the bed. 'Please tell me you are not driving me into the city looking like that,' he said, horrified. 'I'm starting a new life in Greenwich Village, not the A&P parking lot.'

'Relax, Georgina,' Fiona said, looking around the room, making no move to take off her sunglasses.

'Where's Deirdre?' Georgie asked.

'Indisposed,' Moira said, lighting a cigarette. 'Had a rough night.'

'Besides, we got what's-her-name over here,' Fiona said, turning toward me. 'Katie, right?'

I nodded. 'I'll be right back,' I said. 'I'm going downstairs to get a drink of water.' I slid past Moira, who watched me with her cold gray eyes. Deirdre was beautiful, Fiona was crazy, but Moira was the quiet, dangerous one, waiting and watching and then suddenly pouncing when you least expected it. One time, in the smoking bathroom at school, Debbie Maurer had asked her for a drag of her cigarette; Moira had silently handed it over, and when Debbie took a second drag, Moira grabbed the cigarette back so quickly that Debbie had to frantically wave the sparks away from her face. Moira

227

snapped, 'You're going to take two fucking drags, say so.' She became more animated when she drank, but you never knew which way that was going to go, either. She could just as easily do a striptease in the basement of St. Timothy's Church as punch somebody in the mouth. There was something smoldering about Moira; you felt that flames could burst through her pale skin at any moment and paint the air with fire.

I went downstairs to the big yellow kitchen. Sissie, Georgie's grandmother, was at the refrigerator, putting ice cubes into a pitcher of tea.

'How's the packing going?' she asked in her kindly voice.

'It's going,' I said. 'What smells so good?'

'Saints preserve us!' She hurried over to the stove, took two pot holders from a basket on the counter and opened the oven. She slid a tray of cookies out and put it across two burners. 'Good thing you said something, or I would have let them burn.' She smiled at me. 'Getting absentminded in my old age.' She took the cookies and put them to cool on the windowsill. 'Chocolate chip oatmeal,' she said, turning off the oven, taking a spatula from the drawer. 'Off the recipe from the Quaker Oats box. Georgie's favorite, since he was a little boy.' She began loosening the cookies from the baking sheet, sliding them onto a pretty blue plate. 'Figured I'd give him a little care package to take with him so he won't get to missing us too much.' She sighed. 'Poor Bobby left here crying this morning. It's always a – a trauma, you know, when the first one leaves the nest.'

'Have you always lived in Elephant Beach, Sissie?' I asked. She carried the plate of cookies over to the kitchen table and began packing them in a Christmas tin, the kind my parents brought to holiday parties and open houses on New Year's Day.

'Goodness no,' she said. 'We moved here back in, what was it now, '49, after the war. From the West Side, Forty-third and Ninth Avenue. I was always a small-town girl at heart, couldn't wait to leave the city.' She left a few cookies on the plate, then placed the top firmly on the tin, pushing it down carefully to make sure it was sealed. 'And now he wants to go back to that jungle.' She shuddered.

'He likes the city,' I said. 'He's been talking about it for ages.'

She nodded and began moving briskly around the kitchen. 'Well, to each his own, I always say. And really, it's for the best.' She opened a drawer and took out a paper shopping bag. She patted the cookie tin fondly, as though it was human, and put it in the bag. 'You know his father can't stand the sight of him,' she said matter-of-factly. She moved over to the sink and began washing the cookie tray. I watched her for a moment, then said, 'I'll be outside if anyone's looking,' and went out the side door and around the front and sat on the stoop.

Through the open window upstairs, I could hear Fiona's madwoman laugh bouncing off the walls. I lit a cigarette and watched the sky for a while. They said everything came in threes: first Maggie and Matty, then Ginger, and now Georgie. It was unsettling, all this leaving; it seemed more suited to the fall, when the sand began to cool and the wind lifted the curtain of heat and you could almost smell change in the air.

I was about to head back upstairs and say a final good-bye to Georgie, even though we'd planned an outing in the city once he got settled, when I heard footsteps through the screen door on the porch and Fiona came bounding outside, carrying a plastic bag over her shoulder. 'Give me a hand with this,' she said, her voice scratched and blotchy, and I realized she was crying. I had never seen Fiona cry before. She opened the trunk of the car and started jamming things around, rearranging boxes, squeezing the garbage bags in wherever they would fit. At one point she gazed up at the house and sighed. 'I'm gonna miss the shit out of him,' she said. 'But there's nothing for him out here, you know what I'm saying?' She paused to put a cigarette between her lips, and stood looking at the tightly packed trunk.

'You did a great job,' I said, because it was true and I had no idea what else to say to her.

Fiona nodded. 'I've got good organization skills,' she said. 'That's what my boss says. He's giving me a promotion which, hey, I could use the money, because come next winter, I'm blowing this pop shop for good.'

I looked at her, startled. Fiona had practically put people in the hospital for bad-mouthing the Trunk; she'd even gone after teachers who made snide remarks. I'd always thought of her as a lifer, someone who would die on her stool at the counter in MarioEstelle's. She was still working at the insurance agency in town and I assumed the night classes she was taking were in secretarial administration. That's what most of the Trunk girls went to Carver Community College for. Then I remembered how when she'd broken up with Mickey Fallon, he'd gone on a three-day bender and stood outside her house and yelled her name so that the whole street could hear. She'd never even opened the window.

'Where will you go?' I asked.

'Miami Dade,' Fiona said, promptly. 'They'll take my credits from Carver, I already checked. Carver has a great transfer rate, one of the highest in the country, so I can get my associate's degree down there. We have people in that part of Florida, my mother's cousins, so I'll have family close by. It's nice. I went down for my vacation in April. You ever been?'

'No,' I said.

'It's cool,' she said. 'Funky. Too many spics, but they're Cubans, at least they look white. The city's too much for me, man. Miami's more like a – a small-town city. Plus you got the beach, so it's, you know, it's like home, but you're still way the hell out of this shithole.'

I looked at her. 'What are you going to get your degree in?'

She lifted her face to the sun. 'Some type of administration,' she said. 'Hospital, public health, some shit like that. I don't mind starting at the bottom, but eventually I got to run the show, know what I'm saying? I wasn't meant to take orders. That's not for me.'

'That's – that's great,' I said. 'I mean, you – I always thought – you always seemed—'

I didn't want to say the wrong thing. With all the Feeney sisters, you never knew what would set them off.

Fiona tossed her head. She'd taken out the curlers and her hair bounced down her shoulders, clean-smelling and shiny. She'd stopped teasing it into a ratty bird's nest. She took off her sunglasses and through the heavy black streaks of her mascara, the bruise beneath her left eye winced in the sunlight. 'You know how I got this? That motherfucker Jimmy Murphy was whaling on my sister Deirdre and I got in the middle of it. And it wasn't the first time, and it won't be the last and it started when they were going out and still she went ahead and married that animal. What?' she said, staring at me, her eyes searching my face.

'Nothing,' I said. 'I'm just – it's just that Deirdre's so – I mean, it was like she could have had anybody.' The Feeney sisters were all good-looking but Deirdre was truly black-Irish beautiful. Sometimes in church, if the light coming through the stained glass windows hit her face a certain way, everyone stared at her instead of whichever priest was serving mass that Sunday.

Fiona snorted. '"She could have had anybody,"' she said. 'Who? Who's better? They're all the same, think they can go to church on Sunday and eat the wafer and all is forgiven.' She shook her head. 'And people wonder why I drink.' Her face looked softer, sadder for a moment. But when she spoke, her voice was edged with contempt. 'She's just like my mother, Deirdre. But that shit's not for me. That's why I'm leaving.' She turned and looked at me. 'You're smart, you'll do the same.'

Behind us, the screen door slammed. 'What's the big gabfest down here?' Moira said, coming up behind us with a box of LPs. She looked at me accusingly. Georgie was behind Moira, his arms full of quilts. We spent the next minutes packing the car, making room for the boxes, spreading the quilts over the back of the trunk. Finally, Fiona slammed the door shut. She turned to Georgie. 'So that's it, right?'

'Just let me go back up and do one more—'

'One more,' Fiona said, holding up one finger. 'One. And Moira, you go with him, make sure he doesn't linger.' She looked at her watch. 'And then let's get this show on the road.' She put her sunglasses back on, the crest of the bruise visible below the rim. She turned to look at me. 'You're coming with us, right?'

'Of course,' I said. I hadn't known I was going to say that until the words were out of my mouth. I hadn't known I wanted to go until I said the words.

'Darling!' Georgie said delightedly, clapping his hands.

'Shit!' Fiona exclaimed. 'Where's the Cold Duck? Moira, what'd we do with the Cold Duck?'

Moira opened the passenger side of the car, knelt down and began feeling around. She came back up, holding a shopping bag from Carelli's Liquor Store and a paper bag from Godwin's Party Supplies. 'Plastic wineglasses,' she said triumphantly. 'None of that Dixie cup shit. Shows we got class.'

'We should have remembered to put it in the fridge until it was time to leave,' Fiona said.

Georgie peered into the bag from Carelli's. 'Three bottles?' he asked skeptically.

'In case we hit traffic,' Moira explained.

At the exit for the Midtown Tunnel, Georgie began crying.

'Did I call it or what?' Fiona asked, looking at her sister in the rearview mirror. 'I win the pool.'

'We bet that he'd start bawling,' Moira explained. 'I said he'd start when we pulled away from the house, Fiona said before we hit the tunnel.' Georgie ignored them and wept. He wept all the way through the tunnel, at times drowning out the radio. We were listening to the oldies station; to the

Hitters, there was no other music. They thought Jimi Hendrix was a communist because of his hair. It was like Cousin Brucie was in the car with us, playing 'See You in September' and "Sealed with a Kiss'; when he played 'Under the Boardwalk,' I thought we'd have to take Georgie to the hospital. 'It makes me remember that summer,' he sobbed. 'That summer we graduated and I was trying to fall in love with Reeny Coffin, but I just couldn't do it.'

'Too bad, Georgina,' Fiona said, illegally changing lanes. 'If she hadn't been such a crazy bitch, it might have been a whole different life story for you.'

'Oh, what have I done? What have I done?' Georgie moaned.

'Shut up and drink,' Moira said, pouring more Cold Duck for everyone. She looked relaxed and happy. I'd never seen her look this happy before; it must have been the Cold Duck. I was feeling it myself. I didn't like the taste of beer and I could tolerate some kinds of liquor, but this was different. I felt lighter, as though I was floating in place. I wasn't afraid of the Feeney sisters anymore. I wasn't afraid Moira would suddenly whip around and bash my teeth in with an empty bottle. I held my plastic wineglass out for more. Outside, the sky was sun-soaked, golden behind the buildings that lined the streets.

'Sissie's Sunday morning pancakes,' Georgie sobbed. 'How will I live without Sissie's Sunday morning pancakes?'

'You'll get on the fucking train and come down to the Beach for breakfast,' Fiona said. 'Am I better off on Broadway or should I go across Fourteenth Street?'

'Take Broadway,' Georgie sniffled. 'You can take it straight down, then turn on Houston.'

Right then 'Big Girls Don't Cry' by the Four Seasons came

on, and the Feeney sisters began hooting like deranged owls. 'How perfect is this?' Moira screeched, spilling sparkling wine on the floor of the car as she poured another round.

'This one's for you, Georgina,' Fiona said, plucking another Kleenex from the dashboard and throwing it at him, and we all began singing, 'Bi-iiig girls doooon't cri-yi-yi, they don't cry,' and even Georgie blew his nose and joined in. At the end, we all applauded and cheered.

'Will you call me up and sing to me sometime?' Georgie implored us all, twisting around to look at me and Moira. 'So I don't get too lonely?'

'Sing to you? What did we just spend two hours packing that Goddamned stereo in towels for?' Moira asked. 'Fi, pull over for a second.'

Fiona swerved into the next lane, leaving behind an echo of madly honking horns.

'Careful,' Georgie warned. 'This is the big city. We don't know the entire police force here.'

'Don't be such a fucking worrywart,' Fiona said.

'Pull over, Fi,' Moira said, trying to a light a cigarette.

'I'm trying, for chrissake,' Fiona said, careening across the next two lanes, then making a right turn.

'I won't make it to the apartment alive,' Georgie moaned.

Fiona parked in front of a deli with a neon Miller sign. She put her sunglasses on top of her head. We rolled down the windows and blasts of hot air wove around us. The street looked sad and sinister. A young Puerto Rican boy with Ring Ding frosting around his mouth stared at us from the doorway of the deli. I smiled at him and he ran inside.

Moira topped us all off with the last of the Cold Duck. She

clinked her plastic wineglass with Georgie's first, then Fiona's, then mine. She raised it high in the air. 'The Feeney sisters forever,' she said.

'And their friends,' said Fiona. We all toasted and drank, and when I caught Fiona's face in the rearview mirror, she winked at me with her good eye and then threw her plastic wineglass out the window and started putting the car in drive for the last lap of the journey to Georgie's new home.

'Let's take a picture,' Moira said suddenly.

Georgie groaned.

'Fiona? The light's so good now. Where's the camera?'

'I have to meet the landlord by seven,' Georgie said, anxiously. 'I don't want to miss him, he's got the keys.'

'We can take a picture when we get there,' Fiona told her sister. 'In front of the building. Or in the apartment, for that matter.'

'No,' Moira said stubbornly. 'Let's take it now.'

'What's the big fucking deal?' Fiona asked.

'Now,' Moira said, and suddenly her face contorted and then she was weeping, violently, her whole body heaving. She turned away from us so that she was facing the street. No one said a word. Moira wrapped her arms around herself, clutching her shaking shoulders. 'Once we get there, it's too fucking final,' she said, her voice low and raspy.

Georgie put his hand on Moira's shoulder. She reached around and grabbed it, holding tightly. Georgie sighed. 'Where's the camera?' he asked.

Fiona, still staring at her sister's back, put the car in park, then reached into the glove compartment and took out a Polaroid Land Camera. She handed it to Georgie.

'C'mon,' he said resignedly, opening the car door. 'But let's make it snappy so I'm not locked out of my own apartment. And we need to find someone to take the picture.'

Moira took the camera from Georgie. Her face looked pale and raw from all the crying; the tears had left white streaks on her skin that looked like runs in a silk stocking. We got out and stood in the space between the car and the deli. The sun was lower now, and the street was empty. Then the Puerto Rican boy came out of the deli, his face wiped free of frosting. Moira walked over to him and began talking. She knelt down in front of him, flipping open the camera, showing him how it worked. She spoke sharply, the way she had in the smoking bathroom at school that day, when Debbie Maurer had taken an extra drag of her cigarette. 'You see what I mean?' she asked impatiently. 'Do you get what I'm saying?'

The boy looked doubtful, his dark eyes troubled. I walked over and knelt in front of him. I felt I should just take the camera from him and offer to take a picture of Georgie and the Feeney sisters; they'd known each other forever and hung out all the time together, and I was outside the frame. But the Cold Duck and the sunshine and the way we had sung together in the car and even Moira's sob storm turned me away from that thought. I showed the boy how to focus through the little window, how to click the button when the picture looked ready. I looked into his beautiful eyes. *'Por favor?'* I asked. His face broke into a smile. He grabbed the camera and put it right up against his eye.

'Watch out he doesn't steal it,' Fiona called from the curb, and I put out my hand and the boy took it and we walked to the empty center of the street. The air was smoke-stained and steamy, and the heat shimmered up from the pavement like a separate layer you could almost walk on. The boy put the camera to his face, and Fiona said, 'Okay, on three!' and the boy looked puzzled, and I began chanting, *'Uno, dos, tres,'* and he smiled again and clicked the camera, and Fiona said, 'Shit, my eyes were closed,' and Moira said, 'Do it again, one more time,' and the boy, eager now, took another picture and then another and then another. He had to take four pictures before we found one that wasn't too light or too dark, where no shadows lay across our faces, where nobody's eyes were closed and everyone remembered to smile and we finally looked the way we wanted to and would never look again. Once we were satisfied, Moira gave the boy three dollars and he stood there clutching the bills, beaming up at us as the sun melted further into the sky. Then he turned and ran back into the deli.

It's a great picture. The way Fiona's hair waves out in the sudden breeze makes her look like a model in a magazine, and you would never know that minutes before it was taken, Moira had cried her heart out in the backseat of the car. I'm kneeling on the hood behind Georgie, with my arms clasped around his neck just like I'm in love with him, and Georgie's smile is so wide, he looks so handsome and happy, that you just want to reach into the photo and kiss him right on the lips. It's a great picture, and if you look at it long enough, in a certain way, you can almost hear us laughing, hear the laughter floating out behind us until it grows fainter and further away, like the memory of a faded scar.

FOURTEEN

those girls from the dunes

In seventh grade, they came to school in cashmere sweaters and silk stockings, wearing suede shoes from Bloomingdale's in the city. Their clothes were never too big, their teeth never crooked; it was as though they lived at the orthodontist and their blinding smiles made you want to bloody their lips. They thought who the hell they were and seemed to exist only to make everyone else feel like shit. Because of them, junior high was brutal, a nightmare, and everything you'd ever believed to be good about yourself got erased, like you were starting life all over again in a gray swamp. 'If I had to live those three years over again, I'd kill myself,' Liz said. 'I'd kill somebody, that's for sure.'

But in high school, everything changed. Those girls from the Dunes stopped shaving their legs and wearing bras. They stopped wearing makeup and, instead of cunning little outfits from Lord & Taylor, with sweaters and kneesocks that matched, they wore ragged jeans and flannel shirts in winter, and cutoffs and flip-flops in summer. They wore red and blue bandannas around their long, shiny hair. They smoked Kools instead of Marlboros and slept with boys, lots of boys, and everyone talked about it but nobody wrote their names on the bathroom wall at the bus station, like they did with Sheila Mooney, who lived in the Trunk and wore her mother's leopard coat to school so that she looked forty instead of sixteen. Nobody called them 'cow' or 'slut' except for us, and even with underarm hair hanging down to their knees, they still ruled the roost. Even when they spouted stupid shit like 'Free Angela!' and 'Power to the People!' and everyone else laughed scornfully, they held their heads high and believed in their words.

Those girls from the Dunes! We envied them, hated them, and wanted to be them, isn't that always the way? It's an old song, because those girls are everywhere, in every story, in every life; fairy-tale princesses living in castles waiting for the prince to come rescue them (and he always does), carried to school by six shining horses and a gilt-edged carriage, or their mothers' Cadillac Coupe DeVilles. Prettier, brighter, lovelier than everyone else, or at least they think so, and they are never fearful of ridicule or laughter or life.

They tried to befriend us, and publicly we cursed them and threatened them in gym class, but at night when they called us, we'd take the phone into the bathroom or the linen closet and speak in whispers, as though talking to an illicit lover. We were jealous over who called whom, and then began fighting over their attention, and finally, because they'd been clever and we hadn't suspected, we realized it was never us they wanted at all, but the boys, our freckled, blue-eyed, shaggy-haired boys, so different from what they were used to, those boys from the Dunes with their soft, pudgy hands, and their juvenile jokes and girlish giggles, who'd never quite lost their baby fat and wore braces well into their teens. Who were polite and respectful and predictably successful as student council presidents and honor roll students, but still their girls turned away, lowering their sights to strong-limbed boys who held after-school jobs instead of attending SAT prep classes and had to buy their own wheels during senior year instead of getting the keys to a Corvette convertible for their eighteenth birthdays. The boys we hung out with, Voodoo and Billy and Conor and them, made rude remarks and raspberries whenever they walked by, but their eyes followed those girls from the school bus windows as the bus pulled away from the curb. They secretly yearned to put their arms around them, to pin them against the brick wall in back of the high school gymnasium, where they could drop their eyes and stammer something that sounded like surrender. We were furious, enraged at those girls for seducing us into submission, then at our boys for defecting to the enemy, and, finally, at ourselves, for our own stupidity. 'How did we not see this coming?' we asked one another in dismay. The answer was so simple it made us want to cry: we wanted to believe they liked us, that they wanted to be our friends.

Those girls from the Dunes! They were used to being the best, even when they weren't, like the time Michele Apton got a D in Algebra and her mother came to school to talk to Miss Fland, who ended up changing Michele's grade to a C+, not like when Gin O'Connor got a D in Home Ec and her father called her onto the enclosed porch and boomed so loud you could have heard him in New Jersey, 'Dumb ass! Who the hell fails Home Ec? You better straighten up and fly right and stop embarrassing your mother.' When Connie Bescht stole Tommy Malone from Edie Cartwright, we all surrounded Edie in the smoking bathroom, saying comforting things like, 'When we get through with her she'll really be singing those bell-bottom blues.' But Edie begged us not to, not to do anything, please, *please*, it would only make things worse. 'They'll just start that "crazy girls from the Trunk" shit again,' she said, her voice hoarse with smoke and tears. 'Trying to make us look like animals next to them.'

'Like fucking Amazons,' we all agreed.

'Besides,' Edie said, blowing her nose, 'Tommy'll come back. He doesn't know it yet, but he will.' And weeks later Tommy did, meekly following Edie through the halls to class, through the streets of the Trunk to her after-school babysitting job, until she finally turned around and shouted, 'What?' And after she'd tortured him sufficiently and finally asked him what made him return ('though I should be asking what made you leave in the first place, asshole'), Tommy answered, 'Because every time I kissed her, afterward I always ended up wanting to punch her in the face.'

And in their senior year, Tina Kravitz took Tootie Malloy away from Vera Maddox, and Tina was brazen about it, bold, stepping right up next to Vera in the smoking bathroom, running her hands through the long, golden tresses that Tootie seemed so crazy about compared to Vera's kinky red mess, like a devil's halo around her head. Everyone expected Vera to flip out, because she and Tootie had been together since ninth grade. But by then, Vera had an eye to the future; 'No kid of mine's going to end up a beer-drinking, glue-sniffing Trunker,' she would say, yanking a comb through her hair in front of the mirror, her cool green eyes shaded and knowing.

While everyone else sat in the back of Mrs. Doulin's Bookkeeping class, making paper airplanes out of the weekly quizzes, Vera sailed through Merchandise Purchasing, earning an A for her efforts. Her steno and typing were so impeccable that she bypassed the traditional Katie Gibbs secretarial training and skipped school one day to ride the Long Island Rail Road into Manhattan and interview at one of the big insurance firms through a contact of her uncle's. She secured a job as junior assistant to one of the vice presidents at a higher salary than anyone had ever heard of, slated to begin a week after graduation. 'You should see this place,' she said excitedly, her face vibrant, her hair gathered in a knot at the nape of her neck that we thought made her look so sophisticated. 'And the men! God, my new boss is so handsome, if he wasn't married I'd be jumping his bones in the supply closet, which, by the way, is bigger than my whole freakin' bedroom.' We laughed, and Tina Kravitz, standing nearby, smirked and kept playing with her hair, her tiny tits bouncing underneath her tee shirt as she flung herself this way and that. She and her friends were talking about some kind of game, tennis or something, and Tina said in a loud asking-for-trouble voice, 'Sore losing, that's all it was, end of story.' And then, smiling at herself in the mirror, she said, 'I just love winning, man. I mean, when you get right down to it, what else is there in life?'

Vera turned toward her, her huge green eyes blazing, but then she turned back to her own reflection in the bathroom mirror and began rearranging the tendrils that had escaped from the knot at the nape of her neck. When we asked her later why she didn't just deck Tina right there, she told us she was thinking of the wedding picture on the credenza at Tootie's tiny shotgun house in the Trunk, of how beautiful Tootie's mother and father had been at nineteen and twenty, and how now Mr. Malloy sat in front of the television, bleary and gut-blown, speaking only to bark orders at Tootie's mother or yell at Tootie for taking his last beer.

'That depends,' she said finally, staring straight into Tina's face. 'On what you think you won.'

~ ◊ ~

Years later, Vera would wake up next to her married boss in the one-bedroom apartment on East Sixty-eighth Street and walk over to the window where she could touch the tops of the lantana plants and sweet-potato vines, courtesy of the classy florist shop on the ground floor. She would stand there, naked, smoking a cigarette, listening to the church bells peal out over the neighborhood. The sound of the bells would remind her of St. Timothy's and Sunday mornings in Elephant Beach, when her father would stop at Renzi's Bakery and pick up crusty semolina rolls and jelly donuts for breakfast after mass; they never ate before, so that everyone could receive Communion. Vera couldn't remember the last time she'd tasted the wafer, and now she only went to church for midnight mass on Christmas Eve, when she was home visiting her family.

Yet, that morning, for some reason, she thought of getting dressed and walking over to St. Michael's Church and bringing back crumb cakes from the German bakery on Lexington Avenue, oranges from the grocery on the corner to make freshly squeezed juice in the tiny kitchen of the brownstone floor-through that her lover paid for. She looked over at the sleeping figure in the bed, wondering if he'd be able to stay for breakfast. She took a bottle of Shalimar from the dresser and idly sprayed her shoulders, the tops of her thighs, the nape of her neck. Then she lit another cigarette and turned her gaze outward, thinking of the things she'd left behind, the things she'd escaped to get here, to this window, on this street, in this life.

FIFTEEN

conversations with my father

'I heard he walked off Ricky Moore's construction crew second week in.'

'What the – what happened?'

'Ricky says nothing. Says the guys couldn't have been nicer, you know, "Welcome back, man," buying him coffee and shit. Then, middle of the afternoon, he just, like, started punching a wall. Ricky said it was like he wanted to kill the fucking wall, man. And then he just walked off the site. Just walked off the fucking site, you believe that?'

'Shit, I'd give my left nut to get on Ricky's crew. Pays top dollar, health insurance, the whole nine yards. Always has work, too, even when everybody else is slow.'

'Yeah, well dig this: I heard he was with Christa Cutler couple weeks back, couldn't pull the trigger, you get my drift. Left her sitting on the lifeguard chair and then went skinny-dipping at, like, three in the morning.'

'So what? Maybe he wasn't in the mood.'

'How are you not in the fucking mood around Christa Cutler?'

'She's always been a hotbox, man. Maybe he had enough of that over in Nam. Heard those hookers are something else.'

'Luke McCallister. Man, that guy was like my idol. Between the surfing trophies and the chicks – didn't someone tell me he was going to Spain to surf for the winter?'

'From what Conor says, he can barely make it down to breakfast. Told me his old lady goes to mass like every day since he got back, says novenas and shit so he'll be normal again.'

'Lighten up, for chrissake. It sounds like his fucking eulogy. Guy's not dead yet.'

'He keeps this shit up, he might as well be.'

'He was in a war, man, not a keg party. He gets to act any way he wants to. Leave him the fuck alone.'

It wasn't the biggest deal in the world, but this was the first time I had been on the Long Island Rail Road going into the city by myself. Usually, I was with my family, or with Liz and Nanny, to go shopping, have lunch, see movies, walk around the Village. Look at the holiday windows at Lord & Taylor, light candles at St. Patrick's Cathedral. Or we'd be with everyone else, heading in to see a concert at Madison Square Garden. But I had never been on the train alone before. I lit a cigarette and stared out the window as we pulled away from the station. I was glad the sky was overcast and it looked like rain. I would have felt I was missing out if it was a brilliant beach day, wasting time in the city when I could have been lying on the sand with my eyes closed, listening.

Summer was almost over and still nothing had happened with me and Luke. Sometimes I was scared of him. I was scared of the things that Conor said, things I overheard from other people, on the beach, at Eddy's, in the lounge at The Starlight Hotel. Almost every night that I didn't have to work, I'd plan what I was going to say to him while I put on my mascara in front of the bathroom mirror. But when it came time to approach him, I'd get close enough that the look in his eyes would stop me from coming closer. Conor said he surfed alone, during very first light, sometimes leaving the house while it was still dark out. At night, he'd walk by himself, his hands in his pockets, shoulders hunched forward, as though he was trying to shake a chill. I'd watch him walking down Comanche Street and I'd want to catch up with him, but I didn't have the nerve. I didn't want to answer questions, either, from Liz or Nanny or even Conor. Sometimes I'd wonder why Luke bothered at all, why he didn't just stay in his room if he wanted to be alone. Sometimes I'd get angry that he was making everything so hard. And then I'd have to remind myself that he didn't know, he had no idea how I felt, and at times, I barely knew myself anymore.

Now it was the second week in August and I felt like the world was moving too quickly away from me. Some days I felt so jumpy that once at work Good-Looking Freddy asked me was I on black beauties, and did I know where he could get some. I'd always been a sleeper, good until at least noon on weekend mornings, but now I'd begun waking in early darkness, my stomach churning. I couldn't remember the dreams I had, but it seemed like my insides were clamoring for something. Sometimes if I lay still long enough, I would fall back to sleep for a while. Other times, I got up very quietly and went out the back door to the porch, careful not to wake my brother when I walked past his room. I would smoke a cigarette while gazing up at the stars, and the breeze coming off the ocean would soothe me. Once, I fell asleep on the porch, right in the lounge chair, and stayed there until morning, when I woke to the sound of my brother's laughter and my mother standing over me, shaking her head.

'Katie, man, hey.' I looked up to find Luanne Miller smiling down at me. She was wearing a cotton skirt that looked like she'd taken an old sheet and sewn on a ruffled hem, and light blue flip-flops that matched the embroidery on the neck and cuffs of her Indian blouse, much the way her kneesocks used to match her cashmere sweaters and pleated skirts back in seventh grade. She was smiling as though she couldn't believe her luck, finding me on the train, like she'd just been waiting to see me her whole entire life. That's the way Luanne was now, but she hadn't always been that way. She'd been queen of the Dunes girls since forever, and she was still beautiful and had been for as long as anyone could remember and probably always would be.

Luanne had taken the seat right across from me. As the train ground away from the station, she lit up a Kool and I wrinkled my nose. I didn't see how anyone smoked menthol cigarettes; it was like lighting an ice cube on fire and throwing it down your throat. She French-exhaled, crossed her legs, and smiled again. 'So. Where you headed in the big, bad city?'

'I'm meeting Georgie Dugan. He was a senior when we were sophomores. Some bar, Jimmy Day's, in the Village. Then we're going to see his new apartment. He just moved in about a month ago.' I didn't tell her that before I met Georgie I'd be meeting my father for lunch at his request. He was taking me to Luchow's and had insisted on picking me up at Penn Station.

'Don't know him. Don't remember him,' she said. 'But I love Jimmy Day's. Outasight jukebox, man. Great burgers! I'll be spending a lot of time there once I move in.'

'You're moving into the city?' I asked.

She nodded. 'I'm starting at New York University in the fall. Going in today to find some things for the apartment.'

'Are you – will you be living in the dorms?' I wondered how Luanne could always make me feel like she was much older, even though we were the same age and had been in the same algebra class in ninth grade.

She shook her head. 'My family has a place in the city,' she said. 'On East Fifty-seventh Street. I'll be staying there while I go to school, thank God. I am so ready, man. I am so looking for a change.' She leaned her head back on the seat and closed her eyes. 'What are your plans?' she asked. 'You graduated, right?'

'Yeah, Luanne, I graduated,' I said, trying to sound tough and snotty, like Liz. 'I don't know what I'm doing in the fall, yet.' I didn't want to tell her I was going to Carver Community College. I just didn't want to tell her that right now.

'Keeping your options open, that's cool,' she said approvingly. 'Way cool. I kind of wish I hadn't locked myself in so early, but the whole backpacking through Europe thing is so clichéd, you know? And my sister lives in California and I've been there a ton of times, I can go anytime I want. And I was desperate to get out of town, so . . .'

'How's Tyrone? You still seeing him?'

Luanne sighed heavily and opened her eyes. 'I was hoping you wouldn't ask me that.' She took another cigarette from her little fringed shoulder purse and tamped it down before lighting up. She leaned back again and I thought her eyes looked wet but with Luanne you could never tell. 'Ty and I are over,' she said, staring up at the train ceiling.

'Really,' I said, like I was surprised. I had known Tyrone Dancer since we were kids at Central District Elementary, when he came up from Alabama in the third grade. He was always a nice kid, with one of those great Pepsodent smiles. Junior high did a number on everyone, but by the time we were in high school, Tyrone had grown a soft, springy Afro and had founded the Soul Brother Society. All the black boys still in school wore black-and-yellow satin jackets with the letters 'SBS' embossed on their backs and marched through the halls with their shoulders jutting forward and wouldn't talk to white people. When we were sophomores, they got into it with the Hitters and school was suspended for three days while the school board held meeting after meeting with furious parents and had the carnage cleaned up, all the smashed desks and broken cafeteria tables and shattered glass doors. Tyrone was always called to the table as one of the community youth leaders, along with Jimmy Murphy from the Trunk and Raymie Cortez from the Brothers Hispanica.

Luanne was what Rita and Raven and the rest of the city

people called a Saks Fifth Avenue hippie, someone who would spend sixty dollars on a peasant shirt in the window at Bloomingdale's while screaming about the oppression of the masses. 'Oppression' was one of Luanne's favorite words during high school, along with 'revolutionary' and 'Free Bobby.' She was a picture of radical chic in her strategically patched bell-bottoms and hand-tooled Apache leather belt and perfectly faded blue work shirt, and it was a testimony to her holy aura that when she and Tyrone walked the halls with their arms wrapped around each other no one, not even the most hardened Hitter, sneered at them publicly, or made obscene gestures when they were out on the quad, sharing a cigarette. When Jeannette Trevino, who lived in subsidized housing, began dating a black guy from Lefferton, they stoned her right out of the Trunk, standing outside the naked ugly cinder-block apartment house, throwing rocks at her windows. Not pebbles; rocks. Like that might ever happen to Luanne Miller, queen of the Dunes. No one would stand outside the house she lived in and write epithets on the two-car garage door while chanting racial slurs through her bedroom window.

'Since June,' Luanne was saying. 'We split up right after graduation.' I knew she was dying for me to ask what had happened. I lit another cigarette and stared out the murky window as we passed tract houses, developments in other towns, where other lives were being lived. She leaned her forehead against the window. 'He did it for me,' she said. 'Because he knew how hard it was, how much I had to go through because we were together. My parents, the way they treated him when he would come over.' Her eyes widened slightly. 'It was just like that song, "Society's Child," like

Janis Ian wrote it just for us, you know?' She started singing softly, rocking back and forth on the seat. '"Come to my door, baby . . ."'

'What did his mother have to say about it?' I asked. During his Central District days, Tyrone hadn't had a father, but his mother used to walk him and his sister, Tanya, to school in the morning, carrying her youngest baby boy on her hip. She was very black and looked more like their older sister than their mother.

Luanne sighed dramatically. 'It was fraught, man,' she said. 'Way fraught. She had such a deep history of oppression. You know, raising five kids by herself, and then Tanya's baby. Working for the man, that total distrust of *los ojos claros*, you know, the light-eyed ones.'

'Why are you speaking Spanish?' I asked.

Luanne shrugged. 'It fit, man, that's all. It expressed what I was thinking better than English could. I mean, the way Ty's mother looked at me, she looked into my face, man, and all she could see was the plantation mistress. Could I blame her, man? Could you?' She shook her head. 'The things I saw down there, you wouldn't believe it,' she said. 'All the white people in Elephant Beach should have to live in the projects for a – a week, man. Maybe a month, even. See what it's like, what that burden does to you. Trying to rise above it with the man's foot up your ass.' She leaned forward, whispering. 'I used to beg Tyrone to beat me. On those days when I saw the rage building. I could feel the rage in his bones, man, beneath my fingers. "Hit me," I used to tell him, "go on, hit me, I can take it. I can take anything, if it saves you a beating from the fascist pigs."' Her eyes shone with tears. 'But he

253

wouldn't.' She leaned farther toward me, her hands on her knees. You could see the lines of her underwear through her skirt. 'I would have had his baby,' she whispered. 'I would have had his little black baby, kinky hair and all.'

I nodded, not wanting to look around at who else was sitting in the smoking car. I hoped there weren't any black people. Most of the Dunes girls had spent hours in ninth grade ironing their thorny tresses; in high school, their irons went the way of their bras and the razors they'd used to shave their legs. They let their hair frizz out naturally, like kinky weeds trailing down the path of their spines. Luanne's hair never frizzed; it wasn't naturally straight but it waved around her shoulders and rippled down her back like a cornflower sheath.

The conductor came around and punched our tickets. 'Change at Jamaica,' he said, and moved on. Luanne watched him walk away. '"I can't see you anymore, baby,"' she sang in a whisper. She probably thought she looked sad, but really she just looked as bored as she used to in algebra class when Mr. Contini droned on about fractions. She leaned back against the seat and rolled her eyes upward, trying to look years and years older. 'It was a beautiful part of my life, man,' she said solemnly. 'But some things just aren't meant to last.' She closed her eyes and I thought that I wanted to lose Luanne before I met my father in the waiting room at Penn Station. It was just so typical of him to insist on picking me up, like I was still a child. He was always doing stuff like that: coming to basketball games even after I told him there wouldn't be any other parents there; waiting outside in the car after dropping me off at the church dances, even after I'd gone

254

inside and the music started. Showing up places I didn't want him to. Where he wasn't supposed to be.

〜𝟄〜

I saw my father standing in the waiting room beneath the little television when I came out of the bathroom. Before the train pulled all the way into the station, I'd told Luanne I had to run and use the bathroom and she'd wrinkled her nose and said, 'That place is totally gross, man. And that bathroom lady attendant they have there totally freaks me out. Talk about oppression of the masses, right? I mean, can you imagine? She's like the poster girl, man. Poster woman. Sitting there, day after day, smelling everyone's bodily waste. It's like I want to say to her, "Lady, lady, liberate yourself from this smelly bondage, man! Go live in a world where the piss runs free!"'

'I have to go,' I said. I made sure I went in the opposite direction from where Luanne looked like she was headed. I had always felt sorry for the bathroom attendant, actually, but there was something reassuring about her. She looked like somebody's grandmother. I knew it was a crummy job, sitting, staring at those dirty pink tiles all day. Handing people rolls of dry toilet paper, change for the sanitary napkin machine. But then, one time when we were coming home from the Christmas show at Radio City Music Hall, my father told me that hers was a union job with raises and benefits and at least she wasn't on her feet all day, working her fingers to the bone in some dingy factory. I felt better about the bathroom lady after that, and thought her smile might be real at least some of the time. I always made sure to tip her a quarter.

I watched my father watching television in the waiting room. It was what he did most nights at home, after dinner. He was looking up at the picture, some boring news show, and I walked over and touched his arm. It took him a minute to look away. 'There she is,' he said, and gave me his cheek to kiss. He didn't kiss me back. He didn't like affectionate demonstrations; it wasn't his way. I started walking toward the escalator and he pulled me back. 'Where do you think you're going?' he said sharply. I felt the familiar sinking inside me, like something had come loose and was floating to the floor. It was always like this with my father. 'Come this way,' he said, and began walking toward the subway entrance. It turned out they were doing construction and we had to go up to street level after all. 'Ha! Told you,' I said, and then I felt like an idiot. My father walked a bit ahead of me, more in tune to the rhythms of the city. I was still working on beach time.

On Seventh Avenue, the streets were wet and dripping, though it had stopped raining. There was light coming from the sky, but you couldn't see the sun. 'Over there,' my father said, pointing to the IRT kiosk across the street, but right before we crossed, several police cars screamed up to the curb and a bunch of cops came storming out and ran up behind us, up the steps of Penn Plaza. My father and I turned to watch. There was a small group of people in the middle of the plaza, holding signs and marching around in a circle. The signs said 'Make Love, Not War,' 'Draft Beer, Not Boys,' 'Eighteen Today, Dead Tomorrow.' The people were chanting,

'One, two, three, four, we don't want your fucking war,' over and over. Their voices were loud but they didn't sound strong. They sounded tired. It wasn't a big group. The cops stood watching for a minute and then one of them pulled out a bullhorn, even though the crowd was about a hundred yards away. His voice was garbled through the bullhorn, so we couldn't hear exactly what he was saying. The people kept marching around, chanting. The cops went among them, pulling on their arms, pulling them away from the circle. Most of them began walking away, but a few started struggling. 'Take your hands off me, pig!' one woman cried, trying to wrench her arm free. She pushed the cop away with her other hand and then two-three-four police were on her and she was on the ground, and another guy was trying to get her away from the cops and then he, too, was on the ground, and some of the other marchers began shouting at the cops but they didn't move forward from where they were standing and then the cops cuffed the man and the woman and began dragging them toward the squad cars. The woman was writhing around like a long, elegant snake; when they passed us to get to the car I could see she was older than I'd thought. Her long, dark mane was shot through with strands of silver. 'Fucking fascist pigs!' she snarled, twisting and turning. 'Establishment pawns!' the man hollered. The cops wrestled him into the backseat of the squad car. One of the cops put his hand on the woman's head and pushed it down until she cried out in pain. 'Police brutality!' she shrieked. What was left of the small crowd of protesters took it up. 'Police brutality!' they howled from the steps of the plaza. 'Yeah, baby,' a barefoot black man wearing red earmuffs said as he walked by, pumping his fist in the air. The squad cars sped away, lights flashing, sirens blaring. My father touched my arm and began walking toward the subway. 'Fucking pigs,' I muttered beneath my breath, loud enough for him to hear. I watched his lips tighten, but he said nothing, did nothing, except hand me a token for the subway ride downtown.

Raven and the city people made fun of Luchow's, but I secretly liked it because the restaurant reminded me of my grandmother and how much she'd loved their sauerbraten. We used to go there on her birthday every year before she died two Octobers ago, and she always looked so happy, listening to the oompah band that would play in the dining room. It was beyond corny, but there was something touching and familiar about the restaurant, the way the older waiters seated you so solicitously, the way the whole place smelled of cigar smoke and beer.

'We'll need a few minutes,' my father was telling the waiter now, after he handed us the menus. 'In the meantime, I'd like some coffee, if it's fresh, and Kate?' My father looked at me. I would have loved to order a beer just to freak him out, but I said, 'Coffee for me, too, please,' and the waiter smiled and nodded and went away. My father was not the type to have a beer with lunch, or dinner for that matter. He said drinking made him sleepy.

We studied the menu while waiting for the coffee. There was something to love about the menu. You didn't see this type of fare in Elephant Beach restaurants, that's for sure.

Casseroled Spring Guinea Hen in Wine Kraut. Koenigsberger Klopse with caper sauce, which were really meatballs. Pigs Knuckle with Sauerkraut. Seventeen different styles of potatoes!

'So,' my father said, reaching for a roll. 'September is right around the corner. Are you all set for school?'

I nodded. I'd been accepted at Carver Community College. I hadn't applied anywhere else, because my grades weren't good enough, except in English. I'd look at the brochures and college tour books in my guidance counselor's office and feel only anxious; I couldn't think of another place I wanted to be, except the Beach. It was the only life I knew. Carver was about a half-hour drive up the parkway toward the middle of the Island. It used to be an army barracks and now it was a college where you went to class in old airplane hangars with gunnysacks still hanging from the rafters.

'You were accepted on the daytime schedule, as I recall,' my father said. There was more status in going during the day. People tended to think of daytime students as real college students who took things more seriously, as opposed to the nighttime students trying to crunch in their classes between commuting and their jobs. Most of the Trunk kids who'd been accepted at Carver were going at night.

'I've been thinking, though, maybe it would make more sense for me to switch to nights,' I said. 'Work more hours at the A&P. I could maybe go full-time and take—'

'No,' he said sharply.

'"No" what?' I asked. 'Most people would be happy to have a daughter who wanted to work to help pay for her college education. I guess you're just not one of them. I could make one hundred and fifty dollars a week plus benefits. What's so bad about that?'

'I'm not raising you to be Martha Muldoon,' my father said.

'Well, that's cool, because I'm not looking to be Martha Muldoon,' I said, and just then the smiling, red-faced waiter with the waxy mustache appeared with our coffee and asked if we were ready to order.

'I'll have the Saddle of Canadian Hare with Kronberries and potato dumplings,' I said.

'For God's sake, Katie,' my father said. 'Order something you're going to eat.'

'I'll eat it,' I said. 'It's rabbit, right? I love rabbit.'

'When have you ever eaten rabbit?' he asked. 'Do you even know what the hell a kronberry is?'

'Is very good,' the waiter said, beaming.

'There! It's settled,' I said. 'Thank you.' I handed my menu back to the waiter and crossed my arms over my chest. This wasn't like when I was thirteen years old and he told me I shouldn't order the chicken pot pie at Pat Reilly's Chop House because it was all scraps, all garbage. I was eighteen and we were in a city restaurant and I could order what I wanted.

My father sighed and handed his menu to the waiter. 'I'll have the bratwurst,' he said.

'Is very good,' the waiter said, and then he left us. My father watched him go. He selected another crisp, white roll, tore it in half and took a bite. He looked in my direction. The light from the lamps in the room glanced off his glasses, pinpoints of brightness against the smudged frames.

'The A&P is fine for now,' he said in a placating tone. 'It's a fine part-time job while you're still in school. But down the road, you might want something a little different. Something better. You know, Carver has one of the highest transfer rates in the country. Your mother and I were thinking . . .' He trailed off. He took a sip of his coffee. I bit my tongue so I wouldn't tell him that I was sick and tired of hearing about the transfer rates at Carver; it was all well and good, but I mean, it was still Carver, not Harvard. I lit a cigarette, and I could see the expression on my father's face because he hated my smoking. But still he said nothing, just patted his lips with his napkin and then laid the napkin back in his lap.

I was thinking how the mothers were always screaming, but the fathers were silent. Every house I walked into, my own house as well; the mothers were always going at it. 'Over my dead body you'll see him again!' 'Take your sister with you, no arguments!' 'And where do you think you're going? Get back here and do those dishes!' 'It'll be a cold day in hell before you wear that outfit out of this house!'

But none of the fathers talked. They were silent at the supper table, except to bark, 'Be quiet!' or ask for the mashed potatoes to be passed. They spent all day working away from the rest of us, behind desks, on scaffolds, underneath sinks. Yet, they never shared anything with us but short answers; 'Fine,' my father said, when my mother asked how his day was. Or else they grunted and poured a scotch and took it into the den to watch the news in peace, because no one else was interested. They were up early, before anyone else, sitting at kitchen tables, scalding their tongues on bitter instant coffee, reading the paper in lonely silence that they didn't want disturbed. The ones who worked the night shift were

261

still sleeping when their children left for school, and they didn't welcome interruption, either. I watched my father now, across the table, cleaning his glasses with the snowy white edge of the tablecloth, thinking I would never notice him twice if he wasn't my father, wondering why if he went to college he had so much trouble saying things. I could almost see the words stumble before they reached his lips.

'What were you and Mom thinking?' I asked, trying not to sound exasperated. I knew how it would go if my mother was here. She'd be bringing in everything, the A&P, street corners, failing Regents geometry by one point, for God's sake. Her voice rising, waving her hands around until my father took hold of them and held her fingers down and said through clenched teeth, 'Janice, control yourself.'

'We were thinking you might want to go away to school after a year or two at Carver,' my father said.

'Why? Trying to get rid of me?' I asked.

'No, no, nothing like that,' he said quickly, like he was trying to reassure me. 'We just thought that, perhaps after a year or two, you might want to see a little more of the world than Elephant Beach, that's all. Sometimes new experi-ences—'

I snorted. 'You didn't even want me to order the Hare with Kronberries!'

'Sometimes new experiences,' he went on, as if I hadn't spoken, 'give you a new perspective on life. Going someplace different than what you've been used to can open up—'

'I haven't even started Carver yet,' I said. I wanted this conversation to be over. I had been very hungry and now my insides were shaking. I didn't know if I could eat.

'There's no rush—'

'Then why are we talking about it?'

'Because it's never too early to begin thinking about the future.'

'You just said there was no rush. That's, like, a contradiction.'

My father sighed again, and I felt bad. We were rarely alone together and he'd been sincerely trying to have a conversation. It wasn't his fault he didn't know how to talk to me. It wasn't his fault that this was the way it was with fathers.

'Let's see what happens this semester,' I said. 'I mean, I haven't even registered for classes yet.'

'I'd be happy to help you,' he said quickly, looking up at me. 'I'd be happy to go with you to the registration, help you pick out—'

'I'm all set,' I said, just as quickly. 'It's not happening till the last week in August. I've got my ride and everything.'

'Katie, it's very important that you pick the right—'

'I know that, Daddy. I went to the orientation last month. I took notes. I'm all set, really.'

'Well then,' he said, and the way his face looked made me feel like crying, and then the food came and we both looked at our plates and away from each other.

I waited until we finished eating to speak, because I knew my father liked to eat in silence. My meal had been pretty good, but not the best. The kronberries tasted disappointingly familiar.

'You were in the war, right?' I asked. 'World War Two?'

'World War Two and Korea,' he said, looking around the

room as the waiter removed the plates. 'Though that was just a skirmish, compared to the Second World War.'

'What do you think about Vietnam?' I asked him.

'What do you mean, what do I think about it?'

'Well, compared to the other wars,' I said. 'Are we winning? I mean, why are we even there? No one seems to know, not even the—'

My father laced his fingers together and placed his chin on the bridge of his hands. 'I don't know that anyone ever wins a war,' he said. 'When you consider the cost on the other side of the ledger.'

'You mean like – the deaths and everything?'

'The deaths, sure. Those who died fighting. But there's the living, too, don't forget. Men, women, families – it's a tremendous impact on how people live, afterward. Funny,' he said, putting his hands down on the table, 'we act like going to war is a perfectly normal thing, as normal as leaving for work in the morning. But don't kid yourself. There's nothing normal about it. Taking ordinary people, living ordinary lives, thrusting them into – into horrifying situations, really, that they have absolutely no training for. One day you're working in a hardware store, the next you're shipped off to some beach thousands of miles from anything you've ever known. How the hell does working in a hardware store prepare you for Guadalcanal?' He shook his head. 'Some people never recover, and when you think about it, that's the more normal – the more expected reaction. And we treat them as though they're the sick ones, as though you shouldn't be troubled by watching your friends—' He broke off and looked at me. 'I'm sorry, Kate,' he said. 'I shouldn't be going on this way, not to you. Especially not after eating, how was your hare?'

'The hare was fine,' I said. 'But Daddy, did you – I mean, during the war – wars – were you in the – I mean, you don't have to talk about it if you don't want to. I'm just – I'm interested in what you have to say.' It was true. I was listening to my father now. He was saying the same things that Mitch had said, but in a different way. I thought he was saying things that Luke was probably feeling. I heard everything my father was saying, because it made so much sense.

He was quiet for a few moments. When the waiter came by, he asked for more coffee. 'During World War Two, I was an ensign,' he said. 'Because I had a college education, I went directly from school into the navy, at a higher rank than some of the others. It was different than now; everyone enlisted. Everyone wanted to get into the service, to fight for their country. I was in the Pacific. And one of my assignments was to – to transport the men who experienced very intense battle fatigue back to the States from Japan.' He was quiet again.

'So – they were just tired of fighting?' I asked. 'Were they going to, like, rest up and go back to the war?'

'No,' he said quietly. 'They would never go back. Some of them – many of them, in fact – were classified Section Eight, meaning they'd been judged mentally unfit for service.'

After a moment I said, 'So, they like, flipped out in battle?'

My father smiled wryly. 'I guess you could put it that way. It's as good a way as any. The ship was huge, a destroyer, filled from stem to stern with men who . . .' He paused. He stayed quiet for a minute. It seemed as though he was searching for words and couldn't find any. 'Those breakdowns

265

occurred a lot more frequently than most people think,' he said, finally.

'What'd they do?' I asked. 'Like on the ship, did they act crazy? Was it like *The Snake Pit* or something?'

He nodded. 'Some did. Some cases were more severe, they cared for them in different ways. But mostly it was quiet. Almost eerily quiet, considering. Considering the sheer numbers of men on board. What I remember most was their eyes, how they'd follow you when you were walking by. They'd just look at you, not saying anything. At times, it was unnerving, to tell you the truth.'

'I bet it was,' I said. I looked at my father, dressed in a suit for his job as an accountant in a real estate firm. I tried picturing him in a khaki uniform, looking like Henry Fonda in *Mister Roberts*. I tried picturing him giving orders, walking past hundreds of men who couldn't speak or didn't want to. 'Were you afraid, ever? That they'd like, do something?'

My father laughed out loud. 'It was a war, Katie,' he said. 'Every day, everywhere you looked, you had to be afraid someone was going to do something. You just never knew what.'

'Do you think any of them recovered? Like, once they got home, were around their families?'

He nodded. 'Some of them, sure. Sure. I like to think most of them, after a while. And don't kid yourself – a lot of men who fought and weren't classified Section Eight were just as troubled afterward. If you're really interested, there's a movie you should see – *The Best Years of Our Lives,* with Fredric March. It's a bit difficult to watch, but it's a wonderful film. It tells the story of what happens after better than I ever could.'

I nodded. 'I can look for it on *The 4:30 Movie*. Sometimes they run old movies.'

'But I never answered your original question,' he said. 'About the war we're fighting now. Kate, listen to me: You must never underestimate the evils of communism. Despite what you kids think, it enslaves people more than capitalism. God knows this country has its problems, but – in Korea, the lines were drawn. Things were clear. You knew exactly who the enemy was. With Vietnam, there was no provocation, no attack. There's no – no clarity to this war whatsoever. Half the time our boys don't know who they're fighting, or why. Chasing shadows in the jungle. I don't blame them for being terrified, and when you're terrified you do desperate things. We don't belong there. We never did.' My father drank from his water glass. I lit a cigarette. We sat in silence for a while, but it wasn't bad. The waiter came back, pouring fresh coffee into our cups. He handed us both dessert menus.

'What would you like?' my father asked. 'They make a terrific German pancake here. They're famous for it. They prepare it right at the table, set it up in flames and everything. It's a real performance, very dramatic. And delicious. You can have anything you want with it – apples, chocolate sauce. Huckleberries. Though maybe you've had your fill of berries for one day.' He smiled. He was reading the menu and he looked happy. My father loved desserts. My mother was always after him; 'That's enough, Bob,' she'd say, when he tried to sneak an extra sliver of chocolate cake, a final dollop of rice pudding. She didn't want him to get fat. She didn't like fat people; she thought they were sloppy and had no discipline.

I had seen them make the German pancake before, when we'd come here on my grandmother's birthday. It was an exciting dessert, but we'd never ordered it because my grandmother was always afraid the tablecloth would catch fire and we'd all go up in flames. I was full from the lunch, but I said, 'I don't think I could eat a whole one, can we split it? Maybe with chocolate sauce?'

'Of course,' he said, smiling, signaling for the waiter.

—❦—

Outside the restaurant, my father handed me the instructions he'd written on one of the index cards he always carried in his shirt pocket, on how to get to West Fourth Street, where I'd be meeting Georgie. I told him Jimmy Day's was a bookstore in the Village. He wouldn't have approved of me meeting a boy in a bar while it was still light out. He didn't love me meeting my friends in bars when it was already dark. I thanked him, thinking that after he got back on the subway going uptown, I'd just walk over instead of riding the train. The sky had cleared and the sun was out. I liked the way the air smelled, different from the beach, but tangy, intoxicating. I had never walked in the city by myself. I knew I would get to where I was going all right. The streets were filled with people I could ask for help if I got lost along the way.

'You have everything you need? You have enough money?' my father asked.

'Plenty,' I said. 'I got paid yesterday.'

He nodded, staring down Fourteenth Street. I hooked my arm through his, something I rarely did with anyone, but it seemed just the kind of old-fashioned, courtly gesture that went with the rest of the day. With the restaurant and the Tiffany lamps and the mustached waiters and the deer heads hanging from the walls. We walked toward the subway at Union Square, where my father had promised to leave me. We walked slowly, in the sunshine, and I leaned a little toward him and he didn't pull away.

SIXTEEN

death to the working class

No one has as many dead friends as we do. It always freaks me out when I talk to people in their twenties, sometimes older, even, and they don't have anyone who died in their life. I don't know if it's better to get it over with when you're younger, to have that experience of seeing someone you were hanging out with two days ago lying in a coffin, dressed in their best clothes, looking like a figure in a wax museum. But I don't know that it ever gets easier, no matter how many years go by.

The first one was Tess Nolan, when I was seventeen. She was a year ahead, already enrolled at Katie Gibbs in Manhattan, even though she felt she was meant for better things. 'What to do with this life?' she'd moan, examining her face for blackheads in the small mirror she always carried with her, those nights we sat around someone's bedroom, smoking and listening to records. She'd pull her hair back, experiment with different looks, talk about becoming an actress, but she'd never even joined the drama club and Mr. Nolan wouldn't pay for anything but secretarial school. He had five daughters and was hoping they'd all marry rich bosses so he wouldn't be carrying them on his back for the rest of his life.

The weekend right before Halloween, Tess and Paulie Barton, her boyfriend until somebody better came along, were on their way home from a costume party at Paulie's cousin's over in Rockaway. Tess had gone dressed as a nun, and had spent weeks making the costume as authentic as possible. Paulie went as a baseball player, donning his old uniform from the Knights of Columbus summer league. He'd just bought his first car, a Toyota, because it was good on mileage and seemed more classy than a Volkswagen bug. They'd been drinking at the party and Paulie wasn't used to driving anywhere but Elephant Beach. Coming home on the Belt Parkway, he was in the left lane and hit the divider; witnesses said the car swerved out of control and was then hit from behind by another vehicle. Paulie was already dead when the paramedics arrived. Tess died in the ambulance, on the way to Mercy Hospital. We learned later that she'd won a prize at the party for Most Original Costume.

I was home babysitting for my little brother when Liz called. I remember putting the phone down and sobbing so loudly from the shock of it that my brother came running in from the next room, patting my back as I wept, asking, Did I want a drink of cold water? Should he call Mom and Dad? while the brackish laugh track from the television set blared in the background.

The wake at Farrell's Funeral Parlor was jam-packed. The

Nolans were a popular family, but Tess was beyond popular; people idolized her, even though she'd do things like take money out of your wallet when you weren't looking, or throw your biology notebook out the window of the school bus the night before a test. But that was Tess: funny, loud, cruel; once, when we were sitting smoking on the quad, she snatched one of my loafers and wouldn't give it back, holding it up for everyone to see while I limped to Spanish class with a hole in the toe of my green opaque stocking. If you ever did something like that to Tess, though, she wouldn't look at you for weeks, despite notes and tearful entreaties. That was the whole Nolan family, so stubborn they'd eat dirt. One time, Tess and her sister, Peg, didn't talk for two months over a pair of brown gloves.

Sometimes, when Tess's eyes would roam over us looking for a target, I wished she'd go away. I was glad when she graduated and wouldn't be around for my senior year. People who didn't know us often took us for sisters or cousins, claiming we had such similar features and mannerisms. Tess was always quick to point out that we looked nothing alike, that her eyes were darker, my nose bigger. Sometimes I felt insulted when she started these litanies, but other times I smiled inside where she couldn't see. Privately, I thought I was prettier.

Now, looking down at her lying in the coffin, I realized I was glad she was dead, and the sudden, surging savageness of this thought upset me so that I began weeping violently, my tears falling on her white silk burial dress, the silver crucifix she clasped in her hands. Meg Sweeney, a distant cousin of the Nolans', knelt down and put her arms around me. 'She loved you,' she whispered against my ear. 'She always said you knew how to keep a secret better than anyone.'

～δ～

Meg's own mother was next, during one of the mildest Februarys anyone could remember. She'd been running from their house on Myra Lane and had tripped on the high heels she was wearing – she had beautiful legs and wore heels all the time, even to go grocery shopping – and had fallen under a sugar maple tree, where she suffered a heart attack and died right there on the sidewalk. The story was that she and Mr. Sweeney had been talking behind closed doors and she had begged him to stop seeing his mistress. 'I love you,' she said softly, so the children wouldn't hear, even though they were listening at the door. 'I'll do anything you want me to. Anything.' He left the house and got into his truck and she ran after him. But the truck was gone, so she began running through the thick winter mist. They found her outside her parents' house on Winchester Street. Meg's grandparents had never liked Mr. Sweeney and hadn't wanted their daughter to marry him. After she died, their hatred of him was so deep that they refused to see their grandchildren, to have anything near that reminded them of him.

Mr. Sweeney and Mrs. Vitelli, the mistress, had been seeing each other since last summer. They'd met when he'd gone over to fix the leaky kitchen faucet in her apartment; she was a divorcée who lived alone in the Neptune Arms on upper Buoy Boulevard. They were secret about it at first, then more blatant, holding hands at Leo's Luncheonette, driving through

273

town together in Mr. Sweeney's green truck with the gold lettering, 'Sweeney's Plumbing,' written on both sides of the cab. Mr. Sweeney was the only plumber in town who would make calls around the clock, no matter what time of night, and had built up his business so that the Sweeneys weren't country club rich but lived better than most of the other tradespeople in Elephant Beach. Whenever I'd go over to Meg's house, her parents would be sitting on the enclosed porch with drinks in their hands, and Mrs. Sweeney would always smile as though she'd been waiting her whole life for me to arrive. 'Why, Katie, hello!' she'd cry gaily. 'Meg's upstairs getting ready, she'll be just a minute. Sit down and tell us what's been happening in your life.'

It wasn't the kind of behavior you'd expect from a plumber, and it was hard to picture Meg's father, dressed in his dark blue overalls with his name stitched in red over the pocket, as a romantic figure carrying on a clandestine affair. But the most shocking thing about it was that Mrs. Vitelli was short and boxy with stringy black hair and a screechy voice, while Mrs. Sweeney was beautiful and it wasn't just my opinion, everyone thought so. She had green eyes so huge and expressive they seemed almost alive, like separate, living parts of her face, and luxurious black hair with red highlights, caught up and held in place with a silver clip. Even on the coldest days in winter, she wore only a white cashmere scarf over her skirt and sweater. When she stood on the steps of St. Timothy's after mass with her dark sunglasses, she looked like a movie star.

'You could see it, though, these past few months,' Desmond, the manager at the A&P, said. 'Whenever she came in she'd be wandering around the aisles in a daze, like she didn't know where she was. Like I always say, you never know what goes on in the bedroom.'

In my mind I saw her then, running through the icy mist, her eyes frantic, her hair wild, wondering what to do, how she could get her husband to love her again. Thinking as she ran, *Maybe my parents will know. Maybe they can help me. Even if they never liked him, I'm their daughter and they want me to be happy.* And then she tripped and fell under the maple tree and had the heart attack, as surprised by the whole thing as everyone else. There had been no history of heart trouble in her family and she didn't smoke or drink excessively. Maybe her heart had just given out, tired of loving someone who wouldn't love her back.

'I'm going on break now,' I said, putting the wooden divider on my register to signal it was closed, grabbing my cigarettes.

Desmond turned to look at me, at my face. He put his hands up in the air. 'What?' he asked, bewildered. 'What'd I say? What'd I do?'

At the funeral, Liz and I clung to each other, watching Meg usher her brothers and sisters up the aisle. 'It feels like all our mothers died, even though they didn't,' Liz whispered in my ear. Later that year, Mr. Sweeney and Mrs. Vitelli were married. They moved into a big house right over the bridge and tried living like normal people, but whenever they showed up at St. Timothy's, everyone just stared and stared; even the choir stopped singing. Finally, they moved away, to Clayton County, which was like another country altogether. Meg went to New Hampshire to live with an aunt and uncle and attend the local community college, somewhere in the White

275

Mountains. She seldom came home and never answered our letters.

⌐ᴏ⌐

They say it comes in threes, and the following September, Bennie Esposito died in a cell at the Elephant Beach police station. Bennie was a city boy; he grew up in the Bronx and his family was so poor they only had a woodstove to heat the apartment. His mother moved him down to her cousin's house on Sister Lane to get him away from his friends and his drug habit. She thought the fresh sea air would straighten him out but he found his connection two days after they'd opened the house. (We always thought it odd the way city people believed the fresh sea air would cure every ill, when all it ever really did was leave salt stains on the walls of our houses and fill the couch cushions and comforters with the smell of mildew.) Bennie looked like a rock star, with his suede jacket, two-tone platform shoes with five-inch heels, and shoulder-length shag, stumbling around Comanche Street, singing at the top of his lungs, 'Every time it rains, it rains bennies from heaven.' Other times, when we were lying on our towels at Comanche Street beach, he would gaze out at the ocean before his eyes became heavy-lidded from quaaludes, shake his head and say, 'You people out here. You got no fucking idea.'

'I'm cutting you off, Bennie, man,' Raven told him several weeks before he died. 'Your mother did everything but get down on her knees and cry to me.' Mrs. Esposito was a small, tired-looking woman with huge black eyes like Bennie's.

Sometimes she'd come around the corner to Eddy's, stand there in her housedress, arms folded, shaking her head. 'I don't know what you people do to him,' she'd say. Very gently, she'd take Bennie's arm and try to lead him home, while he either slumped against her shoulder or began dancing a frenzied jig, trying to get her to dip and twirl with him, as though they were at the Copacabana in Manhattan instead of the middle of Comanche Street. Bennie was always talking about taking us to the Copa, to clubs in the city. 'That's where it's at,' he'd tell us, 'not like these little shit nothing places out here.'

I had a crush on Bennie when he first moved down. He had an aura of sinister glamour that appealed to me; Luke hadn't come back yet and I was bored with daydreaming. Early in the day, before the drugs took hold, Bennie would start a conga line in the sand, or show us how to tango, or demonstrate the more intricate steps of slow dancing (not the kind of hanging all over each other we'd do at church dances), making the moves look smooth and sexy. When he held me against him, I could feel his rib cage beneath the spangled tee shirts he wore. Desi caught me once, watching Bennie buying a pack of Marlboros, joking around in one of his more lucid moments. Desi waited until he left, then turned to me, his eyes bugging. 'That? That's what you want?' He shook his head disgustedly. 'No wonder your mother's upset. You better get out of here. You better go somewhere far, far away from this corner.'

The cops hated all of us, but they hated Bennie the worst, especially Detective Mickey Conlon; he called Bennie the dancing junkie. 'Go ahead, junkie,' he'd say, lifting Bennie under his arms and shoving him into the back of a squad car. 'Dance.' In May, Bennie had come walking up Comanche Street wearing a motorcycle helmet, swaying in time to some invisible beat inside his head. Detective Conlon pulled up next to him, and without getting out of the car, said, 'What, no dancing today, junkie?' Bennie began frantically tap-dancing around the car, lingering in front, as though daring the detective to run him down. Detective Conlon gunned the motor and began inching toward Bennie, but even he wasn't crazy enough to kill him in broad daylight, while children ran through the streets and neighbors gossiped over their fences. Instead, he leaned out the window on the driver's side. 'Next time I pick you up is gonna be your last, junkie,' he said. 'And you better know what I mean by that.'

On a rainy Friday night two weeks after Labor Day, Bennie stood swaying on the corner of Comanche and Lighthouse Avenue, hitchhiking to Lefferton, a scruffy drug town over the bridge so dangerous that the beach was usually empty even during the day and no one drove over there after sunset. Desi saw the whole thing, he was locking up for the night and saw a black Buick pull up right next to Bennie. He told us that someone got out, opened the back door of the car, shoved Bennie inside and then took off. It was raining too hard for Desi to make out the dark figure in the rain, but he hadn't spent his life on city streets for nothing. *Cops,* he thought. He shook his head and went upstairs to the apartment.

Bennie died during the night in his jail cell. The overdose-from-barbiturates story made perfect sense to anyone who knew him, but what about the bruises on his face, his chest, his legs? Everyone figured that Detective Conlon had picked Bennie up, taken him down to the station and worked him over. Timmy Jones tried talking to his uncle Frank, a retired Elephant Beach cop, who said, 'You want to stay away from that one, you know what's good for you. And what the hell you doing hanging around junkies in the first place, you?'

At the wake, Mrs. Esposito wailed, 'Bennie, Bennie, we lost you, Bennie,' while everyone walked around feeling angry and sad. Voodoo, tripping on mescaline, knelt for too long at the coffin, his eyes huge in his face, whispering, 'Bennie, man, wake up.' The mescaline made him believe it might happen. I walked by Bennie's brother-in-law, a soft, pudgy man with mud-colored eyes, dressed in a checkered suit too loud for a wake, delivering a stunted eulogy to some city people we didn't know: 'I'm telling you, John, he worked her for years, forging checks, taking bills from her purse, she oughta be grateful he's gone before he sent her to the poorhouse.' Afterward, everyone went back to the beach and sat in a line across the sand. The joints went back and forth and finally, Voodoo motioned for everyone to raise their cans of Bud or whatever they were drinking. 'Bennie, man, you were my brother,' he said, his droopy eyes still sad. 'Hope you're hanging tight up there with Jimi and remember: "If I don't meet you no more in this world, then I'll meet you in the next one." For real, my brother. For real.'

⤳

They say that after the first death, there is no other, but of course there is and always will be: Michael Courtney, falling

279

backward off the boardwalk and breaking his neck while stoned on Valium; Cully McKee, drowned with his surfboard when he went wave-catching after Hurricane Elizabeth; the Torreo brothers, two poor, dumb guineas trying to make a buck, who burned to death while torching a house on the bay, an insurance scam gone awry; Tony Furimonte, killed in a bar fight in Providence, surrounded by people who didn't know him. At the funeral, Nanny wept and wailed and clung to Voodoo, whose lips curled into a small, smug smile, knowing that finally Nanny would be all his, at least until the rich boss came along and carried her away to a distant castle. And then there was Raven, diving off the balcony of the Sea Lion Hotel. Poor Raven hadn't been right for years, the drugs eating away at his body, his brain; once, he disappeared for eight months before showing up on Aunt Francie's doorstep, asking for a ham sandwich on white bread with the crusts cut off and a 7Up. Everyone rejoiced over his homecoming until we realized that nothing would ever bring him back, not shrinks or electric shock or the people who loved him. Raven, so good-looking, smiling with his mouth closed so you couldn't see the missing teeth, rotted from speed. We often wondered what drove him off that balcony, what final picture came into his mind. 'Maybe he thought he really could fucking fly,' Rita, his old girlfriend, said with a bitter, twisted smile.

As the years folded over one another, you thought about the dead people occasionally and wondered if they'd been saved from their own lives for something better. Sometimes, you could see them: smiling up at the sun through movie star sunglasses; dancing on a star, wearing patent leather platforms; soaring through the air against a cloudless sky. Best of all was when you heard them singing. The singing was so sweet, you had to stand still and close your eyes to listen. And for a minute or two, you stopped being afraid.

SEVENTEEN

last call

I had just put the wooden divider on my register to signal that it was closed when I looked up and saw Liz and Nanny and Voodoo coming through the automatic doors. I waved and started walking toward them. 'Perfect timing,' I said. 'I'm just going on break right this minute. Let's go to Leo's and get coffee, I'm starving, we can—'

'Katie, man,' Voodoo said quietly. 'Take a walk, okay?'

I looked at their faces. Voodoo's eyes were red, but that was pretty normal. Though his hands were quiet, hanging down his sides. 'What is it?' I asked. 'What's wrong?'

Liz took my arm and we began walking through the doors, out to the street. We walked into the alley between the A&P and the Sunoco station where we usually took cigarette breaks when the weather was nice. Liz and Nanny had joined me here many times.

'What's up, man?' I looked at the three of them, and Liz said, 'Katie, Mitch – they found Mitch in his room this morning.

282

He's – he's gone, sweetie. He died sometime over the past two days, they think.' Liz's eyes filled with tears. She looked away.

'Over the past two days?' My voice scaled up.

'He was in his room,' Voodoo said patiently. 'You know how he gets holed up, drinking, sometimes you don't see him out for weeks. And we had that wicked rain on Sunday and no one was out, so nobody thought to . . .'

'It was Len who found him,' Nanny said. 'Knocked on his door to give him his mail and he didn't answer, and Len said there was a – a smell—' She broke off, crying, and burrowed further into Voodoo's shoulder.

It was a beautiful day. A blue skies, white sails on the water kind of day. It was the color of the sky that made me ask, 'Are they sure? That he's – I mean, remember that time we thought Bennie had OD'd and then they pumped his stomach and—'

Liz broke in gently. 'Sweetie, they're sure. Len called – the ambulance, medics, whoever they were.' She put her hand on my arm. 'They're sure.'

With the arm that wasn't around Nanny, Voodoo pulled me close. 'We didn't want you hearing it from strangers, man,' he said. 'You know how shit gets around.'

At first, no one seemed to know how Mitch had actually died.

'Probably drank himself to death, the way he could put it away,' Raven said. We were all up in the lounge at The Starlight Hotel. I had come down to Comanche Street straight from work. It was still early; the sun hadn't set. Filtered light poured through the windows behind the bar.

'You think he – like he meant to do it?' Rita, Raven's girlfriend, said. Raven had his arm around her, holding his beer in the other hand.

'I don't know, man,' Raven said. 'There should be a coroner's report or something, but Mitch didn't impress me as a suicide kind of guy. And if he did do it, he would have eaten his gun, not taken pills or anything – I mean, anybody know, did he cop from any of you guys?'

Billy and Conor shook their heads no.

'Look, he had the leg thing, and he wasn't the healthiest guy—'

'Yeah, man, the times we hung out, I don't remember him ever eating anything. Never kept food in his room—'

'Len, man, you'd know – he ever order room service? A burger, anything like that?'

Len paused, his hand on the Heineken tap. 'Come to think of it, no,' he said thoughtfully. 'Never sold him so much as a package of beer nuts.'

'Fuckin' guy drank so much, he probably forgot how to chew.'

'C'mon, man, show some respect.'

'I am showing respect. I respect anyone could drink that way and keep it together for as long as he did.'

Raven raised his glass. 'To Mitch,' he said solemnly. 'A true soldier in the battle of life.'

'To Mitch,' we echoed, and everyone drank. Len turned the bar lights up, then dimmed them again. 'You Can't Always Get What You Want' was playing on the jukebox. Mitch had once met Mick Jagger in Golden Gate Park and thought he was the coolest living person on earth.

'What's going to happen,' Nanny asked hesitantly, 'with the – I mean, what about his family? Are they going to take him back to San Francisco?'

'Yeah, what about that? Anyone know anything about his people?' Voodoo asked. 'Katie? You guys were tight. He ever say anything to you?'

'No,' I said regretfully. 'We never talked about family.' It was actually hard to remember what Mitch and I had talked about. Nothing and everything, really. After I'd overheard Mitch and Luke talking about Vietnam that one night, I'd tried to subtly pump him for information about Luke, but he'd just shake his head and say, 'Already told you what I thought about that number. Give it a rest, angel.' I had no idea what he really meant, but he refused to explain and changed the subject, speaking very fast the way he did right before he was completely drunk, and not allowing me a word in edgewise.

'Never said anything to me,' Raven said.

'Well, we should find out, shouldn't we? If he had family?' Cha-Cha asked. 'Because even if they take him back to Frisco, we should do something.'

'Really, man,' I said. 'He was part of our people. We should definitely do something.' I pushed my empty glass forward on the bar for a refill. 'Len, he ever say anything to you about his parents or anything?'

Len filled my glass with fresh ice. He gave me extra maraschino cherries without my having to ask. His fingers touched mine, briefly, as he handed me my drink.

285

'There's a wife somewhere,' he said.

'Get out!' I said.

'No way!' Billy said.

'Are they still married?' Liz asked.

'All I know is there's a wife somewhere,' Len repeated softly. The Stones were singing 'Honky Tonk Women,' and I felt tears sting my eyes. I looked around for Luke, but he wasn't with us. I wanted to see him. I wanted to tell him he had to take care, take care. There were so many ways he could end up if he wasn't careful.

'Maybe my brother knows something, man,' Conor said, like he'd read my mind. 'They've been talking a lot since he came home.'

'Where is Luke?' Rita asked. 'I thought I saw him when we came in.'

'He was in the bathroom, punching the shit out of the urinal,' Billy said, rolling his eyes. 'Screaming "Fuck!" over and over. Surprised you didn't hear him out here, man.'

Conor sighed, set his drink down and walked toward the bathrooms at the back of the bar.

'Fucking McCallister, man,' someone murmured. I thought Raven or Ray Mackey would say something, but nobody did.

It turned out there was a wife, and they were separated but not divorced. Len called her; he'd gotten the number from Mitch's tattered phone book when they were cleaning out his room, not knowing if she was a mother, sister or aunt, only that she had the same last name as Mitch. Her first name was Rosemary and they'd been separated for three years and there wasn't any other family that she knew of. Mitch's father had died years ago and his mother had passed while he was over in Nam. She took the news calmly, not at all surprised that the cause of death had indeed been acute alcohol poisoning, and thanked Len for calling, but said that Mitch had become a different person from the one she had married and she really didn't know him at all anymore. When Len asked her what she wanted to do about the body, the funeral arrangements, she sighed and said that it really wasn't her problem. 'I don't mean to sound cold, but we didn't part on the best of terms,' she said. She thanked Len again and hung up.

'Bitch,' Liz said. 'Talk about cold, Jesus.' It was Friday and we were back at The Starlight Hotel. Mitch had been dead for almost a week.

'Hold on, now, honey, none of us really knows the whole story there,' Len said, and I looked at him and knew he was thinking about his sister and the screaming husband.

'But – but if she won't do anything and there's no other family . . .' Nanny's voice trailed off. 'I mean, how long will they keep him over at Farrell's? They can't just throw him out, can they?'

'Unless there's burial insurance or some kind of policy—' Raven shrugged.

'There isn't,' Len broke in. 'I asked the wife. And we didn't find anything when we went through the room. Except empty bottles underneath the bed.'

'They could put him in Potter's Field, man,' Cha-Cha said softly.

287

'Ah, no,' Nanny and I said together.

'Really, man, fuck that,' Billy said. 'I mean the guy won the Purple Heart, for chrissake—'

'It's not something you win,' Luke said drily. He was sitting in the corner of the bar opposite everyone else, smoking. 'It's not like it was a carnival and you get the third toss free.'

I looked at Luke. The sound of his voice made my heart jump a little. I realized I hadn't heard him speak since he'd been back. Not like this. His voice sounded gravelly, older than before he went away. I had heard him so often in my head, it took me a minute to realize how different his voice was from what I remembered.

'Whatever,' Billy said defensively. 'I mean, shit, what if we called the VA hospital and asked them? I mean, shouldn't he get a – a military burial or something, you know with a flag over the coffin and shit?'

'No,' Luke said quietly. He got up and walked over to the table. Usually, everyone stood or sat around the bar but tonight we were at one of the longer tables, by the fireplace. It was filled with dead cigarette butts.

'What do you mean, no?' Billy asked.

'It's not what he wanted,' Luke said. His hair was caught back in a ponytail. His voice held a note of quiet authority. 'He hated that military shit. He didn't want a thing to do with any of it, you dig? Didn't even like going over to the VA hospital for his meds but he couldn't afford them otherwise. He wanted his ashes scattered on the water. That's what he wanted.'

'Yeah, well, why didn't you speak up before, man?' Billy asked.

'We only just found out about the family,' Luke said. 'Couldn't act on anything until they weighed in, could we? Now we know.'

'We're his family now, man,' Voodoo said solemnly. Everyone looked at him. 'That was me, not Jimi,' he said.

'Really, man,' Conor agreed. He was looking at Luke, smiling. He seemed happy that his brother was participating in something for the first time since he'd come back. Even if it was burial plans for one of our friends. 'So Luke, man, did he say anything else? Like, did he—'

'Why did he tell you that in the first place, do you think?' Raven asked quietly. 'I mean, were you guys just sitting around, talking about the most far-out ways to say adios to the planet? Or you think he really was planning to—'

'It came up,' Luke said, running his hand down the side of his face. 'It just came up. During the course of conversation.'

Billy snorted. 'Must have been a really cheerful conversation,' he said.

'Fuck you, man,' Luke said, like he was tired of the whole thing. 'It came up, it's what he said he wanted. If it was me—'

Billy stood up. 'But it's not you, is it? It's not—'

'Take it easy, Billy,' Conor said, going to stand beside his brother.

'You got a problem, man?' Luke asked conversationally.

'Yeah, I got a problem,' Billy said. 'With guys like you, walking around like—'

'Would you all knock it off!' Everyone turned to look at me. I was standing up now, facing them. 'What's the matter with you? Mitch is dead, laying up at Farrell's almost a week

289

now, and you're sitting here acting like it's showdown time at the O.K. Corral? It's not about you,' I said, looking at Billy. And then I turned to Luke. 'And it's not about you,' I said. 'Not everything is about you. It's about Mitch, about saying good-bye to Mitch, Goddamn it! He's the one who's dead!'

Everyone was quiet. I could feel them all watching me, and the last thing I remembered before stalking off to the bathroom was the startled look on Luke's face as he stared directly into mine for the first time all summer.

~

When I came out of the stall in the ladies' room, Liz and Nanny were waiting for me.

'A showdown at the O.K. Corral,' Liz said, her lips twitching, and then the three of us were laughing hysterically, leaning against the sink, hugging each other.

'I feel like a total jerk,' I said, wiping my eyes, though I didn't, really. I just wanted someone to tell me that I wasn't.

'No, Katie, man, that was great,' Nanny said, blowing her nose. 'It really was.'

'Really, man, what a bunch of assholes,' Liz said scornfully. 'Getting into some ludicrous pissing contest at a time like this.'

But now I was feeling embarrassed. Billy and I were tight, I could make it up to him later, but what must Luke be thinking? I had barely said five words to him all summer and now I'm yelling in his face what I should have been yelling in my own. Because right now it should be about Mitch and somehow it always ended up being about Luke and I was losing patience with it, with myself, with the whole sad, sticky summer.

'Katie, when you ran off like that, Luke kept looking at you, he said, "Who's that chick again?"'

'Really,' I said, like it was no big deal to me.

'Luke fucking McCallister,' Liz said, examining her face in the mirror. 'Man, I don't know. I always thought he was more – more manly or something, right? Instead of this, like – shit, am I getting a zit on my friggin' eyelid?'

'Fuck you, "manly,"' Nanny said. 'He was over in Nam, for chrissake, what "more manly" do you want?'

'Come on,' I said, opening the door, growing impatient with them, with everything. 'Let's get going.'

We walked back to the long table. I went over to Billy, put my hand on his shoulder. 'Hey, Billy, man, I—'

He pulled me down on his lap and gave me a huge hug. 'No, baby, you were right on,' he said. 'Right the fuck on. But don't let it go to your head.'

I stood up and asked, 'So? What's happening? What are we going to do?'

I looked around the table and when I got to Luke, he looked at me again like he was seeing me for the first time. He was twirling a set of car keys. 'I'm going over to Farrell's,' he said. 'Get some info, see where we go from here.' He put the car keys in the pocket of his jeans. I remembered then that Luke had a car; he'd driven a maroon Cutlass black-top that Conor had driven while he was gone. There had usually been a crowd in the car with him, a girl sitting next to him, laughing through the window. The radio blaring. Sometimes he'd had his arm around the girl, sometimes not. Still looking at me, he asked, 'Feel like taking a ride?'

⟶ ૦ ⟵

Mr. Farrell was a short, fat bald man whose head was sweating because the air-conditioning was on the fritz. I had gone to school with his daughter, Patrice; we'd been lab partners in eleventh-grade Earth Science and used to sneak out to the corner bathroom, where nobody hung out, to smoke cigarettes under the ugly fluorescent lights. Farrell's was the most popular funeral home in Elephant Beach; people spoke of Mr. Farrell as though he was the Picasso of the corpse world. He would spend whatever time it took, pulling all-nighters if necessary, to make loved ones look as alive as possible. It was said that his bodies were so lifelike you almost forgot they were dead.

'Luke McCallister!' he cried, coming toward us. He grasped Luke's hand in his own. 'Welcome back, welcome home! You're looking very fit, sir. Very fit, indeed.' I was thinking Mr. Farrell truly was a man of superior talents, in that he managed to successfully combine a hearty cheerfulness with a ghoulish aura that befitted his surroundings.

'Mr. Farrell,' Luke said quietly.

'And who is this?' Mr. Farrell turned toward me with an inquiring smile.

I stuck out my hand. 'I'm Katie Hanson, Mr. Farrell,' I said. 'I went to school with Patrice. We were in the same science class.'

He shook my hand politely and then turned and led us to

292

one of the blue velvet love seats in front of the phony fireplace in the anteroom. You could tell it was phony because the logs were lit and it was mid-August. He stood facing us and his features changed into a sober mask. 'Regarding the deceased,' he said gravely. 'Mr. Ronkowski. We have a slight problem, I'm afraid. I have to have a family member sign the release forms.'

'He has no family, man,' Luke said. 'There's no next of kin. His wish was to be cremated and have his ashes scattered over the water. That's what we're here to arrange.'

Mr. Farrell cleared his throat and tugged at the collar of his wet white shirt. He looked stifled in his black suit and I wanted to tell him to take off his jacket and tie and be comfortable. But it wasn't my place. He was not my guest, I was his. By comparison, Luke, in his faded jeans and flip-flops, strands of his honeyed hair falling out of a rubber band, looked as cool as if he'd just walked out of the ocean.

'I'm afraid it's not that simple, Luke,' Mr. Farrell said, his face a sympathetic study. 'There's no will, no written directives, and there's the matter of—'

'Mr. Farrell, the man was a member of the United States military.' Luke spoke crisply, as though delivering a report. 'He served two tours in Vietnam. He was at Khe Sanh. He lost his leg in battle. He earned a Purple Heart. He spent the last days before his untimely death living in a fleabag hotel that cost three dollars and fifty cents a night. He drank himself to death and now he's been dead almost one week. He's laying up in your funeral home and, for some bullshit paperwork that means nothing, we're delaying his last wish.

His last wish, in the form of a verbal command to me, was to have his ashes scattered over the ocean. Are you going to deny a serviceman who sacrificed a limb for his country his last wish on this earth, sir? Are you really going to do that? Because there's no written word, no fucking family signature from a family that doesn't exist?'

I looked at Luke, amazed. He spoke softly, mechanically, his words slicing the air like small knives. His face never changed expression the whole time he was talking, but I watched his left fist clench and unclench and Mr. Farrell saw it, too, his glance flickering downward. I'd seen the way his face flinched when Luke said 'fucking.' You'd think a funeral director would have heard those words before, would be used to them.

'Luke, now, of course I respect the man's service record,' Mr. Farrell said. 'Of course we all want to do as much as possible for our boys—'

'We're not boys,' Luke said, and something loosened in his voice. His body tightened.

'Mr. Farrell,' I said quickly, 'we're Mitch's – we're Mr. Ronkowski's only people. He doesn't have anyone else. We're his people, Mr. Farrell. We just want to remember him well. We're having a ceremony on the beach, and then we're having a dinner for him, for his friends who – who loved him. Can't you help us, please? Mr. Farrell, can't you please help us?'

Mr. Farrell looked from me to Luke. He looked back to me again. 'Of course I'll help,' he said, so sincerely you wanted to believe him. 'Of course I'll help you honor this man who sacrificed so much for his country.'

'Just burn the fucking body,' Luke said, and Mr. Farrell's

face finally collapsed so that all the careful signs of counter-feit emotion came together in surprise and anger and contempt and sorrow.

～δ～

'What'd you tell him?' Luke asked.

We were sitting in the Treasure Chest Bar and Grill, not far from Farrell's, by the marina under the bridge. The long, polished bar faced the water and the boats rocking the harbor. It was the kind of local place you came to for birthdays and other special occasions. They were known for their soft-shell crabs. I looked around for Charlie Brennan, Marcel's father, who practically lived at the Treasure Chest, but it was prob-ably too early for him to be there. I had been to the Treasure Chest before with my family, but I'd never sat at the bar, drinking vodka and grapefruit juice, watching the sun drag the dregs of daylight across the bay.

Luke was drinking Jack Daniel's on the rocks. I sipped my drink slowly. I wasn't used to drinking this early in the evening and I'd had only a coffee ice-cream cone with sprinkles since breakfast.

'I told him you were really cut up about Mitch's death,' I said carefully, not looking at him. Luke had stormed out to the car, after telling Mr. Farrell to burn Mitch's body. 'I told him you had both been in the war and he had to make allow-ances.'

Luke laughed. His laugh sounded dry, dusty. He fumbled for his cigarettes. '"Allowances,"' he said. He held the pack out to me and I took one, even though I had my own. He lit

295

us both from the same match. We sat, smoking, and I was surprised at how comfortable I felt, how calm. *This is Luke,* I thought, watching his velvet eyes staring at the boats outside the window. *This is Luke.*

'He liked you,' Luke said suddenly, his eyes on the sunset outside the windows. 'Mitch.'

'I liked him, too,' I said.

'No, man, you're not getting my meaning,' Luke said. 'I mean, he dug the shit out of you.'

It took a minute for what he was saying to sink in. 'No,' I said quietly. 'It wasn't like that.'

'Was for him,' Luke said.

'I never—' I started. 'He never—'

'He didn't tell you because he thought it would get weird, and he didn't want that. "That little girl is my sunshine," that's what he said about you.' Luke grinned. 'Little girl with a big mouth.'

Tears came to my eyes, fell down my face. Luke looked over at me, startled.

'Hey,' he said. 'Hey, I was kidding, man, I just—'

'It's not that,' I said brokenly. I thought about that last time I'd sat with Mitch, talking about Luke, the construction workers hassling him. All the times we'd hung out, he'd never said a word. Even his eyes had stayed silent. I thought about the rolled-up cuff of his pants, the wooden leg. 'Five fingers of love,' he'd said, laughing.

I wept.

Luke didn't say anything. He let me cry. He handed me a stack of cocktail napkins from the pile in the little box on the bar. He dropped some, and as he bent over the barstool to retrieve them, his tee shirt rode up his back and I caught a glimpse of the scar, a shiny crisscross of what looked like tiny hearts sewn together in a jagged line across his back.

I wiped my nose carefully and stuffed the cocktail napkins in the pocket of my cutoffs. 'Do I look like I was crying?' I asked Luke. He laughed. Then he took a cocktail napkin and leaned forward and brushed my right cheek. 'Not anymore,' he said. He put the napkin underneath his drink.

'What about the rest of it?' he asked. 'The ceremony on the beach? The dinner? Is any of that really happening?'

I shrugged. 'Beats me,' I said, but the more I thought about it, the better an idea it seemed. I could see us, all our people, on the beach at sunset. Everyone who wanted to saying his or her piece, sharing a stoned memory, whatever. And then we could head over to The Starlight for some kind of buffet supper spread that I'd seen them put on when the Chamber of Commerce held one of their meetings there when they were tired of the VFW hall and wanted a view of the water.

'I mean, really, man, why not?' I said to Luke. 'I think Mitch would have liked it,' and hearing myself say the words, I knew it was true.

Luke sighed. It had a heavy sound. 'What?' I asked, and then it occurred to me, like a sudden hard slap on the shoulder. 'Oh God, did you – was it – was it something he asked you to do for him? Like, by yourself? Is that what—'

Luke held up his hand. 'No, man. Really, no. Look, we were drunk. He was shit-faced, which apparently was pretty normal for him, right? Cat kept a bottle in his pocket, a bottle in his room, and lived on top of a bar. Total coverage every hour of the day and night.'

I asked what had been on my mind and everyone else's. 'Luke,' I said. I stopped to savor the taste of his name in my mouth. 'Did he say anything to you? Was it just drunk talk or was he planning to – to kill himself and giving you, like, last-minute instructions?'

He rubbed the bridge of his nose and shook his head. 'We were talking about body bags,' he said, in the same dry voice he'd used at The Starlight Lounge, which made him sound older than everyone else. 'The indignity of body bags. Like how stupid they look, like big, shapeless pieces of shit instead of human beings. That's what we were talking about, man. That's what led to his historic statement. Is it what he really wanted? Is it what he would have said if he knew it was going to be last call for real? How the fuck should I know? I mean, dig it, I barely knew the cat. But since it was the only reference to his own demise anyone remembers, and since he apparently never was sober, it's the only intel we've got to go on.' He looked at me with a little half smile. 'That's army talk for—'

'I know what it means.'

'You want another drink?' Luke asked, opening his wallet, laying a ten-dollar bill on the bar. I nodded. 'Sure,' I said. I looked out the wide windows. The sun was gone but it wasn't full dark yet. The sky was a deep blue, with splashes of orange on the horizon. I looked up at a lone star glowing so brightly in the sky that it had to be a planet, Venus or Mars, something. I shivered at the beauty of nights like this, remembering other nights as beautiful when I'd looked up at the stars and made a wish.

I went for my own wallet, an Indian braided piece I'd gotten at Heads Up. Luke put his fingers over mine and pushed them down. 'I've got it,' he said, as the bartender brought us our drinks. The skin on my knuckles felt electric. I could feel the brush of his fingers along my spine, light as feathers falling from a dream. This first touch. Luke.

~⚬~

Len sighed, running a hand through his silvery hair. 'I miss him, you know?' he said, staring out the porthole window behind the bar. 'Sometimes it was a pain in the ass, the way he'd get tanked and just go on and on. He used to come in first thing when I opened, I'd be trying to count out the drawer and he always made me lose my count. But now it's like I'm waiting for him to come through the door, start his infernal yakking.' He shook his head and moved down the bar to his other customers.

We were passing the hat to pay for the cremation and any extras for Mitch's ceremony. Everyone was into it, from the derelicts that lived in the rooms at The Starlight Hotel to Desi and Angie, up at Eddy's. 'We used to shoot the shit,' Desi said, handing me a twenty from the register. 'He was good people.' Fiona Feeney came into the lounge one night and handed me an envelope filled with bills; the Hitters had taken up a private collection spearheaded by Jimmy Murphy, who'd liked listening to Mitch's war stories. He himself had wanted to be a Green Beret but was kept from enlisting because of a heart murmur. When he was drunk, he would play 'The Ballad of the Green Berets' over and over again on the jukebox. 'His idea of a vicarious thrill,' Fiona said.

'Listening to tales of blood and guts and bayonets.' The cremation was going to cost three hundred dollars. Len said he'd
throw in the buffet, with a couple of pitchers of beer, maybe
some sangria. 'Tastes like cat piss, but it seems to be popular
with the ladies,' he'd said, winking at me.

'That'll work,' Luke said. 'That's great, man, really. Thanks.'

'Really, Len,' I said, and meant it. He was doing everyone
a solid.

The ceremony was going to be on the Friday night of the
weekend before Labor Day weekend, on Comanche Beach. I
had run into Luke on my way up to Eddy's for an egg cream
and he'd asked me to come with him to talk to Len about
the party afterward. It was the third or fourth time in my
life, being in a bar during daylight. I felt daring and deca-
dent, even if I was only drinking ginger ale. We were sitting
in the corner by the jukebox. Otis Redding was singing 'Sittin'
on the Dock of the Bay.' It made me think that summer was
all but over; you could smell it in the lift to the wind at
night. You'd wake up at five in the morning, looking for
blankets, when for months you'd slept with only your sheets
for shelter.

'Here's something, though,' Len said, making his way back
down the bar to us. 'The wife called, what's her name,
Rosemary. She wanted to know what was happening with
the, you know, if there was going to be a funeral or some
such.'

'Fuck her,' Luke said serenely. I loved the way he said
things like that, as though he was just making conversation.
'I mean, pardon my French, but what's it to her?'

'Well, technically, they're still married,' Len said. 'She's

300

entitled to his benefits. Maybe the thought of his disability check softened her up, made her more sentimental.'

'Does she want a funeral now?' I asked. 'Does she want to take him back to—'

'I told her about the, you know, the cremation,' Len said. 'Reminded her of our previous conversation, in which she wanted no part of it. Asked her, did she have other plans before we went ahead with the actual, you know, the cremating. She said she was just looking for some kind of closure.'

'Closure,' Luke said, snorting a laugh. 'We should have sent her his wooden leg.'

'What about Mitch's leg, man?' I asked suddenly. It bothered me, now that I thought of it, what would happen to his leg. 'Did they – did they take it with him?'

'I don't know,' Luke said, sounding as surprised as I felt. 'Shit. Len, did you—'

'I didn't notice at the time,' Len said. 'And what does it matter now? It would be a kind of creepy souvenir.'

'I guess,' I said, after a minute. I had the insane thought that Mitch might miss his leg, and then I thought about the wood burning and I shook my head because the sun was high in the sky and such thoughts seemed out of place.

'Though I was wondering,' Len said hesitantly. He reached underneath the bar for something and came back up with Mitch's cane. I stared at the silver dragon's head and my eyes flooded with tears. I took a deep breath and blinked them back. It wasn't the time, I told myself. This wasn't the time.

'You think he would have minded—' Len looked at both of us. 'I don't know who to ask,' he said apologetically. 'Maybe the wife, I don't know. But I was thinking, maybe I could

301

give this to my brother-in-law? The one that's a vet as well? He's had some trouble walking, and I was thinking—' He broke off, staring down at the cane. He ran his hand over the wood. 'Maybe I should ask the wife, you think?'

'No way, man,' Luke said firmly. 'I mean, who was closer to him at this point, right?' He turned to me. 'What do you think?'

I loved that Luke had asked me. I no longer felt like crying. 'You take it, Len,' I said, just as firmly. 'He would have liked to know it was going to another soldier, don't you think?'

'You think his wife is really coming in all the way from Frisco?' Luke asked skeptically.

'Fresno,' Len said, putting the cane back beneath the bar. 'And I got to tell you, the way it sounded, she just might show up. Asked me what time things would start happening, how far we are from Kennedy Airport.'

'You talking about that one-legged nut job? One was in here mouthing off a couple weeks ago?' We all swung our eyes to the voice. It was familiar to me. I saw it belonged to the fat construction worker who had been in the lounge that day with me and Mitch.

'Shove it, Jimmy,' Len said quietly. I watched his shoulders flex. 'Guy passed away last week, so lay off.'

'Yeah? What from?' another voice asked. They were clustered at the far end of the bar, by the door that led to the piazza.

'Choked on his own bullshit,' Fat Jimmy said, chortling fatly, meanly. Nobody else laughed.

'You know them?' Luke asked me in a low voice.

'I'll tell you later,' I whispered.

302

'I said, lay off, Jimmy,' Len said sharply.

'Hey, hey, rest in peace, all right?' Fat Jimmy said. 'But you got to admit, the guy was a—'

'He was an American,' I said loudly. 'An American who fought for his country. And now he's dead and we're planning his funeral, so please, man, show some respect, okay?'

It was quiet again. Jay and the Americans were singing 'This Magic Moment.'

Luke put his empty bottle of Bud down on the bar. He paid for his beer and my ginger ale. 'Let's cop the breeze,' he said. On our way out, the younger construction worker who had sung along to 'Fly Me to the Moon' that day when Mitch was still alive stepped out in front of us.

'You gonna wake him or what?' he asked quietly.

I explained about the ashes, the party afterward. 'He had a lot of friends,' I said, making sure Fat Jimmy could hear. 'A lot of people who loved him.' Luke and I walked out to the patio, where we paused to light cigarettes before heading to the beach. He cupped the match so that when we bent over together for the light, our foreheads touched. We heard someone call, 'Hey!' The match went out. The young construction worker walked toward us, quickly, and when he reached us, he handed Luke a small wad of rolled-up bills. 'For the, you know, whatever,' he said. Close up, he looked older. In the sunlight you could see the wrinkles around his eyes.

'Thanks, man,' Luke said. 'But I do believe we're covered.' He didn't want to take the money. He tried handing it back, but the construction worker pushed it hard into Luke's hands. He looked from me to Luke and back to me again. His eyes were sorry. 'Must be something,' he said. 'Buy a round, after. Maybe some bagpipes, right? Something.'

～ⴰ～

The day of the ceremony, a soft, light rain was falling. There was a strip of gold light lining the horizon, which meant the rain might stop, and it did. The afternoon fog rolled out to sea and the air was dry and smelled like clean clothes and seaweed. All our people were there and some others. Len had closed the bar for the occasion and Desi and Angie came down from Eddy's. There were some regulars from the lounge at The Starlight Hotel who Mitch would drink with during the day, men and women with bad teeth and putty-like complexions who may have been meant for better things but never moved far enough off their barstools to find them. And Mitch's wife had shown up after all, had taken a cab from Kennedy Airport and was staying in Mitch's old room until Sunday. She stood now at the edge of the half circle that had formed close to the shore, near the jetties, a faded-looking girl who used to be beautiful and whose eyes told you that she knew it and missed her beauty. She wore a long granny dress and a fringed shawl with delicate flowered patterns across the back. She was barefoot and so were most of the rest of us, though the sand was damp and cold. Our flip-flops lined the seawall at the Comanche Beach entrance, a delicate barrier proclaiming the privacy of the occasion.

'So. You and Luke, man,' Liz whispered, as we shared a cigarette before.

'There is no me and Luke,' I said, though there had been

304

other remarks over the past few days, raised eyebrows, knowing glances.

'Oh, please,' Liz said, rolling her eyes. 'You think we're all blind? You think we never noticed the way you act whenever his name comes up? I'm just happy you finally got up off your ass and did something about it.'

'It's not like we're going out or anything,' I said. 'It's just – I don't know, man. I don't know what it is. The whole Mitch thing, you know?'

Liz nodded. Her face had lost weight since the abortion. She looked thinner, older, and was working a lot of hours at the dealership, 'saving up enough so I can finally split, man, get out of that fucking house.'

'Go for it, man,' she said now, her gaze cool and knowing. 'But don't be stupid. Go on the Pill, it's practically foolproof. You want me to go with you? There's the clinic over in East Cliff, we can go before school starts, have lunch at Cookie's—'

'Liz, man, slow it down,' I said, looking around to make sure no one had heard. I wanted to tell her. I wanted to tell her, but I couldn't because she did have a big mouth, which was why Nanny and I held back from her, why she still thought Nanny was a virgin, why she never knew that when Nanny was stoned enough on ludes she still did it with Voodoo on his stained sheets beneath the Jimi Hendrix poster, and that she felt doubly dirty, balling someone she didn't love, with the *Electric Ladyland* album playing in the background and Jimi and his flaming penis hanging over the bed. But neither Liz or Nanny knew that I planned to make love to Luke that very night, in one of the empty rooms at The Starlight Hotel, and that I was prepared through the rhythms of my body and the box of rubbers I'd bought two days ago, since I didn't have time for clinics and pills. I hadn't told either of them that I wanted Luke's honey-colored baby inside me someday, that sometimes, when I thought about it while lying awake at night, I put my hands on my stomach, imagining its shape.

But not now. I didn't want it now, when things with Luke were first beginning. I didn't want to end up like my mother, having to make that kind of choice before I was ready. I wondered had she been careful or careless; did the rubber break, or had she been so carried away by passion she just didn't care? I wondered if she ever thought about me on my birthday, or wanted to forget the day I was born because it made her sad, or angry, or if she never gave it a second thought. I knew who I was, though. I knew if I carried Luke's baby around for nine months and had to give it up, I'd give it a second thought. I'd think about it until it drove me crazy.

Liz was gazing at me, smirking. 'You and fucking Luke McCallister. Wouldn't that be something, man. Wouldn't that be a trip and a half.' There was love in her eyes, and something else, but I turned away from it and began walking closer to the shoreline.

Billy faced everybody and coughed a few times. Luke stood farther apart, holding the small silver urn. He'd asked if I'd wanted to ride back over to Farrell's to pick up the ashes; I'd wanted to get out of my shift at work but I had already gotten this weekend off, both Friday and Saturday, and didn't want to push my luck. 'It's cool,' Luke said. 'I think the cat's afraid of me, but hey, fuck him if he can't take a joke.' I wanted to kiss him right there, in front of the A&P, where he'd come looking for me. I smiled, but I felt a small clutch of something when I looked into his eyes. I saw the shadow of the strain there, as if he was trying really hard and unsure that his efforts were succeeding. And then he smiled and the shadow was gone.

'Okay, man,' Billy said loudly. 'We want to do this while it's still light out, so we can see what we're doing. So let's – let's get going.' Billy was usually the best speaker, a natural master of ceremonies, but he was standing awkwardly in the sand, looking like he'd lost something. His voice sounded too high. I looked around at everyone, waiting. We wanted it to be beautiful, but it was strange, not having the priest, the organ. The limousine out front, waiting for the coffin.

Then Billy turned to me. 'Katie, man, how about you say a few words, start the ball rolling?' And I saw Liz's eyes slide over, saw that something in them that made me turn away. I stepped forward. I was wearing my cream-colored peasant shirt and most faded jeans. I had washed my hair with Herbal Essence and the juice of half a lemon. I wore mascara and Bonne Bell Musk Oil on my wrists, my throat. Between my legs. I looked out at everyone. Some people were mildly high; out of deference to the occasion, it had been informally decided that hard drugs would wait until after the ceremony. Even Bennie Esposito's eyes weren't yet at half-mast. I looked out at my friends and wanted to feel sad, but I felt something else instead.

'We all know why we're here tonight,' I said. 'I can hear Mitch now, telling me, "Keep it short and sweet, sugar, I got a drink to catch over at the lounge."' There was laughter in the crowd. In back of me the shadows were lengthening in

307

the sand. 'If anyone has a memory to share or something you'd like to say . . . just say it, man. We can go down the line.' I cleared my throat. I spoke too quickly, talking about that day in the bar with the construction workers. I didn't tell about why I'd wanted to speak to Mitch, or what Len had said about the screaming. I just told how he'd handled the construction workers, how they'd done a turnaround at the end. 'It wasn't just because of his leg,' I said. 'It was because of Mitch. You know how he was, no bullshit. One of those guys even chipped in for tonight. Told us to get some bagpipes.' More laughter. There were bagpipes at practically all the funerals at St. Timothy's, somebody's uncle from Knights of Columbus dressed in a kilt, playing 'Danny Boy.' I was starting to feel choked up. 'Good-bye, Mitch. I loved you, and I'll miss you.' I stepped back and turned to look at the ocean. It was all right to cry. A friend was dead, and other friends were close by.

Almost everyone took a turn. A lot of shared memories: the last joint smoked; the last shot bought. A day at the track. Mitch singing along to the jukebox in a surprisingly clear tenor, belting out 'I Left My Heart in San Francisco.' The books that lined the windowsill of his room, Hemingway and Steinbeck and Richard Brautigan and Kurt Vonnegut. 'Mitch, baby,' Bennie murmured, swaying lightly on his feet from force of habit; he hadn't stood up straight in a long time. 'He always came in the store, he'd tell me, "Hello, beautiful," like it was my name,' Angie said, her voice quavering. 'No disrespect, I dug him like everyone else did,' Voodoo said, when it was his turn. 'But I'm gonna give a quote from Jimi that sounds exactly like what Mitch would have said if he was here: "It's funny how most people love the dead. Once you're dead, you're made for life.'"

Billy went last. He took a crumpled piece of paper from the pocket of his jeans, saying, 'I remembered this from when we did Shakespeare in school, man. Can't remember which play, but I felt it was right on for this – for Mitch.' He read, '"Now cracks a noble heart. Good night, sweet prince; and flights of angels sing thee to thy rest."' I stared at Billy, but he was still looking down at the piece of paper, putting it back in his pocket. I was thinking how life went on and on and for weeks and months on end nothing ever seemed to change, and then suddenly people would amaze you.

Everyone fell silent, and we thought we were done, but then Mitch's wife stepped into the line, hesitantly, and said, 'Is it – if it's not too late.' She cleared her throat nervously. 'I have something, but if it is too late, that's fine, I don't want—' She threw her arms out, as if she could draw meaning from the air without having to speak. 'I don't want to intrude,' she finally said, looking around the circle, trying to find our eyes.

No one spoke at first. Everyone had heard the story of her first reaction to Mitch's death. But she'd been a part of his life that none of us had known. She was already retreating, her ankles sinking backward in the sand, and I stepped forward and said, 'No, it's – it's cool, it's fine, please . . . please. Go ahead.'

She stepped forward again, standing between Conor and Raven, hugging her shawl tighter around her shoulders. 'It's a poem he liked,' she said. 'He liked it very much, and it

309

seemed to fit the occasion. It's called "The Valedictory," by José Rizal, but it's also known as "*Mi último adiós*." Mitch used to call it "Crown 'n' Deep.'" She cleared her throat and began:

> Land I adore, farewell. . . .
> Our forfeited garden of Eden,
> Joyous I yield up for thee my sad life
> And were it far brighter,
> Young or rose-strewn, still would I give it.
>
> Vision I followed from afar,
> Desire that spurred on and consumed me,
> Beautiful it is to fall,
> That the vision may rise to fulfillment.
>
> Little will matter, my country,
> That thou shouldst forget me.
> I shall be speech in thy ears, fragrance and color,
> Light and shout and loved song
>
> O crown and deep of my sorrows,
> I am leaving all with thee, my friends, my love,
> Where I go are no tyrants. . . .

She trailed off and bowed her head. You could hear weeping in the crowd. Something about the words, the high, sure timbre of her voice, had been deeply affecting, and she was right. It was totally fitting. I heard someone murmur, 'Beautiful, man,' and then Luke turned and climbed up on the jetties and began walking out to the farthest point, where the waves licked the sides of the rocks and all you could hear was the surf pounding. The rest of us followed. He opened the urn, took a handful of ashes, stared out for a long moment at light pouring down from behind a pink cloud, and threw the ashes into the roiling water. He turned and handed me the urn. We looked at each other, unsmiling. I took a small handful of ashes and flung them into the ocean. One by one, everybody took a turn, except Bennie, who had held out as long as he could and now could barely hold his head up and nobody wanted him dropping the urn. 'So long, pal,' Conor murmured, gently tossing his ashes into the ocean. Mitch's wife was last. She took the urn and tipped it upside down so that the remaining ashes rained into the wind until the urn was empty. She stared out at the horizon, a slight smile playing on her lips, and began walking back down the jetties, balancing carefully on the jagged rocks.

Slowly, everybody filed off the jetties, jumping down to the wet shoreline. I looked backward, once, but it was too dark to see anything. Someone in the crowd began singing 'Dead Flowers,' off the Stones' *Sticky Fingers* album, and soon everyone was taking it up: 'Send me dead flowers to my wedding / And I won't forget to put roses on your grave . . .' It had started softly, then dipped and swelled until we were one voice practically shouting the words, raucously, joyously, in peculiar but definite harmony, as we made our way off the beach toward the bright lights of the lounge at The Starlight Hotel.

'That was a beautiful poem,' Nanny said. We were jammed up in the ladies' room, which had only two stalls. Rosemary, Mitch's wife, was examining her face in the mirror as she washed her hands. It was hard to pinpoint her looks; at first glance on the beach, with her long dress and flyaway shawl, she looked like she could have been one of the girls from the Dunes, and I was surprised because I had never pictured Mitch with a Dunes girl. But now, even in this dim lighting, the hard lines around her mouth were evident. She looked around for paper towels to dry her hands and of course couldn't find any; the holder was always empty. We usually dried our hands with toilet paper, but the stalls were both full, so she began shaking her hands to dry them. She stood facing us and smiled. 'There are other, longer versions, but that one was from the Tillie Olsen story "Hey Sailor, What Ship?" From *Tell Me a Riddle*. Have you read it?'

'Never heard of it,' Liz said.

'Mitch loved it,' Rosemary said. 'He used to like for me to read it at night, before we went to bed.' She stopped shaking her hands and crossed her arms so that they held her elbows. The fringes of her shawl hung down to her waist. She was telling us something, but I wasn't sure what. There were things she might have known, but she didn't know how girls from the Trunk could be when it came to outsiders. Nanny had only been trying to be polite under the circumstances.

'Yeah, Mitch used to tell some great stories,' Rita said into the stony silence. Her voice sounded very loud in the tiny bathroom. Her face was slack from drinking. She hadn't liked the way Raven had been glancing at Rosemary. 'Never told us he had a wife, though. Must have slipped his mind.'

Rosemary was lighting a clove cigarette. She crossed her ankles and leaned back against the wall, exhaling. 'Really,' she said, her voice bright with interest. 'Did he tell you the one about how he built a fort out of beer cans in the living room and refused to come out, even to use the bathroom? Or how he made a pyramid of empty whiskey bottles in the dining room and shot them up, one by one, with his trusty Colt 1911? And how one of the bullets went through the open window and almost hit a two-year-old sitting in a stroller?' She spoke with the same low, musical lilt she had while reciting the poem on the beach. 'Have you ever tried cleaning shit out of a shag carpet?'

It was dead quiet in the bathroom. The stalls were empty, but none of us moved. It was as if our bladders had frozen.

Liz shrugged. 'For better or worse, man.'

Rosemary looked down and shook her head. The same small smile played on her lips. She took a drag from the cigarette and then ran the butt under cold water. She threw it in the overflowing trash can and turned to leave. She turned back once, though, with her hand on the doorknob. 'He wanted to go,' she said. 'He enlisted, he wasn't drafted.' She looked at all of us, her eyes like low-beam searchlights. Then she hugged the shawl closer to her body and went through the door, closing it quietly behind her.

The night wore on, like so many other nights, but different. A long table had been set up against the wall with a buffet of deli cold-cut platters, plastic dishes of pickles and coleslaw, aluminum-foiled pans of baked ziti and tossed salad, and a platter of party cookies tied in orange cellophane from Renzi's Bakery. Maybe because of the food no one seemed quite as wasted as usual, except for Bennie of course, who was passed out underneath the pool table. Toward midnight, there were more shot glasses lining the bar and Len rigged the jukebox to play a long Rolling Stones riff. Everyone was dancing up a storm. I danced with Billy and Conor and Liz and Nanny and Voodoo and even Len came out from behind the bar, to great cheering, and boogied down to 'Jumpin' Jack Flash' and 'Brown Sugar.' Rosemary had been sitting most of the night in a corner of the bar, primly sipping cranberry juice, but Cha-Cha and Conor surrounded her and soon she was downing tequila shots and laughing hysterically at anything anyone said. Now Ray Mackey was twirling her around the dance floor. She was a very good dancer. I wondered if she and Mitch had gone out dancing before he lost his leg, to clubs, maybe, or divey bars with good jukeboxes, or maybe they just danced around their living room while people passing by peered into their windows and watched. Now I knew what Len had meant when he said he kept expecting Mitch to show up; every time I looked at the corner of the bar by the jukebox, I kept expecting to see him sitting there, talking, laughing, his amazing eyes taking everything in until the booze made the click happen and he zoned out to his own private hemisphere.

Looking around the lounge was like looking at one of those freeze-frame photographs. People were laughing and singing and dancing and, whenever there was a jukebox lull, raising their glasses in a toast to Mitch. His wife, Rosemary, was

314

weaving toward the door that led to the rooms above the lounge, surrounded by Ray and Raven and Cha-Cha, her arms around Rita, who'd decided to love her after many shots of tequila. Rosemary turned in the doorway and her shawl slid to the floor as she lowered her head and held out her arms and announced, 'Now I am home, and you are my family.' Everyone applauded and she blew a kiss to the crowd and then she was gone, floating up the stairs to her dead husband's bed. Raven and Cha-Cha went out to the piazza to smoke a joint. Nanny and Voodoo were wrapped around each other, their eyes closed, their lips locked, as though they were alone someplace, a desert maybe, trying to stay warm. Outside, Rita was getting sick in the clump of sea grass behind the patio. Angie had left long ago, and now Desi, wearing a lopsided smile, was making his unsteady way home to the rooms above Eddy's, probably dreaming of unbuttoning a thousand tiny buttons on a sky-blue sweater. Liz was swaying against the bar with a happy look on her face, maybe thinking about the pile of dog shit she'd left on the driver's seat of Cory's Triumph TR6 on Tuesday night. Billy and Conor had run out of money and were begging Len to let them run a tab. Ray Mackey was sitting outside at an abandoned table on the patio, his head resting on his arms, a lit cigarette falling from his fingers. I looked around and felt like crying, not from being sad but because everything went by so quickly and I wanted it back, even my days of being an outsider, trying so hard to belong. Even the days of longing for Luke, because they had all led up to this, this night, so thick with stars and music and ashes. I wanted it to last, but it was late and soon the lounge would be closing. And some little bit of something would be lost, even though we'd probably be here again on another night very soon.

I felt a light touch on my arm and turned to see Luke standing next to me. He'd been drinking as long as everyone else had, maybe doing other things, too, but his eyes looked clear. 'That was cool, what you said on the beach,' he said. 'That was very cool, man. He would have liked that.' He put his hand underneath my elbow.

'Yeah, I think he would have,' I said. Over Luke's shoulder, I watched the photo freeze-frame one more time and then the picture became clear and fluid and all the colors came together and for that exact moment, I had the feeling that everything would be all right. That even after the music stopped, we'd all still go on dancing.

if i knew you were going to be this beautiful, i never would have let you go

'Steps from the ocean!' 'Waterfront views!' That was how the ad in the local yellow pages described The Starlight Hotel, that late great fleabag that enjoyed its real heyday during the twenties and thirties, before everything went to hell. Oh, it was never like the grand palaces that lined the boardwalk farther uptown, with their stained glass windows facing the water, the sounds of their orchestras drifting out over the ocean. No, The Starlight Hotel was the crown jewel of the honky-tonk part of town, a pink stucco building that stood out from the weathered bungalows that lined Comanche Street, jalousied windows covered with sateen awnings, tasseled umbrellas shielding the cocktail tables on the small piazza, where people of interest came in taxis under cover of darkness and never signed their real names to the register. It was a discreet location where bellboys could be bribed to bring back a bottle of gin fresh off the boats during the Prohibition years, where (local legend had it) Starr Ames, the silent-screen actress, ended her life after Franco Giselli told her she had been a Goddamned fool to think that he, a practicing Catholic with six kids, would ever leave his family for an over-the-hill hussy such as herself. They found Starr in the bathtub, eyes staring up at the tin ceiling, polished toes peeking out from the bloodied water, palms lank but curiously turned upward, as though waiting for a fortune-teller to come along and read her life line. It was this faded tragedy that started The Starlight Hotel's slow decline, so that by the seventies, like the rest of Elephant Beach, it stood drenched in decay, the stucco walls flaked and chipped under coats of white paint used to deflect the sun, sateen awnings shredded or sold, jalousied windows missing panes, art deco screens scratched and shattered, and the once festive piazza now a weed-choked vacant lot with a few rusted patio tables that once held gaily striped umbrellas. It was said that even the ghost of Starr Ames, glamour gal of the silent stage and screen, done in by talkies and brandy Alexanders, wouldn't deign to haunt the penthouse on the top floor, where she'd taken her final bath; it chose, instead, to walk the shoreline in bare feet, holding a pair of Ferragamos in one hand and a white fox fur (a gift from Franco Giselli) in the other, singing at the top of her lungs, 'I got something, something, something, for my baby and he for me, / We got something, something, something, yeah! / My baby and me.'

But over the years they never did change the ad in the

yellow pages, and we used to scream with laughter, wondering what would happen if some family from Elmhurst or Philadelphia, even, lured by the promise of waterfront views and proximity to the beach, pulled up in their station wagon expecting a brief respite from the city heat and found instead – well, The Starlight Hotel. What would they think, we wondered, seeing the collection of funky losers sitting out front in their sagging beach chairs, with their fifty-cent sunglasses and torn visors, the cracked and calloused soles of their yellowed feet tipped toward the sun? There was Silvester, palsied from some unknown malady, who would stutter into the lounge after a day at the track, waving a fistful of bills, crowing, 'It was a cool, cool, pigeon blue, and my baby rode it all the way home'; Jay, a retired English teacher who could read tea leaves and write letters of recommendation for the price of a Schlitz; and Amos, a leathery specimen who, when drunk, would give away his silver rings and then stagger up Comanche Street, screeching, 'Which one of you Goddamn bedbugs stole my jewels?'

And if the family was brave enough to venture inside, what would they make of the nameless waitress who wandered the halls hoisting an empty tray high in the air with one arm, stopping random visitors to ask, 'May I take your order?' and then turning abruptly to continue her solitary sojourn? Or the young mother with three children who lived on the ground floor and would go out at night, leaving her babies asleep in one bed underneath an open window, their bare bottoms dotted with mosquito bites the shapes of tiny half-moons, as if waiting for someone to walk up Starfish Alley and steal them? And Roof Dog, the mangy German shepherd who lived in the hotel

319

and would make his way up to the roof if someone left the door open, howling long and loudly as he galloped from one end to the other?

Well, where else were they all going to live in such sordid splendor for three dollars and fifty cents a night? The Starlight may have been little more than a flophouse, but the rooms were saved by the water views and the smell of the ocean crouched right outside the windows, and the gaily colored Japanese lanterns strung around the ceilings, whose dim glow provided reading light and hid the true crustiness of the surroundings. Because of its proximity to the Comanche Street beach entrance, it seemed somehow less sinister than it would have in the city, say, or on a more isolated stretch of road. And because of that proximity, and the cool, dim lounge with its long mahogany bar, and the cheap drinks, and Len, the bartender, who was generous with buybacks, and a jukebox that played an eclectic mix of Santana, Frank Sinatra, the Doors, and the Wild Irish Tenors, among others, and because of some bizarre notion we had that hanging around a seedy dive with marginal lunatics made us somehow superior to our high school counterparts, with their pastel, split-level palaces and Velveeta lives, that last summer before everyone left, The Starlight Hotel became our headquarters, our nocturnal home away from home. It was where Billy Mackey stayed when his parents discovered the stash of quaal-udes beneath the loose floorboard in his bedroom and threw him out; where Kenny and Joanie Kramer held their wedding reception when it became clear her parents wouldn't contribute a nickel after finding out she was three months pregnant; where Carlie Slattery slept the night of her miscarriage so that she could bleed safely on the hotel's moth-torn sheets without her mother finding out. It was where I thought I might find my mother, not the one who stood in the doorway of the bathroom while I applied lip gloss before heading out to Comanche Street, screaming that someday I'd regret this attraction to the seedy side of life, my father had a master's degree, for God's sake, but the mother who had given me up for adoption when she was sixteen years old, younger than I was that final summer. The Starlight Hotel seemed exactly like the kind of place a woman who'd given birth to an illegitimate daughter would be living, and on graduation night, while everyone was dropping acid or smoking angel dust or snorting heroin in the men's bathroom, I wandered, lightly stoned, through the vacant hallways, dreamily pushing open doors to empty rooms, imagining my mother lying down on one of the lumpy double beds, her long hair fanning down the stained chenille bedspread, her flesh smooth and uncurdled against the flimsy slip she was wearing, gazing up at the ceiling while the smoke from her cigarette curled out the open window. I would be standing at the foot of the bed, and she would rise slowly and stare at me, at my hair, my face, the shape of my nose, and then she'd smile wide and hold out her arms, and say, 'If I knew you were going to be this beautiful, I never would have let you go.'

That night of Mitch's wake, standing next to Luke, I grew tired of waiting, and when Frank Sinatra began singing 'My Way,' I took his hand and led him out to the patio and said,

321

'Dance with me,' and we moved into the music, our faces so close I could kiss the small scar on his left eyebrow, but I didn't. I had my arms around his neck and he held me around my waist, pressing lightly against the small of my back. At one point I thought there were tears on his face, or they could have been my tears leaking onto him, or maybe they were stars casting shadows, it was a bright night, the exact kind of night I'd pictured a thousand times over, Luke and I slow dancing, then breaking slightly, sneaking up the back stairway, Luke's hand cupping my ass as we climbed up to an empty room and finally closed the door on the rest of the world. The next morning, the waitress who wandered the halls would fill her empty tray with chocolate cake and orange slices and bring it to us for breakfast, and in late afternoon, Jay would read our tea leaves and we'd spend our nights swaying to the music, to the sound of the ocean practically on the door-step, and on nights when the clouds hid the moon, we would lie under the patchwork quilts that smelled of salt water and mildew and tell bedtime stories against each other's skin.

I could see it all so clearly that I thought it had already happened, and when the song ended and we broke apart, it took me a minute to understand that this was Luke, *Luke,* and nothing had happened, we had barely kissed yet. He stood there, suddenly looking so lost, so empty, that again it was I who took his hand, and led him up the hotel's back stairwell to the floor where the rooms were sometimes unlocked, and I found one and went in and opened the window, and we lay down together on the stained chenille bedspread, and for a moment I could smell my mother, what I thought she smelled like – cigarette smoke and lilies of the valley. I

322

turned toward Luke and smiled, relieved that we were finally here, and I closed my eyes and waited for him to kiss me, hold me, waited for it to begin. But then I heard a strangled sound, and my eyes flew open and it was Luke, leaning against me, sobbing, tearing at his hair, and I didn't know what to do, I had no idea what to do. I tried to lift his tee shirt and kiss his scar, but he pulled it back down again. 'No, no, please don't,' he choked out, so I put my arms around different parts of his body through his turbulent thrashing until he felt dead in my embrace. I leaned in close, to make sure he was breathing, and when I saw his shoulders rising and falling, I settled back and held him, through the night sweats that soaked the bed while he slept.

It was a long night. A thousand thoughts ran through my head but I couldn't tell you what they were; I don't remember. I was too conscious of Luke, of thinking he might wake up any minute and want to talk to me about things. I thought maybe he'd wake up and we could go for a walk on the beach and watch the sunrise. My arm was becoming numb, electric pinpricks all over, but the whole time I was hoping he'd get up, I still wouldn't move for fear of waking him. I tried lighting cigarettes with one arm and almost set the sheets on fire. Still, I smoked an entire pack of Marlboros and longed to go downstairs and buy more from the temperamental machine in the lobby, which sometimes worked and sometimes didn't, but still I wouldn't move away from Luke. My arms were beyond tired, and Luke's tee shirt was as wet as if he'd stood out in the rain, but his face looked peaceful and his breathing was even and his occasional whimper never rose to a scream. At one point I tried turning so that I was facing him, so that

I could watch his face while he slept, and I heard a soft rustling beneath me. I reached down and felt the lonely weight of the crumpled condoms I'd bought at Coffey's Drugs in the pocket of my jeans.

It was a very long night. Below us, I heard the jukebox stop playing. I heard Len telling everyone, 'You don't have to go home, but you can't stay here.' I heard everyone moving out of the bar and onto Comanche Street. I heard voices fading. Above us, I heard Roof Dog bark twice before settling down to sleep. I heard Len closing up downstairs, bottles banging, the clang of the cash register as he counted out for the night. I heard him lock up, start his car and begin driving back to Rockaway. I heard the silence on Comanche Street, interrupted by a muffled cough somewhere in the hotel, a lone cry from a child's nightmare in the bungalow across the street from the bar. But then the quiet completely covered everything, and right before I finally fell into a short, dreamless slumber, with Luke's breath warm on my neck, I heard faintly, through the window, a woman's whiskey voice, playful, almost laughing, singing: '. . . something, something, something, yeah! / My baby and, my baby and, my baby and me.'

When I woke up shortly after daybreak, Luke was gone, the sheets still damp from his night sweats. I hadn't felt him slip from the bed or heard him walk across the room. I hadn't heard the door close. Two days later, I learned that he'd left town. He'd told Conor that he needed time away from everyone, everything, that until he was at home again in his own skin he couldn't be at home anyplace else. He was heading west, and he might stop in Boulder to see Maggie and Matty, or he might just keep going until he found a place he'd never

324

been before, where he didn't know anyone. Conor, perpetually stoned or drunk or both, shrugged his shoulders, heading for the beach, his surfboard hooked under his arm. 'It's cool, man,' he said. 'My parents are, like, freaking out. But I can wait until he's ready to be my brother again.'

But I was done waiting. I was ready, now, ready for those arms that had tried to hold me before Luke came back and went away again, ready to embrace someone, something that would hold me through the night when I needed to be held. But then Labor Day came and summer was over and everyone was talking about leaving, taking off for communes in California and New Mexico, moving to the city to get better-paying jobs, to Canada to avoid another draft lottery. Time to get real, man, people were saying, which made me sad and anxious, because all along I thought it *had* been real, that the whole point of being together was that we wouldn't be like everyone else and that for all our summers we would lie next to one another on the sand at Comanche Beach, a chain of sun-kissed flesh that would never break. And years later, Liz, like a sister to me, only better because our blood didn't get in the way, said half scornfully, half pitying, 'It's like we all knew it was this big myth, but you were the only one who really believed it.'

And I did, *I had,* I'd bought the myth, even when I finally left I still thought I was leaving something behind and kept coming back to find it, and a few years later, when they started pouring federal funds into dissipated seaside towns on the East Coast and Elephant Beach received its fair share, and The Starlight Hotel was sold to developers and its ragtag crew of tenants cast out, and Conor and Billy, winos in waiting, tried petitioning Comanche Street residents to keep it open so that the crew of funky losers would have a place to live, or perhaps concerned about their own hazy futures, the neighbors slammed the door in their faces, saying, 'What are you, crazy? Let that Goddamned rattrap burn to the ground!' Which it almost did, the blaze set by someone's careless cigarette or the phantom owner's hankering for insurance money, no one ever found out. And when I brought a sun-bleached boyfriend home from school, and insisted on driving past it, charred and boarded now, waiting to convert to luxury condos – Steps from the ocean! Waterfront views! – and selling for less because they never could quite get the smell of funk and mildew out of the walls, because I wanted my new love to know something of my past and be charmed and delighted by it, when we parked and, after looking around, the only thing he had to say was, 'If we get out of the car, do I need to lock the doors in this neighborhood?' I knew then that it was over, and I chose, instead of him I chose the part of me that was trapped forever inside The Starlight Hotel, along with all the dreams that never came true, and some that did.

acknowledgments

Special thanks to John Freeman for opening the door that led to *Granta* and my excellent agent, Sarah Burnes; to Amy Einhorn for loving the book and opening yet another door; and to Liz Stein for taking it over the finish line. Thanks also to the rest of the amazing team at Putnam/Penguin Random House: Ivan Held, Katie McKee, Lauren Truskowski, Kate Stark, Mary Stone, Lydia Hirt, and Arianna Romig, and to the lovely folks across the pond at Headline: Marion Donaldson, Emma Holtz, Georgina Moore, Yeti Lambregts, and Jo Liddiard. Additional thanks to former *Granta* editors Patrick Ryan and Ted Hodgkinson; André Aciman and the Writers Institute at the CUNY Graduate Center; the Writers Institute first-fiction class for feedback on "Babies"; Karen Spear Ellinwood for her insights on "Catholic Girls"; and Barbara Greenwood and the New Bedford nightbirds for their input on "Adventures in Zombie Land"; always loved the image of you all on overnight, reading aloud. Love and gratitude to all the friends who have been there and been there, especially the ladies of the beach: Susan Allen, Linda Allen, Deborah Emr, Jenny Briggs, Glynnis Burke, Patricia Slattery, Mitty Smith, and Jean Sondergaard, and to Joe Becker, Cindy Burch, Tim Chandler (RIP), Lynn Duffy, Hank Kattan, Marcia Klugman, David Laibman, Linda Nahum, Maite Reyes, and Irene Roberts. Big love and tremendous thanks to my husband, David, who told me now was the time to go for it, for all the reading and insightful editing, for riding around Brooklyn listening to Jimi Hendrix, and for the support that helped this book get written. Much appreciation to the New York Writers Coalition and to Melody Brooks and New Perspectives Theatre for providing spaces that helped keep the creative fires glowing. And finally, thanks to all the funky East Coast beach towns that served as home over the years and came together as Elephant Beach.

about the author

Judy Chicurel grew up in Long Beach, Long Island. Her work has appeared in national, regional and international publications including the *New York Times*, *Granta*, and *Newsday*. Her plays have been produced and performed in Manhattan and India. She lives in Brooklyn, New York.